THE
RELUCTANT
DETECTIVE

A Martin Hayden Mystery

Adrian Spalding

Cover designed by Allison Rose
allisonthewriter.wordpress.com

This book is a work of fiction. Names, characters, places, and incidents either are products of the author's imagination or are used fictitiously. Any resemblance to actual persons, living or dead, events, or locales is entirely coincidental.

Adrian Spalding
Visit my website at www.adrianspalding.co.uk

OTHER MARTIN HAYDEN MYSTERIES

The Reluctant Detective Goes South.

The Reluctant Detective Under Pressure

Acknowledgements

If a novel was a ship, then the author could well be described as the Captain of that ship. It then follows that there must be an able crew, ready and willing to help the Captain get to the final port. So before this story begins, I would like to draw your attention to my brave crew members who donated many hours of toil towards the passage across the seas, helping me navigate through some choppy waters and the occasional calm.

Thank you to my crew: Irene, Angela, Claire, Anthony, Peter, Brian and Gavan. Plus, a special mention to my long-suffering wife, who spent hours and hours making sense of my writing. Thank you all.

In memory of Soko

CHAPTER ONE

Martin, with tired blue eyes, looked at the telephone on his desk; it rang louder than he had ever noticed before. It had to be Jenny calling to apologise, and so she should. He had treated her to a very special meal at her favourite restaurant, 'Ceviche Soho', followed by an energetic evening dancing at a nearby salsa club. Jenny loved the salsa and had insisted Martin take lessons in the techniques of the Latin dance. After the club, they took a cab to her luxury Bayswater flat to make what Martin liked to refer to as 'Salsa sex'.

She knew he would not creep home with the ever-present danger of waking his mother. Such action would require Martin to explain why the overnight work assignment he was supposedly on was cut short. So instead, he had walked back to his office in the centre of London.

Martin had been sound asleep next to Jenny dreaming about race horses when she started shaking him vigorously and speaking with an urgency.

"Get up now, Martin, you need to go!"

Martin liked to take his time waking up. Today, there was to be no such luxury.

"Martin, wake up!" Jenny's sense of urgency had increased. "Ian caught an earlier flight; he has just landed at Heathrow. Move Martin, for Christ's sake, move!"

Jenny was now out of bed and getting dressed. He was about to turn over and snuggle deeper under the warm, cosy duvet when he recalled Ian was married to the same Jenny that was now pulling the duvet off the bed, leaving him naked and a lot less cosy.

Jenny drove to collect her husband from the airport, leaving Martin standing on the pavement, alone, cold and sleepy. Thankfully, he had dressed, albeit in last night's crumpled clothes. He looked for a cab to take him to his office.

Yes, it had to be Jenny. Who else would even consider calling him at this unearthly time of the morning? He would, of course, accept her apology; he would be mad not to. She was attractive, rich, enjoyed the company of younger men (Martin was ten years her junior), had a great sense of humour, long, attractive legs, plus a strong imaginative sex drive. The only down-side was her marriage to Ian, which made the relationship, on the one hand, exciting and on the other, at times, complicated, 'go with the flow, stay close to the bank, enjoy the ride,' that was one of 'Martin's Mantras', as he liked to call them.

There was a small, vindictive part of him that was tempted to leave the telephone ringing until the answer machine kicked in; he could then repeatedly replay her apology. But he thought of her amazing breasts coupled with 'making up sex', so he grabbed the phone before any mechanical voice had a chance to kick in.

It was a woman, just not Jenny. A young-sounding woman, asking about the job vacancy that he had advertised. 'Great', Martin thought, 'that's all I need at seven-thirty in the morning!'

* * *

'Shit!' thought Susan; she had not expected to hear an actual, real human voice from the other end of the telephone. There again, she could never have expected or imagined that she would be inside a cramped coffee shop at seven-thirty in the morning, sitting next to a man she had only just met and ringing for a job interview. Sometimes life throws unexpected things into your face just for the fun of it. Susan was fast learning that life must have a weird sense of humour.

It had really started going very strange just a couple of hours earlier when Susan left Heaven. Not the place where angels hang around chatting and discussing the latest set of gossamer wings or laugh about if an angel really appeared every time a bell rang, how crowded their home would be. The Heaven that Susan stumbled from was a nightclub located under Charing Cross railway station. She stumbled because she had had just a little too much to drink in too short a time. She fell onto the damp pavement. Susan felt the pain as she grazed her knee, plus the indignity of her low-cut dress moving in such a way that it exposed most of her cleavage and a high proportion of one of her breasts. Even as she gazed very closely at the dried chewing gum on the pavement, she could feel eyes looking at her and judging her.

A moment later, she felt a strong pair of hands helping her to her feet. Then those same hands started feeling other parts of her body, including her now very exposed breast.

"Enough of that!" Susan pushed the hand away and yanked up her dress to regain her modesty. "There's helping a lady and groping a lady, so thanks for the first part."

He was taller than her, well-built and standing a little too close for comfort; there was clearly alcohol on his breath. Susan could not complain about that as she guessed her own breath was not exactly fresh.

"Just a cuddle and kiss as a thank you," the deep voice pleaded, with a smile that looked to Susan a little creepy, as she noticed his hands were once again sneaking over her body.

"Piss off, weirdo!" Susan was always one for the blunt approach. She then felt his hands tighten on her arms.

"You'd enjoy me; I have some special talents that young

ladies love."

"Just let me go!" There was, for the first time, a hint of fear in her voice, which she tried to hide unsuccessfully. The fear only seemed to encourage the young man. Then she noticed the two others standing behind him smirking and leering.

"I think you should be a little more grateful. I did help you up. Who knows what might have happened if I'd just left you there?" He laughed before his head moved towards hers, his lips primed and aimed at hers.

She tried to struggle, but his grip was just too much for her. She wondered if she could jerk her knee into his private parts to make it clear she had no interest in joining lips. As he was so close to her, she was not sure she would be able to generate enough force behind her knee. The result would possibly feel like she was rubbing her knee against him, sending all the wrong signals.

"Just a little snog, darling."

Susan was beginning to run out of ideas when she heard another voice chime into the conversation. A strong, commanding male voice that forced everyone to turn and look. Susan felt relieved; a knight in shining armour was going to rescue her, and he would save her from these drunken louts, who had nothing more than a lot of dirty thoughts on their minds. The tall drunk now released her to see just who was calling.

"Let the lady go. Then we can all be on our way without anyone getting hurt, or any tears being shed."

The tall drunk just laughed loudly at the man striding towards him. Susan looked at her knight in shining armour. Well, actually, he was dressed in a printed floral dress, black court shoes, pearl-drop earrings. He had clearly bleached blonde hair and had an old, slightly wrinkled face with eyes that were surrounded by black eye liner, lips bathed in a deep rouge lipstick and a strong chin that had dark stubble appearing. Susan was a little disappointed, to say the least.

"Oh, so what is the little poof going to do? Hit me with his handbag?" The comment brought an outcry of laughter from his two associates.

"No, the handbag goes onto the ground," which it did, only emphasising Susan's disappointment in her saviour. "Then I ask you again, politely, to get on your way, so no one gets hurt."

The tall drunk had now lost interest in Susan. The thought of punching this man dressed as a lady seemed to be a more fitting end to a good night's binge drinking than just fumbling with some drunken slag. It was lucky that Susan did not hear that thought as he moved away from her, or else she would most certainly have kicked him in the nuts.

"You do know your make-up is going to get really messed up when my fist lands on your face."

The two men squared up to each other, although to any passer-by, it would have looked like a man and a woman. They edged closer and closer. Their eyes locked on each other. It was then Susan noticed the man in the dress. His eyeshadow had little glittery bits that reflected off the street light; she liked that effect and wondered if she would get the chance later to ask him where he had bought the eyeshadow.

The tall drunk dug into his pocket and pulled out a knife, which also glinted in the amber street light.

"Come and show me what you got, Lady-Boy!"

"Oh dear, that was not the best move on your behalf. You are going to regret drawing a knife on me."

The tall drunk lunged forward, his only intention to stab the transvestite.

"Have some of..."

Before his sentence was finished, the man in the floral dress sidestepped the lunge. Firmly he grabbed the assailant's wrist with one hand, while the other hand pushed on his elbow joint, then he pressed even harder. In a moment, there was a loud cracking sound, followed by a scream of pain from the tall, drunk man, as the man in the dress let him fall to the floor in agony.

"You've broken my fucking arm!"

"You are the observant type. Now I'd run along if I were you."

"You're going to pay for this, bastard!" He turned to his now, not so brave looking companions, "Get the Fed's. Let's get this fucking old tart arrested."

The man in the floral dress picked up his handbag and walked towards Susan, who was thinking that she was in a weird dream as a result of too many cocktails in the club. He took her by the hand and then turned towards the drunk with the broken arm, writhing on the grey pavement in pain.

"Please feel free to call the police. They will take at least eight minutes to get here, in which time I could have broken your other arm, both of your legs and be working my way through your friends. Take it as a lesson learnt, young man."

So that was how Susan ended up in this busy coffee shop with a man she had only just met, whose name turned out to be Colin.

The reason she was telephoning for a job was equally weird. It had started with Colin asking a question that had been bothering him ever since he first saw Susan in the club. Colin was not the sort of person to shy away from awkward or blunt questions either, making them almost the perfect pair, although Susan preferred her men in jeans, not dresses.

"Why were you flirting with so many men at the club? You do know that Heaven is a gay club. The men there tend to prefer well-hung men, not flirtatious young ladies."

"Of course, I knew it was a gay club; that's why I was there, looking for a gay man to live with."

Colin picked up his skinny latte, drank a hearty mouthful to give him time to figure out exactly what Susan was planning or if she was still very drunk.

"Maybe this is none of my business, but why would you be looking for a gay man to live with?"

"Well, not live with in the sense of a relationship, more flat-mates. Share the rent, household bills, cleaning, cooking, and all that sort of stuff, without any of the bedroom stuff that is bound to rear its head if I just had your average 'hetero' guy as a roommate. Plus, gay guys always seem flush with cash, good jobs and the like, so it seemed like a good idea. Colin, I need a job. I don't have one, and the only way of paying next month's rent, unless I find a gay flatmate, is to sleep with my overweight landlord with his suspect personal hygiene regime, something I have no plans or desires to do."

Never one to shy away from a challenge, Colin stated, "Right young lady, let's see if we can find you a job which doesn't involve lying on your back." Grabbing the paper, he donned a pair of half-lens reading glasses and began trawling through it, "So Suzie Baby, what qualifications do you have?"

"None."

"Well, that's an easy answer; sadly, it does limit our options. Experience?"

"Four years working in shops and two years in an office."

"I guessed as much. Maybe you would be better off lying on your back," Colin commented whilst peering over the top of the London Metro.

Susan ignored him, dropped six cubes of sugar into her coffee, and then stirred the syrupy mixture with the provided wooden stick before burning her tongue as she sipped on the drink. Susan watched the bloodshot eyes of the man dressed as a woman scan the job section; occasionally, he made small sounds as he weighed up the jobs on offer.

"If you're not going to perform blow jobs on your landlord, would a job which demands no qualifications and no experience, plus is well paid into the bargain, be of interest to you?"

"If you can find me a job like that, Colin," she said, blowing her coffee in a vain attempt to cool it down, "I'll take you for tea at the Ritz with my first pay packet."

Smugly he handed her the job section of the Metro and pointed at a quarter-page advert.

"I wonder what I should wear. Sequins and diamanté, I think, they always look kind of Ritzy, don't you think darling?"

Personal Assistant Required
Hayden Investigations seek a PA to the Senior Director

Based in a prestigious office suite located in central London, the role will include organising the director's diary, his travel arrangements, liaising with clients, field agents, and managing a small administrative office. Some UK and European travel will be required, so a passport is essential.

It is important that the successful candidate fits into a small, dedicated team, so personality will take precedence over qualifications and experience.

Remuneration is negotiable for the right person.

Please contact, by telephone, Martin Hayden for an informal discussion.

Susan read the advert three times to check she understood it. She had, after all, been up a little over 24 hours, plus the vodka and Red Bulls that she had drunk had yet to clear totally from her system.

"Sounds very high powered, and it doesn't say 'no qualifications'," she emphasised the 'no qualifications'.

"Suzie Baby, it's a golden opportunity, just read between the lines. This high-flying detective, director, person, thingy wants a young tart to take around on his business trips, be with him in posh, foreign restaurants, and then shag once in a while. That is why he wants an 'informal' discussion first, to check out the talent and get a few personal details. The last thing he wants is some fat butch PA who does a great job in the office, but he wouldn't be seen dead in a restaurant with. You'll love it. You might have to sleep with him once in a while, but what hardship can that be. Just lay back, close your eyes and think of the money."

Susan finished her coffee; its sweet warmth gave her a cosy feeling. Really, she just wanted to sleep. Even so, it was a job, or a possible job, what was the worst that could happen; she'd get turned down.

"I'll give him a call later; I really do need some sleep before I start doing telephone interviews with directors."

"God, you women! I might dress like one, but I'm so glad I don't think like one." Colin straightened his dress, drained his cup and stood up. "Ring him now; you'll get an answer machine; it is only seven-thirty in the morning. Give him your number using that husky voice that lack of sleep, smoke-filled rooms and alcohol gives you, and I'll wager he'll be on to you like a shot.

"Another Americano?" without waiting for an answer, he minced off to the counter, "I'll get you a Danish. Keep your strength up. Ring him now, Suzie Baby, ring him now," he called without looking back at her.

Under the eagle-eye of Colin, flanked by a fresh, steaming Americano coffee with six sugar cubes in it and a freshly baked, or so they say, apricot Danish, Susan, against her better judgement, called Hayden Investigations. For some reason, her new transvestite friend seemed to be more excited about her calling than she was. Maybe she was becoming a fatalist, thinking the worst, devaluing herself. Susan had received too many turn downs, refusals, letters which simply said, 'sorry but you have been unsuccessful on this occasion'. Everyone had a point at which they thought, 'shit, will I ever get a job?' For some, that point might take one thousand refusals; others maybe just two or three. Susan had lost count of the number of jobs she had applied for and had not got, but she was beginning to reach that point.

Susan heard the phone ring almost six times before, to her surprise, a human voice answered. 'Shit!' thought Susan.

*   *   *

Martin always thought advertising for a personal assistant was a bad idea; it would only complicate what for Martin was a very acceptable situation. His mother, on the other hand, disagreed emphatically, which at times seemed to be her default position in all matters concerning Martin.

If nothing else, Martin had manners. His nanny, who had looked after him during his first few formative years, had instilled in him that good manners and polite behaviour were the cornerstones of a civilised society. She also took a leather strap to him when he missed out a 'please' or a 'thank you', so that helped the learning process dramatically. So he put aside the disappointment that it was not Jenny calling him.

"So you are interested in the position here at Hayden Investigations?"

Susan composed herself, sat up straight in her chair before replying, "You're in early; I was expecting an answer machine."

"Well, I'm terribly sorry about that, would you prefer to speak to my answer machine? I would pass you on to my personal assistant, but for the fact that that is the role I am advertising and hoping to fill."

"No, you're fine. And yes, I am very interested in the position."

"Well, let's see if we can take some basic information from you, then if you sound the sort of person that we could employ, I'll ask you to attend an interview so we can meet face to face. First of all, what is your name?"

"Susan Morris, but you can call me Sue. Most of my friends always call me that, amongst other things," her nerves caused her to over answer the question.

"OK, Sue. Well, you might have guessed from the newspaper that we are an investigations agency, dealing with blue-chip clients across Europe, so you will not find our company splashed all over yellow pages. Discretion is our motto, so I hope you are the sort of person who can be discreet?"

Susan wondered if sitting in a now very crowded coffee shop alongside a transvestite, who was leaning against her head so he could listen to both sides of the conversation, and whom she had only just met, would be considered as discreet. She was not sure, so she just answered, "Of course."

She began to answer his somewhat odd questions as honestly as possible, questions which she figured were those psychological ones she had read about. Clearly, a detective agency had to be very careful who they employed; even she could understand that, so the questions, strange as they were, she was happy to answer, after all, she needed a job. She found Martin's voice calming; his voice definitely contained a public school twang. As the questions moved on, she began to dream about herself in the job: modern offices, booking trips, dealing with clients, phone calls, letters to write, maybe a small team of other office staff. Travelling with Martin, who did sound cute, if he asked her out to a restaurant, would she....?

She stopped herself daydreaming when he asked, "Are you in a stable, current relationship?"

Offbeat question, she thought but was still happy to answer.

"No." If he had met her semi-regular boyfriend, no way could he be described as being stable.

"Would you object to travelling around Europe in the course of our business?"

"No," she said calmly. 'Hell no!' she thought with excitement. Going to pubs and clubs abroad with an expense account now that was just the sort of work she could handle with ease.

"Would you describe your alcohol intake as moderate?"

"Most certainly." The first three glasses of wine she would consider moderate; after that, she just didn't give a monkey's.

The questions became ever more psychological, although Susan didn't mind in the least. With his posh accent, he sounded like Hugh Grant. Hopefully, his hair was better groomed. She wondered if he was married; she guessed he might well be or in some long-term relationship with some heiress or other.

"All of our staff need to be physically fit, so how tall are you, and what is your current weight?"

"Five foot three and eight stone," she lied a tad as she was nearer nine stone; well, to be brutally honest, nine and a half was a more accurate description. She had planned to go on a diet as soon as she had a job and could afford a better, healthier diet. "I'm a size ten if that helps you picture me."

Colin raised his eyebrows at that response. He could see, without any doubt, she was at least a size 12.

This was getting easier, she thought, and just hoped she was building up a high score in the test. She really needed this job. If there was going to be a choice of sleeping with her landlord or this Martin, Martin would win out, even without having ever seen him.

"What do you think is your best attribute?"

Colin was now pressed against her ear like a teenager on heat, trying to listen in. His earrings were leaving a red welt on her neck; his perfume was no less obnoxious.

"My breasts, people say they are small but perfectly formed. I am often complimented when I wear low-cut tops." She stopped, her cheeks now burning; Susan was not often embarrassed. It was an odd question, but she really needed this job.

"What I actually meant was what your best quality is, you know, good shorthand, excellent communications skills, that sort of thing."

"Oh shit, I'm sorry." Susan had a habit of speaking first, then thinking, then regretting. She couldn't help it; it was just something she had done all her life; it came to her as naturally as breathing.

"No, don't worry, it was an interesting answer."

Susan tried to make up for her misinterpretation of the question by trying to dilute her previous answer but instead managed to make things worse, yet another quality she had.

"When I say my breasts are my best part, there's nothing wrong with the rest of me; my legs aren't bad; in fact, I'd say they were as good as my breasts, maybe you should see both and decide for yourself." 'Shit!' she thought again. Did I actually say, 'let him see both'?

Colin gave her the thumbs up before standing up and thrusting his hip backwards and forwards in a fornicating motion, much to the confusion of the three businessmen who decided they should conduct their meeting elsewhere.

"OK, Susan, I think that's enough about your physical side for now. Well, Susan, you certainly seem to be the sort of person that Hayden Investigations would be interested in employing, so with that in mind, I would like to invite you to our offices for a formal interview."

Colin hugged her like an enthusiastic auntie.

"Hurdle one cleared darling, time for clean underwear, then hurdle two. Tea at the Ritz, here we come."

* * *

For the third time since leaving Oxford Street tube station, Susan checked the address as she stood outside the imposing

Victorian building. Being so close to the BBC (British Broadcasting Centre), she kept a vigilant eye out for celebrities. If there had been any walking past her in the street, then they were not that famous as far as she was concerned, as she had not recognised anyone. The address, One Duchess Street, looked to her like a palace. It was no such thing, just an imposing white four-storey building that once had been home to a rich Victorian family. No longer a home full of family, servants and maids, it had now been separated into plush office suites where small companies, who could afford it, had an office with an impressive address. Susan took a deep breath, then pushed the glazed, black, wrought-iron door and stepped into a grand, ornate hallway with a wide carpet. Ahead of her was a staircase leading upwards and to the left of it was a small, elegantly carved wooden desk with an elderly man, in a type of grey uniform, seated behind it. He looked up from the computer screen and smiled at her.

"Can I help you, Miss?"

Susan approached the desk; her shoes seemed to sink into the deep-piled carpet.

"I'm here for an interview with Hayden Investigations."

"Then you'll need to knock on that door over there. Mr Hayden is already in." The elderly man pointed to a black-painted panel door just to her, right at the foot of the staircase.

"Before I go in, can you please tell me if there have been any other people turning up for an interview today?"

"Not that I know of Miss, but good luck anyway."

Susan tapped firmly on the door just below the brass plate that had the words: 'Hayden Investigations' engraved on it. A moment later, the door was opened by a cute young man, maybe in his thirties, who ushered her in before closing the door behind her.

"You must be Susan." He offered his hand, and they shook hands formally.

"That's right; I'm here to see Mr Hayden."

"And now you've met him. However, please call me Martin; I hate calling people by their surname. Grab a seat; can I get you a drink? Tea, coffee, water?"

She looked at him and compared him to the mental image she had drawn during their telephone conversation. He was taller than she had imagined with a slender figure and his hair was better groomed than Hugh Grant's.

She looked around the room for the first time, becoming aware of her surroundings. The room was perhaps twenty feet by twenty feet square, although Susan had never been good at judging sizes. The office was decorated with boring beige-painted walls and just two desks facing each other in the centre of the room. One desk was being used and had a smart looking laptop on it. A brown paper bag with a half-eaten bacon roll was lying beside a branded take-out coffee cup. Opened out across most of the desk was a broadsheet newspaper, not the sort that Susan would ever consider reading; she was a Daily Mirror sort of person as had been her parents. There was a leather settee to the left of a small door where, from what she could see, there was a small kitchen area.

"Water's fine," she finally replied.

"That's a relief; they supply a water machine here. I haven't got around to sorting out the kitchenette yet, so I rely on the many takeaways around here for my coffee fix. Sit down, Susan. Thanks for coming."

She sat down at the desk facing his cluttered desk; it was totally empty, just a plain bare desktop.

Martin sat down, pushed the paper to one side and picked up the bacon roll.

"Late breakfast," he confessed before continuing.

"So, after our interesting and very revealing early morning telephone conversation, what more can you tell me about yourself? Maybe not too intimate this time." He smiled warmly,

15

then proceeded to take a large bite from the roll and ate while he waited for Susan's reply.

Susan was not inclined to answer at once. From her new viewpoint, she continued to take in her surroundings. The beige walls were still as boring, emphasised she now realised, by not a lot else in the room. No office machines, no filing cabinets, no bookcases, nothing that you would expect to find in a modern office. There was a long, black leather settee on which someone had thrown their coat; she guessed that would have been Martin. Not even a picture or a poster on the wall, Susan would describe the office to be an empty office, certainly not a busy office. Just one cluttered desk, one empty desk, one settee and two now occupied chairs.

"I think you'll find all you need to know in this." She passed him a well-presented CV, a CV that Colin had spent time revising, rewording, and in his own word, 'reinventing'.

Martin glanced over the document, all the time rolling his ear lobe between his fingers. Susan sat nervously. She did not have possession of the most sought-after curriculum vitae in the kingdom. In fact, it had been compared to a wet, wilted lettuce leaf, which had been how one potential employer had described it to Susan when she had rung up demanding a reason for not getting the job as a chartered accountant with PricewaterhouseCoopers. Clearly, she understood that she was not qualified to be a chartered accountant, but that was six months ago when she had been a firm believer in the 'don't ask, don't get' frame of mind. Since then, her self-confidence had plummeted to the point where when she failed to get a job at McDonald's, her only reaction had been to shrug her shoulders and walk away eating a complementary Big Mac.

Now at twenty-nine years old, she still had at least forty years of possible employment ahead of her; unless the Government continued to raise the retirement age, in which case she could have fifty to sixty years left. Her qualifications consisted of a 'D grade' in Home Economics, a St John's Ambulance first aid certificate, plus an overnight badge she obtained from the brownies after spending twenty-four hours under canvas when she was seven. Otherwise, her educational days had been spent chasing boys, applying make-up, wearing clothes which her mother described as inappropriate and the occasional bit of shoplifting with three other girls, all of whom, as soon as they left school, became professional single parents.

Susan had been lucky, or unlucky, whichever way you wanted to look at it, as her teacher, Mr Stokes, well, in fact, Mr Stokes's wife, ran a small, street corner mini-market, and she had provided Susan with a full-time job when she left school. This gave the sixteen-year-old Susan the chance to begin a career in shopkeeping, as well as affording the opportunity for Mr Stokes to grope her in the stockroom whenever his wife was out front serving.

Susan put up with his wandering, mostly harmless, hands for a year before leaving Mr & Mrs Stokes to begin a new life with Boots the Chemist. She stayed three months at the chemist before moving up the high street to work at HMV, followed by another change, Thomas Cook (four doors along from HMV). So, by the time she was twenty-one, Susan had run out of shops in Tooting High Street in which she could work. So, at that point, Susan jumped on the tube and headed for Bayswater, where the streets are longer and contain more shops.

Longer streets were not the only reason Susan had jumped on the tube to Bayswater. She was lucky enough to have an aunt who worked there for a family whose business was selling stationery to companies both large and small. For close on two years, Susan settled down to work by day and enjoyed some nights out. Life was tolerable until the family business went bust. The first Susan and her aunt knew of the calamity was when they arrived one cold November morning to find the doors locked and some long, legal notice pinned to the door. Auntie returned to a small market town in Suffolk where she had grown up, leaving Susan to fend for herself.

Martin looked up and spoke to her across the desk,

"I see you spent a lot of time in retail management, it sounds like a very good scheme being seconded to so many different companies, and it must surely have broadened your horizons tremendously?"

Susan smiled again, "Yes," that was all she could muster by way of an answer. She was not too sure what else Colin might have mentioned about her retail experience.

Martin looked over the type-written pages again, wondering what sort of questions he should be asking. This interview business, both the telephone and in-person versions, was turning out to be a lot harder than he could have imagined. He wanted to come across as able, director-like, decisive, comfortable ordering people around, developing strategies, making serious business decisions. Yet having never read the instructions, he totally screwed up the answer machine. He had pressed all the wrong buttons and had been left with two recorded calls after the advert appeared: one from an agency who wanted to run the advertisement in some other publication, then one from a dragon of a woman who sounded a lot like his mother. So now his main and only candidate for this job was the attractive girl sitting in front of him. Looking at her CV, she could most likely run rings around his business sense and tie him up in little knots.

Martin looked over her qualifications once more. She had seven 'O' levels (Colin had told her that no one ever checks these things) and had spent five years on a retail management course that involved her being seconded to a number of high street chains; Boots, WH Smith, Sainsbury's etc. Colin had assured her that if they asked, she could always say the company which ran the management course had closed down. Then two years as a Commercial Business Finance Consultant, (Colin was confident a

Commercial Business Finance Consultant could, in fact, be anything as long as at some point you touched an invoice or handled money), working alongside the Finance Director of a large stationary company as it merged with a larger group and her post had then become redundant, (Colin thought it sounded cool and powerful, plus references might be difficult as records do get lost in these moves). At present, according to Colin, she was a freelance consultant working for PricewaterhouseCoopers in their Global Communications Directorate. Colin guaranteed her that there were over a hundred people in that department, with a revolving carousel of consultants that jump on and off all the time. He should know because he knew one of the guys who worked there, Derek, a tall, sweet-talking Aussie with big biceps, who in his spare time wore make-up and was thinking about wearing women's clothes as well; he was just not yet sure.

Yes, Martin thought, she was well qualified, possibly too qualified for what he wanted. Even though she had the looks and the walk, he was tempted to be upfront with her, give her the chance to leave then and there, but that would mean Martin would be back to square one, and his mother would still be pushing him to get a personal assistant.

Without looking up from the CV, Martin asked, "How's Zoe nowadays? I haven't seen her for, oh, must be about six months."

Susan had a blank look on her face. Who was this man talking about, Zoe? Were things about to get even weirder?

"Who?"

"Zoe, Zoe Harris, Comms. Director at PwC."

"I'm sorry, Mr Hayden, you have lost me there."

"Call me Martin. I said this was an informal interview, and we are an informal company. Zoe Harris, Communications Director at PwC, your boss," he smiled.

Susan had one word in her mind on a continuous loop: 'Shit! Shit! Shit....!'

"You know Zoe?" Susan laughed to hide her fear at being tripped up and her urge to stuff Colin's drop-earrings down his throat the next time she saw him.

"Dated her for about three months. I might even have walked past you in the office, small world. So how is she?"

There is always a danger that a small lie that is found out leads to another slightly bigger lie, which in turn, when that one is found out, leads to another even bigger lie, and so it goes on and on until, before long, you are telling the person you are lying to, that the earth is flat, and you have positive proof in the form of a written affidavit from God. Unless, of course, you stopped the lies in their tracks by confessing the moment the first lie is found out. Susan, on the other hand, believed there was a saying that states two lies make a truth as long as the second lie moves you away from the first lie.

"I never had much to do with Zoe, and spent very little time in the London office, mostly out with clients, spent a long time travelling the country," she added. She was a firm believer in if you are going to lie, embellish and make it work for you.

Martin tossed her CV onto the desk; the weight of the fiction it contained made an audible thud in Susan's ears. He leaned back in his chair, intertwined his fingers and looked at Susan's physical attributes; all of them were very nice, he concluded, maybe she had a natural streak of honesty in her. Maybe, he thought, he should be honest with her.

"Susan,"

"You can call me Sue."

"I would prefer to stick with Susan. First, I prefer the name to the shortened version, and there was that stupid song: 'A Boy Named Sue'; and you are, I can see, no way a boy. So, Susan, I'll be honest with you for the simple reason that I like you, and I would hate to be complicit in you making a wrong move in your career. There are a couple of things that I need to explain to you about the post here at Hayden Investigations, which were not properly explained in the advertisement. I hope you'll understand the reasons why the advert was not as full and frank as it should have been."

Susan felt her back straighten. She wondered how strange this was going to get and, as a precaution, checked the quickest way out.

"When the advert spoke of prestigious clients, that was not strictly true on a number of different levels, the main one being we have no clients at all. Not one client, not one case, our customer base is non-existent. Then the small administrative unit, same thing, there is a desk, just no people. So strictly speaking, it should be I not we, I have no clients, prestigious or otherwise."

"Field agents?"

"Likewise, yet to be established."

Susan thought the job advertisement had a lot in common with her own C.V., lies or, as Colin would say, 'not altogether factual'.

"So, there is no job here then?"

"Well, there is a job, just not what one would describe as a conventional one."

"You have lost me totally. Is this a job or not a job?"

"First, before I go into too much detail, I just want to say that I would like to offer you the job."

"Which is not a job?"

"Correct."

"So, is this job the same one you advertised or is there something else that I might need to do for this job that is not a job?"

"OK. A full and frank explanation; let's start with me. Martin Hayden, stinking rich parents, sadly my father died leaving me a very generous monthly allowance. Well, sad that he died, the allowance part was not so sad until my mother decided that she wanted to interfere. Interfering is something she is a professional at, and she works at it tirelessly. In her opinion, I should work, find a job, and if I did not find myself a job, she was going to stop my allowance. She has some sort of legal control over my father's last will and testament. Frankly, my future hinges on when my mother dies, and I have full access to the family fortune, which is unlikely to happen in the near future. That makes me sound mean and cruel, which I would like to reassure you I am not."

Susan moved her chair back ever so carefully, saving her time in getting to the door if required; cute Martin was beginning to sound a little bit odd.

"So," he continued, "if I take up a real job, say in banking, then I get my generous allowance. The flip side is not only do I have to toil daily; I have to work every day with a load of twats in the City, and Susan, that is not how I see myself. So, I compromised with my mother. I started my own business; hence Hayden Investigations, and I continue to get a regular income from my inheritance."

Susan thought she understood, although she was not entirely convinced, so asked, "Why a Detective agency?"

He leaned forward on his elbows and smiled at Susan, at which she relaxed just a little.

"I'm glad you asked that question. I think it shows how cunning I can be. Being a private investigator stops Mother from asking awkward, prying questions around the dinner table. 'Hello Martin', she might say, 'how was your day, anything exciting?' 'Sorry, Mother, my cases are all confidential; I just can't talk about it,' so my day is mine to do as I please. If I say so myself, brilliant!"

"Maybe," was Susan's verdict.

"Trust me, it is. However, Mother has insisted that I get a personal assistant to help me with my workload, which will allow me to cut down on all the overnight assignments that I take on."

"Now you are confusing me; you have no work, so why are you doing overnight assignments?"

"My overnight assignments are very much social and pleasure, that is all I'm going to say. Nevertheless, if I don't employ a P.A., then Mother will become even more suspicious of my agency than she is already. Hence the job, which is not a job, if you're interested. Although looking at your CV, if you wanted a real job, then I'd understand if you just wanted to leave right now."

Five minutes ago, Susan was tempted to flee. Now, this cute young man, whose eyes seemed to twinkle, appeared to be offering her paid employment with a job description that contained just one sentence, 'do nothing', now that was the sort of job that Susan felt she could handle, maybe even succeed at. Now it was time for her to ask some serious questions and get serious answers.

"So, what star sign are you?"

"Pardon?"

"What star sign are you?"

Martin paused for a moment to consider the question, "I have absolutely no idea what star sign I am. Is that important?"

"Of course it is. When were you born?"

"Second March, nineteen eighty-two."

"Mmm, thought as much, a Pisces, you seem a friendly sort of person. Just can't believe that you didn't know your star sign; I thought everyone knew their star sign. Still, there is always a first time, I suppose. So this job, which is not a job, where will I do this non-existent job?"

Martin finished his coffee, "I assume you'll be here for most of the time. You could still do secretarial type stuff: make restaurant reservations, order cabs, book theatre tickets, that sort of thing. I think it could be fun."

"I am getting paid as well?"

"Of course, market rates for a personal assistant to a company director."

"Then I'll take the job," Susan concluded, not believing what appeared to be her good fortune in landing a cushy job, which if it did get a little too weird, there was always the unlocked door she could walk out of.

CHAPTER TWO

Susan knew from bitter experience that the first day at any new job was always going to be a little surreal. She recalled her previous jobs being introduced to countless members of staff. They all smiled and welcomed you, even those who, in the fullness of time, you learned to hate. Then you were given some basics as to your job, plenty of reading material, and lots of support to enable you to learn how to perform the tasks. Of course, none of that applies when the job you have just started has no work associated with it and just one other person in the company. Even so, Susan wondered as she looked across her empty desk at Martin reading a newspaper if he was actually going to say anything beyond the polite 'good morning' he had uttered when she first arrived.

Susan looked down at her well-worn desk, a simple desk with three drawers on the right. She opened the top drawer, the smallest of the three, and examined the abstract contents, which included four very thick elastic bands, a Chinese takeaway menu, three ballpoint pens, one was clearly broken with a well-chewed end which lay against an unopened pack of pink post-it notes, which in turn sat on a business card that Susan picked up and read.

"So, who are Maw Graphic Designers?"

Without looking up from his paper, Martin replied, "They rented this office before me."

"So, you haven't tidied up the place since they left?"

"Why would I? Nothing actually happens in this office except for a few telephone conversations."

Susan dropped the card back into the drawer and closed it, and then looking towards the window, she spotted a wilted plant that must have once possessed some green healthy leaves and not the brown brittle leaves it now comprised of.

"I suppose they left the plant behind as well?"

"No, my mother gave it to me with the express expectation that I might water it. She should have known I cannot live up to any of her expectations."

"So, what shall I do?" She asked, drawing Martin's attention away from the entertainments page, where he was trying to decide which film Jenny might like to see.

He looked across at her as if to say, who are you exactly? Instead, he told her, "What you want, I guess."

"Normally, the boss tells the worker what they should do!" Susan pointed out.

"Normally, the job involves work of some description; you might recall this job description had no work attached to it, so there is not much I can tell you." Martin returned his gaze to the entertainments page.

"I can't sit here all day doing nothing."

Without looking at her, Martin replied, "Actually, that is exactly what you agreed to do."

"I'm going to make myself a drink," Susan stated as she stood up from her desk and walked towards the small kitchenette.

"Black coffee and no sugar please," Martin called from behind his paper.

"I thought you said there was no work involved with this job; now, when it suits, I get work. Typical boss changing rules to suit themselves. Where's the sugar?"

"There is none. I don't take sugar."

"Well, I bloody well do!"

"Well, bloody well, go and get some!" Martin responded, neatly folding his paper and walking towards Susan with his empty, disposable cup. If Susan was going to start making coffee in the office, it would save him the trouble of walking around the corner to buy it.

"I see; I'm going to have to do your errands all day."

Martin was now standing close enough to Susan for her to smell his aftershave.

"It's not easy being a boss of a high-powered, successful detective agency, you know. Here's a tenner, get sugar, tea, coffee, whatever you think the kitchen needs."

"You're not the boss of a high-powered, successful detective agency."

"I never said *I* was the boss of one. It's bad enough having one employee. Oh, don't forget chocolate biscuits."

Luckily for Susan, with her many experiences of first days at a new job, she had quickly learned that even though she had no work, there were still things to do and ask for. Cups for the kitchen, a cafetière, pictures for the wall and a spare set of keys for the office; for each and every request she made, Martin simply gave her some cash and told her to go and get it. She cautiously asked about a laptop, if she was going to sit all day at a desk, she was at least going to get onto Facebook and do some online shopping without using her personal mobile phone data allowance.

"Well, go and get one," was all he said.

"You mean I have to buy my own laptop for work?" Susan was not planning to do that; she'd rather drag her obsolete Dell laptop into the office.

"No, I'll pay for it, of course. Just get one, and I'll give you the money."

"Until I get my first pay packet, I can't afford one. Can I choose it, and you go online and pay for it?"

Martin looked exasperated, pulled his wallet from his jacket and handed her a credit card,

"Just pop along to John Lewis and get one."

Susan rolled the credit card around her fingers,

"I can't use your card."

"Of course you can, silly girl. Walk in, choose a laptop, hand them the card; my pin is 6969, then, hey presto, you have a laptop. Although don't expect me to set it up for you, you'll have to sort that out yourself."

"You trust me with your credit card? I could cause havoc in Oxford Street with this and your pin number."

Martin looked down at his paper.

"You have honest eyes, plus if you do, I'll just tell them you stole the card. Now run along and get yourself sorted, and just leave me in peace."

If Martin had expected peace to continue in the Hayden Office after employing Susan Morris, he was wrong. If Susan was not texting friends, sending Facebook messages or talking on the phone, she was talking to Martin, asking him, in his opinion, mindless, pointless questions. 'Have you ever met the Queen?' 'Is that really a Rolex watch you're wearing, not a Turkish fake?' If there were no questions to ask, then Susan would not hesitate in sharing her life with him. Then, when all else failed, she would read his horoscope, none of which Martin listened to.

By the second week, Martin had accustomed himself to sharing his one-time quiet office with a young lady who shared everything. She made good coffee, was adept at booking restaurants for him, happy to do just about any errand he asked. In return, he walked in each day with not only his bacon roll, but he also now purchased a sweet vanilla Danish that Susan enjoyed eating as they had their first office coffee. During which, like it or not, Martin learnt what was going to happen that day to Pisceans like himself, all over the world.

During their often-one-sided conversations, Martin was intrigued to learn about modern social media, Facebook, 'checking in', he thought you only did that at hotels, the posting was no longer done just at a red pillar box, then 'shares' that were not bought and sold. Fortunately, he learnt that the initials 'WTF' did not stand for Welcome to Facebook. With Susan's help, he opened his first Facebook account, searching for old school friends as well as a few previous female companions.

Their relaxed situation could not even be disrupted by Martin's interfering mother, who called at least twice a week to speak to her son. Susan, polite, contrite, explained that he was out with clients, thus unavailable. Then Susan would ask about Mrs Hayden's health. Often they spent several minutes chatting, even to the point that Susan learnt about some of Martin's previous girlfriends. She warmed to Mrs Hayden, even though Martin had warned her not to get too friendly with his mother, but Susan guessed that was more about the secrets that Mrs Hayden shared with her.

Nothing in life, however blissful, stays the same for long; change is always waiting around the corner. For Martin and Susan, that change came their way one Tuesday. It had started like any other day at the office. Martin had arrived a little later than usual after an appointment with his shirt-maker to ensure his range of fashionable summer shirts fitted correctly. All of Susan's boyfriends had only ever bought shirts by collar size, so a made-to-measure shirt was somewhat of a novelty for Susan, and she mentally crossed off a Marks and Spencer shirt for Martin's Christmas present.

As Martin finished his coffee, he leaned back in his chair and said, "You're hungover, aren't you?"

"Not so much hungover, just knackered. Last night was a very late night with some of the girls. We found this really cool cocktail bar in Streatham that serves well into the early hours. The real plus point is the three blokes behind the bar shaking cocktails with muscles that just ripple. To be honest, that would have been why we were all drinking so fast, just to get to order some more. Anyway, how did you know I was a little the worse for wear?"

"Your jumper is inside out, seams and labels showing all over it. See, that's why I am the detective!" he teased.

Susan looked down to see that indeed Martin was correct. She had rushed out this morning when not fully awake, an easy mistake when you are hungover.

"Well, I'm off to the ladies to correct my error."

As Susan stood up from her desk, there was a loud knock at the door. Martin and Susan both looked up to see the door open wide and a woman, maybe in her sixties, stride in confidently.

"I'm here to see Martin Hayden."

"You're speaking to him. What can I do for you?"

Without hesitation, she closed the door behind her, looked around, walked across the office, pulled a plastic chair from beside the kitchenette, placed it alongside Martin's desk, sat down and introduced herself as Mrs Grace Holburn.

"I want you to investigate my maid, who I know is stealing items from me, nothing too valuable, you understand, just small trinkets that disappear. I know for a fact that it is her taking them as I have had a small camera installed in certain rooms, and I now have photographic evidence of her stealing my belongings."

Martin looked at the woman; her grey hair pulled back into a bun, which only served to emphasise her rounded, freckled face.

"So why do you need me to investigate? It sounds as though you have evidence enough to go to the police."

"Young man, I am aware of the evidence that I hold on her. But first, I would like to know what she is actually doing with these items. I presume that she is selling them, as I could not find any of them when I searched her room. I am concerned that she has a secret family or relations that she has not told me about somewhere in London, who she is supporting by stealing from me. That is why I want you to investigate."

Martin noticed the large diamond engagement ring next to her wedding ring and compared it to her very plain, simple clothes. He wondered just why she was so keen to discover if her maid had a family in London.

"The thing is, Mrs Holburn, we do currently have a very full client list, and it might well be difficult for us to fit in your case for a while."

She looked around the office with a disapproving look that she had perfected over many years of giving out disapproving looks.

"You don't look exactly busy here, plus I am sure it would only take a morning of your time. She has Tuesdays off, so that will be the only day that she has any chance to sell any items or pass them onto the family, which I am sure she is concealing from me."

"I am still not sure we would be able to help you. We deal mostly with large scale investigations, plus our rates are amongst the highest in the sector. I would also add...."

It was then that Susan interrupted,

"Mr Hayden, there is an urgent email from our Newcastle field agent that you should read."

Martin looked at Susan with a quizzical look. He would have liked to tell her that however hungover she might be, there were no field agents anywhere. He refrained, deciding that it would not give a good impression to Mrs Holburn, not that he was that bothered about Mrs Holburn or her thieving maid; he just wanted her out of the office.

"Thank you, Susan; I am sure it can wait."

"No, it can't, Mr Hayden. It is very urgent and need only take a few seconds to read and act on."

Susan tried to be as forceful as she could, knowing that her jumper being inside out would not add anything to the gravitas of her words.

A little aggravated, Martin apologised to his first potential customer, who he was doing his best to put off. Then he turned to read the message in his inbox, wondering what Susan had sent him, as he knew there was no such thing as a Newcastle Field Agent.

Subject: *YOU NEED TO READ THIS*
Maybe she has been sent by your mother to test you out. It could be a trap!!!!!!!

"Please tell him that is fine, Susan." Martin then turned back to Grace.

"It's a her in Newcastle, Martin, not a him; Jo is Josephine." Susan smiled at Mrs Holburn, "We are employing more and more female agents; they are softer, so much better than their male counterparts."

"Thank you for reminding me, Susan. I know our female agents like to turn things inside out to get to the truth. Now, Mrs Holburn, your maid, if you are sure that she sells these small items and then meets up with her family on Tuesdays, I possibly could, as a special favour, fit you in sooner rather than later, maybe next Tuesday?"

Mrs Holburn left the office satisfied that the truth about her maid would be uncovered; she also left two stunned people behind, trying to come to terms with having just been engaged to investigate something.

The rest of that day, Hayden Investigations had a very different dynamic. Talk of work and toil came into the conversation before Martin asked the inevitable question.

"So, just exactly how do you think you follow someone?"

The other question they had bantered about was just why Mrs Holburn turned up at the office asking for the help of a private detective; Martin assumed that his mother would be involved somewhere along the line.

Susan drained the last of her afternoon coffee and considered the question.

"Well, walk behind them, I suppose. Jim Rockford always used to walk a few yards behind, stopping once in a while to tie his shoelace or look in a shop window. I don't think anyone knew that Jim Rockford was following them."

"Jim Rockford?"

"'The Rockford Files'. Christ Martin, have you not lived? Eighties private detective on TV worked in Los Angeles with his father, a retired truck driver. You must have heard of it. Anyway, whether you did or didn't see the Rockford Files, that's what private investigators do when they follow people. He always got the bad guy."

Martin screwed up his brown paper bag with the remains of his sandwich lunch and threw it across the room, bouncing it off the edge of the wire waste-paper basket and landing it on the floor.

"Susan, television is not real," he spoke as if he was addressing his younger daughter, "they are made-up stories. If I've got to follow this maid, then I'd like to do it correctly and not get compromised."

"I'll Google it. Plus, for your information, a lot of TV is real; in fact, reality TV is becoming the norm. Think of those 'fly on the wall' documentaries; they're all real."

"If it was an actual fly on the wall doing the filming, then I might have some sympathy with your viewpoint. However, there will be at least one person in the room filming, possibly another directing, and even a third to take notes, not a normal family dinner by any stretch of the imagination."

"Whatever. Here we go, 'How to follow someone like a P.I. without getting caught', that I'm sure, will tell you all you need to know to be the Jim Rockford of Oxford Circus!"

So, Martin spent the rest of the day learning how to be a private investigator or at least achieve a basic level in 'following a target', as it was described. It sounded easy enough; after all, a parlour maid was not exactly a violent criminal, so he should be reasonably safe on that count. Plus, the amount of work involved would be to simply walk behind someone, which could not be too difficult.

That night he had been tempted to ask his mother if she had sent a client his way, as both he and Susan were confident that Mrs Holburn was no more than a trap laid by Mother. Of course, to ask her could compromise his position, almost admitting that having a client arrive at the door of Hayden Investigations was an unusual occurrence, so in the end, he maintained his dignified, 'Good day at the office, handling confidential cases,' which seemed for the most part to satisfy Mother, who made no mention of, 'Did a Grace Holburn come to your office today?' No doubt Grace would have reported to Mother by now, and she would have been aware that her son had taken on the case, as indeed he had, hoping that just a couple of hours walking behind some Filipino maid, would put him in the clear and back to a full social life.

The next day, with the first-ever work-related entry in Martin's Outlook Calendar, he prepared for lunch with Jenny. A quiet lunch was all that she wanted today, something to get her out of the house, which Martin was pleased to assist with. So, it was no surprise when, just after noon, there was a knock at the door. The surprise was the woman who walked in, who did not have Jenny's long legs or her rather ample bosom; definitely, the woman standing in the doorway was not Jenny. In fact, both Susan and Martin looked at the lady and thought to themselves, 'Who on earth are you?'

"I want to speak to Martin Hayden please," her voice was both well-spoken and bellicose.

A distinct feeling of Groundhog Day floated over Martin.

"You are speaking to him. What can I do for you?"

"I need to speak to you privately about a very confidential matter." Although she was speaking to Martin, she looked down her nose through her broad-rimmed glasses at Susan, clearly implying that she wanted the girl removed from the room.

"My personal assistant, Susan, can be trusted totally."

Martin hoped that he came across convincingly, as he doubted that Susan could be discreet about anything that she classed as good gossip. He knew that from personal experience when Susan had shared with him the very explicit details of one of her girlfriend's exploits of bedding two men at the same time. Although somehow looking at the woman standing in front of him, with her grey hair cut in a straight fringe across her high forehead, he doubted it would be anything to do with sex.

"Very well, may I sit?"

It was not intended as a question, so she did not wait for an answer; she simply sat down at Susan's desk and looked across at Martin in a way that made Martin feel uncomfortable and made him wonder if it was a sexual issue after all. This left Susan standing awkwardly by the kitchenette door, eagerly waiting to hear what was said.

"I am Mrs McLaughlin, although you may call me Paige. I wish to enlist the services of Hayden Investigations to follow my mother."

Now Martin had two distinct and very separate thoughts. First, following people was something he now knew a lot about; although he had not actually followed anyone just yet but he knew the theory. Secondly, 'her mother'? Martin estimated that Paige was in her mid-sixties, so her mother would be at least in her eighties; how hard could it be to follow an old lady?

Without waiting for a reply, Paige continued; she was used to people carrying out her wishes without question.

"My mother goes abroad regularly on those awful coach trips around northern France. Each time, I know she takes a large sum of money with her and never returns with any. I am concerned that she is being taken advantage of; being ninety years old, I am sure she is seen as a very vulnerable lady."

Ninety, Martin thought, following behind a wheelchair cannot be that hard. Paige continued, "I want you to go on her next trip, which leaves this Friday, watch her, and see what happens, then report back to me. It is a five-day trip, so I am happy to pay your daily rate for the five days; I trust there will be a discount. Plus, I will pay your expenses, as long as you have receipts to verify your spending and do not exceed one hundred pounds per day. No one needs to spend more than that. I will expect a full report on the sixth day."

Martin looked across at Susan.

"This sounds a lot like the Newcastle case that we had recently."

Susan nodded. "Very much the same, I would say."

"Mrs McLaughlin, or Paige if you prefer, if I am required to start this case on Friday, I will need a little time to organise my diary. I will call you later today to make final arrangements."

Susan asked as she showed Mrs McLaughlin out of the office, "Just one more question if you don't mind, it will help with our marketing. Where did you hear about our company?"

Paige looked slyly at Susan, having already made her mind up that this young lady was not the sort of person she would employ if she ran a detective agency.

"A friend recommended your service. I do hope that you live up to my expectations." She turned to speak to Martin, "I look forward to meeting you again."

Without waiting for a reply, she strode out of the office.

As the door closed, Martin slumped forward onto his desk, his head in his hands.

"Without a doubt, Mother recommended me. Why does she persist in running my life for me?"

Martin knew two things: his mother would never stop interfering in his life and the other thing that was never going to happen to Martin Hayden was that he was going on a five-day coach trip to France with a load of old ladies. Some things he could handle, old people were not one of those things. Old people have a habit of telling you what to do, think they know what's best for you, and totally do not understand the modern world, applying their outdated experiences to a time that they do not and cannot fully understand. So, when Susan asked if he was going, the answer was a definitive 'no'.

"I think you should go," Susan countered, "that way, your mother cannot say you are not working."

"Susan, no way am I boarding a coach, pre-packed with pensioners. You, on the other hand, I am sure would get along fine with a bunch of old dears."

"Can't."

"Why not? I thought part of your mantra for getting a job was anything is possible."

"Part of my getting a job was saying I had a passport, which I do; it's just it's out of date."

She smiled as Martin scowled back at her.

"I am beginning to think that your CV was not as frank as it should have been."

"But you love me now, so let's move on."

A moment later, the door swung open again. This time a tall, blonde woman stood smiling at Martin.

"Ah, at last, I get to meet Susan." Jenny stepped into the office, her tall stiletto heels digging into the carpet. She undid her jacket and embraced Susan with an air kiss to each cheek. "I cannot understand how you put up with his ways; I know he drives me mad at times. A true gentleman would have picked me up in a cab. Instead, I have to walk past shops, which I find terribly hard to do."

"Well, you're not laden down with bags," Martin observed, standing up and collecting his jacket from the back of his chair.

"Delivery service darling, delivery. I'm sure the expensive restaurant you have planned for me would not take kindly to me arriving with an armload of shopping bags."

"Do you want me to book your coach trip?" Susan asked before Martin was able to exit the office.

Jenny stopped, wobbled on her heels, and turned back to Susan,

"Coach trip? Not for my Martin?"

"Well, I can't, as I don't have an up-to-date passport, it will have to be Martin on his first international case."

"Pray, explain Susan. I am sure Martin will not share this amazing piece of news. Does this mean you get to do some real work, Martin?"

Jenny stood in the office, a silent Martin beside her, as Susan explained the arrival of clients they had had. It amused Jenny to learn that Martin had not just one but now two clients that he would need to satisfy. In fact, Jenny thought it hilarious that Martin might have to actually do something that came close to being described as work.

"Well, I'm not going, and that's that. End of discussion," Martin stated. "I'll have words with Mother tonight, she can tell Paige McLaughlin that we are unable to help, and I'll be sending Susan out to follow the maid. Thus, I will remain untarnished by real work. And before you start moaning about following maids, Miss Susan Morris, take it as punishment for telling white lies on your CV about your passport."

Jenny ran her hands through Martin's hair,

"Susan, do you not agree that this young man should put aside his fear of old people and embrace a coach trip?" Susan simply nodded and smiled in agreement. "There, Martin, we both agree, best start packing. Nothing too raunchy mind, can't have those old ladies having heart attacks, can we?"

"Jenny, I am not going."

"Maybe you don't want to work, which is fair enough; why should we if we have enough cash to live our lives? That's the only reason anyone would want to go to work. However, Martin, consider this old lady, ninety years old, going off to France with a bagful of cash, coming back with nothing. Someone I suspect is taking her for a ride. A frail little old lady being conned should not be allowed to happen anywhere on this planet, let alone on a coach trip to Monet's garden, did you say? Maybe you don't want to, but you have the chance of stopping this old lady from getting conned. Martin, you should, as a decent human being, go and stop whatever is going on. Even though some might describe you as a lazy, self-centred individual, it's a chance for you to redeem yourself. It would make me very happy to see you as a decent, caring human being."

"She has a point, Martin; it does sound from what Mrs McLaughlin said that there is a little old lady, her mother, being conned out of her life savings. What would you do if that was your mother, with your inheritance dwindling into the pocket of some scoundrel?"

"I'm hungry; if you want lunch Jenny, you had best follow me. See you tomorrow, Susan."

Jenny smiled back at Susan and followed Martin out of the office.

* * *

There was going to be no good time to ask the question. Martin knew that when he did, he would get her glaring eyes from across the large pine-wood table that he and his mother used for their meals. It was the informal dining table, located along one wall of the large rectangular kitchen. It was easy and convenient to cook, serve, eat, and load the dishwasher with the least number of footsteps taken. There was another much grander dining room in the house with a finely polished table and matching plush upholstered chairs. A dining room that could accommodate twelve people with ease, giving room for guests to eat, drink and converse comfortably. That room was reserved for special occasions; everyday eating was carried out in the kitchen. Martin's mother insisted on doing all her cooking; even though she had many opportunities to employ someone to cook for her, she always refused. 'How can you expect foreign people to cook proper English food? It just cannot be done.' She had famously commented at a dinner party. This was ironic, really, as, at the time, she was serving a very spicy Indian Biryani. From the looks around the table, many thought she was a little confused or maybe not confused, but just a bit misguided.

"So, you asked her?" Susan inquired.

"Yes, 'Mother,' I said, 'did you recommend some of your friends to my service?' Then I covered my bland sausages with some brown sauce to give them some flavour. She always buys the cheapest, insipid sausages saving pennies. I have told her time and time again, 'cheapness comes at a price'; that is one of my long-standing mantras."

Susan was sitting on the side of Martin's desk eating her Danish breakfast and dropping flakes of pastry onto his desk. Normally he might well have mentioned that he did not want food crumbs on his desk, but today her tight jeans and floral perfume out-trumped the crumbs.

"Mother said she did bring up what I do for a living during a small lunch with a couple of friends, clearly the two old biddies who turned up at our office. Mother said they were both having difficulties and wondered how they might get discreet help, so she put my name forward. Of course, Mother emphasised that she was only doing it to help my business grow."

What she actually said to Martin was that she had little faith in her son ever becoming a business entrepreneur without her behind him constantly pushing and cajoling him to take action. She had always wanted him to go into banking, a career move that she was sure would have suited him. Sitting in an office making phone calls, playing with figures, in fact not needing to do a great deal in order to make stacks of money. After all, that is just what bankers do; take a bag of money from one person and pass it to another, skimming off a percentage in the process. Not real work, unlike her husband, who bought cold steel and turned it into screws of all shapes and sizes that people wanted. Martin knew what was coming next; he had heard it countless times during his childhood and adult life. Your father built up a worldwide respected company manufacturing screws, screws of all types, shapes and sizes. The English Screw Company started in a small workshop, and through hard work, razor-sharp business acumen, and a supportive wife by his side, it became a world leader, which pays for everything you have. In her mind, Martin had a lot to thank the simple steel helix for. Martin did not see it that way at all, mainly because he never really understood how a screw actually worked or why you needed so many different screw heads and screwdrivers. For Martin, a good old-fashioned hammer and nail seemed to be as efficient, although Martin wouldn't, or any of his friends for that matter, ever describe him as a DIY expert.

So, much to her disappointment, Martin shunned the banking industry and started his own company, which he seemed to have no ambition to grow and expand. So, without a supportive wife, which was another thing that disappointed her about Martin, it was going to be up to her to keep him on his toes. Hence, she had insisted on a Personal Assistant and was now directing friends to help increase trade; next, she would be insisting that he employ additional private detectives. Mrs Hayden had plans for her son; he just was not fully aware of them as yet.

"So, I asked her to let me know next time she advertises us, which she said she would, although I doubt she will, it's just the way my mother works. At least we can now turn down anyone else who arrives on our doorstep."

Susan slid off the desk, brushed the crumbs from her jeans onto the carpet and walked back to her own desk.

"At least she cares for you; so many parents couldn't care less about their kids."

"Didn't your parents care for you?"

"Hell yes, Mum and Dad loved me. I have no idea why; I was the dumb one of the family. Both my sisters had brains and my share as well, I reckon. I was always bottom of the class, was always getting caught smoking or shoplifting, but they still appeared to love me, even though I must have been one big disappointment."

"Shoplifting?" Martin was surprised by the admission.

"Nothing serious, packets of sweets, lipsticks, just things me and a group of girls did for excitement during lunch breaks at school. Come on, have you never nicked anything in your life?"

"No, never!" Martin declared firmly, "I went to a boarding school, so lunches were spent inside the hall eating, not prowling the high street for victims."

"Well, I have changed since being a teenager."

"Thank goodness for that."

"So, our two clients, what's the plan, are you going to France? Did Jenny convince you yesterday over lunch?"

Jenny had indeed been most persuasive. She had first appealed to Martin's compassionate side, pleading that a lonely, frail, ninety-year-old lady was getting scammed out of her savings, maybe by some French scoundrel, or even worse, someone on the coach trip itself. Jenny could see no reason why a 'con artist' could not be in their sixties or seventies. This argument did not change Martin's mind one little bit. Five days trapped with a coach load of pensioners was not high on his list of priorities. Her second reasoning was a change of subject.

Jenny's husband, who she always said she loved but just did not find exciting, owned buildings across the capital, buying them up cheap, refurbishing them and then renting them out. Both residential and commercial properties could be found in her husband's portfolio, including 'One Duchess Street', the base for Hayden Investigations.

"The arrangement we have regarding your office space. It will make me feel a lot more comfortable if you do help the occasional client. If you were actually working from your rent-free office, it would make it seem a lot less like stealing, more like a friend doing a favour for a friend."

To be fair to Martin, the rent-free office had been Jenny's suggestion, following a very passionate night early in their relationship. Martin, with Jenny laying her head on his chest, had been talking about how he wanted to start his own company, but the financial burden of renting office space in London was a big downside. At once, Jenny suggested that as her husband had a shed load of office space in London, she was sure she could find one that they could 'manage' in such a way that Martin paid no rent; hence, the rent-free office at 'One Duchess Street'.

Although Martin had never considered it as stealing, it was clear that she was going to review the arrangement unless he helped the frail, old lady. Five horrendous days on a coach was the price he was going to have to pay. In his own words, 'cheapness comes at a price' or, in this case, rent-free office space comes with conditions.

"Yes, Jenny and I had a long conversation, and I could see that there is a vulnerable old lady here who needs help, so I'm off to France on Friday. Which leaves you with the maid next Tuesday if that is OK with you?"

"Of course, it sounds exciting, Susan Morris, PI, just like Jim Rockford."

"Now, I do not want you taking this the wrong way but consider for a moment you are following her to where, we have no idea, so I am a little uncomfortable about you doing this on your own. Is there anyone you could take with you to make sure nothing goes wrong? I don't want you getting hurt or into some sort of bother."

Susan walked around behind Martin and hugged him, "You're so sweet at times. I'm sure Colin would love to help."

"That guy who helped you outside the club?"

"The very one."

"Well, he sounds like a tough cookie and can handle himself. I'll be a lot happier with a strong man beside you; he sounds just the ticket. Well, Martin Hayden Investigations will be, for the first time, doing some actual investigating. Hopefully, it will also be the last time."

"That is," Susan added as she walked over to the window checking the weather to see if she needed to wear a coat when she went shopping at lunchtime, "unless your mother has other ideas."

* * *

Sitting on a luxurious fifty-two-seater coach that was crawling through the traffic-clogged streets of Chelsea reminded Martin of that dark, autumn day he left home, a timid eleven-year-old boy, on his way to boarding school. Back then, he sat alone, scared of what might lie in store for him. He had heard so many horror stories of life in dormitories, with strict masochistic form masters and older boys treating the younger new boys like slaves. Those fears had etched themselves into his memory so well that sitting here today, he felt a shiver of dread ripple down his spine. It was his mother who had insisted that her young son be sent away for his education. It was the expectation that all well-bred boys should spend their school days learning: Latin, Mathematics, English and, importantly, how to live away from their family and be independent. Although his father finally agreed, he did so reluctantly, of that Martin was pretty sure. He had overheard his parents discussing his schooling arrangements on many occasions, with Father saying how much he had hated his days at boarding school and that he had hoped his son would never have to go through the same ordeal. In the end, as always, Mother got her way, and a young, terrified Martin was on his way to boarding school.

Around him, back then, were boys of all shapes and sizes dressed in pristine school blazers, each with newly pressed white shirts and school ties; conservative school ties that would be worn as a status symbol of their education for the rest of their lives. Some boys chatting non-stop with excited voices; others, like Martin, sitting quietly, avoiding eye contact, trying to stay within their own safe world, not wanting to socialise or engage in mundane conversations.

Today, as they stopped outside South Kensington tube station to collect more travellers, Martin could see the similarity to that school coach. However, this time the coach was mostly populated by grey-haired women instead of young boys. Some of them had been eager to talk to fellow passengers and at once had begun to share their experiences with voices that were full of excitement as they began their adventure. All of them seemed to be a lot older than Martin, yet he could still see those who, like himself, would prefer to just sit and watch the world go by. So far, he had no one beside him, a situation he hoped he could maintain.

He watched three people step onto the coach, a man and a woman who were clearly a couple, maybe in their seventies, although Martin would always be the first to admit he was not a good judge of age. The third person boarding at South Kensington should be Beatrice Cook, Paige McLaughlin's mother. If she was Beatrice, Martin was impressed. She was tall, very straight-backed and well dressed in a pale green trouser suit. She acknowledged both the courier and driver and then walked to the very back of the coach without acknowledging anyone further. She was going to be one of the quiet ones, Martin assumed.

That could not be said for the couple who had just got on and who had now settled in the two seats directly in front of Martin. Before the driver had even managed to rejoin the congestion on Cromwell Road, the woman who had taken the window seat turned around and spoke to Martin through the gap between the headrests.

"Hello, I'm Fleur, and this is my husband, Ron. I thought we were going to miss the coach as Ron was convinced that we should be at Gloucester Road tube station, weren't you Ron? We were on the tube between Putney Bridge and Parsons Green, that bit of the underground that is not underground, although Ron has always said that there is more overground to the underground than there is underground. I don't travel much on the tube, even though I have my freedom pass, I still prefer the bus. So, I was sure we were meeting at South Kensington, but Ron thought it was Gloucester Road. I always was sure it was South Kensington because I can remember thinking when we got the booking confirmation that it was near the Science Museum, not that I have ever been there. So, we were searching through our cases for the booking form, which turned out to be in Ron's pocket. I was right, so we stayed on the tube and just about made it here. Where did you get on?"

Apart from her voice coming through the gap, Martin was struck by a very strong perfume that could never be described as a fragrance. Martin suspected that she may well have spilt it whilst talking to herself in the dressing table mirror.

"Victoria coach station was my boarding point."

"We thought about that too, yet it's just so busy, I would get lost with all those stops and different buses and things. As I said to Ron when we booked this, South Kensington was going to be a lot easier than Victoria coach station, and I was right. There were just us and that other lady, the tall one.

"You're a bit young to join all of us old 'fogies'. We've been on a few of these tours; we try and do one a month if possible. It gets us out and gives us the chance to meet people. Ron likes to stay at home, but I tell him, you need to get out and see the world. We've been to this part of France before, although that was for the D Day beaches tour, which Ron didn't mind going on. Ron likes his war history, don't you, Ron? So, what brings you on this coach load of pensioners?"

Martin was tempted to lean through the gap and see if Ron was still alive, as he had not heard a word spoken by him yet, although Martin did suspect that being married to Fleur did not give you much opportunity to get any words in. The temptation for him was to tell her the truth; he was having to follow an old lady to prove to his overbearing mother that his business was active, thus allowing him to retain his monthly unearned income. Clearly, it made better sense to lie; Fleur did not seem to be the sort of person who could keep a secret.

"I like the company of older people; they have so much wisdom and experience to share, I find it refreshing. My peer group tend to enjoy getting drunk and making fools of themselves."

"Well, you haven't been on one of these trips before. I'm sure by the end of our five days, at least two old dears will have arrived back at the hotel drunk, and a few more will have made fools of themselves. We were on a Paris weekend trip, and two old ladies had gone missing one night. The whole hotel was in uproar with worry for them; even the French police were called. They were so nice and helpful, not that I am saying our police are not helpful, it's just that you don't expect foreign police to be the same as a London 'Bobby'. Well, those foreign police carry guns for one thing, which I think is so frightening. What if one of them went mad or something? It's not unheard of. Anyway, they searched high and low for these two old dears; one was eighty-four and the other eighty-five. It was after three in the morning when they arrived back at the hotel in a police car, having been discovered in a seedy bar in the red-light district. Both of them were very drunk, having decided that they wanted to try that strong French drink, Absinthe. I wouldn't try anything much stronger than a sweet sherry, although Ron likes a whisky at Christmas. The next day both of them were hungover, serves them right, that's what I say. So, you can expect some of the same on most of these trips."

It had become clear to Martin that Fleur could not answer a question in less than a hundred words; short, sharp answers were not something she was capable of. So, he needed a diversion to break the conversation. He pulled out his mobile telephone from his pocket,

"Excuse me, please, I need to take this call."

"I didn't hear it ring, and I know I have very sensitive hearing; the doctor was very impressed when I had my hearing tested. Not because I had anything wrong with my hearing, far from it; it was just that I was getting some dizzy turns, so they wanted to check everything out."

"It was on vibrate in consideration of others." Martin wondered if Fleur had a vibrate setting. Before she could answer, he held the phone to his ear, "Hello, Martin speaking."

Fleur turned away from the gap she had been peering through and moved her attention to the couple in front of her. Martin had a one-sided conversation with his telephone and realised he had only been on this coach trip for less than thirty minutes and already he was talking to himself.

* * *

"Please do join me; it will make a pleasant change to be
opposite an attractive young man while I dine. I am sure you will
be a lot more interesting to talk to than some of these dreary,
old people." Beatrice waved in the general direction of the tables
around her occupied by their fellow passengers, who were
having their first meal in France.

Martin took up the invitation to sit down facing Beatrice
Cook as she finished her entrée of thinly cut ham decorated with
small onions and gherkins on a bed of green lettuce. He was not
sure what Jim Rockford might have thought of dining with the
person that you were meant to be following; it just seemed a
better way than skulking in the corner with watchful eyes and
looking like some sort of weirdo. Martin had observed Beatrice
getting off the coach, carrying her luggage and collecting her
key from reception without any form of hesitation. She did not
look to be the sort of person who could be easily conned out of
anything, let alone her money. Compared to the other travellers,
she did not look her age and seemed to be different to the other
'old dears' as she described even those younger than herself. Her
eyes had a sharpness to them, a street-wise look. Martin
doubted that she would be taken for a fool. So, ignoring the vast
amount of advice from the aspiring private detective websites he
had read on the internet, he decided it might be useful to join
her for dinner and learn a little more from her and not just her
daughter. Martin knew from experience there were always two
sides to a mother and child story.

"I'm Beatrice or Trixie if you wish. I'm not too bothered
what people call me." Beatrice offered her hand to Martin by
way of a greeting.

"I'm Martin, pleased to meet you," he said, shaking her
hand.

Martin, on the recommendation of Beatrice, ordered the

entrecôte, cooked rare, as she had pointed out that: 'if you want vitamins then go rare, if you want iron, go well done, so unless you're pregnant, go for rare every time'. As Martin passed on the entrée, both their main plates arrived simultaneously. Beatrice cut into her meat and began consuming it with youthful gusto.

"I always find it amusing that red meat you can eat raw, yet the way they talk about poultry, you have to burn it to get it anywhere near clear of salmonella. Yet the powers that be, so-called experts, still maintain that red meat is bad for you; what do they know? I have often wondered what it would be like to kill an animal then eat the meat while it was still warm. I hope you don't think I'm weird; I just question things too much sometimes. For example, what is someone like you doing here, clearly underage for one of these placid trips?"

Martin felt he was on the spot here, mainly because naively, he did not expect before he started this trip to be asked just why he had joined a bunch of people who, for the most part, were at least twice his age.

"I just wanted to get away from everyone I know for a while, a bit of time out."

"Sounds like woman trouble to me; I will ask no more. I understand the need sometimes to get away from those that hang around us."

"Is that why you are on this trip?"

"Partly. I like my own company, time to read, contemplate, relax. Back in the smoke of London, there is a constant line of boring invitations to lunch, coffee, dinner, knitting circles, all that sort of crap old people are expected to do. To be honest, one has to accept some of those invitations, but here on these coach trips - I now do a few each year - one can disappear into one's own life. What do you do back in the UK? I guess you haven't retired yet unless you're living off the family fortune?"

Martin was beginning to wonder if Beatrice was a better detective than he was. It was instinct that made him answer.

The food was good, he was a little tired, and the red wine was starting to relax him. Plus, it was an answer that he automatically had given many times in the past.

"I'm a de......" he stopped himself mid-word, frantically thinking of a word that was not detective but began with the same syllable he had already blurted out., ".... deputy..." he added, which was not much help at all, and he felt he was now beginning to sound like an imbecile, "a deputy security manager. I shouldn't really say any more than that. I'm sure you understand."

"Sounds exciting. I'll ask no more. Shame though, I like a bit of excitement in my life."

Martin was now planning to pry more into her life, learn a little more about Beatrice when he heard a familiar voice from behind him.

"Can we join you?" Fleur did not wait for an answer; she just sat down beside Beatrice and ushered Ron to sit down next to Martin.

From then on, Beatrice, Martin and Ron listened to Fleur. She talked about children, grandchildren, decorating, and gardening, 'which Ron does most of, spending a lot of time in his greenhouse'. Martin could understand the attraction of the quiet solitude of the greenhouse for Ron.

During her soup, Fleur launched into reasons the country was in the state it was. Why her local council was better before the poll tax changed everything, followed by schools that do not teach children the things they should know. Immigration was bringing the country down, and as for asylum seekers, well.... If some of them had listened to Fleur before coming over, then they might well have stayed in France or even returned to their newly liberated iron curtain country. Fleur had an opinion on anything and everything, no opinion being exactly well thought out or based on tolerance. Even poor Ron was lampooned as he ate his plain omelette and chips.

"Ron doesn't get on with this foreign food; he likes an English roast, meat, vegetables, something which you can recognize, isn't that right, Ron? Still, he likes an omelette, don't you, Ron? He wouldn't dream of having one of those Indian curries; you don't know what goes into them."

Ron nodded as he sprayed more tomato sauce onto his chips.

Martin wondered what it was with the English and their distrust of foreign food. Fleur and her kind did seem to have a complete distrust of any food, which might be deemed 'foreign'. Martin had no scientific evidence, although he would have liked to point out to Fleur if he could have got a word in that the rest of the world seemed to have survived on 'foreign muck' for a good few thousand years. So why doesn't Ron want to try the faux fillet? After all, it's only beef? Still, the main thing was that Ron was eating his omelette. He did not seem to be that enamoured with it, or maybe that had more to do with Fleur talking about washing his 'y' fronts in non-biological washing powder. It was at that point Beatrice stood up and politely left the table, leaving Ron and Martin to the verbal broadside of Fleur.

Beatrice had gone up to her room, but Martin wondered if she might make an appearance later in the evening, so with that in mind, once he had seized a short break in Fleur's talking to excuse himself from the table, he sat quietly in the reception area, sipping a cold beer and reading one of the French newspapers hoping to refresh his schoolboy French. Having decided that the sports pages are by far the easiest to read, he happened to glance up and see Beatrice leaving the hotel, slide into the front of a taxi that was waiting in front of it, and drive away. Martin went up to the reception desk.

"Do you know where that lady has gone? The one who has just gone off in a cab."

The male receptionist shrugged his shoulders,

"She just wanted a taxi," his English was laced with a strong French accent, which Martin thought sounded almost put on.

"Is there any way to find out? I really need to know where she has gone."

"Maybe if I get you a taxi, then your driver, he might know. He might be able to speak to the other taxi driver, who knows? I am not a taxi driver. You want le taxi?"

It was not like hailing a London cab; a quarter of an hour later, a blue, well-worn Peugeot pulled up outside the hotel, and Martin jumped into the front seat. The driver smiled, displaying a row of crooked teeth, and then asked in an even heavier French accent than the receptionist had,

"Where to Monsieur?"

"A taxi picked up a lady from here, say twenty minutes ago. I want to go to the same place as she went to."

The driver with the crooked teeth, even though he had limited English, continued smiling. His foreign vocabulary was limited to keywords all associated with going places and getting paid; for him asking to follow someone was a little more complex.

"I not understand" was his fall-back phrase in these situations.

Martin took a deep breath and tried to explain in broken French that he wanted to follow a ninety-year-old lady who had taken a taxi earlier and if there was any way that they could find out where she had gone. Of course, that was not the type of phrase you learn at school; teachers just did not plan for their pupils to stalk old ladies across France.

"Suivez la vieille dame dans le taxi qui a quitté ici, il y a un peu de temps." Martin thought that was a pretty good attempt, and his French teacher, he hoped, would have been impressed.

Not expecting such a request, the crooked-toothed driver, assumed he had heard wrong,

"You want zee old lady? I find you young, beautiful lady, better, n'est pas?"

Instead, Martin used his schoolboy French to ask the driver to wait while he sought the help of the receptionist and so avoid what the taxi driver might be offering him.

Five minutes later, all three were grouped around the driver's door, Martin with the receptionist, who was called Henri, and the taxi driver, whose name appeared to be Luke. Martin thought he heard some words that could have been describing him as a little mad. Even so, Luke made some phone calls, laughed a lot into his mobile phone and said a number of times, 'oui, un peu bizarre.' Eventually, he looked proudly with his crooked smile and announced, "Get in, we go."

After that, Martin was being driven through several dark backstreets, across traffic lights just flashing amber, before they left the street lights and drove into dark, winding, narrow lanes.

"A quelle distance?" Martin asked more than once, each time getting the reply, 'pas loin', 'not far', he translated.

The dark roads seriously made him wonder if he should have asked Susan's guardian angel, Colin, to join him on this coach trip. He had no idea where he was going or who he was going to meet. It was another ten minutes before they joined a road with street lights again. The town sign showed Deauville, and once again, other traffic made Martin feel a little less vulnerable.

The cab pulled up in front of a grand, white building with the word 'Casino' emblazoned in white lamps over the wide, pillared entrance. After Martin had handed over what he considered to be an excessive number of euros for the trip, he walked into the grand, sumptuous entrance. The doorman dressed in braided uniform, white gloves and shoes which you could check your make-up in nodded politely and opened the door for him.

Martin entered and made his way past the cloakroom and

through a heavy glass door which led into a glittering room of lights, tall arches, heavy drapes and hundreds of slot machines which were being worked frantically by numerous men and women. It took Martin the best part of ten minutes, wandering between the slot machines and into blackjack gaming rooms, before finally walking into a spacious room with six busy, roulette tables. He spotted Beatrice standing beside a roulette table and leaning across to lay some coloured chips on it.

Martin stood beside a noisy, colourful slot machine and watched Beatrice as she continued to place chips on the table, wait for the roulette wheel to stop, and then place more chips on the table. At one point, she clapped her hands, and Martin watched as the croupier pushed a small pile of chips her way, no doubt that time she had chosen the number correctly. Then the routine of laying chips on the table continued. She chatted with the other gamblers, laughed, pointed and was clearly part of the group that surrounded the table picking numbers.

He continued to watch her, an elderly lady, well dressed, clearly enjoying herself a little too much. Martin had always assumed that by the time you reached your nineties, evenings would be spent at home in front of the TV, preparing for an early night, not standing beside a roulette table close to midnight, putting your pension on red and black numbers. He began to consider his options. He guessed he had now achieved the objective of his trip to France and could see that Beatrice was not being conned out of her money. Well, that might be a matter of opinion, but she was not being deceived. She was just enjoying giving it away freely to the casino owners.

As the wheel stopped, without any preamble, she strode away from the table directly towards Martin, with a beaming smile on her face.

"So, is this how you deal with woman trouble, Martin, hanging around slot machines?" Beatrice laughed. "Picking up a bit of strange or just gambling the night away?"

"Could say the same about you; reading a book, relaxing, contemplating."

"Hey, I told the truth, young man. I read books about how to win at the roulette table; I contemplate which numbers will come up and then relax as the wheel spins. I'm always open and honest; it's just that some people, those who don't know me, assume an old lady like me would not be spending her nights at the casino. Come and buy me a drink. I'm having a break; let the wheel spin without me for a while."

They sat in purple velour armchairs in a quiet corner of the casino with a low table in front of them. Beatrice had a large gin and tonic, no ice. Martin sipped his cold beer before he asked a question.

"So, is this your holiday treat, a night at the casino?"

"You are so naive, Martin; there I was thinking that you were a man of the world. I spend every night in this casino. I'll be back tomorrow night, the next night and every night until we go back to the UK. By the end of the week, they will be giving me free drinks, and there will be tears when I leave, assuming I have lost plenty. If I win big, they will be glad to see the back of me."

"Do you win big?"

"Oh yes." Beatrice stirred her drink with a bright pink plastic stick on which a lemon slice was skewered. "I win big, but that is offset by losing even bigger. Gamblers never win. Who do you think pays for all these plush and garish surroundings? Everything they do, roulette, blackjack, craps, poker, all the gaudy slot machines over there, all programmed and weighted in favour of the casino. This isn't a charity, Martin; this is a big money-making business. I give them my money, and I get, in return, excitement. So, in the end, we are all happy, getting what we want."

"Why come all this way? What's wrong with London casinos?"

Beatrice emptied her glass and caught the attention of a passing waiter so she could order another drink.

"And G&T for my friend here," she added. "If you're going to be with me all night, you have to drink something more exciting than a plain beer. I can't have you being too sober now, can I?"

Martin accepted the offer of a gin and tonic, guessing it could be a long night.

"So why not London?" he repeated.

"Banned, not allowed in them. Well, to be fair, that is not exactly true, but I am as good as banned. The rule there is that I cannot spend more than a hundred pounds a night, so a bloody waste of time. Hence I have now boycotted all the London casinos in favour of the more relaxed French ones."

"You must win really big back in London?"

"I wish. No, it's my interfering daughter who decided that I should not lose so much and applied some pressure to the casinos."

"So isn't that a good thing, cutting your losses, not gambling too much?"

"No, Martin, it is not. Let me explain further to you. I gamble, I always have, and I always will; it is what I do. Let's take roulette, my preferred game. I like the conflict in my mind, debating where to place my chip, then deciding, placing that small slice of plastic against a number. That is followed by the anticipation of the wheel rotating and the small ball rolling in the opposite direction. My heart really does start beating faster as the wheel slows. The time is now coming. Will the ball land on my number? My pulse starts to race. When the ball starts to bounce around the numbers, everything is slowing but for my pulse."

The waiter interrupted by placing two large gin and tonics on the table. Beatrice placed twenty euros on the waiter's tray, then waved him away, picked up her drink and continued.

"Finally, the ball decides where it wants to land and who it is going to favour on that spin. The croupier calls the number, did I win, did I lose? If I win, then I have planned everything correctly, I have forecast the future and now have thirty-five times what I put on the table. I am a winner. On the other hand, more often than not, I will lose. I will watch as the casino staff scoop up my stake; I have failed to predict the number. So, what do I do? I go back to square one, thinking where I might have gone wrong. Is there a pattern forming? How close was I? Again, with more information, I debate and consider where to place my next chip. So down it goes, and the whole process starts again as the wheel begins to spin. At times it is better than sex, not that I have had that in a number of years. Trust me, Martin; it is the closest any ninety-year-old can get to an orgasm. Come on, grab your drink, let's get you some chips, and we'll work the tables together. I sense you have a lot to learn."

Over the next three hours, Martin learnt just about all there was to know about roulette. He learnt that he was playing the French version, which is subtly different to the European and American versions. He could see the stick man clearing the table of the cash chips and paying out the winning bets. According to Beatrice, much slower than the English, but there again, she said, when have the French ever rushed anything. Martin was mocked by his new gambling friend for playing just five euros a time. He, on the other hand, thought she was mad for placing bets of one hundred euros. That was until she picked the correct number twice in a row and had seven thousand euros in front of her.

It was three o'clock in the morning, with the casino closing when they both left, getting into one of the many taxis that were waiting patiently outside. Through dark, winding lanes, they were driven back to the hotel.

"Thank you for teaching me how to play roulette, Beatrice."

"It was my pleasure. It's not often I am able to get such a young, handsome man beside me at the table. Same again tomorrow night?" She saw the hesitation in his eyes. "Come on," she encouraged, "you are only young once. I know that from experience."

Martin smiled, "Sounds like fun, and I might splash out and maybe place a ten euro bet tomorrow."

"Last of the big spenders, are you? Can I suggest that if we are hitting the tables tomorrow night, that we eat at the casino? I could not bear to get trapped at the dining table with that 'talkie' Fleur person and her wimp of a husband. It kind of puts you off your food, don't you think?"

"That sounds like a good plan to me, plus I will treat you. What about one of those big plates of seafood that you can share, crab, lobster, oysters? They look so appetizing. I might not yet be a fully-fledged gambler, but I do like to enjoy my seafood, especially when in Northern France."

"I like sea food, as long as it is a fish. The lobsters and oysters you can keep; I hate any sort of seafood that comes in shells. I am convinced that if God had meant us to eat such things, he would not have encased them in rock-hard shells that are a pain to open."

Sitting in the back of that cab, Martin wondered what Jim Rockford would have thought about the Hayden investigation technique; he hoped that he would have been impressed.

After that, Beatrice and Martin slipped into the routine of arriving back at the hotel around three in the morning, sleeping in till midday, missing all the excursions, having lunch before heading over to the casino for a couple of hours in the afternoon, taking a break for dinner in 'Le Cercle' restaurant, which overlooked the gaming tables. Then it was back to the tables to spend the evening watching that little ball drop into, hopefully, your number. Apart from losing money, Martin soon realised that his behaviour and that of the ninety-year-old Beatrice was now the subject of many conversations among their fellow travellers, who they rarely saw. It was on the last day in the afternoon as he came down to join Beatrice to take their waiting cab to Deauville that he saw Beatrice with another old lady, whom he had seen around. They were having a very heated conversation. The shorter woman, who he knew as Florence, was waving her arms around and pointing at the face of Beatrice, who appeared to be giving as good as she was getting. Martin approached them to hear Florence say with venom, "You have always been selfish; nothing changes."

Beatrice looked and saw Martin beside her, "Come on, Martin, our cab is waiting; I have no more to say to this woman."

In the cab, Martin asked what was going on. Beatrice told him bluntly that it was none of his business. For the rest of that last night, Beatrice was not as happy as she had been, even though she left the casino that night with over a thousand euros profit. Twice Martin returned to the subject of the conversation with Florence, twice he was told there was nothing to tell. In the end, he had to settle for not knowing.

* * *

"Oh my God, she's gambling the money away. These old people, you've got to watch 'em all the time."

Susan brought Martin's coffee over to his desk, spilling some of it on the way, the revelation that Beatrice Cook was a gambling ninety-year-old having distracted her.

"Oh yes, and she knew how to gamble. Over the week, I think she must have lost the best part of five thousand pounds. Ugh! Sugar Susan! I've been away a week, and you have already forgotten how I like my coffee."

"Yeah, the same way you forgot to bring any duty-free wine back with you. What will her daughter say?"

Martin looked across at Susan.

"You've changed your hair colour; it's a lot blonder now."

"Colin suggested it, thought the colour might suit me. I'm not so sure now."

"Never take fashion tips from men; we just can't do it. Going back to Beatrice's daughter, she must have known that she gambled, so she lied to us. Beatrice told me that it was her daughter that contacted all the casinos, telling them that they should limit what her mother could gamble and pointing out that an old lady losing thousands could be seen in a bad light if it ever found its way to the press. A veiled threat if ever I heard one. So, they took the hint and limited her gambling, which did not please the old lady one little bit, hence the reason she goes abroad."

"So why go to the expense of employing us, just to find out something she must have already guessed?"

"That is a question that I think we should ask. Talking of investigations which it would seem is something we are doing, hopefully, only in the short term, I might add. How did you get on with the maid?"

"Where shall I begin?" Susan pondered.

Susan thought about starting at the beginning of what had happened yesterday, when she had first met up with Colin as planned in a small park opposite Mrs Holburn's house in Saint Georges Square, to await the exit of the maid through the front door. However, she thought that part of the day was not something she should share just yet with Martin.

* * *

Colin had been eager and was already there, sitting on a slightly damp bench, wearing very baggy trousers which resembled something a Turkish sultan might wear, together with a very heavy and equally baggy navy-blue roll-neck jumper which contrasted with his bright red lipstick and almost matched the blue eyeshadow he was wearing. Colin waved her over, moving the large canvas tote bag from beside him and placing it on his lap.

"No sign of her yet, although it is only just ten-fifteen. Take a seat; I'm sure it won't be long before she appears."

Colin took a small notebook out of his back pocket and proceeded to write in it. Susan looked over his shoulder and saw the words: 'ten-eighteen Susan joins Colin on the bench.'

"That's a bit precise and over the top. We're only going to walk behind her, not write her life story."

"Suzie Baby, my dear, we need to make notes of what we are doing, timings and places, what we see, who we are with. You never know when you might need to rely on these things."

"Maybe, but ten-eighteen, I would have said around quarter past ten."

"Try saying that in a court of law. What if the police do get involved? Heaven knows what she might be doing, buying drugs and then selling them at a profit; we have no idea, Suzie Baby? So, I'm making good solid notes of our activity, just in case it ends up in court. On another matter, I saw just the hair colour for you yesterday. I just know it will suit you. Here, silver-blonde, it is so you, Suzie Baby."

Colin handed her a box of branded hair dye. Susan looked at the model on the box, not sure about the colour.

"Do you think so?"

"Oh yes, Suzie Baby, it will make you look really sophisticated. That shade is all the rage, you know, I would wear it, but I think I am a little too old to carry it off. Look, here we go."

Colin pointed over to the large, green-painted open door and the short woman clutching a blue plastic shopping bag coming out of it. The woman walked down the three broad steps onto the damp pavement, then began walking in the direction of Pimlico tube station. Both Colin and Susan began to follow her, Colin noting the exact time they began, Susan still unable to see the point.

They followed the maid past the tube station; she seemed to be walking with a slight limp, her jet-black hair flowing in the slight breeze that was chilling the morning. Against the cold, she wore a lightweight mackintosh with a thick knitted scarf around her neck. Soon they were walking along a small parade of shops on Lupus Street, where she entered a small second-hand shop, the doorbell tinkling out onto the street. The shop presented itself as a bespoke antique shop. Susan followed the maid in and looked around the dusty, cluttered shop. Colin was correct in his description that it was more of a pawnbroker than an antique shop. Even so, Susan took a liking to a painted trinket box, ideal for some of her bracelets. It reminded her of a similar trinket box her older sister had had. A box Susan had coveted, but her sister had refused point-blank to give to her, even though it sat empty and unused. Susan had always been happy to share anything she had with her sisters, yet they were so different, possessive and jealous of each other. Susan opened the box. It had that musty, unused smell which would soon change once she began to use it, then it would have a hint of perfume, a loved and treasured smell to it. She stood close to the maid, an innocent shopper, watching the tubby grey-haired shopkeeper, as he examined a porcelain figure of a woman holding balloons, which Susan thought quite ugly.

"I'll give you twenty pounds, and that is a generous offer as I know you. Is that a deal?"

The maid, twisting the blue plastic bag nervously between her fingers, nodded, then held her hand out, upon which the tubby shopkeeper placed a crisp new twenty-pound note. Without a word, the dark-skinned maid scurried out of the shop, the bell tinkling with a sharp note as she left.

Susan stepped up to the counter and offered cash for the painted trinket box. Tempted as she was to ask about the maid, she resisted, knowing that Colin would be outside waiting impatiently for them to continue following the maid, as indeed he was.

"Jeez, Suzie Baby! Can't you go into any shop without buying something? We're meant to be following someone, not on a shopping spree."

"You can be such an old woman at times, Colin."

"Given the way I dress, that should be no surprise to you. It is just fortunate that our young maid has slipped into that mini-market across the road. I think I had better go in and see what she is up to, save you getting distracted and doing your week's grocery shopping!"

Colin strode off across the busy road and disappeared into the shop, leaving Susan to scrutinise her newly acquired trinket box.

Inside the claustrophobic mini market, it was not hard to see the maid who was already at the counter. Colin grabbed a wire basket, threw a couple of items in it and stood close to the counter, looking as if he was torn between the large packet of cashew nuts or the spicy Bombay mix as he appeared to slowly read the ingredients of each. Instead, he watched and listened as the maid filled out a Western Union transfer form, handed over the twenty-pound note, then waited for her receipt, which the Asian shopkeeper handed over with a smile.

"See you next week."

The maid nodded and left the shop without a word. The shopkeeper was used to that. She came in each week, offered a small amount of money to be sent via Western Union, and then left without a word. He knew she would be back next week. He then turned to serve the odd-looking woman, but all he saw was a wire basket containing a bottle of ketchup, a box of brillo pads and a bag of Bombay mix, the strange-looking woman had already left.

"There's nowt so queer as folk," he spoke out loud to himself, his deep, strong Yorkshire accent echoing off the shelves.

The Philippine maid continued her journey onto Vauxhall Bridge Road. At a distance behind her, Susan and Colin continued to track her as she turned off the main road, along a residential side street, heading towards Victoria. Each turn, Colin noted in his small book.

Susan tried to summarise the morning so far.

"So she has taken a pottery figure from the house, sold it to the guy in the second-hand shop for twenty pounds, crossed the road, sent that same twenty pounds off, we assume to the Philippines, and now she is wandering towards Victoria."

"You only assume it has gone to the Philippines. As I told you, I couldn't quite see the destination or the currency. He did tell her that the money was about a thousand odd, whatever the currency was, but the guy behind the counter had the strongest Yorkshire accent I have heard for years, so I couldn't quite make out the name of the currency. Now she is walking the streets, not exactly flush with cash. And if we do end up in Victoria Street, can you please keep your credit card tucked away and restrain yourself from shopping? We are working, you know."

"That was never part of the deal with Martin; the job was to involve no work, so this is not what I signed up for."

"But it is fun; you have to admit."

Susan smiled broadly, "I will agree it's pretty cool following someone for real, just like being a detective."

They continued to stay behind her as the maid criss-crossed the back streets between Vauxhall and Victoria. Finally, she stopped and walked into a small working man's cafe that was squeezed between a dry cleaners and an art gallery.

"Well, there's a result; we get to have a sit-down and a coffee," Susan smiled.

"Maybe we should stay outside for a while in case she is just popping in for a sandwich and not staying. No point in us going in and her walking out as we sit down to a full English breakfast," Colin contended.

"Don't be daft. Let's go in."

"I'll wait a while."

"What's up, Colin? Why don't you want to go in, a bit of history for you inside?" Although Susan joked, she could see that Colin was genuinely hesitant about going in. "OK, let's wait a moment or two, at least until we can see her sitting down, then we go in whatever."

It did not take long for them to see the maid settle herself at a window table. There she sat with a cup and saucer in front of her, as she looked out across the street with an expression which suggested her thoughts were far, far away.

Colin and Susan sat at a table towards the back of the cafe, where they could easily see the maid as she stirred her drink aimlessly, staring out into the street, appearing to be in a world of her own. The minutes ticked by; builders came in and ordered food at the counter, bacon baps, fried egg sandwiches, portions of chips, all taken away in polystyrene boxes. Others sat in and tucked into plates of fried food. Office workers came in, ate sandwiches and drank latte coffee before returning to their work. Still, the maid sat, once in a while sipping her now cold coffee. Colin and Susan sat and watched until a man dressed in a white apron approached the maid. He was clearly the owner as they had seen him directing operations behind the counter, making sure orders were taken, food prepared and paid for correctly. In one hand, he carried a large plate of food, a roast dinner: beef, roast potatoes, carrots, peas, a large Yorkshire pudding, and in the other hand was a cup of coffee. He laid it in front of the maid, who turned away from her dream and smiled at him before ravenously tucking into her dinner.

"Now, can we order a full English breakfast? She's eating; I think we should."

Colin did not respond at once; he was thinking, mulling over what he had seen. Having considered it, he spoke, "That is most odd, Suzie Baby, she never ordered that. You don't come into a greasy spoon cafe like this and order a coffee and then order your dinner to arrive half an hour later. You get it sooner rather than later. These cafes are the original fast food places. All the customers we've seen here have come in for takeaways or ordered food which got delivered to their table within minutes, five or six minutes at most, yet her dinner arrives half an hour later? She never ordered that meal; it was given to her."

"Why would he give her a meal?"

"That is the question we need to answer, Suzie Baby. That is the question."

As the tall owner walked back towards the counter and his busy kitchen, he wiped his hands on his apron, looked around the tables, making sure his customers were happy and the tables fresh and tidy. He prided himself on a pristine café, and it was that pride and attention to detail that made his café both popular and profitable. His eyes, scanning the tables, glanced and fell upon Susan sitting beside Colin with their empty cups in front of them. He moved towards them.

"Colin, you old tart, I haven't seen you in ages. When did you slip in unnoticed? No fry-up, tut-tut, not another diet?" he laughed, collecting the two empty cups. "Same again?"

"Thanks, Graham, mine's a skinny latte coffee, and Suzie Baby here is having an Americano. How's business?"

"Good, I'm pleased to say. Whatever we're doing here, it seems to work. Plus, you must have seen all the building work going on around here, concrete office blocks coming down and new glass towers going up, so there's always a long line of builders burning lots of calories which I can replenish for them. You two not eating today?"

"Mine's a full English without the black pudding," Susun answered at once.

"A fried egg sandwich will do me today, please Graham, thanks."

"Pleasure's always mine, Colin. It's just good to see you again."

"Just one other thing," Colin ushered Graham closer to the table. He leaned over to hear Colin as he asked quietly, "that woman over there by the window, was that a free meal you gave her?"

"Interested in Tala, are you?"

"Tala, Philippine name?"

"Yes, means 'bright star', or so she tells me, and I have no reason to doubt her. She seems genuine enough."

"So the free meal, what's the story?" Colin insisted, looking for an answer to his question.

"She started coming in here about six, seven months ago. Just bought a cup of coffee and then sat herself down and watched the world go by. Spent most of the day here, with just the one cup and left just before we closed. That was her pattern, to arrive here about eleven, sit with her one cup until just before four, every Tuesday without fail. Well, you know me; everyone has a story and not always a good one. So one day, I asked, 'Do you want anything to eat?' I could see the fear in her eyes; maybe she thought I was going to throw her out. She got out her purse and asked, 'Can I have a sandwich?' She held out about eighty-five pence in change. So I got her a hot meal, which she wolfed down as though she hadn't eaten properly in days. I told her to keep the money and come back next week. The following Tuesday, she arrives, orders her coffee and a bit later, I serve her a meal. Once again, she offers me a handful of change, which I refuse, and I get a big hug, and I notice a few tears in her eyes for my trouble. Well, since then every Tuesday, - we call her, 'Tuesday Tala' - sits at her table in a world of her own, we feed her and then she leaves about four as always. Where she comes from, what she does, I have tried, but she prefers not to talk too much. Her English seems good enough, so maybe she's just shy or ashamed of what she does; I have no idea. But at least I can sleep easy, knowing that she gets at least one hot meal a week. She's not on the streets, I'm sure, too clean and tidy for that. There must be a story behind her of that, I'm sure. I bet you know a lot more than me?"

"That is so sweet of you to give her a meal," Susan commented.

"Well, as I said, darling, everyone has a story behind them, sometimes a bit of kindness can make all the difference. I'll never make a fortune, but I'll never starve, plus I can rest easy at night."

As they ate, Susan and Colin discussed what they should do next. They had been employed to follow a maid called Tala, a name never mentioned by Mrs Holburn. She had only referred to her as the Filipino maid. They had followed her and could now say that she was stealing, which everyone already knew, the proceeds from which she was sending somewhere and then accepting a charitable meal.

So Colin was all for leaving the cafe, then passing that information onto Mrs Holburn to do with as she wanted. Susan was not so sure. Why was Tala stealing? Why did she have to accept charity hand-outs? Why was she spending the whole day sitting in a cafe, her only day off, wasting it watching passers-by through the window? Susan wanted to probe a little deeper. She wanted to go and talk to Tala, ask her directly and get the answers to her questions. Colin advised against that, 'don't get personally involved, you can't solve all the world's problems on your own'. Susan often received advice, and she often ignored it.

Tala was startled when Susan sat down beside her. Susan could see there was fear in her eyes as she recoiled away from her.

"I just want to have a few words with you," Susan tried to reassure Tala, whose only response was to ask,

"You police?"

"No, it's a concerned friend who can see that you are not enjoying your life, and maybe talking to someone like me could help."

"I have no friends, and I do not know you for sure."

"But I know a little about you and want to know a little more. I know you take things from Mrs Holburn, and I know you sell those things, and then I also know you send the money out of the country back to your family."

"You know Mrs Holburn? She will throw me out if she knows I take things."

"Maybe she won't if she knows why. Why do you steal? Tell me; I sense you are an honest woman, church-going, believe that God is watching over us all, you cannot be stealing for yourself. I know you get free meals here, so the money goes somewhere."

Tala looked down at the table. She could not look Susan in the eyes; she was too ashamed that she had been caught and was now going to be called a thief.

Finally, she had the courage to answer. "Back to my family. I send the money to Manila, the Philippines. They need the money to pay their rent and eat. They all rely on me, my grandparents, my mother, my four brothers and three sisters; they are all waiting for the money each week. I have to send it to them, or else they could lose their roof."

"It's still stealing, even if it is to help your family."

"I have to; I have let my family down. I cannot tell them the truth. I came here to England so that I earn money, more than I could earn in the Philippines, and help them live."

"Well, what do you do with your wages, what you get paid for being a maid? Can't you send that back to them, or at least some of it?"

Tala was now looking at Susan, tears trickling down her bronze cheek, twisting and fidgeting with a tissue between her fingers.

"I don't get wages."

"No pay, you must do, you work."

"It was in Manila that I was offered this job. All I had to do was pay my air fare. My family scraped together to pay. So I come to London, to be maid for Mrs Holburn. In Manila, they say I would get a living wage, a London wage which is so much more than I could earn in Manila. My family were pleased for me, and I was happy for my family. So when I arrived at big house, I was excited to be with such a rich family. But I was not told that I would have to pay for my own food and bedding. Mrs Holburn explained that rent and food is very dear in London, the government set the level for a maid's wage, and she cannot change it. So my wages would only just cover the rent, as a favour to me she would provide my food. Yet I know back in Manila, my family are waiting to get money, some of my wages, to pay back my air fare and then pay for food and rent. But I have nothing now to send back. I was such a fool; I should have thought about paying rent over here. In Manila, maids like me live in the house free; I just thought it was the same here in London. I have sold my jewellery, my watch. I had nothing else to sell, so I take small items, so I can send money back to my family. What else can I do? I cannot let them starve; I have no money to go back. I have let my family down." Her tears were no longer trickling; they were flowing as she tried to control her sobs. Susan put her arm around her to try and comfort her.

"So you work six days a week, get nothing but a bed to sleep in and some food, although clearly, they don't feed you on your day off. Tell me, how long a day do you work?"

"I get the family breakfast at seven in the morning; then I finish once I have cleared all the dinner plates and pans in the evening, maybe ten o'clock."

"You work fifteen hours a day, six days a week, and I thought the slave trade had ceased."

* * *

"It sounds to me," Martin replied as he heard just the significant parts of Susan's day, "that the slave trade is very much alive and well and living in the heart of Pimlico. I'll give Mrs Holburn a call later and tell her what we now know. The maid does have a family, just in another country."

"There's no need to call," Susan admitted, "I've already spoken to Mrs Holburn."

Martin let his head rest on his keyboard, his voice slightly muffled and clearly frustrated, "Tell me you just spoke to Mrs Holburn please. Don't tell me that you have given her a piece of your angry mind; using such words as slavery, despicable, Victorian working conditions."

"I might not have used despicable, not too sure what that means, I've seen the film, and that was fun, so didn't actually use that word. I did, I will admit, use bitch, tight-fisted, Scrooge, uncaring human being, and compared her to shit on the street, but by then, I was rather annoyed and not really keeping track of what I was saying. Sorry." She then added, "she did mention, I'm pretty sure, that she had no intention of paying us."

"Well, all I can say is, it is lucky that we do not rely on paying clients. Maybe I should speak to Beatrice's daughter, just in case you decide to have a rant about daughters curtailing their mother's gambling habits."

CHAPTER THREE

It had been a calm relaxing three weeks since Hayden Investigations had carried out any work, either paid or unpaid. Martin had firmly resisted Susan's idea of reporting Mrs Holburn, the slave driver, to the police. He cited that it was 'not really any of our business,' plus he had previously heard of servants under investigation being mislaid, suddenly moved off to another family, so it might not be the best course of action. Susan had then called him a self-centred, uncaring 'Hooray Henry' before she stormed out. Just like a forgiving old married couple, the next day, she was making him coffee, and he was buying her apricot Danish pastries. Soon they were back into the normal routine of daily work or their special variation of it. Susan had not entirely forgotten Tala; it was just that she had been distracted by going out with the girls, planning her holiday in the sun with the girls or finally thinking about one of her friends who was getting married later that year, so Tala was no longer foremost in her mind.

Martin continued his social lunches, attending evening premiers and taking Jenny dancing whenever the opportunity arose. Even though she was extremely interested to know how the very first two investigations for the agency had concluded, he was a little cagey about what he told her, as he sensed that she might, like Susan, push for some action to help out Tala, something he preferred to avoid.

Nothing was what he was always preferred to do, to avoid difficult decisions or making choices that would compromise his relaxed, easy-going lifestyle. Although over the past few weeks, he had been pushed to get involved with other people's lives which made him uncomfortable, in the end, there was no real harm done to his envious lifestyle. Maybe he thought of Tala a little more than he might have, given the fact that he had never actually met her. He could not help thinking about the young Philippine maid, what she might be doing in Mrs Holburn's house: cooking, cleaning, being shouted at, commanded to do things. Even Martin would admit, although only to himself, that he found Mrs Holburn intimidating, but what could he realistically do? Report her to the police, who might get around to paying her a visit in the fullness of time. Then what? Martin had heard stories before about illegal maids and man servants. They were often presented to friends and neighbours as 'just a friend of the family', 'we met him/her on holiday, and they so much wanted to spend time in London, how could we not open our arms to them?' Martin had heard it many times whilst dining with his mother's friends. No one around the table would admit in their well-spoken, well-bred voices that the person now serving you dinner is just unpaid labour. He admired Susan, who had simply walked out of that cafe, straight around to Mrs Hoburn's house and banged on the door until she got an answer. That was passion; that was raw emotion which was brave. It might not have achieved anything yet; it might never, but he was sure that Susan had felt a lot better for telling Mrs Holburn the way it was.

"You read the Telegraph, don't you?"

Susan's question interrupted Martin's thoughts. Actually, it was more the regular sound of Susan's phone as messages came into it, which she read and then responded to in an instant. A moment later, the sound of the reply tone pinged out across the office.

"I'm sure it would be a lot easier just to talk to your friend instead of constantly writing messages to him or her?" Martin said.

74

"She's at work, as a receptionist, so she can't be seen to be on the phone all the time; hence we message each other. So, do you read the Telegraph?"

"Yes, and why do you want to know, thinking of moving up market from your tabloid?"

"I read the Daily Mirror newspaper, which is all I need, good, honest news and to the point." She ignored Martin's smirk. "My friend, the receptionist, tells me there's a bit in there about Margery Lawrence, and I would like to see it."

Martin folded the Telegraph and handed it across to Susan as he asked, "Margery Lawrence, who is she? One of your friends?"

Susan unfolded the paper and laid it out on her desk, turning over the pages, looking for the article.

"No, she's not. She died years before I was even born; she's an author. I would have thought someone like you, with your upbringing and expensive education, would have known all about her."

"When you are at an all-boys boarding school, unless the books have pictures of naked women or erotic stories in them, you are not always that interested."

"No change there then." Susan continued to look through the paper.

"So what did this Margery write? Romantic novels?"

"There you go again, stereotyping us women. She was not a Mills and Boon writer, if that's what you're getting at. Her most famous book was: 'Number Seven Queer Street', about an occult detective called Dr Miles Pennoyer; think of Sherlock Holmes does supernatural and then you'd be close."

"You have lost me if you're telling me the truth."

"I have most of her books that you can buy. I like her because I think I am a reincarnation of her. We share the same birthday, just 98 years apart. Which if you add together makes seventeen, add those two numbers and you get number eight, a very special lucky number if you are Chinese."

"Susan, I hate to point this out, but you're not Chinese."

"Maybe not born there, but they are a very cosmic race. Anyway about Margery, when she was young, she said she was visited by a dead relative who told her the whereabouts of some important papers, which turned out to be exactly where the ghost had told her they would be. I also, when I was young, had an auntie visit me soon after she died. She didn't tell me anything important, but she stood at the bottom of my bed, just as if she was alive and told me not to carry on seeing a boy I was seeing."

"Did you carry on seeing him?"

"Yes, and I regretted it. He turned out to be an arsehole, which most of my boyfriends tend to be. So, what sort of book do you have on your bedside table, some posh Latin thing, or Playboy magazine?" Susan laughed and looked back down at the broadsheet as she continued to turn pages.

Martin did have a strange book on his bedside table, one he had held onto for many years, a simple story that he often read; he understood the moral of the tale. He considered not telling her, but Susan, he guessed, would find out in the end. Plus, he quite liked sharing some of his life with Susan; it made him feel close to her.

"Promise not to laugh if I tell you?"

"Cross my heart." Susan duly acted out the cross just to prove her sincerity.

"A Ladybird book called: 'Chicken Licken'."

Susan instantly burst out laughing, "Tell me it's not the children's book?"

"Yes, it is the children's book, and you said you weren't going to laugh."

"You told me it was going to be a book, not a baby book. 'Chicken Licken'. I have heard some weird stuff in my life, but well, that proves your education was a total waste of your parents' money. Why is it your favourite book? There are no naked females in it; I'm sure unless you're into farm yard animals?"

"Do you know the story of 'Chicken Licken'?"

Susan looked up from the paper, took a large mouthful of her coffee before she answered, "Yes, some chicken thought the sky was falling down 'cause an acorn or nut fell on its head. So it went off to tell the king, met a group of other animals along the way who joined in until they met up with the fox that promptly ate 'em all. Weird kid's story, but most of them are."

"So, what's the moral? What is the lesson to be learned?" he asked in a serious tone.

"Christ, Martin, how can you critique a Ladybird book for kids? It's just a simple story."

"I will tell you. Most people think the moral of the story is not to believe everything you are told. I think of the moral as being more don't get involved and avoid getting drawn into something you cannot control or even understand. If only 'Cocky Locky' had told 'Chicken Licken', 'don't be stupid, the sky is still up there, look for yourself.' But oh no, 'Cocky Locky' joined in, and in the end, got eaten; serves him right. So for me, the moral is, do not get involved in things. It makes for an easier life, and you don't get eaten by the foxes."

Susan turned back to her paper. "Sometimes, I worry about you being part of the ruling class."

Before she could continue to ridicule Martin for having a children's book beside his bed, and she really wanted to, she noticed an obituary in the Telegraph of a name she recognised.

"Beatrice Cook has died," was all she said.

Martin, who was about to ridicule Susan in her belief that she had been reincarnated, stopped what he was going to say and looked over to the obituary that Susan had now turned towards him.

"That's the same woman that you went to France and gambled the nights away with."

"Yes," Martin agreed as he read aloud the announcement:

"**_Beatrice Cook_** _died peacefully at her Hereford Square home, aged 90. A devoted wife, loving mother to all her children and grandchildren, she was an extraordinary woman who lived her life in her own way, to the full. She will be greatly missed by family, friends and colleagues. Funeral Service to be held at Kensington Crematorium. Donations, if wished, to St Anne's Church._"

"We should send some flowers," Susan said without any hesitation.

"Why? She was only a client, or at least her daughter was the client. Why should we send flowers? It is not as if we are going to need to follow the old girl again. Flowers would be a waste of time."

"You are such a selfish prig Martin," Susan spoke as she put on her coat, picked up her handbag and powered down her computer. "It's just nice to be nice once in a while; we're all human, no matter how rich our parents are. The loss of a parent is painful, whatever your income bracket. I think even you, although you would never admit it, will be sad when your mother passes away. So whatever you think, I am off to buy some flowers and a sympathy card and then drop it round to Paige McLaughlin. If you don't like it, tough!"

Martin watched as Susan left the office, feeling like he had been told off by his mother. At least he could console himself knowing that he was having lunch with Jenny. With her husband away on business somewhere in Europe, he was hopeful of some afternoon delight.

* * *

Jenny had chosen the restaurant where they were going to have lunch. Martin would not have described it as anything like a restaurant at all. Martin's idea of a restaurant was a place where you are greeted politely at the door and then shown to a table; a table that was ready-laid and prepared for your arrival with crisp white starched table cloths, fine damask cloth napkins and polished cutlery laid correctly; cutlery of a traditional design, Martin always favoured the bead pattern. There should also be wine and water glasses ready on the table. Once seated, the waiter, after placing a bottle of water on the table and laying your napkin on your lap for you, offers you the menu and wine list from which you choose your favoured meal and wine to accompany it, which is then served to your table, by the continuously attentive waiter, allowing enough time between courses to enjoy relaxed, stimulating conversation.

Granted, at Jenny's choice today, you were greeted at the door, handed a menu and invited to choose a vacant table, but there the restaurant feel ended for Martin. He looked over and saw a partly occupied wooden bench along with an extended wooden refectory-type table. Jenny told him it was a Euro-chic eatery. Martin would have described it, not to Jenny, of course, as a cafeteria. Still, he was not always one to complain, so he smiled and began to enjoy the company of Jenny, who he struggled to hear over the racket of the other diners. Martin was also a little put out when he learnt that once he had chosen what he was going to eat, he would have to go up to a counter point, where each one had its own chef, to order his food and then wait while it was cooked. Granted, they were all pasta dishes; even so, it was not that far removed, Martin thought, from school dinners. Once he had received his Salmon Carbonara, it was back to the bench. Then he had to scurry off to purchase a bottle of wine and collect two glasses, having been told by Jenny that he was being silly if he expected service, this is much more fun. Martin was not so sure, but he kept telling himself that later he would be lying naked next to Jenny, so eating in a cafeteria he would just have to put up with. Jenny, on the other hand, thought it hysterical that Martin was so uncomfortable sitting at the bench with other diners close enough to overhear their conversation. She called him, as she often did, a spoilt little schoolboy, which was a form of endearment. She liked Martin; he was usually good fun, able to take a joke and was a lot more attentive to her needs than her husband.

Jenny flicked back her blonde hair, revealing drop-earrings with small cats on.

"So what position do you favour this afternoon?" she teased, "any preference?"

Martin felt the conversation the two strangers were having next to him stop; he guessed they also wanted to know. He replied, playing along, in a serious voice,

"I thought the straps you used last time were a little too tight; chafing on my wrists, maybe go back to the silk ribbons?" If Jenny was going to play games, then so was he, it might not be his first choice of a place to eat, but he was not going to back down when Jenny started playing games.

"So we are thinking in the doorway position?" she responded.

"In the doorway, or the claustrophobic atmosphere of the wardrobe was very invigorating, I thought."

Martin realised that the couple next to them, a young man with an even younger woman, turned their heads ever so slightly to get a better look at the two people discussing sexual positions. Jenny looked up from her Spaghetti Bolognese.

"Maybe we should ask your personal assistant if she has any ideas?"

Having already finished his meal, Martin pushed his plate to one side and took a drink from his wine glass.

"I gather she has had a lot of experience with different positions, so I guess you could ask her advice the next time you see her if that's what you want."

"No, not me, you ask her, here she comes," Jenny nodded her head towards the door.

As Martin turned round, coming towards him, was Susan looking flushed, and he could see anger in her eyes; he was not too pleased either at having his lunch interrupted. The silent eavesdropping couple were waiting with ghoulish anticipation as to what would happen next.

"What are you doing here?" Martin asked with an irritated tone.

She did not wait to answer but just squeezed in beside Martin, forcing the eavesdropping man to move up, then took hold of Martin's glass and, without asking, finished his wine.

"Hello Jenny," she said, almost ignoring Martin, who continued to question his Personal Assistant.

"How did you know I was here?"

Susan turned to look at Martin, giving him a quizzical look. "Who books your tables? Jenny, why do you go out with him?"

"I've asked that question of myself at times. Maybe he is just interesting."

"Susan, I'll ask you again, what are you doing here?"

Jenny, Martin and the eavesdropping couple all waited to hear.

"Jenny, did he tell you that the ninety-year-old lady he went on holiday with has died?"

"He tells me nothing."

Martin would have preferred to explain to the couple next to them, who were no doubt starting to get the wrong impression of him, the exact circumstance of him going away with a ninety-year-old which was not being made clear.

Susan continued, "Well, she died at her home. So I thought it would be a nice gesture to pop round with some flowers and a card. The old lady's daughter, Paige, answered the door, looking down her nose at me. 'I'm so sorry to hear about your loss,' I start. Well, to be fair, she was polite to me, she wasn't going to invite me right inside that was clear, did I mind, no of course not, I was only showing my respects, I didn't want to have tea and cakes with the old dear. As it was raining a little, she let me stand in the hallway, which made me feel even more awkward. So I asked, 'was her mother ill or was it sudden?' 'Very sudden,' says Paige, 'she was found dead in her bed one morning'. Now, at this point, it is starting to feel like I am getting blood out of a stone. I know when my mother died, that was after an illness, I was happy and pleased that people asked me about her, it helped me a lot. So with my caring nature, I ask, 'what was the cause?' Very reluctantly, she tells me it was food poisoning. 'Oh dear,' I say, 'that must be terrible for you. What had she eaten?' Reluctantly she tells me, 'oysters during the previous evening and no doubt she died during the night'. Then, I recall something that Martin had told me after his week away with the old lady; she didn't do seafood, well, not shellfish. I recall you telling me that Martin, 'cause I loved the old girl's comment about God putting shells around food for a reason. So I say to Paige, 'I didn't think she ate shelled seafood', to which she gives me this look of daggers and says, 'have you met my mother? No, young lady, you have not, so I think I would know my mother a lot better than you.' 'Bitch', I thought, calling me a young lady in a not nice way. 'Thank you for the flowers,' she says to me, 'but I have to let you go now as I have, I am sure you understand, a number of things that I need to attend to.' So there I am, almost pushed out of the door but not before I notice on this little table thing in the hallway a letter from her bank agreeing an extension to an overdraft of thirty thousand pounds. As my mother would say, 'all show and nowt to show it with'."

"What is your point, Susan?" Martin asked.

"The daughter needs money and killed the old lady, her mother!"

"Before she gambled it all away," Jenny added with a smile.

"Exactly," Susan agreed. "Martin, you need to confront her and get a confession from her."

Exasperated, Martin poured himself another glass of wine.

"I know your hero, Jim Rockford was it; he would have found a motive and uncovered a murderer, but, as I have told you before, that is TV; it is all fiction. Beatrice died, maybe it was a bad case of food poisoning, but murder, I doubt it."

"She has a point, Martin." Jenny added, "you told me that the old lady never ate shellfish and was clearly gambling and losing loads of money. Maybe her daughter saw her inheritance dwindling away and decided to take action. Greed is a strong motive, and I think I read somewhere that most victims are killed by someone they know. I love Jim Rockford re-runs too, and he would have, without a whisker of a doubt, looked a little deeper. Plus Martin, I have noticed that you always talk about her warmly. I think that you had a soft spot for the deceased lady."

"Thank you, Jenny," Susan smiled at Jenny, before turning to Martin, "so Martin down to you."

Martin glanced at the eavesdropping couple who were going to offer him no support at all.

"Let us all calm down and apply a reality check to what is fast becoming a bizarre conversation. I cannot just knock on Paige's door and accuse her of murdering her mother unless I have some real proof. If I did have real proof, then I would hand it to the police, and they can knock on her door."

Martin knew from bitter experience in his life; women tended to be able to influence him more than they should. It was not a weakness, he would argue; it was, on the whole, the easy option. It was just that by taking the easy option now would mean facing up to a fierce Paige at some point.

＊ ＊ ＊

"Would you like milk in your Earl Grey or lemon?" Paige warmly smiled at Martin as she offered him a small white milk jug.

"Thank you; I take it without any additives. I prefer just the refreshing perfumed flavour of the tea, of which this one that you serve is especially fine," Martin tried not to make his reply sound like a dramatic irony.

The last time they had met was in Martin's office when he had reported back to her on the activities that her mother was taking part in during her French coach trips. It had been a very business-like and formal meeting, with Paige listening and occasionally nodding as Martin recounted the trip.

Now, sitting in her home, there was a different atmosphere. Martin had been forewarned by his mother that Paige was both vain and eccentric, a dangerous combination. If that was not a bad enough mixture, his mother had added another warning that Paige, although married, liked to think she could turn the head of any young man that might speak to her. Martin was often amused and surprised at how much gossip and knowledge, of often very personal habits, his mother knew about other people, especially as she had added that Paige had never had an affair in her life, but that it was not for want of trying. He had asked his mother point-blank, 'Do you think that Paige McLaughlin would consider murdering her own mother?' His mother was surprised on two counts, first that her son was actually asking her advice on anything, plus he was clearly asking her for guidance about one of his normally confidential investigations. She tried to conceal her excitement at getting involved, not least because he had mentioned murder.

"You are such a kind young man with very alluring eyes." Paige returned the milk jug to the push-up bench that had a range of weight-lifting paraphernalia next to it, most of which Martin would struggle to lift.

Both Martin and Paige sat in what could only be described as a living-room come weight-training, fitness room. They sat beside one another on a very wide, sumptuously upholstered, floral-patterned settee with red braided cushions that made it awkward to lean back. Also, within the room, built on either side of the open fireplace, were tall bookcase units full of dusty tomes, nothing modern to be seen, just row upon row of leather-bound books. The settee on which they both sat faced the broad bay window, in which stood two running machines that looked out across the street. The empty water bottles beside them and the towels draped over the side bars indicated that they were used and not just for show. The other clue that Martin had to convince him that this room was an active household gym was that in the air hung a faint yet distinctive odour of sweat.

"I always buy my teas from an American company: Harney and Sons, they are of course expensive, but they are all wonderful to taste. So, what do I owe the pleasure of your company to, Mr Hayden?" Her words had a sinister tone, but her smile continued to be warm.

"Firstly, to apologise to you on behalf of my assistant; I understand that she visited you at a very inopportune time and may have caused you some distress. I am truly sorry for that. She is just a little, how can I put it, volatile sometimes. She meant no harm at all; she was, like yourself, very upset to hear about your mother's untimely death; such a shock to us all."

"That is so sweet of you, Martin, thank you. Maybe, I must admit, I could have been judged to have been a little hard on her at the time. I am sure you understand the loss of a parent can be distressing and can make any of us act a little funny."

On his way to see Paige, he had sat on the District line tube train and played out in his mind the different scenarios that might transpire. Most of those he had imagined would involve Paige ranting and raving; he had not thought that she would have taken the apology without question. Clearly, his mother was right; younger men were Paige's weak spot. His next question might well change that.

"Secondly, I really do wonder why your mother was eating oysters. When I was with her in France, she did seem adamant that shelled seafood was never going to be for her. So I think it strange, unusual, maybe impossible, to think of her tucking into oysters."

Martin stopped and awaited the expected reaction from Paige, who sipped her tea slowly, her eyes lingering a little too long on Martin's Chino's, before working their way upwards to stare at his eyes. Her expression seemed neutral, almost as if her mind was elsewhere; possibly, she was thinking how to respond.

"You must understand," she began as she ran her finger around the rim of her cup, "that my mother was ninety years old. At that age, the odds of going to sleep and not waking up again are very short; indeed, at ninety, death cannot be far away. When I heard that she had been found one morning, dead in her bed, it was neither a shock nor a surprise." Paige put her cup down and rested her hand on Martin's knee. "It did surprise me that there were empty oyster shells on what was her dinner plate from the night before. She must have eaten them, and then perhaps they had disagreed with her, and she had died, maybe there had been a bad oyster. Maybe deep down, she knew she should not eat them; she had almost a natural instinct to avoid shellfish. We all have basic instincts that we should not ignore," the double entendre was not lost on Martin. "I always thought my mother did indeed detest shellfish, but she had been a rebel throughout her life, going against convention, trying new radical experiences; to her, that was the same as gambling. So I imagine that something or someone encouraged her to eat oysters, or maybe it was a straightforward challenge that she took up, and it sadly killed her. I doubt we shall ever know the truth. More tea, Martin?"

The explanation she had given seemed plausible. Just because you believe you dislike something does not mean you never try it. Then you either change your opinion and end up liking what you had thought you did not like, or you confirm what you already knew. He refused the offer of a second Earl Grey, so Paige continued, her hand now resting just above his knee.

"She had visited her doctor just the week before. Mother had been feeling tired and washed out, so I thought it would be for the best if she visited her GP. The doctor told her there were some irregularities with her heart and was planning to send her for some more checks. I believe that is why he suspected that her death was, in the end, due to heart failure. Although he did add that a severe bout of indigestion could have antagonised it and that Mother would have felt as though she had an upset stomach, which was confirmed by the indigestion tablets that were beside her bed. So the doctor was happy that it was simply old age and a heart that had had enough of living.

"Would you like to stay for some lunch Martin, my maid is about to prepare mine?"

Martin was about to refuse her invitation and leave before her hand had a chance to travel any higher when a small dog pushed open the door and proudly pranced across the room, ignoring both Paige and Martin. The dog, which Paige referred to as Minsky, calmly stood in front of one of the running machines, positioned his paw above the switch on the white four-way extension lead then swatted downwards. The red neon light came on, and in turn, Martin heard the sound rumble of the running machine as it burst into life. A moment later, Minsky, a grey terrier of some description, jumped onto the black moving belt and began trotting away as if he was human.

Martin was concerned that Paige had laced his tea with some substance that was making him see things; either that, or it would lower his resistance to her advances.

"Don't mind Minsky, he loves walking, and to be brutally honest, it is so much easier for him to use the machine than wait around for us to take him across the square. My husband thinks he enjoys it more, staying warm and dry, Minsky, that is, not my husband." Paige laughed at her joke.

Now he was reassured that he was not losing his mind, he bluntly asked, "Who inherits your mother's estate?"

The smile that Paige had on her face ebbed away.

"My mother's estate? Martin, I need not tell you that my mother had been a gambler all her life. Money just slipped through her fingers into the hands of casinos across the country. Any money she might find she did have would end up on the green baize of the roulette table. I tried my best to curtail her gambling, but she was, as I am sure you know, a very strong-willed woman."

Paige stood up, then turned off the running machine, much to the disappointment of Minsky, and ushered the now panting dog out of the room.

"There may well be some assets, paintings, objets d'art from her house, but I doubt I will be able to retire on anything that my mother leaves me, even if I am mentioned in her will. For most of my life, my mother has been a disappointment to me; I cannot see that changing now she is dead."

It was at that point that Martin's mind recalled her being in his office. After he had told her all about her mother's gambling, he had then asked her, 'You must have guessed your mother was gambling on those trips, why employ me to tell you something that you, no doubt, already suspected?' Back then, in the meeting, Paige had just smiled formally, yet there was still a sort of warmth to it, almost as if she had expected the question to be asked of her. Her reply had been, 'I will admit that I did suspect she was popping over the channel to play the tables, although she, of course, denied it emphatically when I asked her. So it was at a lunch I was having with your mother when I expressed my concerns. Your mother, being the caring person that she is, said that you are a detective and would be happy to help and be very discreet about anything you found out. Hence, I asked you. I did not want to taint your thoughts by sharing my suspicions. Now I know she gambles abroad, I will look into ways of curbing her activities, like I always do and always find a way to achieve my goal, for her sake.'

As Martin hailed a cab, he wondered just what Paige might have done to curb her mother's gambling. At the same time, he vowed that should he have to go back to visit Paige, he would seek the services of a chaperone, just in case.

* * *

"Do you want your stars for today, Martin?"

With a grimace, he looked over his laptop towards Susan, who was staring at her own screen. Martin knew from bitter experience that the first internet site Susan would visit was that of 'Stars are Us' or some site similar to that.

"No thanks, Susan, I'll risk the unexpected today."

"You really should listen; it says here for a Pisces like yourself...."

"I said no. I really do enjoy being surprised by my day, so let's avoid the stars and those bizarre conversations that we always seem to end up having."

Susan closed the lid of her laptop and looked directly into Martin's eyes. "What bizarre conversations do we ever have?"

her voice was full of indignation.

"You want an example? One good example of the weird conversations that you try and engage me in: disappearing poo. Good enough?"

"Disappearing poo is a fact, as I explained to you previously, a phenomenon that no-one ever talks of."

"Can you blame them?"

"We should address these things; have you checked recently?"

"As I told you before, do you seriously think that I would finish doing a poo, then stand up and turn around to look into the pan, just to check what I have done? Cats might, I'm human, lid down and flush."

Susan would not be put off by his reluctance to accept her hypothesis, "It happens you know, you sit down for a poo, and I know for a fact it is done as I hear a splash, then once I'm finished, I turn around, look into the pan, and it's gone, literally disappeared. It must have gone somewhere."

Martin folded up his newspaper, "Susan, I think that some bodily functions should not be discussed outside of the room that they occur in. Can we move on?"

"I'll read your stars then."

Martin sat back in his chair, resigned to the fact that he was going to learn what the day had in store for him.

* * *

Samuel Parker was the Hayden family solicitor, he had been for just about forever, or that was the way Martin saw it. In fact, Samuel had only taken over from his father twenty years ago, inheriting all his father's clients, including the Hayden family.

The offices of 'Parker Phelps' were just off Trafalgar

Square, where they had been located ever since Mr Parker (Samuel's father) and Mr Phelps started the business in the late nineteen-fifties. When Mr Phelps died in a tragic skiing accident close to Lake Annecy in the early sixties, Mr Parker Senior continued using the name of Parker Phelps. Nothing too big, just a reliable family firm that looked after a number of rich clients, helping them buy and sell property, ensuring they avoided taxation where possible, as well as aiding the eviction of tenants when required.

When Mr Parker Senior decided it was time to pursue his passion for sailing, he handed the business over to his only son, Samuel, who continued to serve the elite of society. Samuel specialised in inheritance laws and taxation; he was the favourite point of contact for those who wanted to ensure that the vast majority of their family fortune remained in the family. When Samuel's father drowned in the Mediterranean during a particularly severe summer storm, Samuel Parker, at last, took full control of the company. The first thing that Samuel wanted to do was change the name to Parker Solicitors; that is until he found out just how much the change would cost him. His frugality getting the better of him, the name Parker Phelps remained.

Martin and Susan crossed Trafalgar Square then walked up Whitcomb Street, already, thanks to a delay on the District line, ten minutes late for their appointment with Samuel Parker.

"I still don't understand just why you want me to hold your hand to talk to your family solicitor," Susan whined, as she had been doing ever since they had left the office. She had planned to pop along to Top Shop in Oxford Street to purchase some cut-away jeans that were in the sale, knowing that they only had two pairs in her size. She was convinced that this meaningless visit was going to result in her losing a real bargain.

They both stopped outside a small medal and coin

collectors shop window. Martin turned to face Susan, unusually irritated by her moaning,

"I need you beside me because I am after a big favour from my family solicitor. I am going to ask him to do something that could get him struck off."

"He's not a doctor, is he?"

"It's not just doctors that get struck off; it's a term for when a professional gets thrown out of the profession's 'old boys club'. But all that is beside the point. My plan is that with you beside me, he will melt a little. He has an eye for a young lady." He then turned and continued to walk towards their destination.

Susan did not move, "You're not planning to pimp me out, are you?"

"No, Susan, but let's say he would enjoy impressing you by doing me a favour."

"You make no sense at all. Why not just ask him?"

Martin stopped, turned and looked at Susan amongst the steady flow of pedestrians before taking four steps so that he was beside her. Calmly he spoke, "I need to ask him if he can find out who is handling the last will and testament of Beatrice Cook, then I need him to try and find out who will benefit from the will and who stands to gain the most from her death, none of which is ethical. I am hoping that a man of fifty might just do it, solely to impress a young lady wearing a low top."

"A top, I wish to point out, you asked me to wear. Fifty! Is he a pervert or something? Anyway, you said yourself that gamblers have no money."

"Most don't, that's very true, but I thought about it and your murder theory. Beatrice lived in a flat that must be worth the best part of a million pounds; if she had gambled it all away, she would not still be living there. She might have been a gambler, but I think a shrewd one, so I just want to know who is getting her money. We're already late, best foot forward, old girl." He smiled, "plus the theory of murder is yours and yours alone, I'm just doing as I am told."

"If he is fifty, then I hope he is tall and handsome," Susan called as she followed in Martin's wake as he pushed his way through a tide of French tourists.

A woman who Susan considered should have retired years ago led them through the dingy office, with its dark, old-fashioned filing cabinets and cupboards that had been bought by Parker and Phelps when they had first started the business. A dusty fax machine stood at one corner beside a tired-looking grimy photocopier machine. Susan considered that the little old lady opening the door to Samuel Parker's office was not the only thing that was past its sell-by date. Susan was equally disappointed to see that Samuel was short, grey-haired, nothing like she had hoped for as his eyes, which were almost covered by wild bushy eyebrows, latched onto her cleavage.

Samuel greeted Martin with a warm, friendly handshake before offering them both a seat in front of his dingy well-worn desk, which contained pillars of papers and buff folders on either side, framing the small solicitor in his double-breasted suit.

"This must be Susan, your personal assistant, so pleased to meet you at last. I hope Martin is looking after you well."

She did not like his shifty look or the dusty shelves around her. The slightly musty damp odour that lingered in the room did nothing to enamour her to Samuel. In fact, she took an instant dislike to the man, although to her, it was clear that Martin trusted him, as his family had done over many years, whilst looking after their affairs. Martin and Samuel exchanged social pleasantries. Samuel asked after Martin's mother, and Martin asked how Samuel's wife was. All very cosy, Susan thought.

Susan only entered the conversation after she noticed a large mug on the desk that Samuel took small weasel-like sips from. The mug displayed a picture of a bull that appeared to be dancing through a galaxy of stars.

"Are you a Taurean?"

Samuel lifted the cup away from his lips, holding it as if it was a trophy that he had just won, looking at the raging bull.

"Bit of a clue, Taurus on my tea mug. Yes, the twenty-third of April, nineteen sixty-seven, busy day for birthdays; St George's day, Shakespeare, plus yours truly. Not that I am in the league of killing dragons or writing sonnets, I just spend my time being pedantic over words, very boring indeed, some would say. Although I do have an interesting riddle for you about my name, which I am sure Martin has heard several times before."

"More of a pub quiz question than a riddle, I would say," Martin added politely.

"Nevertheless, my dear, if I said that my father wanted to call me Geoffrey, and my mother was adamant that no way would she be calling her son Geoffrey. Why do you think my mother didn't want to name her son Geoffrey?"

Susan thought to herself, what a bloody stupid question. How would I know why your parents argued over your name? Don't all parents fight over names? She knew her parents had, luckily for her, the name Penelope had been beaten by Susan.

"I have no idea." Susan wanted what seemed to be a pointless conversation over as soon as possible.

"Well, apparently, I was conceived on the day England won the World Cup, so my father wanted to call me Geoffrey after Geoff Hurst, who scored on that day. Mother blocked that choice and called me Samuel." Samuel laughed; Martin smiled politely at the story he had heard on many occasions. Susan still thought it was bloody stupid. She guessed there would have been a whole batch of children named after the World Cup team, knowing the mentality of football fans. She surmised that today there were several women in their fifties called Bobby, who wished that England had lost that match.

Once the polite laughter had subsided, Martin brought up the reason for his visit.

"I am after a favour; a big favour from you, Samuel."

"Ask away."

"A friend of mine, well, I have not known her for that long, has died, and I wanted to try and find out who is handling her will."

"That shouldn't be too difficult to find out. What's your friend's name?"

"Beatrice Cook, she died recently, aged ninety."

"Beatrice Cook was a friend of yours? I know you like the mature woman, but Beatrice?" Samuel asked, his leather chair creaking as he leaned back.

"She wasn't that sort of friend. I met her on a trip to France. She reminded me of my grandmother, feisty and fun."

"Actually, she was one of my clients. Well, to be honest, like most of my clients, they were all customers of my father and have stayed on with the firm all their lives. So to answer your question, I am handling her estate now she has died."

Susan stepping or rather jumping in with both feet, asked, "Who gets her money?"

Samuel turned to her and allowed his eyes to wallow a while on her figure before answering the blunt question.

"Are you asking as Martin, the friend, or as Martin, the private detective? If it is the latter, what possible reason could you have to want to know who inherits her estate?"

Martin made sure he answered quickly, avoiding Susan talking herself into a hole.

"Her daughter was concerned about her gambling; I have been helping her to try and avoid any large debts being made public and embarrassing the family."

"Bullshit!" Susan opened the hole and jumped in. "We think she was murdered. Maybe someone named in the will did it. I still think she gambled it all away as all good gamblers do, but Martin now thinks otherwise. So, who gets her cash, her daughter?"

"Susan, can you leave this to me please," Martin sounded like an annoyed parent that was chastising a small child.

"I must say, Martin, your personal assistant does get to the point. Murder you say, young lady," he looked at Susan, happy to talk to her directly and take in the visual benefits. "Have you told the police of your suspicions?"

Martin pointed out, "an old lady dies in her bed of heart failure; I don't think they would look at that as a priority case."

"So why, young lady, do you think Beatrice was murdered?"

"The night before she died, it looked as though she was eating raw oysters and champagne. Her doctor surmised that she might have eaten an oyster that was contaminated with some sort of bacteria, which might have killed her, or at least the stress of the infection killed her, therefore natural causes. There is just one thing that does not add up to us; she never ate shellfish of any kind, raw or cooked."

"Interesting hypothesis. So you think that someone deliberately fed the old lady raw oysters to kill her. Sounds very much like a hit and miss plan to me. Visually there is no way of knowing if an oyster is contaminated or not. But I do see your point."

Samuel sipped his now cold tea once more and looked up at the yellowed ceiling; his father had smoked a pipe all his life, and his son had been unable to bring himself to redecorate, far too expensive. He continued,

"You know Martin, as I recall, your detective agency was set up for the sole purpose of ensuring your monthly unearned income continued, so I am intrigued that it now looks as though you are doing some real work?"

"Mother's interference! Hence the P.A. sitting beside me and having to do some detecting, so not turning out exactly as I

96

had planned." Martin scowled at Susan, although deep down, he wanted to find out what the truth was behind Beatrice eating oysters, even if it was not murder.

"Murder," Samuel repeated, talking to himself, before looking up at the couple in front of him. "That is a serious allegation, and you think that maybe a beneficiary of the will might have hastened her death?"

"It's a thought," Martin said, having given up on the diplomatic approach.

"Well, as you know, I cannot make the will public until after the funeral; that was her wish. Anything else would be a breach of the confidentially that I have been entrusted with. Yet, I would be foolish to ignore what you are saying to me. Beatrice approached her life in a, shall we say, different way to her contemporaries; her will reflects that. So when I add your allegations to what I know of the construction of her final requests, maybe there is something that you should know." Samuel leaned forward and picked up his phone, "Audrey, could you bring in the Beatrice Cook file, please?"

They all sat in silence for the few brief moments that it took for Audrey to enter the room, hand Samuel the file and leave without a word being spoken.

Samuel spoke as he simultaneously opened the blue folder, pulled out a group of papers from it and slid on his reading glasses, "I do hope, in fact, I ask you not to tell anyone just where this information came from. I feel I am doing the right thing morally, especially as I have known you and your family for many years. However, my professional body might well take a dim view of my revealing some of the contents of Beatrice's will."

Martin leaned forward and spoke softly, "Thank you, Samuel, you have my word."

Samuel removed his glasses, noticed Susan's frown, then looked at the rest of her. He would love to employ younger women in his office; the visual benefits were obvious to him. The negative side of such an action would be younger women would ask for a competitive salary, whereas his current part-time office staff, consisting of Audrey and Margaret, were both receiving state pensions so were more than happy to be paid what was considered a competitive salary ten years ago.

"I know it will not surprise you when I say that Beatrice liked the roulette tables; only the most naïve in her circle of friends were not aware of that fact. Beatrice, I guess, often won, although more often than not, she lost, often very large sums, large cash losses that she could not afford on her limited income, which was derived mostly from her husband's shares in a number of blue-chip companies. So, her solution to this shortfall was simple, she had assets, so mortgage them to release the cash held within those assets. I said that Beatrice was unconventional, so the last place she would go to was a bank. She knew full well that any bank manager worth his salt would know where the money would end up, so a conventional bank mortgage was not on the cards. Plus, she was not planning to repay any form of loan with monthly repayments that would impinge on her gambling."

Samuel finished his tea and continued, with the slightest hint of a smile on his face,

"So she arrived here telling me she was cutting out the middle man, 'by doing some futures'. What she actually meant was that she planned to sell part of her property in Hereford Square, yet the contract with the purchaser would allow her to live there until her death. A practice that is quite common in France."

"So it's no longer her house now she is dead?" Susan asked.

"Not exactly, as I mentioned she was a shrewd old girl, she sold just ten per cent of the property to an estate agent on the understanding that on her death, the estate agent could cash in their investment, which looking at the way property in that area has gone up, should make the estate agent a good return. I think Beatrice also had an ulterior motive as well. She knew that when she died, the estate agent would want the money, and that would mean that Paige, her daughter, would either have to sell the house or take out a loan to pay off the estate agent, and that thought amused Beatrice no end."

* * *

Susan and Martin walked across Trafalgar Square, dodging between the bustling tourists, vendors and street performers that had appeared as the sun was drying up the damp pavements. They had the name and address of the estate agent, having reassured a nervous Samuel that they would not reveal their source. Even though Martin was pleased with the outcome, Susan was not so sure. All across the square and then past Charing Cross Station, she was moaning about the lecherous old solicitor who she did not trust one little bit. Apart from his obvious meanness, why would anyone trust him to handle any of their affairs? For the most part, Martin ignored her gripes.

"Just because he is one of your old cronies, why should we......?"

Martin interrupted her, "Susan, just think back awhile, will you. Who was it that thought it a good idea to look a little deeper into Beatrice dying? In fact, as I recall," Martin sounded sarcastic, "there were two people who encouraged me: you and Jenny. I was more than happy to let the Cooks sort things out for themselves and leave me to enjoy my relaxed lifestyle without having to do anything. Plus, I think we both agreed that knowing who benefits from the will is a good starting point. So my old crony, not a friend of mine, I should point out, has given us a lead. If you have any better ideas, please let me know.

Alternatively, we could just wash our hands of the whole thing and go back to the way we were." Martin secretly hoped that Susan would not accept the last option.

"Well, Colin said that we should find out where she bought the oysters if we think that's what killed the old girl."

Standing on the District line platform at Embankment, Martin replied above the roar of the approaching tube train, "Well, maybe you should go off and do as Colin suggests, while I go and sink a few glasses of 'bubbly' with some friends. I need a break from this work."

"You know your trouble, Martin."

"I sense you are going to tell me however I answer that question."

"You just live in Martin's world, somewhere one day you'll have to leave because, believe it or not, Martin, there are other people on this planet who, in the end, you just cannot avoid. At some point in your privileged life, you are going to have to acknowledge their existence and once in a while do something that doesn't only benefit Martin."

Martin shrugged his shoulders, looked down at his phone and ignored Susan for the rest of the journey. Not put off, Susan pointed out that he was behaving like the spoilt child he was.

Not wishing to give up on the case, Susan did go and speak to Colin. They met up the following day to try and establish the origin of the oysters. What Susan did not give any thought to was just how Colin planned to go about it.

* * *

Susan pressed the door buzzer to Beatrice's flat and waited for a reply; there was none.

"Let's go around the back instead," Colin suggested.

They found a small alleyway at the back of the house and slipped unnoticed into the very small garden.

"I don't think anyone is in. She did, as far as we know, live alone," Susan observed.

Colin ignored her and examined the white PVC handle on the patio doors. Susan, standing alongside him, watched as he pushed a thin metal strip between the gap in the middle of the patio doors. It was time for Susan to ask the obvious question, a question that she had wanted to ask ever since they had walked into the hallway uninvited.

"Are you sure we should be doing this? You do know it is illegal to break into someone's house?"

Colin continued to manoeuvre the blade, lifting it upwards against the lock. Today Colin looked more like the mature gentleman that he was in his normal attire: bootleg denim jeans, a chunky-knit grey jumper, no earrings, and just a hint of mascara and eye liner with a discreet shade of lipstick. The lock released its hold; both white double-glazed doors opened inwards.

"Here we go, quick, get inside and let's get these doors closed again. No point advertising that we are at home."

Illegal or not, they had now broken in. They stood together in one corner of the room, silently looking around what was obviously a large kitchen/diner. Directly in front of them was a doorway. To the right were wooden kitchen units that ran along the wall and then turned the corner until they abutted a closed door. In the centre of the room was a large dining table with six oak chairs around it. The air was fresh, the whole kitchen tidy and ordered. The sink was empty, worktops clear but for a red and chrome food-mixer and a silver microwave. The ceramic hob was clean and shiny; there was not a stain anywhere. Only an empty glass vase was on the kitchen table.

"Seems we are the only ones at home," Colin whispered. "You check the kitchen cupboards over there; I'll do the drawers here." Colin pointed towards the large welsh dresser that was on the left-hand wall close to where they stood. Plates, cups, dishes of various designs were randomly displayed on the dresser shelves.

"So, what am I looking for?" Susan asked.

"Who knows, a receipt for twelve oysters would be a great find. Look for anything that might indicate where Beatrice shopped, carrier bags, till receipts; anything which might help. Of course, if you find either a signed suicide note or a confession from a killer, now, Suzie Baby, that would be very useful."

As silently as they could, Susan and Colin worked their way searching through the kitchen. Being quiet and careful was something that Susan was not that good at, Colin decided, as she knocked over the washing up liquid into the sink.

"Did anyone tell you," Colin maintained a hushed yet clear voice, "that you are a shit burglar?"

"It is my first time. Breaking into houses is not something I do much, and how come you are so accomplished at doing this?"

"Darling, when you have lived my life, there are few things I have not done, some I'm proud of, some I'm a little ashamed of. Either way, I have done them, so why not learn and make use of our life experiences. I should say, by way of defence for breaking into dear old Beatrice's flat, that we do think she was murdered. So, when you are dealing with people who are happy to break the law - murder is still not lawful here - sometimes you need to step outside of the law yourself because that is where the perpetrator will be."

They continued moving through the kitchen, opening cupboards, moving cans and packets aside, pulling out drawers, searching between tablecloths and cutlery for something, though just what that was, they were not sure. Susan was now on her knees looking under the sink.

"No Waitrose bags, but plenty of blue plastic bags in this bucket."

"That's a start. Blue plastic bags equal local shop. You know what," Colin stopped what he was doing and looked around the kitchen, stroking his smooth, shaved chin as he considered what he was observing. "You know Suzie Baby; you say she was a gambler, a serious gambler who did a lot more than the odd flutter on the Grand National. Well, all the gamblers I have known, the real hardened gamblers, gave little thought to anything other than how they were going to beat the bookie. So their homes tend to be chaotic and messy, whereas this one is pristine, polished and prim. I would say that someone has been through this place having a good clean-up."

"Getting rid of evidence?"

"Maybe. You finish off the cupboards; I'm going to look around a couple of other rooms. Hopefully, I won't find anyone asleep in the bedroom."

Susan opened the fridge and understood at once what Colin was saying. The fridge was empty but for two bottles of champagne and a jar of Tiptree marmalade standing alongside an unopened bottle of Lea & Perrins Worcestershire sauce and an empty cheese dish. Every shelf appeared clean, not a crumb or any evidence of it being used. It was, in fact, the reverse of Susan's fridge back home, which was stuffed full of half-empty packets and cartons, some squeezed in at the back, well past their sell-by date and some even showing signs of green furry growth, which was the reason that every time she thought about cleaning out her fridge, she diverted herself with a less onerous chore. Yes, Beatrice Cook's fridge was immaculate and almost clinically clean; Susan could see what Colin was saying. Maybe Paige had been in the flat and cleaned it up, removing any possible evidence of what really went on the night Beatrice died.

"I've struck gold!" Colin returned to the kitchen, waving a chequebook over his head. "Her bureau was a total mess, much more in keeping with a gambler's desk. Fortunately for us, our old lady still believed in the old way of paying her bills, by way of an old-fashioned, very retro cheque book, so I now know that on the last day of each month she paid: 'Wilson's Grocery Store' a few hundred pounds, no doubt her monthly shopping bill. Quod erat demonstrandum."

"Quad what?"

"Q.E.D., 'thus it has been demonstrated'. We know where she shops."

"So, where exactly do we find this grocery shop?"

"Wilson's Grocery Store third shop along from the underground station where we arrived. Considering you work for a detective, you are not very observant."

* * *

"What's wrong with your eyes?" Martin asked.

This was the first time he had seen Colin in person. He had already heard a lot from Susan about this superhero. Saving her from a gang of thugs, supporting and encouraging her to apply for the job at Hayden Detective Agency, even reading over her C.V. 'just checking for typos is what Susan admitted to. Then there was the practical advice he had offered her. Apparently, he offered advice on following people as well as other hints and tips on detecting that Susan passed on. So, in Martin's imagination, he wondered if Colin and Susan were becoming closer than just good friends. As a result of all he had heard, he had in his mind a very different image to that of the man who now stood in front of his desk. He had been expecting to see a young, strong-looking man, with steely incisive eyes, definitely not eyes that were surrounded with what looked to Martin like mascara; he hoped he was mistaken about that.

"Nothing, as far as I know, unless you mean the mascara and eye liner," Colin answered, what to him was a question that he was often asked when people met him for the first time.

"Mascara?" Martin repeated. The original Colin image in his mind had disappeared in a puff of smoke.

"Yes, you know, make-up makes my eyelashes look thicker. Do you like it?"

"So I guess that on your lips is lipstick and not the natural colour of your lips?"

Colin puckered his lips, "Don't you think it looks natural? Shame, I was trying to be a little more discreet today, toning things down a bit as I did not want to stand out in the crowd. You should see me when I am all dolled up for a night on the town; then you would see what lipstick should look like."

"He does look an absolute dish when he is all dressed up, puts me to shame," Susan admitted.

"Still, let's tell you what we found at Beatrice's flat," Colin directed the conversation away from his looks which was very much not like him. Colin liked to talk about Colin; he could keep it up for hours if need be. However, he sensed disapproval in the look that Martin was giving him.

Martin raised his hand, indicating to Colin that he wanted to continue the conversation about make-up.

"So why would you want to wear make-up?" Martin asked. "You're a man."

"Where have you been for the last fifty years, Martin? The male cosmetics industry is growing faster year on year. We men are caring more and more about our appearance and using moisturising creams, face scrubs and body sprays. The boundary between what men and women wear is becoming more and more blurred, not just in what we apply to the skin, what we wear as well: jeans, tee-shirts, hairstyles. Years ago, men wore socks and women wore stockings, now women often wear socks and men, well, not all of them are wearing stockings just yet, but a lot are. More young men are dumping socks, and that is currently considered to be the height of modern fashion. Give it another fifty years, Martin and who knows where we will be."

"So, are you just very fashionable or a transvestite?"

"I prefer to think of myself as a fashionable transvestite. Don't worry, Martin, being a transvestite is not compulsory yet!"

Susan and Colin laughed; Martin was not so amused. Martin always considered that he was open-minded and tolerant, which is easy when you are surrounded by people who share your values, dress according to convention and follow the median path that society lays out. So being confronted by someone who is challenging those values, dressing unconventionally, and not following the path society expects made Martin start to feel uncomfortable. Martin could never really decide if he was just disgusted by those who stood outside of accepted normality (not just transvestites, people riddled with tattoos or body piercings were another group he thought to be weird), or if he was jealous of the freedom of expression they all seemed to have.

"Grab a seat, Colin." Susan invited him to sit beside her. "I think we have made some progress, Martin; we have a good line of enquiry as we say in the business, don't we, Colin?"

Again, Martin remained sullen-faced as Colin and Susan shared their joke.

"The inside of Beatrice's flat is pristine; nothing seems to be out of place. It looks just like it had been cleaned to remove any evidence. Colin said a gambler's house is usually chaotic. Mind with two bottles of champagne in the fridge; the old girl did have style. As I said, we think someone has made a point of thoroughly cleaning the flat; we think in an attempt to wipe away any fingerprints or other evidence."

Again Martin raised his hand, like a form teacher silencing his class. "Hold on, hold on a minute. Who let you into her flat?"

Colin went to answer, an enthused Susan beat him and spoke first, "Colin did, he had this great tool thingy that 'kinda' unlocks doors. It was really easy and so, so cool, a bit like you see on the telly."

"You unlocked the door?" Martin spoke methodically, just to be sure he was hearing Susan correctly.

"It wasn't locked," Colin butted in, which only made matters worse as Susan added,

"Don't be so coy; you took ages wiggling that bit of metal around before the door opened. I was getting a little nervous, as I've never broken into a person's house before."

Colin decided to remain silent; he hoped that was the best option as he watched Martin's already sullen mood grow even darker.

"And do you know why you have never broken into anyone's house before, Susan? It will be because it's illegal, not allowed, the wrong thing to do. Decent people do not break into other people's houses, those who do are usually burglars, and burglars get caught and end up in prison."

Susan, feeling like a schoolgirl that has just been told off by the teacher, looked at Colin for some sort of help. He tried his best.

"We were looking for clues that might reveal the old lady was murdered."

"Might reveal, Colin? Might reveal, I very much doubt, is a strong defence. What on earth were you thinking of breaking into the flat? I was expecting you might pop along there, ring the bell, no answer, knock on some of the other flats, see what you could find out. I did not think for one moment that you would decide to break in and rummage around her place. That is the most stupid thing I think I have ever heard. If you get caught, though I won't shed a tear for you, with Susan alongside you, she'd be sent down as well. How do you think she'd survive in a women's prison? Plus, what do you think it would do for my

107

reputation? How could I look my friends in the eye, all of them thinking I have overseen some sort of illegal break-in. I'd be out of business within days."

"She wouldn't go down for a first offence, under section 9 of the 1968 Theft act. It would only be trespass, and we didn't take anything."

"What about the cheque book?"

"Thank you, Susan! Evidence, which we did not actually remove, we had no intent to steal."

"Cheque book? It gets worse, don't tell me you then opened the champagne and had an impromptu party?"

"There's no harm been done."

"No harm, I think there has. You have crossed a line no one should cross. Actually, I think it would be better if you just walked out of here and did not come back. Stay well away from me and do not get involved in anything that Susan might well be doing that is connected to her work here. Get out, Colin, just go before I decide it's better to just call the police now and tell them what you did. At least that would put me in a better light."

"Martin, I think you are overreacting a bit here; we were doing it for the right reasons. We found out some interesting things about Beatrice which might help your investigation."

"He's right," Susan added, "there was nothing taken. We did no damage. I doubt if anyone knew that we were even in there."

"You cannot see the point, can you? Nice people from our side of society do not go around breaking into other people's houses, whatever the reason."

Colin stood up and walked towards the door calling back, "I think it best I leave now, see you soon, Suzie Baby. I'll give you a call."

"What's the matter with you Martin, Colin's been helping us; we're not exactly expert detectives, are we?"

"No, but at least we don't go around breaking the law."

"Watergate became a film!" Susan said, then stood up and followed Colin out of the office.

As the door slammed, Martin called out, "even those burglars got to see the inside of a prison."

The office fell into silence. Martin wondered if he would ever see Susan again. He hoped she would be back soon. Colin, he was not sure about, even so, he did Google the 1968 Theft act, just out of interest.

* * *

For Martin, dinner with Mother that night turned out to be a quiet affair. Well, not so much from her side, Mother spoke almost non-stop, telling her son, who was only half-listening, that Camilla Westenburg had finally divorced her husband after fourteen years of marriage.

All Martin could think of during the over-detailed information that his mother was giving about the Westenburg family was whether Susan might decide to hand her notice in. Clearly, she was angry with him today for throwing out Colin, yet what could he do? The man, or woman, depending on your viewpoint, did break into a flat. Whichever way you looked at it, that was an illegal act.

After the dishes had been loaded into the dishwasher and his mother had retired to the sitting room to watch a programme about nasty neighbours, Martin sat in the kitchen and regarded his phone. For only the second time in his life, he logged onto Facebook. With just four friends, Susan, Jenny, Brian and Michael, he did not have many updates. It was the status of Susan Morris that he looked at first.

'Shit day today with the boss being the boss' was her current status, which had stimulated a number of replies. The first was from a female friend with, in Martin's opinion, a very attractive profile picture. His first thought was to send her a friend request, then thought better of it and just read her reply.

'Chin up, Hun, it's another day tomorrow.'

Susan; *'Hope so, you try yer best and he still shouts.'*

Another friend, less attractive than the first, chipped in, *'Sounds horrid, just give him some verbal back, that should shut him up!'*

The first attractive friend added: *'Just like that waiter in Lloret de Mar!!!!'*

That enigmatic comment gathered over ten likes and a number of what Martin now knew to be emojis.

Susan: *'I bet that poor waiter is still shaking! Can't do that to my boss he's to cute."*

Martin did not take in fully Susan's comment, having found himself distracted by the poor grammar in all the posts. Young people, he thought, in the digital age with all sorts of spelling and grammar checks, have no idea whatsoever about good grammar. A missing comma or an out of place apostrophe brought a tirade of verbal abuse from his grey-haired English teacher, whose black gown made her look like an oversized crow as she swooped down between the desks of the terrified pupils. That should read 'he's too cute', Martin thought. Then it dawned on him, 'she thinks I'm cute,' which brought a smile to his face, which then fell away as he wondered just what Susan did to that waiter in Lloret de Mar to make him shake so much?

CHAPTER FOUR

The next morning Martin walked into his office unsure of whether Susan would be there. The aroma of fresh coffee as he opened the door reassured him that she was indeed at work, that is, unless he had coffee-friendly burglars in the office.

During the morning, they rarely spoke. Martin felt that he was getting the cold shoulder from her. Both maintained a degree of politeness, but there was none of their normal laughter and banter. They sat in mutual silence, staring at their computer screens to avoid eye contact, Susan typing away, Martin reading his paper.

After an hour, it was Susan who had to speak, as was often her default position when silence was called for, she made a point of speaking.

"Colin is only trying to help us, maybe he was a little too enthusiastic breaking into the flat, and alright, I should have been stronger and stopped him. I'm just keen to find out what happened to Beatrice as I'm sure you are as well. Colin has lots of good ideas. He watches all the detective and police programmes on TV. He's really a bit of a geek when it comes to detective work and, well, to be honest, Martin, we're not exactly highly trained Private Eyes are we?"

"Well, he does seem to know his stuff, and you didn't take anything, so according to the bit of the law Colin mentioned, it was more trespass and not burglary."

"There you go, Martin, no harm done, nothing illegal."

"Well, trespass is still not exactly legal, is it?"

"And since when have any of us been totally legal in everything we do. I admit I've done a few things that sail close to the wind of being legal."

"Like shoplifting?"

"Maybe, and are you perfect? I bet you're not. I bet you've broken the law a couple of times."

Martin thought about what she said, smiled, and without saying a word, thought to himself, 'yes Susan, you are correct', although he would never admit out loud just how he had broken the law. To avoid the inevitable question that Susan was going to ask, Martin moved the conversation on.

"Next time you see him, tell him I forgive him. I was a bit over the top. Maybe it was the way he was made-up that rattled me. If he is that much of a TV detective expert, he could be useful."

It was now close to lunchtime. Martin folded up his newspaper and leaned forward, fiddling with his right ear lobe, which, Susan had learnt, was a sign that he was a little nervous.

"I'm off to see the estate agent, who it turns out to be a she, not a he, to find out how much she might have made by Beatrice dying."

Susan answered without hesitation, as though she had been planning her response all morning,

"Knowing that you like to avoid getting involved with people, or should I say helping people, I thought you were planning to give up work once and for all and let the Cook family fight over the inheritance."

"True, I do prefer to avoid real work; life is just a little too short to enjoy all the hedonistic pastimes that man has made for himself; there are a lot of vices to get through. My problem is that once I say I will do something, I will do my very best to do it, however much it might curtail my planned lifestyle. So I am going to see the estate agent and see if I can find out anything of interest. I do not plan to break into her office during the night; I prefer to talk directly to people and ask them questions," he added sarcastically.

Susan was about to say: 'Fuck you, how could I have asked Beatrice where she got the oysters from? She's fucking dead.' Sensibly she thought of her current employment status with Hayden Investigations, the relatively easy-going workload, although not true during the past week compared to when she had first started. Yet she was confident that this investigation would peter out soon enough, and she would be back to a job description that comprised of shopping, lunch and coffee.

"I'll come with you, learn the right way. Plus, I guess she must be attractive, so I'll be there to keep you out of mischief."

Martin ignored the sarcasm in her voice. Together they left the office to make their way across town to Driscoll Estates.

* * *

Taking up two prestigious shop units on the Cromwell Road, the wide glass-fronted estate agents shouted opulence, richness and success; two shop units do not come cheap in this part of London. In the sparkling window were selected properties for sale, large properties, small properties, self-contained flats, both purpose-built and converted. Not one had any indication of the price as that would be far too crass. The interior was no less stylish, wide desks, chrome-framed leather chairs, deep, practical carpet, plus space; lots of open space making you feel so relaxed, you felt you could waltz around the office area, although you would not want to disturb the quiet calm as the occupants of the four desks spoke on the telephone. The fifth estate agent was talking warmly to a couple as they flipped through a glossy, colourful property brochure. Over to the right of the office were more white leather chairs, a low coffee table and slow filtering coffee, a sanctuary for potential customers as they considered their purchase.

"Good afternoon. Can I be of help?" A young woman, maybe in her early twenties, dressed in a black skirt with a contrasting white cotton blouse, smiled with whitened teeth.

"Yes, I hope to be able to speak to Melinda Driscoll if she is available?" Martin asked.

"Of course, can I ask what it is regarding?"

"Beatrice Cook, I understand that Melinda has an arrangement with Mrs Cook which needs to be expedited."

She gestured towards the sanctuary with the leather chairs and coffee.

"Please take a seat, and I will see if Ms Driscoll is available. Do help yourself to coffee."

"Expedited? What's that all about?" Susan asked, grabbing a packet of shortbread biscuits as they sat down.

"Well, makes us sound important, I hope."

After a few minutes, they were both ushered into a discreet office that was no less plush than the rest of the agency. Melinda Driscoll eyed them both with suspicion before inviting her guests to sit down, thanked the young girl with the white teeth, who gave everyone one last flash of the teeth which must have cost a fortune to be that bright, before closing the door behind her, leaving them all to talk without being disturbed as she had been instructed.

"You both look too young to be close relatives of Beatrice Cook unless you are grandchildren, and as I recall, she had little to do with them, or them with her for that matter. So, what interest do you have in Beatrice Cook?"

Martin was impressed by her direct, no-nonsense approach, although her stunning facial features framed by heavy-rimmed glasses impressed him even more. Shoulder-length blonde hair, sharp blue eyes, with just the merest hint of make-up, high cheekbones, soft-looking kissable cheeks, a small button nose and with a tiny dimple in the centre of her chin. Maybe her mouth, if Martin was going to be supercritical, was a little thin-lipped. That flaw would not stop him from asking her out, even though she was possibly about his age, an age group he tried to avoid when seeking romantic dates.

"We believe you have entered into an agreement with Beatrice that concludes when she dies."

"I have been told you are Susan Morris and Martin Hayden. First, I would like to know a little more about just who you both are before I answer that question."

"Something to hide, Melinda?" Susan chimed in, convinced that was just the sort of question Jim Rockford would have asked. It was Martin who spoke next to take the edge off that blunt, sharp question.

"Beatrice has died in potentially suspicious circumstances, and we want to establish who would benefit from her death."

Melinda stood up, she recognised the way Martin was looking at her, walked around to the front of her desk and sat on the edge, allowing her skirt to ride a little high, displaying her legs for his benefit.

"If you were police, you would have waved your warrant cards around by now. Revenue Inspectors, no, you look too kind to be one of those creatures. Maybe you are from one of the many casinos that Beatrice frequented, looking to settle her tab. Suspicious circumstances, you say, mmm, an investigator for the family?"

"Private investigators; just bringing together some loose ends for the family, ensuring that everything is handled discreetly."

"If you want to know, I was not aware the old lady was dead. What is it that you want to know?"

"More about your arrangement with Beatrice."

Melinda looked over towards Susan, examining the girl's clothes, none of which looked to be of any real quality, pretty mundane, Melinda thought. Martin, on the other hand, clearly ensured the contents of his wardrobe were of high quality. Odd contrast between the two, she thought.

"The fact that you are here tells me you know all about my arrangement with Beatrice, a mutually beneficial arrangement; I should point out. Two years ago, I effectively bought ten per cent of her house in cash, with the understanding that I could not redeem my investment until after she died, which I am sorry to hear that she has now passed. The longer she lived, the bigger the profit on my investment. With house prices on the up and up way ahead of anything the bank would give you, I am, or should I say was, doing well, that is assuming the family sell up the house, and I can then collect my ten per cent. Maybe they might not sell, happy to leave the arrangement as it is, keep the status quo, and I can watch my ten per cent grow and grow in value." Melinda smiled and then returned to her chair, having given Martin enough time to appreciate her legs.

"How did you and Beatrice meet up in the first place?" Susan asked, her tone a little less confrontational.

"She just walked in one day, said she was doing some shopping and apparently had a brain wave. She asked me if I would buy part of her house and told me why she wanted the money. If I agreed, she'd get in touch with her solicitor to make it all legal and above board, as I said, a good opportunity to make some money that I was not going to turn down. It was going to earn more than it would just sitting in a bank. Plus, I liked her, a bit of a rebel if you ask me."

"So you're not bothered about cashing in your part of the house?" Susan asked, having decided that she did not like Melinda. The term 'rich bitch' came to her mind.

"As I said, the longer it stays tied up in bricks and mortar, the better; my investment will grow a lot faster than if it was in my savings account. So her death, suspicious or otherwise, is not in my interest. Now Hugh Alexander is a totally different scenario." She noticed the frown on Martin's brow, indicating Hugh Alexander was a name he had not heard before. "You don't know about Hugh and Beatrice?"

"Tell us what you know?" Susan again asked what she thought was a good Rockford question.

Melinda wanted to laugh at the girl with the rough edges that sat next to Martin but thought better of it.

"Beatrice told me about him during one of her many visits here to have a good chat; she was like that, often at difficult times, although I needed to keep on the right side of her. Anyway, she had some sort of valuable painting at her house by some artist that I had never heard of. She got Hugh Alexander, an artist friend of hers, to create an exact copy of it so she could replace the original, and none of her family would be any the wiser. Hugh then paid her half the market value for the painting on the understanding that he could not sell it until she died. Now, if you ask me, when have you ever heard of a rich artist? He might well need to cash in his investment, plus artworks do go up and down, not a solid investment like property. He has a small shop in Victoria, with a small flat above it."

Susan and Martin left the estate agent, turned left along the crowded pavement and then made their way towards Gloucester Road Tube station. They had Googled Hugh Alexander, so they now had his address in Victoria. Martin was keen to strike while the iron was hot to get this whole time-consuming affair cleared up so that he could go back to his previous life relaxing in restaurants and chatting in bars. Susan still had questions about the estate agent that she wanted Martin to answer.

Susan asked, "Why did you feel the need to ask her date of birth?"

"I was taking a leaf out of your book. You never know; her star sign and mine might be the perfect match."

"You're a Pisces; she's an arrogant Sagittarius; no way is anything happening between you two. However long you might think her legs are, it will end in tears, trust me. Now before we talk to this artist, I need feeding. Those biscuits did nothing for my hunger, plus it is well past my lunchtime, and there is a curry house just up ahead, so let's eat."

Martin followed her into the cramped restaurant like an obedient puppy. He was sure the iron would stay hot until after lunch.

* * *

The waiter was short, in fact, very short, very dark-skinned and incredibly short. Even with Susan sitting down looking at her menu, the Indian waiter who spoke with a slow, strong Liverpudlian accent was still only at her eye level. Susan wondered at what height a dwarf becomes a non-dwarf and where her Indian waiter was on that scale. Looking him in the eye, which was not hard, Susan asked, "Can we have a bottle of red wine as well?"

Martin looked at her with raised eyebrows,

"You can't just ask for red wine, Susan. It is like asking for a curry; there are so many different types, you need to be specific or else you have no idea what you are going to get. What is the house wine?"

The waiter looked towards the kitchen door behind him, then returned his gaze to Martin, pen still poised over his notepad. He had never been asked about the house wine before.

"Do you want red, white or rosé?" He looked for some clarity, people who came into their slightly scruffy Indian restaurant only ever asked for red wine, a beer or a Kingfisher.

"What I meant," Martin explained slowly and carefully, "was what type of red wine you have: Merlot, Shiraz, Cabernet Sauvignon?"

The waiter thought for a moment then answered with as much information as he could muster. "I can recommend our Bangalore red wine. My cousin personally delivers it here."

"I think you'll find that Bangalore does not have an indigenous wine industry."

"I think you'll find India has moved on since the days of British rule. We are more than just punkah wallahs nowadays. We even rule ourselves; I hope that doesn't surprise you too much. I should also point out that the cheaper house wine, if you are after a red, is a Merlot from the south of France, cheap and acceptable. The Bangalore wine, if you want to try it and see how your ex-subjects have been faring without your imperial help, is a red; Big Banyan, a Cabernet Sauvignon, it's a complex wine, smooth, yet full-bodied. I should point out that it is one of our more expensive wines even for those who profiteered out of India's misery."

"Big Banyan, what sort of name is that for a wine? I think you are playing mind games with me. If India does produce wine, I would have thought the wine would have more spicy tones." That was Martin's attempt at humour which fell on stony ground. "I'll stick with the French Merlot house wine. I'll try your so-called Indian wine another time."

"Google it; you'll be surprised."

"Just get me the wine and drop the sarcasm." Martin was short with the waiter, an appropriate tone given his lack of height, Martin thought.

The short waiter smirked and turned away, waddling his way towards the kitchen. Susan leaned forward across the table to speak quietly to Martin.

"I think you should be a little more cautious; he has L.M.S."

"L.M.S? What are you talking about?"

"Little Man Syndrome; it gives him an attitude. I should also point out that if you are going to piss off the waiter, please do it after the food has arrived. I don't want to think what they might be doing to our food out there in the kitchen. I've heard some horror stories about the things waiters and cooks do to customers' meals once they have been upset."

It was the wry smile that the waiter had as he served Martin his Rogan Josh, which convinced Martin to eat just the rice as that looked innocent enough. Susan had no such worries, telling Martin that during her life, she had eaten at many very dubious establishments, and she had a stone-lined stomach. There was not anything they could put in her curry that she had not already swallowed at some time or other. As Martin watched Susan eat with unnerving enthusiasm considering her warning, he began to think about just what he had said to Melinda with the long legs: 'we are Private Investigators, just tying up some loose ends for the family'. He could not tell exactly why; maybe it was the first time that he had asked a total stranger questions about Beatrice, but it began to dawn on him that they were actually investigating a death. He felt a sense of responsibility for Beatrice; if she had died of natural causes, then the next few days would be a waste of time; time he could have better spent with Jenny.

Yet the question is: 'was she murdered and if so, why'? A detective has to think, has to understand the facts, question the evidence, dig deeper into stories that were offered by those around Beatrice. He started to think of those Agatha Christie stories he had read and the American detectives, the fictional investigations, then he turned to the murder documentaries he had watched over the years. Thinking of the questions, they might have asked, had he asked them yet? Did he have any answers yet?

"Beatrice was found dead on Wednesday afternoon, but we don't really know the last time anyone actually saw her alive."

Susan mopped up the last of her Lamb Bhuna sauce with a torn-off piece of naan bread.

"Tuesday," she said between bites, "her daughter spoke to her; don't you recall her telling us that? Sorry no, she didn't tell us; the guy at the shop did."

"What shop?"

Susan burped. "Pardon me, that was a good curry. I would try and finish yours as you seem to have lost your appetite, but I'm really stuffed. Yes, the shop where Beatrice bought her groceries. Oh, I meant to tell you, but what with the fracas with you and Colin, it went clean out of my mind. We found out where she shopped to see if she had bought any oysters. I'll gloss over how we got the address; I think you know the basics. So me and the man with the make-up walked over to the shop where she had an account. I don't think Beatrice was the type of person to trail around supermarkets looking for bargains, so she appeared to get all her shopping from Wilson's Grocery Store, which is just around the corner opposite the tube station.

"We asked for Brian, that's the shopkeeper, which is weird, him being called Brian Wilson like the singer from the Beach Boys. But he was not around at that time; he is the owner or something. So one of the shop workers there told me and Colin that he had not seen Beatrice in a while, but he was full of the story of a customer being found dead. He said Beatrice was found dead on Wednesday afternoon. The police were called to break into the flat where they found her in her bed. Then he told us; do you mind me saying us as in Colin and me, or shall I just say me?"

"I don't care, Susan; just tell me what you found out."

"Well, he told us that she had been found dead in bed with a pile of dyspepsia mixtures and tablets by her bed."

"How did he know? Was he there?"

"Oh no, Paige had spoken to the manager, that's Brian Wilson, not the Beach Boys Brian clearly when she came into the shop to settle Beatrice's account. Paige told the boss, who then told all his staff it would seem about the stuff on the bedside table and told them that there were oyster shells on the kitchen table. So, Paige thought her mother must have eaten them, and one might have been off or something like that. Apparently, she was very upset and told him that she had only seen her mother the morning before she died. Hence Tuesday morning Paige saw her if she's telling the truth, that is. I still think she did it somehow for the money. As you say, if the blonde tart had part of the old girl's house that would shrink Paige's inheritance and now we are about to talk to an artist who does forgeries, if Paige found that out too, well, she might want to stop her mother gambling away the family fortune."

"We need to find out if she really was alive on Tuesday. Although I trust Paige, she's from a good family, I can't see her fretting over her mother's money, and I do think she was more worried about her mother's reputation as a gambler. Let's go and see what Hugh Alexander has to say."

* * *

They exited Victoria tube station, walked along the back streets behind the shops of Victoria Street, across the plaza in front of Westminster Cathedral, along Howick Place and were very soon walking down Horseferry Road.

"There it is," Martin pointed to the art shop, "Alexander Art".

"That's spooky," Susan commented as they crossed the road towards the art gallery. "The café next door is where Tala, the maid, spends her Tuesdays. That's where Colin and I met her, small world!"

Visitors to 'Alexander Art' were few and far between, exactly the way that Hugh Alexander liked it. Shuffling around in his cluttered shop with its dark and dusty corners, there hung a dry ambience of odours: pipe smoke amalgamated with turpentine, tainted with the ever-present smell of oil paint, which Hugh had thickly applied to the canvases that were untidily stacked against the walls. Not that Hugh spent much time in the shop; he spent his days in his adjoining mews studio with its glazed roof that flooded his cramped workspace with seasonal light, enabling him to create loud, nebulous, abstract paintings, canvases which were bold in both colour and texture, expressing those emotions that Hugh felt trapped within his soul. He had left art college with the youthful belief that his art could galvanise society, show a better way and enlighten those whose vision fell upon his stunning abstract works. In those early days, he found it easy to sell his small canvases to friends, relations and the occasional collector who might stumble across his works and felt they showed potential.

Hugh never managed to fully realise that potential. His brushstrokes became audacious. The painful, vivid hues of his work clashed with each other. He found it harder and harder to relate to people and found his personality being absorbed into his art which had become a vortex for his feelings, draining his moods and in turn stirring a greater passion within him to create a canvas living with human emotion. He sold less and less, as friends, relations and collectors shunned him. They left him to his own ends, alone with his cluttered shop and paint-splashed studio.

From his studio, Hugh could hear the knocking on the locked glass door of his shop. Why bother unlocking it in the morning and then locking it in the evening when no one used it; he would argue with himself. Hugh shuffled through the narrow corridor to his shop. As he moved towards the shop door, his leather and wooden paint-stained flip-flops rasped on the tiled floor. He wiped his paint-stained hands with an equally paint-stained turpentine-soaked rag. Martin and Susan waited as Hugh scrutinised them through the glass before partly opening the door and greeting them with a brusk, "Yes?"

Martin spoke through the gap that Hugh had left between the door and its frame, the odour of turpentine overwhelming his sensitive nose.

"I understand that you purchased a painting from Beatrice Cook, and we wanted to talk to you about it."

"Was it stolen?"

"No."

"Then what is there to talk about? I bought it legally."

"Maybe that is so. However, I know you can't sell it until Beatrice dies, and she has now died."

On his face, Hugh showed no emotion. He opened the door wider, allowing some fresh air into the cramped shop.

"Come in."

The three of them stood uncomfortably close in the limited space afforded to them by the shop. Susan thought that Hugh must be well into his seventies, when in fact, he was just sixty-three years old. The slightly arched back he displayed added years to him, as did the wild, unkempt grey hair that covered his head. His rotund face, mostly covered in a grey beard, reflected the wildness of his hair. Martin explained that Beatrice had died in her sleep a few days ago, and they wanted to confirm that he still had the painting or if he was planning to sell it in the near future as Mrs Cook's relatives might consider buying it back. Martin had lied, which surprised not only Susan but also Martin, who had found it easy to make up a lie. His mother had told him that when dealing with people that you wanted something from, you should approach them as you would a game of poker, do a bit of bluffing, and never lay your cards on the table until the end of the hand. Martin consoled himself that he was not lying; he was just bluffing.

"My legal agreement with Beatrice forbade me to sell the painting while she drew breath. I am a man of my word, I can assure you, and so to that end, I still have the painting."

"You were not that surprised to hear that she had died, so I presume that you have already heard," Martin pointed out.

"We live in London; people walk around in their own individual silos, unaware and mostly uncaring as to what is happening to those around them. I am not different; unless it is broadcast on Radio Four, the Black Death could have started across the road, and I would not have heard of it. Yet I did, in fact, hear of it. You know I am Hugh; can I ask your names?"

"Susan Morris, and I am Martin Hayden."

"Hayden," Hugh recalled the name, "would that be the same Hayden that sold off the British Screw Company?"

Martin nodded, "Yes, my father."

"Your father was a good man. I knew him many years ago when we were both a lot younger. So, what do you do now, now the family business is being run by some Asian Investment company?"

Martin held back for a moment, wondering which cards he might need to show. Susan stepped into the void.

"We work for an insurance company. So how did you come to buy the painting off Beatrice?"

"And replace it with a copy is what you want to say. Obviously, her daughter has now found out about the arrangement I had with Beatrice. An agreement which, I should point out, was mutually beneficial to both sides." Hugh threw the spoiled rag into a corner beside a canvas that had broad textured brushstrokes of red over a background of blue.

"I have known Beatrice for a good few years now; not well, you understand, but have met her at some social gatherings over the years. So when we found ourselves in the same queue at the post office, we started to talk. We chatted about the dull queues you always find at post offices. You might just want to purchase a simple stamp, only to find yourself backed up behind people taxing their car or arranging registered post; I'm sure you have both been in such a queue. She asked me how my painting was going, not that I would describe it as painting. I am an artist, and I create art. So I mentioned to her that I now owned an art gallery, and she invited me over to her house to see the paintings that she had, maybe be able to identify some of the ones she could not. So, a few days later, I spent a very pleasant afternoon in her flat examining and admiring her intimate collection of paintings. Not just oils and watercolours, but she also had some very nice pen and ink drawings. I was able to help her identify a few that she did not know the origins of. After that, we spoke on the telephone a couple of times, or if she was passing, she would put her head around the door and say 'Hello'. I never visited her again, that was until last year when she called into my shop and asked if I could value one of her paintings. It was one that I had shown an interest in; admiration is most likely a better description. She had a Russell Drysdale painting, an Australian artist I admired when I first started at art college. Once I had valued it or given her a very rough estimation of its worth, she asked me if I could make a copy of it, something I was not expecting her to say. Surprised as I was, I thought about it briefly and said I could. Then she offered me the strangest of deals: if I made a copy of the Drysdale which only needed to pass the scrutiny of her family, none of whom were art experts, then I could buy the original for half the value I had just given it on the condition that I did not sell it into the art market until after she had died. Having just valued it at four hundred thousand, I was surprised by her offer, which meant, in fact, I was going to be paid in the region of two hundred thousand pounds for making a copy. Although the exact time and amount I would receive would depend on her death. I, of course, agreed, and she arranged for her solicitor to draw up the agreement which I signed. I then completed the copy, and the original Drysdale hangs in my studio."

"Did she say what she wanted the money for?" Martin asked as he got used to the smell of turpentine. He detected another smell; pipe tobacco was now aggravating his nostrils.

"Is that the insurance company asking, or your private detective agency?" Hugh looked at Susan and smiled. "Not Radio Four telling me, good old-fashioned grapevine."

"The Agency," Susan admitted. Secretly she did enjoy owning up to it. Calling it the agency felt to her really cool.

"So you have suspicions about her death?"

"Why would we?" Martin asked.

"Because when people mention money and mortality in the same sentence, murder is usually at the end."

"Did you know what she wanted the money for?" Martin asked again, worried as Hugh pulled a curved pipe from his pocket, examined the half-full bowl, pushed down the tobacco and placed it in his mouth. Martin did not want him to light it as that would have the same effect as fumigating the shop.

"Of course, I did. Beatrice never hid the fact that she liked or rather had an insatiable passion to play roulette. Before you criticise me for feeding her gambling habit, or even my profiting out of her habit, I should point out that in my opinion, gamblers are more religious than some of our most pious citizens. The average churchgoer has faith that if they do certain things in their lives, then their reward will be to pass through the Gates of Heaven with a smug smile on their face. That demands a certain trust and belief. Can you imagine spending the whole of your life living by the guidelines set out in the Bible, only to find out the whole book was total fiction with Heaven only inviting those who showed no love for their fellow human beings to be the chosen ones? That would be ironic, don't you think? Gamblers display that same trust and belief, yet they go further in that they actually put money behind their beliefs. A gambler believes that their chosen horse will be first past the post. They put their hard-earned cash behind that belief, reinforcing their commitment. The big plus point with being a gambler is that you do not have to wait until you die before finding out if your gamble has paid off. I don't gamble, either on horses or getting to Heaven. Funny, I wonder if Beatrice has found the Pearly Gates open for her, I hope so; I liked her."

"Even so, you gambled on the painting going up in value before she died. I think we all know that artworks go down as well as up," Martin pointed out, relieved to see that Hugh did not appear to be planning to light his pipe but just holding it in his mouth as some form of security.

"A Russell Drysdale is very unlikely to go down in value. His works, when they come up for sale, are commanding an ever-increasing premium. Let's not forget, I, in effect, purchased my painting for half the market value."

"When was the last time you saw her alive?" Susan asked, trying to avoid a direct imitation of Jim Rockford.

"Given what I have been told about when she died, young lady, it was the Tuesday afternoon which is going to do nothing to allay your suspicious mind, is it?" Hugh adjusted the pipe that he still held in his mouth located in a gap, worn down by his pipe smoking over the last few decades. "So, I shall explain why I visited her after having said to you we were just acquaintances who passed conversation when we met in the street." He removed the pipe and returned it into his pocket to ensure what he planned to say was fully understood. "As I mentioned, I had been to her flat a couple of times to value and view her collection of paintings, so I knew the range that she had. As well as the Drysdale which I had copied for her, I knew that she had a painting by T.F. Simon, a Czech artist, a painting that her mother had acquired when Beatrice was a young child. I was interested to see if she would consider making it part of our arrangement if I provided a copy for her. Sadly she declined. The portrait was of her mother, and so she did not feel that she could part with it, which was completely understandable. So, I left disappointed. That was the last time I saw her." Hugh paused, allowing a brief moment for any comments from his two guests. They remained silent, so he continued, "I would add that she did seem a little on edge when I saw her that afternoon. Before, she had always shown warmth towards me when we met, insisting that I visit her for tea and conversation, which never actually happened; it is just part of social etiquette. Yet that afternoon, no such warmth was shown; she didn't offer me tea. I would say that she was happy to see me go."

"So you stand to make a lot of money now Beatrice is dead?"

"I stood to make money the moment I agreed to help Beatrice. I will only realise that money if and when I sell the painting. Her death makes no difference to that scenario, of that, I assure you."

"Just one other thing," Susan started, "who told you Beatrice had died?"

"This does sound a little like an interrogation. Someone popped in a few days ago; he told me she had died and asked about the last time I saw her. He was some sort of local reporter, odd-looking chap, wearing eye make-up and lipstick; it shocks me sometimes who local papers employ nowadays."

* * *

Martin and Susan sat on a bench in St John's Gardens, a green oasis in the middle of busy Westminster. They took deep breaths to clear their lungs of the stale tobacco and turpentine that they had been forced to breathe in while they spoke to Hugh. Neither of them liked him; in fact, Susan went so far as to say, 'maybe, he did the old lady in'. Martin was not as blunt.

Together they wallowed in the late afternoon sunshine, Susan relaxed, still bloated from her Indian lunch, Martin now starting to feel peckish, having eaten virtually nothing at all. For a few moments, they sat without conversation, Martin listening to the traffic passing a few yards away, Susan texting a friend and struggling to read the screen in the dappled sunlight. Once she had finished, the phone was slipped into her oversized fake Dior handbag. She stretched out her legs and arms.

"This is the life. I love the warmth of the sun; it makes you feel cosy and safe."

Martin did not answer; he was thinking about Beatrice. He felt a tinge of sadness as he recalled their brief friendship and nights of roulette. He hoped that he would be at the tables when he was ninety, and he hoped that if his death raised a few questions, someone would take the time to see if they could answer those questions.

"Martin," Susan broke into his thoughts, "where would a poor artist like that smelly old man get a couple of hundred thousand pounds to give the old lady in cash?"

"His bank account, I guess. Why do you ask?"

"So you mean that he had in his bank account a load of cash just sitting there?"

"I don't know," Martin sounded a little peeved; he was happily recalling the moment that one of his roulette numbers came up much to the delight of Beatrice. "I am not his accountant; he most likely had it in a savings account, maybe some sort of investment that he could cash in and pay for the painting."

"Doesn't that surprise you to have so much spare cash?"

Martin turned his body towards Susan, his arm stretching out behind her; to the casual observer, they could have been lovers talking.

"Some people have money, some people do not, and it is that simple, Susan, not rocket science."

"It's strange though; we live in a place where we are told that we are pretty equal, a western society that is fair to all. Yet, just a few months ago, I was struggling to pay my rent, fighting to keep a roof over my head. My friends have to use credit cards and hire purchase agreements to buy the things they want. Loads of my mates are always in debt, moving between credit cards, paying just the barest minimum. Sometimes, if they've bought a car, say paying monthly, there comes a point where they just stop paying and then wait for the car to be taken away, which gives them a few months of free motoring. They all seem to spend their time working out ways to get out of paying or securing a new loan to pay off all the others. Yet him over there just dips into his bank account and pulls out enough money to see me out for a few years, just to buy a silly painting. Where is the fairness in that?"

"Who said life was fair? Then again, if life is not fair, I can assure you that society is far from fair and equal. That is the way it has to be and has been for centuries."

"Does it have to be that way? If we shared the wealth around, I'm sure everyone's life would be better. You've had a privileged life, rich parents, private school, not exactly working hard to maintain your extravagant lifestyle. Don't you ever feel guilty?"

"What's got into you, Susan? These are very deep philosophical questions you are asking."

"But I'm right; some have it easy, some, like my friends, have it hard."

Martin waited as an ambulance passed by, siren blaring out, weaving between the traffic.

"Money alone does not make life hard or easy; it just makes things possible which is not always a good thing. A sword will kill a person, a machine gun makes it possible to kill more people, and a bomb makes it possible to kill still more. Making things possible is not always good. Yes, my parents were rich, I

lived in a big house, and lots of things were possible. Take
education, you went off to your school each day and came back
after a few hours. I went off to a private boarding school and
stayed there. That was only possible because we had money. I
hated every minute of my schooldays, from the moment my
mother waved goodbye to me. I was eleven years old, alone, and
did not know one single person at my school. I was terrified
unpacking my small suitcase in a small dormitory surrounded by
strangers, all the same age, but nevertheless strangers. I felt as
though my parents had decided that they were fed up with
seeing me around the house, so had me shipped off to some far-
off land, where I struggled to learn, simply because I hated it.
Dusty, dark, old classrooms with masters that were not
dissimilar. Fellow pupils who would ridicule you if you knew the
answers and poke fun at you if you did not. On the sports field,
the masters took great pleasure in watching us boys scrabble
across the rugby field, being kicked, beaten and bruised, just
because you can get away with that in a rugby scrum. Cross
country running being pushed and tripped into dirty, wet,
muddy ditches face first. Then there were the hot steaming
showers afterwards when boys who liked touching other boys
came into their own. Yes, Susan, money made all that possible.
So how were your school days?"

"I thought they were bad; I'm not so sure now. Although
we still had bullies and perverts amongst the girls and the boys,
it was a mixed school."

"I'm not saying you had it any worse. I'm just trying to
highlight that your perception of the life of another person, rich
or poor, can be a lot different to the reality that the person
experiences. So, was that deep and meaningful question about
distracting me so I would not ask you, 'who do you think the
local reporter in lipstick might have been?'"

"He does like to get involved; I'll speak to him."

They took a cab back to the office; Martin could not face another trip on the congested underground. Being up close and personal with the general public was not where Martin wanted to be at any time. He began conversing as the cab navigated the Victoria one-way system. It was a conversation he had not planned to have, but circumstances were driving him in a direction he had no control over.

"So, Hugh Alexander, is he telling us the truth? Did he leave Beatrice alive and well, or did he stay and have oysters with her?"

"If you're asking me, he killed the old girl for that picture she was not going to sell. He looks the sort of person who always wants to get what he wants, spoilt, I reckon."

"So, Melinda and Paige are now off the suspect list?"

"Why ask me? You're the boss. It's your detective agency, not mine."

"You're the one with the Jim Rockford experience and Colin as your backup."

Susan slid on the leather seat closer to Martin as the cab turned a corner. She liked being close to him; it felt good; it was as though he had a warmth that radiated out from him, making her feel safe.

"It hurts me to say it, but Melinda does not have any need to see Beatrice dead unless she was desperate for some cash. The longer she stayed in the agreement, the more she would make. Paige, I think, is a suspect. That sounds so cool, a suspect. Anyway, I think she still had good reason to stop Beatrice gambling away the family fortune. But I'd put the smelly artist at least second on my list with Paige still at the top."

Martin said with a smile, "Unless there were other arrangements that Beatrice made in her lifetime that we still need to learn about?"

Susan pulled out her phone for what was now becoming a daily ritual and read Martin his stars. She would always politely ask if he wanted to hear what was going to happen in the next twenty-four hours, but however he answered, she would still tell him regardless.

"Do you want your stars, Martin?"

"No."

"I'm not sure your stars are very good today, Martin."

"Why do the stars foretell my death?"

"Worse maybe, 'your hard work....', it says here, so that's wrong for a start, 'Your hard work has not only enriched your social-economic standing but your friendships as well', so as you don't actually do any work at all, let alone hard work, you're going to have no friends, and your social-economic standing, whatever that might be, will also not happen."

"In that case, I had better do something, perhaps answering some questions that we have."

Martin paid the cabbie and turned towards Susan as she stood waiting on the pavement. He had a frown across his forehead.

"Did you get overcharged?" Susan asked.

Martin ignored the question and instead asked one of his own. "I was wondering how Colin found out about Hugh Alexander?"

Susan insisted that they just needed to stick to their own lines of inquiry as she liked to describe them. The first line was going back to Beatrice's solicitor to find out, if they could, who else might have had arrangements with Beatrice, enabling her to finance her gambling through releasing equity. A concept that Susan was finding hard to understand until Martin compared it to pawning the family jewels, which made Susan snigger like a schoolgirl. She knew an alternative meaning for 'pawn' and 'family jewels'.

The second line of inquiry was trying to find out who visited Beatrice before she died. Hugh had mentioned that she seemed keen to get him to leave, which suggested she was expecting someone else that evening.

The third line was the woman that Martin had seen Beatrice having strong words with on the coach trip. Almost an argument, yet not quite, Whatever the conversation they were having was about, they clearly knew each other from a time other than that coach trip. Martin wanted to find and speak to her.

Fortunately, he recalled her memorable name: Florence Gibbons Howard.

"Her name is alphabetical, F,G,H, easy to recall," Martin admitted.

For Susan, alphabetical or not, it was useful that it was such an unusual name; there were not going to be too many in the phone book. In fact, there was just one living in sheltered accommodation off South Norwood Hill.

It did not take long for Susan to find the full address which she insisted on driving to, in what Martin considered to be a very old pale green Ford Fiesta, which indeed it was. It was not so much the age of the car that concerned Martin, more the way Susan drove it through the London rush-hour traffic; driving close to parked cars, braking far too late, missing or just ignoring some traffic signals and appearing not to fully comprehend the term 'give way'. During the drive, she continued to talk about the holiday that she was planning to take with her girlfriends, at what she described, to be a holiday camp in Bognor that was holding an 'eighties' weekend, explaining it as a chance to dress up, get drunk and have a laugh. Martin could not begin to imagine what a weekend in Bognor might be like, let alone a holiday camp.

"Have you actually passed your driving test?" Martin asked as the pale green Fiesta under the unsteady command of Susan lurched forward at a crossroads, only just missing a black cab.

"Yes, third attempt. They say that it makes you a better driver if you fail a couple of times. The first I failed when I hit a curb, well I say a curb; it was the roundabout curb that I hit. The second time I waved to a friend at a bus stop, who would have thought I would have been failed for being social. So it was third time lucky, although I did dress in a certain very feminine way, which might have covered up a few driving errors and little else," she smiled.

Situated alongside the busy South Norwood High Street, Shakespeare Court was not exactly an oasis of peace and tranquillity for the pensioners that lived there. Twenty-four self-contained flats where a mixture of elderly men and women lived as neighbours, all of them residing beside the constant flow of traffic. Some of the residents were able to look after themselves; others relied on social care and family support. Age was not a decider in who was frail and who was strong; it was just the hand that had been dealt to them.

Florence Gibbons Howard lived in a second-floor flat. Now aged sixty-four, she was one of the younger residents and was happy to help those around her who were less able. Despite her hands that now showed the first signs of rheumatism with her knuckles becoming painful, she would be out along the High Street buying newspapers, running errands, doing a little bit of shopping, and at least twice a week she would cook dinner for Mrs Granger who lived next door to her and who was now almost bed-ridden through arthritis.

Florence was surprised that the young man from the coach trip wanted to speak to her. Having seen him spend most of his time with Beatrice, she was tempted to ignore him, but curiosity got the better of her. She smiled warmly as she invited him and his young lady into her flat.

As she did with all her guests, not that she entertained much these days, she offered tea and cakes. The tea was old-fashioned tea leaves, brewed in a porcelain teapot that was hand-painted with yellow roses. The cakes were always Mr Kipling's Country Slices, which she both enjoyed and, as they were individually wrapped, meant she always had some fresh cakes to offer visitors. Florence would have liked to offer more choice to her infrequent visitors, yet now she was in her early sixties, she liked to watch the pennies and appeared more frugal than she had during her younger days. Her one-bedroom flat consisted of a combined living-dining area, with an attached small kitchenette, partly shielded by net curtains that were drawn back to form an archway. All around the cosy flat were framed photographs, trinkets and tiny crystal glass animals, artefacts and pottery, for Florence, all reminders of her past. The walls were crowded with paintings, one very large watercolour overshadowing the other framed oil and watercolours that were fixed to the wall in no particular pattern.

"I do recall seeing you on the coach trip. I'm sorry I never got around to speaking to you. It can be so difficult to speak to all those on the tour," she admitted as she carefully poured tea into Martin's cup using an ornate silver tea strainer. "I really enjoyed walking around Monet's Garden; it was so colourful, which should not have surprised one given that he was an artist." She laughed and offered a sugar bowl to her guests. Martin refused; Susan took the opportunity to place three heaped spoonsful of sugar into her cup. "I never realised until the visit to Giverny that so many American artists lived around there at the same time as Monet. It was such a shame that you didn't manage to make that part of the tour."

Martin thought it sounded as though she was reprimanding him, or at the very least, being sarcastic. He guessed that most of the others on the coach trip had gossiped about the antics of the old lady and that young man.

"I guess I missed out on a lot of those tours, although I did enjoy the nightlife."

"That is because you were just too young to be on such a trip. Young men like you should be off to the sunshine and sandy beaches with young ladies in tiny bikinis, drinking wild cocktails and dancing all night in clubs, not hanging around a bunch of old fogies on a coach trip."

"Sometimes one finds oneself in a situation, and you just have to make the very best of it. I'm sure you noticed I spent a lot of time with one person, in particular, Beatrice Cook. In the same way that I noticed, you did seem to have strong words with each other on the last day. I wondered what that was about."

"Now, why would a conversation I had be of any concern of yours? Didn't Beatrice reveal all to you?"

"She just passed it off as a minor disagreement."

"Well, if that satisfied you then, what brings you now to my door asking about a private conversation? Just ask her again; I am sure she'll divulge all in the end."

Martin finished his tea and refused a second cup before he revealed that Beatrice was dead. As he spoke, both Martin and Susan watched the facial expression of Florence as she heard the news. They both hoped her face might give something away, but what that might be, neither were sure. Her face did not change; she simply said, "Ah, so there is a God after all. I would love to hear the conversation between Beatrice and Saint Peter when she gets to the Gates of Heaven. I'm sure she'll complain of being dragged up there too soon. Well Martin, if she is dead, there is even less reason to worry about a conversation that I had with her a while back."

Susan answered on his behalf as he finished his third country slice and considered if taking a fourth might seem to Florence being greedy. His lack of lunch had left his stomach crying out for food of any description.

"We're investigating her death which on the face of it appears to be natural. However, there are just a couple of loose ends that we need to tidy up for the family. That's why we wanted to know what you both seemed to be arguing about."

Florence had always been the perfect hostess. In her younger days, she arranged large successful dinner parties for her husband's friends and business acquaintances. So she noticed Martin eyeing a fourth country slice and encouraged him to continue eating. She guessed it must be some sort of motherly instinct that delighted her to see younger men eating heartily.

"Investigators, how exciting, so how did she die?"

"Food poisoning, brought on by an infected oyster that put such a strain on her frail heart that she slipped away in her sleep."

"There's no need to try and be a polite young lady. She over-indulged and died, which just about sums up Beatrice. Oysters, you say, no wonder you're investigating. Is Paige not happy with the verdict, or does she think the old girl committed suicide just to spite her? I wouldn't put it past her."

Martin tried to speak, which he could not, as he was only halfway through eating another country slice. So it was Susan who continued the conversation.

"You knew she didn't like Oysters?"

"Unless she could stick a fork in something and put it straight into her mouth, then she was not that interested; I think most people knew that. Time spent digging out the meat from a lobster claw was time wasted, time that could have been used at the roulette table. I presume you know she gambled, well, of course, you do Martin, you were off to the Casino each night with her; I do hope you did not lose too much." Before either Susan or Martin could continue, Florence added, "Investigators, so were you on the job in France, Martin or was it purely a social event?"

Having cleared his mouth of the cake, Martin avoided her question by asking one of his own.

"I would rather ask you how well you knew Beatrice? You know of her daughter, Paige, so it sounds to me as though you knew Beatrice before the Monet Garden tour?"

Florence grinned warmly at Martin and then turned to Susan. "Please be a dear and pass me that photograph."

She pointed towards a gleaming silver-framed photograph, which stood amongst several others, a number with cars and people, some old black and white family groups, as well as portraits of people, no doubt relations and friends all laid out with love on an old mahogany sideboard. The colour photograph was of two adults with a small child beside them, the three of them standing beside a car. Florence took the frame from Susan, turning it to face both her guests.

"This was taken in 1960, the car, a brand spanking new Jaguar. I'm the little girl at the front, eight years old and so excited that my father was about to take me out in his newly delivered pride and joy; a maroon Jaguar Mark Two. I can still recall the newness and smell of the leather when he took us on a ride around the country lanes, the gleaming paintwork reflecting the trees as the car glided effortlessly past them. My mother just could not understand the excitement my father and I felt. She spent the whole journey playing down his pride and joy, although to be fair to her, she never drove. I, on the other hand, could not wait to drive. We were lucky in that we had a large house in the country, so my father encouraged me to drive around on our land to ensure that my love of motoring was firmly entrenched in my soul. I was eight years old and could not wait for my seventeenth birthday, as then I could take my driving test and drive on public roads. You might not recognise the woman in the photograph after all this was taken over fifty-five years ago. Beatrice did lose a lot of weight after this photograph was taken; she never really put it on again. So to answer your question Martin, I knew Beatrice very well indeed; she was my mother."

Florence handed the photograph to Susan, allowing her to examine it more closely. Although Susan had never met Beatrice, she could see that at the time the photo was taken, she was on the plump side.

"So Paige is your sister?" Martin asked.

"Dear Lord, no, that would be a horrendous thought. The woman is totally loopy and an absolute bore. Did you know that she has a gym in her living room? I ask you; what sort of warped mentality decides that it is a good idea to put a gym in your living room. Paige is my step-sister."

Susan placed the photograph back from where she had taken it, noticing there was no dust shadow, which she always saw when she moved things around in her own flat.

"So what happened? Did your parents split up?" she asked.

"Beatrice's gambling habit has been around a long time; I think all her life. She married my father in fifty-one, and I arrived the following year, spending most of my childhood with nannies and governesses. Of course, as a child, I did not understand that my mother was off working the blackjack and roulette tables. When they divorced, I was only eleven; by that time, I had a better understanding of what had been occurring throughout my childhood. Gradually and consistently, Beatrice was gambling, not successfully, and our family fortune was slipping away. Well, I say our family; it was Father's family money; Beatrice only married into it and then successfully frittered it all away. When they did divorce, Father was left with nothing. He took me, and he managed to afford a small semi-detached house, which was OK, just nothing like the one we had left behind and all because, to be blunt, of what my mother had lost at the roulette tables. I did not get to take my driving test until I was nineteen. Fortunately, I was working by then and able to pay for an almost new Triumph Dolomite Sprint out of my savings. Lovely car, but the days of brand new Jaguars were long gone, thanks to Beatrice."

"Did she ever keep in touch with you? She was your mother after all," Susan asked.

"Do you keep in touch with your mother?"

"My mother died a few years ago," Susan admitted.

"I'm sorry to hear that. My point is that young people drift away from their parents as they forge a life for themselves. Any friction between parents only serves to drive the children further away." Florence took a sip of her tea before continuing, "You should understand that Beatrice only really cares for Beatrice. If her stepdaughter Paige was sending detectives after her, no doubt to see where she was gambling, I know Paige had seriously curbed her gambling in the London casinos, so as I said, I would not put it past Beatrice to top herself just to spite Paige. My mother was that sort of woman, very spiteful if you went against her. So I made a point of avoiding my mother whenever possible. Of course, I could not deny her presence at my wedding or the opportunity to meet her two grandchildren. Although she did turn up at my wedding for a few hours and did attend the christenings of my two children, we did not see her on other occasions. So, it was odd to bump into her on that coach trip, an ugly twist of fate. So, when you saw me talking to her, I was, how I shall put it, Martin, I was giving her some home truths, not that it would make much difference to her, but it did me a world of good."

Martin put his teacup down carefully on the table.

"I thought Beatrice's first husband, your father, had an affair, and that's what started Beatrice gambling; she used it as an escape. She told me that she stayed in the marriage for as long as she could for your sake. She seemed to put the blame squarely on your father."

"Well, of course, she would, yet you have to ask yourself if she loved me that much, why leave me? Whatever the rights and wrongs of their marriage, both of them were left penniless. She married back into money; my father had to earn it."

* * *

Martin, wisely he thought, took the train back to the centre of London and then took the tube which would take him home. Even though Susan was more than happy to drive him there, he firmly insisted that it would take her well out of her way. Instead, he relaxed on the train and thought about Beatrice's children, one daughter and a stepdaughter.

Susan, as she drove towards her flat, thought about her current boyfriend, Bradley, calling round tonight. The relationship was not so much strong and stable, more irresponsible and irregular, which was a good description for most of the men who had made an appearance in her life. Her choice of boyfriends was also the reason she preferred to be out drinking and dancing with her female friends, who were more fun, more loyal and did not want to sleep with her at the earliest opportunity, although she did have suspicions about Judith.

All her life Susan had placed a lot of faith in star signs and their compatibility to decide how suitable a potential boyfriend might be. So when, just two years ago, she had met Ryan, who was born under the star sign of Gemini, she was all aflutter as she read about their compatibility:

"When *you think of Gemini and Leo, you can instantly imagine two children playing. One of them is full of ideas and always on the move. The other is a leader, secure and strong, ready to move mountains for their game. They are a very good fit when it comes to sex, for Gemini gives their relationship ideas and excitement, while Leo brings in energy, creativity and love. Their sex life can be stimulated by their intellect and communication, for they both rely on their conscious self and their mind. If Leo feels right in intimate relations with their*

Gemini, as a fixed sign, they will give them stability and a chance to last together for a very long time."

That had left Susan in no doubt that Ryan, with his strong tattooed arms and regular income working as a plumber's mate, was the one for her *'to last for a very long time"*, it was written in the stars. Together they made plans for their future life. When settled, Susan was going to go back to college to secure some qualifications that would help her become something more than a failed retail assistant. She was not exactly sure what career path she wanted to take as she was torn between being a nurse, a human rights lawyer, or maybe a social worker. The final choice could wait until she had English and Mathematics qualifications. Ryan was sure that he would be able to make the grade as a fully qualified plumber. His future plans were to have his own business and employ at least six other plumbers so that he could then sit back and watch the money roll in. Together, Ryan and Susan felt it prudent to set up home in a small flat so that it would make it easier to save and they could have even more hours together in each other's arms. They found a small flat just off the Balham High Road, not far from Tooting, where Susan had been brought up as a child and where her widowed father still lived. They were heady times, Susan felt intoxicated by love, Ryan worked as many hours as he could so that they could buy a new white van for Ryan and still manage the rent. Susan helped supplement her wages by working behind a bar three evenings a week at the Harper Arms in Clapham. Then close to midnight, as Susan was leaving the pub, Ryan would be waiting outside in his new white van to take her back to their cosy love nest.

Looking back at those days of love and roses, Susan should have seen the clues. They were there, just unseen by her. When she returned with Ryan after working at the Harper Arms, the flat would be clean and tidy, bed made, dishes washed, and her favourite glass of red wine waiting for her. She might never have seen them had she not left work a little early one night, so for a change, she was waiting outside when Ryan arrived. Out of the passenger door stepped Stacey Hemlock, a fellow barmaid, who worked the same night as Susan once a week, leaving two evenings a week for Ryan and Stacey to get it together. Susan later learnt they got it together at her flat; hence the bed being made, the flat tided, and the red wine waiting for Susan, which was poured out of guilt and not love.

Ryan and Susan argued and shouted at each other long into the night. The following day, Ryan had moved out using his new white van to carry away his belongings. That same evening, Susan was working back at the Harper Arms, as was Stacey Hemlock, who rented a flat above the pub. It was not long before the two of them were shouting at each other, and Susan poured a whole bottle of Pernod over Stacey. She would have poured a whole bottle of whisky as well, but for the fact, she could not get the optic off.

Although the local drinkers were pleased and enjoyed the unplanned entertainment, the Pub landlord was not so impressed; he sacked Susan on the spot. He then added insult to injury by telling her that he was keeping the barmaid with straighter teeth and was only upstairs if he needed additional help at the bar. So, she lost her part-time job, lost her boyfriend, and was now stuck with a flat she could not afford. Even so, it did not shake her faith in star signs; she just needed to read them with a little more care, as it did actually say, '*a chance to last together for a very long time.*' That night sitting alone in her flat, tears rolling across her flushed cheeks, Susan knew she had missed that chance.

One of the regulars from the Harper Arms who had watched the whole episode knocked on her door the following evening. Bradley told her that it was simply not fair as she was the innocent party in the whole episode, and so he wanted to offer his sympathy, and if there was anything he could do to help, he would be happy to. Susan did think about asking him to kill both Ryan and Stacey, ensuring it was a slow and painful death for each of them. Sensibly she also thought it was a little too much to ask of someone that you barely knew. She did, however, invite him in for a glass of white wine and then discovered that he was a Taurean. As luck would have it, another very compatible star sign for a Leo. So over the following week, Susan and Bradley met up a few times for a drink, but never at the Harper Arms. They got on well enough; he made her laugh, tried, but did not succeed in getting her into bed, and so was not a bad replacement for Ryan. The only problem with Bradley was that he was not that consistent. They would arrange a date, and he would either be late, very late or call to cancel.

"Sorry, Babe, got to work late tonight, so I'll catch you later."

Meaning she would not see him for a week before finally getting a text or a call. He was a boyfriend, just not always around, which for Susan did have its plus points.

"Wow, you've got Sky TV back; your new job must pay well," Bradley's voice seemed to be overcome with emotion at the thought of the cable television being available.

"I told you I'd got it back on. You're so forgetful at times," Susan commented as she poured him a large chilled white wine.

"Tell you what, Babe, do you mind if we see the European qualifiers tonight, I just remembered that it's on Sky."

Together they started the evening watching, Susan thought, two foreign teams, playing for no good reason, meaning boredom was starting to set in for her. She began texting some friends to distract her from the ball being passed around the pitch, with what appeared to her little intention of anyone trying to score a goal, when the doorbell rang. Colin stood in the doorway.

* * *

Martin decided not to go home after all. Sitting on the train, he had begun to think with greater acuity about what Susan had felt about Hugh Alexander. She had placed him second on the list of suspects. An artist with a shop and flat in a very expensive part of London who was able to pull out several thousands of pounds from his bank account in order to secure a very profitable deal with Beatrice. Martin also wondered just how Hugh might have known his father. The name Hugh Alexander meant nothing to him, which was not any great surprise, as he had never taken any great interest in the friends of his parents. There was someone who would know: Frederick Van Houten, or as he was commonly known at school: 'Freddie the Frog'. The nickname was earned through his habit of leaping from social gathering to social gathering to ensure he was getting the very best of any free food available.

So, when Martin called him and offered him dinner at the exclusive: 'The Bell Tower' restaurant, Freddie, without any hesitation, dropped his planned engagement with a minor celebrity to meet up with Martin and enjoy a sumptuous, expensive meal, with the bill being picked up by someone other than himself. That was the way Freddie liked things to be, not that anyone berated Freddie for this habit; his humour, conversation, and quirky view of life, always made for an entertaining evening.

Wherever he went, Freddie liked to be noticed, and the first stage in that process was his attire. Tonight he wore a blazer, bright blue with white stripes finished off with a bright red handkerchief flopping out of his top pocket, an open-necked casual shirt, white with large black dots and casual cream twill trousers. Then there was his deep gravelly voice which carried across the restaurant as he greeted and hailed Martin.

"Over here, Martin, I've warned the waiters you like a large glass or two of red." Once Freddie was assured that the fellow diners knew of his existence, his voice dropped a number of decibels into normal conversation mode, "So, to what do I owe the pleasure of this treat, woman trouble or mother trouble?"

"We'll eat first and talk business later," Martin instructed. "Let's enjoy the fare here."

Both Martin and Freddie had been at the same boarding school together. Freddie, just a year older than Martin, was instructed to be the new boy's buddy, as all new boys were given an older boy to help them adjust and learn the complex rules and traditions of the school. Way back then, Freddie had seen the same fear and trepidation in Martin's eyes that he had felt the previous year. So, when they were paired up, Freddie showed extra kindness and consideration to the young Martin as he showed the new boy around the school.

They would never have described themselves as best friends. They had, over their school years, developed a friendship which neither of them was keen to break or let dissolve, so they met up from time to time or when one of them needed a helping hand with something.

Martin looked down the menu. After a very meagre lunch, he was ready to eat heartily, so he gave his order of 'Saumon Fume', to be followed by 'Souris d'Agneau', to the tall waiter in his starched and stiff white apron, who duly noted it down and then patiently waited while Freddie decided on his meal. While Freddie was making his mind up between the 'Cote de Veau' and the 'Filet de Boeuf', Martin noticed that the restaurant served oysters or huitres as they were described in the menu, Jersey Royal Oysters.

"Philippe?"

"Yes, Mr Hayden," the waiter replied. He knew both of these men, regular diners who always left a generous gratuity.

"Have any of your oysters killed anyone lately?"

Without any sign of emotion or delay Philippe answered, "Not that I am aware, Mr Hayden, although I was off at the weekend, so I cannot speak for the weekend staff. Is there any reason that you are concerned about the potential perniciousness of our oysters?"

Freddie looked over the top of the large menu.

"You're not pissed already, are you, Martin?"

"No, I just wondered what the likelihood of getting a bad oyster is. If I bought some from the market, what are the chances that one might kill me?"

Philippe, still holding his notepad at the ready, answered Martin. "I have yet to hear of anyone dying from a rogue oyster. There have, of course, been some cases in the past of restaurants, some famous, serving oysters that have caused a bout of illness. Norovirus is the most common bacteria found. The key is in the way and frequency there is the monitoring of the waters where the oysters are farmed. Our supplier tests water quality once a week. We are as yet to fall foul of any diners reporting illness."

"Thank you, Philippe, that is reassuring. Even so, I'll stick with the 'Saumon Fume'."

Martin and Freddie concluded their meal with a selection of French cheeses and a glass of port, while Martin explained the events surrounding his investigation into the death of Beatrice. Freddie listened intently, surprised that Martin appeared to be really working, something he had previously always successfully avoided.

"A shrewd old girl," Freddie concluded about Beatrice, "financing your hobby through selling off your inheritance. I hope to God that my old man does not do that as I am relying on him leaving me a heavy cash injection when he dies."

"So, what do you know about this Hugh Alexander?"

"You are talking about the old artist Hugh, in his sixties, has a place in Victoria?"

Martin agreed they were talking about the same Mr Alexander.

"Well, he comes from a wealthy family; lots of old money and titles. His old man was the fifteenth Earl of somewhere in the Midlands, not that being an Earl in the Midlands means much. The family has been around a while; maybe even related to the Sheriff of Nottingham, good family history, well respected. Hugh, being the younger son, does not get his hands on the title. So he did his own thing, which was being an artist, or at least he always planned to be an artist, which was not what his family had wanted for him. I think they were hoping that he would take over the management of the family estate. They have a couple of big dairy farms. The family sensed that Hugh, as a bit of a hippy environmentalist, might well take to it. His older brother was a lot more cut-throat and suited to looking after the family fortune.

"Hugh had other ideas and took himself off to art college, which really pissed off his old man, who then refused to help him financially. In the end, Hugh financed his own education in art by selling marijuana and amphetamines to his fellow art students. Luckily for him, his old man never found out or the police for that matter. Once he left art school, or whatever you want to call it, he went travelling with his friends and customers to explore the world and find themselves. I think it is just a way of avoiding real work. No offence Martin, but at least you admit your reluctance to it."

"No offence taken, old boy. Carry on; our Hugh sounds a rum character."

"When his old man died, his mother forgave him like all good mothers should and gave him a part of the family fortune to continue with his ambition to become a famous artist. When he heard that bit of news, he came rushing back from Goa or whatever part of India he was in at the time, took the money and bought his studio, shop, flat, whatever way you want to describe it and set himself up as a bit of an art dealer."

"So, did he continue the drug dealing?"

"Can't be sure, but the gossip is that he dropped the dealing as the police in London are a lot more vigilant than they are on the Indian sub-continent. The gossip factory does, however, mention that his approach to dealing with art is a lot like his cut-throat brother's approach to investment banking. I am reliably told that when he sells a painting, he offers the buyer the chance to pay for part of it in cash, no receipt, lessens the VAT and income tax for him, all of which pleases the buyer as they think they are getting a bargain. They're not really, as all his paintings are overpriced, although, to be fair, I think all art is overpriced, but that is another matter. The thing is, the poor artist only gets a share of the price that shows in the receipt, and Hugh forgets to mention the cash he has also picked up, shrewd but not exactly fair or honest. No wonder he jumped at the chance of picking up a painting half price; I bet he loved that."

Martin put the last piece of Camembert onto his bread, looked at it, then looked at Freddie, who was just finishing his port and calling a waiter over to have his glass refilled.

"Murder, do you think he might murder someone?"

"Sticky question, old boy, maybe an outside chance, but I really don't think he is the killing kind. He loves money and stashing it away. Not being married, maybe he gets off by counting his cash each night, but Hugh is a wimp; he likes money but does not like the thought of getting caught and ending up in a six-by-six prison cell without access to it. I guess that's why he gave up the drug dealing, too much risk of getting caught. But doing the Chancellor of the Exchequer out of a few thousand pounds, well, not much chance of getting caught there. Can't see him killing the old girl, plus if, as he said, she had a number of paintings he was interested in, well, over a period of time, he could have been onto a winner, doing fakes and getting the original at half price. Killing her would be like killing the goose that laid the golden egg."

* * *

"I had a very enjoyable and relaxing evening with my boyfriend last night; thank you, Martin, for asking," Susan replied in a monotone to Martin's question as he brought a coffee from the kitchenette into their office, carefully placing it on her desk before commenting.

"As you are not sharing all the graphic details, I guess you had a boring night?"

She did not want to admit to either Martin or her friends or even to herself how it seemed to her that when Bradley wanted something, then he would be at her door all smiles, kisses and cuddles. Apart from those times, she never saw him; last night had been no different. They had been sitting together, Susan cuddling Bradley and nibbling his ear, which did nothing to distract him from the football he was watching on her cable TV. It was not the romantic evening Susan had hoped for. In fact, it was totally boring, so the arrival of Colin did brighten her mood. As for Bradley, he was not in the least bothered by the fact that another man had turned up wanting to speak to his girlfriend or alleged girlfriend. Susan did think that perhaps it was the fact that Colin was in his sixties and wearing a very attractive dress with a light woollen cardigan over his shoulders that her visitor's presence had done nothing to enrage Bradley into a fit of jealously.

Colin, by his own admission, had drunk a little too much and was concerned that he had spoilt things for Susan at Hayden Investigations. Together they sat down in the cramped kitchen, sharing a bottle of white wine, leaving Bradley alone with his football.

"I've done a little digging around; I hope you don't mind."

"Hey, I'd love you to help more; it's just that Martin does not seem that keen. It's not as if you can be discreet. The artist

152

described you to a tee, which did nothing for yours and Martin's relationship."

"You found out about the artist; Jim Rockford would be impressed; you're both getting to be very much the professional investigators. Mind, I didn't get much out of him, well, to be honest, I didn't want to stay too long in that smelly shop - hideous place. And did you see the state of his fingernails? They need either a bloody good scrubbing or amputation."

"Martin hated the smell too. Well, we met an estate agent, which we found out about from the solicitor who is dealing with the will that Beatrice had drawn up. The estate agent, some tart named Melinda, what sort of name is that I ask you - told us about the artist, Hugh Alexander, so I don't think we are that good just yet. So how did you find out about him?"

"I noticed it on Beatrice's notepad on her cluttered desk next to the cheque book, 'Hugh Alexander five o' clock', then recalled seeing a shop next to the café with the maid having the same name, simple really. So, what's the thing with the estate agent?"

Susan explained how Melinda and Hugh Alexander were involved with Beatrice. Colin listened closely as she enlightened him about the estate agent and how she had purchased part of Beatrice's flat, releasing the equity as Martin called it.

"So did you and Martin get to see her grocer, the one who supplied her shopping, like I said you should?"

"No, I kind of got distracted after you and Martin had a set-to. Well, to be honest, I forgot," Susan admitted.

"Well, I know what you're like. I did pop in the next day and have a little chinwag with the staff and a very worthwhile conversation indeed. Although I was only able to speak to one of the shop workers, the boss himself was out when I called in, I was told that Beatrice would always order her groceries by telephone. They would then make sure the order was prepared, and the next day, depending on Beatrice's request, someone would deliver it or Beatrice herself might well collect it, or if not, get this, her young maid would collect the shopping. Now, did we know she had a maid?"

Susan thought for a moment; she could not recall any mention of a maid; on the other hand, she did not recall anyone asking the question.

"Well, I think, Susan, the maid might well have a wealth of information about Beatrice. It's highly likely that the maid would have prepared the meal for Beatrice, and if she is nowhere around, well, I'd be very suspicious. Maybe worth a visit when the owner, Mr Wilson, is in residence, he might know more."

* * *

"So who told you she had a maid?" Martin asked, seeing that Susan was uncomfortable sharing what she had learnt. He need not have asked her; he had already guessed that Colin, her transvestite friend, must have told her. After all, he had already been to the artist's shop, so what was to stop the old cross-dresser snooping around elsewhere. It just seemed to Martin that Colin seemed to be ahead in this investigation.

"Colin told me," Susan admitted.

"When?"

"Last night."

"During your romantic evening with your boyfriend? That's a bit kinky inviting a cross-dresser for a three-way date."

"It was not a three-way date. Bradley was watching the football," Susan protested.

Martin smiled. "Sounds to me as though your conversation with Colin was a lot more interactive than any you had with your boyfriend, possibly even more romantic than a football conversation. Doesn't your romantic boyfriend have cable TV?" Martin teased her.

Susan did not see the funny side of something that she had thought but never spoken out loud; she had always pushed the suspicion to the back of her mind.

"What's it to you how me and my boyfriend spend our evenings?" she snapped back at Martin.

"Whoa, whoa, hold on, I am only teasing. I just thought if I was taking you out for a romantic evening, I would at least give you my undivided attention, plus I would actually take you out, not sit in front of the television."

"You would never take me out; I'm not from your class."

"What's class got to do with it? Romantic evenings are about two people sharing time together. It's got nothing to do with class or background."

"I'd only show you up if you took me to one of your posh restaurants with all those fancy-named dishes."

"You wouldn't show me up; you gave me some very good advice yesterday in the Indian restaurant. Plus, you're fun to be with; I enjoy your company." Martin wondered just why he had said that out loud. He had never meant to, even though it was true, he had not planned to tell her, ever. Now he had, why stop as she had told her Facebook friends that he was cute.

"Tell you what, Susan, to prove that I have total faith in you not showing me up, if you tell me what you said to the Spanish waiter to shut him up, then I'll take you to a posh restaurant."

Susan looked at him quizzically for a moment as she racked her memory about a Spanish waiter that she had told to shut up. Finally, she recalled, "You've been reading my Facebook page."

"They are public. So what did you tell him? It sounds an intriguing story."

"The Lloret de Mar waiter?"

Martin nodded.

"Promise you won't think any less of me if I tell you and don't tell a soul; it is a little embarrassing."

"Oh, I like embarrassing stories. Tell me more." Martin smiled and rubbed his hands with delight.

"It was one of those hen-type weekends, you know, a load of girls go away just to drink and get drunk. Charlotte was getting married, so ten of us flew over to Spain dressed in matching tee-shirts and with balloons to give her a hen party to remember. Well, I'm sure you can imagine, ten girls, all dressed to kill, drinking and laughing, attracts the men, obviously. Actually, you don't need to imagine; I bet you have seen such wild female parties. Anyway, we're in this restaurant in Lloret de Mar, the wine is flowing, and we are having a bit of a wild time when this waiter comes over and starts chatting me up. 'Beautiful girl, I take you to show you the sights of the town,' or some sort of Spanish dribble, I don't actually recall exactly as I was a little tipsy. Of course, I do have some standards; as low as they might be, this waiter was nowhere near meeting them. So, he keeps going on about taking me out then adds, which I am sure he regrets now, 'as a lover, you will find nothing bigger than me.' Cheeky, I thought, however big he might be, he was still not up to my standard. Now before I go any further, do you recall me telling you this was a hen weekend?"

Martin nodded; he was eager to hear the conclusion of what was turning out to be a good story.

"So, from the bag that was beside my feet, I take out a vibrator, not just any vibrator, a super-sized vibrator, a very realistic replica way above normal. I turn it on, then poke the now shocked and speechless waiter in the ribs and tell him, 'if you're bigger than this, then I'll see you later.' I have never seen a man run away so fast, and after that, we never saw him. I must say it took a long time for the laughter to stop at our table. So that's the story of the Spanish waiter. Do you still want to take me out?"

"As long as I can check any bags that you bring along to ensure they are vibrator free."

CHAPTER FIVE

Susan and Martin rang Beatrice's doorbell, hopeful that a maid might answer it, but there was no response. So, it was across the road to Wilson's grocery store to see what they could find out.

Earlier Martin had decided that it would be far safer to call Paige McLaughlin by telephone as this would have two distinct advantages. First, he would not need to be alone in the same room as her, thus avoiding anything weird happening, be that hands-on knees or dogs on running machines. The second advantage would be that Susan would not need to speak to her, get into an argument, which could possibly open old wounds and make a total enemy of Paige McLaughlin. Martin was sure that he needed to keep Paige close or at least be on civil terms with her. It was still within the bounds of possibility that she had had a hand in the death of her stepmother.

Paige was at first excited to hear from Martin again. She became amused when he asked her if her mother had a maid. Her mother would never dream of having a maid, Paige reassured him. Her mother would never have considered asking someone else to carry out chores that she was not willing to do herself, 'so what's the point of a maid' Beatrice used to say. Beatrice believed that the only reason anyone would want a maid or any sort of servant was to show off to the rest of their upper-class friends. It meant nothing; in fact, Beatrice often called maids and ladies that do for other ladies as no more than posh pets. Paige was adamant that her mother would never employ a maid.

Paige then suggested that Martin should visit one afternoon for tea and sandwiches as she had enjoyed his company before. Martin ignored the invitation by changing the subject to the fact that he had spoken to Beatrice's other daughter from her first marriage. The admission from Martin created an instant negative reaction from Paige, who asked just why he persisted in asking questions about her mother's natural death; she emphasised the word 'natural'.

"It should be of no concern to you, and I do not appreciate your continued interference in what is a very sad time for our family." She then added a very curt goodbye and put the phone down.

Martin and Susan were now standing outside Wilson's Grocery Store, hoping for a more amicable conversation from Mr Wilson, plus a little more information about the maid that Beatrice might or might not have employed.

Mr Wilson was present this time and was more than happy to talk about Beatrice. Standing amongst his neat, well-stocked shelves of groceries, Mr Wilson stood tall and erect with shoulders pushed back. His grey hair, neatly trimmed, and the wrinkles around his eyes suggested that he might be in his late fifties or early sixties. Everything around the shop looked as though it had been placed with military precision; there was nothing that appeared to be out of place.

Not only was Beatrice a regular customer who bought all her groceries and household items from his store, which he appreciated in today's age of branded supermarket shopping, she was also very polite and pleasant to talk to, happy to spend time chatting with him. They would often talk about the serious issues of the day before moving on to the good old days, which they both warmly recalled. Mr Wilson regretted the way the country had lost its way since joining the common market and the heavy burden of regulations that were put upon small shopkeepers like him.

"I get regular visits, you know, from the bods at the council poking their autocratic noses in everything I do, checking this, checking that, ticking boxes on their forms. I tell them the minute my customers start dying from the food I sell them, I'll soon quickly lose my trade just from word of mouth, with or without their bloody forms. What really rankles me...."

Martin and Susan stood in front of him, humouring him for no better reason than he might have something they needed to know about Beatrice; what that might be, they had no clear idea.

"What really rankles me," he continued, "is I get all the visits, yet all the bloody twenty-four-hour ethnic food shops get away with murder. Not politically correct to tell those that their floor needs a damn good wash or that they are selling what looks to be rotting meat, and as for the bananas, they might be called Plantain, but they are still a health hazard of that, I'm sure. Now you might think me a racist, but I am far from it. I have served all over the world and had to work with all sorts of skin types as well as eat their food. But here in London, they should be made to stick to our standards, not their bloody low third-world ones."

"So, how did you get on with Beatrice?" Susan asked, steering the conversation away from the bigotry he was showing.

Mr Wilson told them that most Tuesday's Beatrice would telephone with a list of her requirements for the week. Then the following day, she might call in to collect her order personally or otherwise, her maid might collect it. Although more often than not, Mr Wilson would arrange someone to take it across to her as she only lived a short walk away. Martin pressed the shopkeeper a little more on the maid, as this was where their real interest lay. There was not a lot he could give. He assumed she was a live-in maid, as there had been times when he had delivered the groceries personally, and the maid would take in the order. She was obviously foreign. She came from somewhere in Asia, Indonesia, he thought. He was sorry that he could be of no more help.

Then he added, "No, almost forgot, sadly the memory is not what it used to be, I still cannot recall the maid's name, but she first came in here one day, a couple of months ago, asking if there was any work that I could offer her. English was not the best, and some of my customers do like to hear a clear English voice when they ask a question, so no chance of me putting her on the front-line, so to speak, but there is still plenty of backroom work to be done. Logistics of keeping the shelves filled can be a nightmare at times, no point in having fresh ham out the back; it does not sell there at all. So, when the maid asked if I had any work, well, I'm always on the lookout for extra hands in the stock room, so I suggested there could be. Even so, I did have my suspicions about her. She looked a little too timid. I do pride myself on being able to judge a man. Then I asked her outright, do you have a national insurance number and are you legally allowed to work in the U.K. The look she gave me told me that she was not. What can I do? I am not going to start employing people unless they have the right documents. There are some rather hefty fines for those of us employing, shall we say, people on the black market. She turned and walked out. Aurora, that's her name, it's just come back to me because it was as she was walking out that I noticed Beatrice had walked into the shop and she spoke to her, 'Aurora, I'm sorry I missed you, let's go back and have a cup of tea'. Well, the poor girl looked terrified, yet she still left with Beatrice. Not sure what that was about, but since that day, she has clearly been working for Beatrice. How the old lady was getting around the tax laws, I dread to think, there again some of these old dears around here have plenty of vim and vigour."

"So apart from her popping in once in a while, there was nothing other than her asking you for a job, nothing out of the ordinary." This time Martin asked the question.

Mr Wilson pondered and rubbed his smooth chin.

"Depends what you're after, really. She did meet up with one of her friends here once. Thought she, the friend that is, was a shoplifter hanging around the tins of meatballs, popular line with the homeless, slips easily into your pocket and plenty of goodness. Anyway, she was looking furtive, so I was keeping a watchful eye on her when the maid came in. Aurora gave her a big friendly hug. Now you can't trust these immigrants. They could have been hugging and passing things between them; if not my tins of meatballs, they could be passing drugs and things. So, I went up to them both just to make it clear that I had been observing them. Aurora smiled at me and told me the other woman was her friend, Tala. They then both left, and I never saw the other girl again. I think they might have been up to no good, and I made it clear I was going to have no-nonsense in my shop."

"I'm sorry, Mr Wilson, you say that Aurora came in asking for a job. Wasn't she already working for Beatrice at the time?" Martin asked, trying to make things clear in his head.

"Absolutely, as far as I knew she had been working or at least staying with Beatrice for at least a couple of weeks when she came in asking about work, made no sense to me either."

"Just one other thing, the other girl, her friend, you say her name was Tala?"

"One hundred per cent she was called Tala, unusual name but I learnt during my tour of duty in India that a Tala is a musical measure, clapping or striking small cymbals, so that's why it stuck so well in my mind. Although she did not appear to be Indian, she was certainly from that part of the world."

* * *

It was Tuesday afternoon, so Susan knew exactly where to find Tala. There she was as they stepped out of the car, sitting in the café window looking without seeing the world passing by before her.

Fear was Tala's first expression as Susan sat down beside her. Martin sat opposite Tala. Fear was the default expression and emotion that Tala felt most days. Fear of the authorities finding her now that her visa was long expired; fear that she could no longer send money to her family now that she had been confronted with her petty theft, and fear that any day she might be thrown out as Mrs Holburn had been furious that she had been stealing small items.

"Hello Tala, remember me?"

The maid gripped her teacup tightly and looked at Martin.

"Yes, where is the other woman?"

Susan paused, confused, and then recalled who was with her the last time she had sat next to Tala.

"Ah, Colin, he couldn't make it today. This is another friend of mine, Martin."

Martin smiled and nodded exactly as Susan had instructed him. The other instruction had been not to say a word.

"I want to ask you a few questions about a friend of yours, Aurora?"

Tala looked at Susan, then turned to Martin; fear glazed her eyes. Susan reassured her that Martin was a friend and had nothing to do with the authorities, that they were not going to report her or Aurora, and they just needed to know where Aurora now worked. Tala shrugged her shoulders, unsure if she should answer; the less she said, the less wrong she could be. Susan began to explain that they had come from Wilson's Groceries and that they had called at Beatrice Cook's flat, but there was no one there. They wanted to know if Aurora worked for Beatrice as if she did, then maybe she might be able to help Susan and Martin find out if anything wrong had happened with Beatrice.

"We know that you know her, the shopkeeper told us. We just want to help."

Tala looked down into her half-empty cup, looking at her reflection, longing to be home in the Philippines.

"Aurora work for a lady called Mrs Cook, near Gloucester Road tube."

"Do you know her well?" Susan asked. Martin was content to listen to the conversation just as he had been told.

"She come from Philippines like me, not from Manila Aurora from Marikina, that's why she has a love of shoes. Marikina make lot of shoes."

"Where does she live now?"

"The same place the last time I was there."

"Why did she ask about a job at the supermarket? Wasn't she happy with Mrs Cook?"

"Aurora has in UK three years. Her first home was with man and wife, but man made Aurora do things. She is good church girl. They were not nice things. When wife find out, Aurora is told to leave. She have nowhere to go. She in here with me one day, sitting here crying. She cannot go home, no money, she has nothing to stay at. Then an old lady sits down and asks what is matter. She take Aurora home with her."

"Was that Mrs Cook?"

"Yes, a gambling lady."

"That's just what we have heard!" Susan smiled.

"But one day, wife comes to house where Aurora is and start to scream and shout, saying bad things about Aurora to Mrs Cook. So, Aurora leave, she not want to make trouble for Mrs Cook. But Mrs Cook take her back in and forgive her."

"Does she still live there?"

Tala nodded. She had not heard from Aurora for about three weeks which was not unusual as maids have little time for themselves, and on the rare days they might get off, it was hard to meet up. Although Tala told them, Aurora had much more freedom than other maids and seemed to be very happy at Mrs Cook's.

Susan wrote down the telephone number and address of Hayden Investigations and asked Tala to let them know if she saw Aurora or to ask her to call as they had some questions about the days before Mrs Cook died.

* * *

Once again, standing outside Gloucester Road tube station, Martin and Susan talked about what their next move should be. Was there a maid at Beatrice's or not? Had she now left because Beatrice had died? Had she killed Beatrice? Susan decided that there were just too many questions. Maybe they should ask at the flats, maybe one of the neighbours would have seen her, possibly spoken to her, know something about the mysterious maid. Martin planned to go home, shower and change before their dinner tonight. He had booked the table for eight o'clock, and he was planning to be on time and hoped that Susan was also going to be on time for their dinner together. Susan, as ever, had other ideas and pointed out that it was only just gone half-past five, so they had plenty of time to knock on a few doors, get back to their respective homes, change, and then still be at the restaurant in plenty of time.

"So Martin, let's do this. We'll either get a lot of blank stares from the residents, or one might come up trumps."

Against Martin's better judgement – he much preferred taking his time getting ready and doing this might mean he would have to rush – he followed Susan along the road towards Hereford Square.

Both Martin and Susan stood side by side on the white stone steps leading up to the large communal door of the building. Together they looked at the six doorbell buttons.

"Well," Martin asked, "shall we try some doorbells, or shall we just break in, which is all the fashion nowadays, I'm told?"

"Sarcasm is not your style; we'll ring the bells. Where do you want to start?"

"Let's think about this for a moment. The last time you were in Beatrice's flat, you said there was no sign of a maid, and you also got no reply, although she could, of course, have been out. There again the police had to break into the flat, so she was not answering the door when they called. And let's not forget the opinion of Paige, who says there is no maid. So maybe it's safe to assume that Beatrice and her maid do not reside in the same flat. She could, however, be in a flat in the same building."

"She'd have to be a bloody rich maid to afford the rent; do you know how much they charge around here?"

"Beatrice was a shrewd old biddy. I am sure she could have come up with a solution."

Martin pointed at the doorbell to one of the flats, number four. It was the only one without a surname against it.

"Could be empty, or the tenant has a really long name and can't fit it on the little label these bells have," Susan prompted.

"We'll see." Martin pushed twice on the button.

Soon after, a timid voice spoke from the intercom. The accent could have been foreign; the distortion of the speaker did not help.

"Yes?" The voice was young, nervous and female.

"Hello Miss, it's Wilson's Grocery. I have the order for flat three but can't get a reply. Could you let me in, and I can leave it by their door?" Martin tried to disguise his boarding school accent, much to the amusement of Susan.

"No," the curt reply crackled out of the grill.

"Come on, Miss, I have a box full of groceries here which I can't leave on the doorstep."

"No, I must not let people in unless I know them."

"Well, we are always delivering here, did a lot for Mrs Cook before she sadly died."

"No," she repeated. The crackling sound from the intercom stopped as the young voice had released the button and cut Martin off.

"That was well handled," Susan commented, trying to contain the laughter that she could feel welling up inside her. "What next, lay siege to the flat and starve her out? That is assuming she is the maid in question."

"Very funny. So, what would Jim Rockford do in his scripted television world?"

"This." Susan turned her attention to the keypad below the speaker and pressed four numbers, seven, one, nine and three. The door buzzed, the lock was released. Susan opened the door and held it back, waiting for Martin to walk through. "Tradesman's entry. Impressed?" she asked.

"Who taught you that, or can I guess?"

"Colin mentioned in passing that every intercom with a push-button does have a code for tradesmen like the postman or the meter reader, the numbers do vary, but often they are the four corners of the keypad. He showed me last time we were here together."

"What exactly does he do for a living?" Martin asked with a suspicion that Susan might say he was a professional burglar. She said that he was some sort of office worker but was not certain. Martin wasn't sure that he wasn't correct in his assumption.

Together they stepped into the hallway. To the right was the door to Beatrice's flat. To the left, there was a mirror on the wall under which was a bow-legged table strewn with letters and flyers. They continued ahead up the stairs, the deep-pile maroon carpet dulling the sound of their steps. At the top of the stairs was a small landing with another set of stairs going up, and to their right was a small corridor leading to a door painted red with a brass number four glinting. They walked towards the door, Susan leading the way.

Susan wrapped on the door gently,

"Aurora, can we speak to you? We need to ask you some questions about Beatrice Cook. We are friends of hers. Beatrice told us that we should help you if anything happened to her, so we are here to help you."

There was only silence in response, so Susan tried again,

"Beatrice told us that she has been looking after you, helping you. We're not from the police or the authorities, that's why Beatrice wants us to help you. You might need someone to look after you, and we're those people. I have also spoken to Tala; she is a friend of mine."

The door opened slowly, a chain limiting how far it could go. It was just enough for a pair of timid brown eyes to inspect who it was that wished to gain entry to her domain.

"You know Tala?"

This time Martin spoke,

"Yes, we have just come from the café where she spends every Tuesday. We're nothing to do with the authorities; we just need to ask you about Beatrice. It would be better if we came in Tala, and Mrs Cook would want you to help us."

Without a further word, Aurora opened the door fully and stood back to allow them to enter.

The flat was small. Maybe once it had been a large bedroom, now it had been converted into a cramped bedsit. With one large window that looked over Hereford Square Green, the room benefited from abundant natural light. It contained a small kitchenette with a table-top grill and oven, and a cluttered white worktop ran down the left-hand side of the room. Under the window was a bed-settee in the position of a bed, an unmade bed with pillows and a crumpled duvet printed with a design of pink rose petals. On the right-hand side of room was the door to the outside world, and alongside it was a door to the shower and toilet. Finally, there was a small table and two chairs; the table was cluttered with sewing paraphernalia and materials.

"Please, sit down." Aurora gestured towards the two scruffy-looking wooden chairs beside the table; both Martin and Susan took up the offer. Aurora sat on the bed in front of them below their eye-line, waiting silently and obediently for their questions. She looked afraid, unsure of her visitors, but she had not dared to keep her door closed and not grant them access. If Mrs Cook and Tala knew these people, they should not be any danger to her. Ever since she had arrived in England six years ago, she had kowtowed to those English who spoke so well, were so rich, who she felt she could not afford to antagonise. Her first employers had told her in no uncertain terms, ' when you talk to me, the word 'no' should not ever be used'.

"My name's Martin, and this is Susan. We were so sorry to hear about Beatrice dying, so sad. I just wanted to hear about how you came to be employed by Beatrice."

Aurora heard the voice, the accent and the precise pronunciation; she was compelled by experience to answer. It was that compulsion that had led to her being cast out into the streets by her last employer. The lady of the house had confronted Aurora as she finished loading the dishwasher after she had cleared away the lunch things. 'Aurora, have you let my husband fondle your body?' Aurora looked up at her employer. She had not come across the word fondle before and wondered what it meant so innocently asked for the meaning. 'Have you shown him your tits, girl? Is that plain enough for you, you dirty little whore? Let him squeeze and kiss them, touch you all over your greasy dago's body?'

Now that Aurora knew what fondle meant, she had to be truthful and could not deny it. Her employer's husband had indeed 'fondled' her. The first time he just came up behind her one day, squeezed her breasts and smiled. She could not say no;

it was not in her nature to upset her employers, so she just let him manhandle her breasts. The next time he uncovered her to expose her chest. Then it continued, each time he pushed the boundaries a little further. He showed her parts of his body, and that scared her even more. What he wanted to do, she knew, was wrong, but she could not refuse. It was either kneel in front of him or be out on the streets. So, when his wife confronted her beside the dishwasher, the confession brought relief to her Catholic conscience.

"My previous employer no longer required me, so she asked me to leave her house. I was without job, no papers, I could not get job. For a few nights, I sleep in park. Friends help me. I sleep at some houses. I start to see if anyone help me with small job; anything, I have to earn some money to get my flight home to the Philippines.

"I was with Tala in that café. I was crying. I could see no way out of being homeless when Mrs Cook sat beside us and asked what was the matter. We told her everything. I went home with her that night, slept on her couch, and the next day, she put me in here, my own flat. She gave me this flat and money each week. I did not do much for her, just a little bit of cleaning and shopping when she was away. Beatrice was kind to me. She was even trying to find a way of getting me papers and a national insurance number."

Aurora caressed her Rosary all the time she spoke. Her long dark hair, clean and shiny, draped around her slightly bowed head. She looked, as she always did, ready to receive a dressing down or to be disciplined for some minor indiscretion.

"Yes, Mrs Cook was a wonderful woman. I only knew her briefly, but even so, I could see that she was a special person. When did you last see her alive?"

Aurora began to look even more worried; she looked up; her brown eyes began to water.

"I didn't know; I didn't know."

"What didn't you know?" Susan asked, putting a reassuring arm around Aurora's shoulder.

"That when I last saw her, she was dead."

This time Martin asked a question.

"Aurora, let's go back a little way, put things into context. Did you see Beatrice the day before she was found dead?"

"The Tuesday, yes, I saw her that day."

"OK, so tell us about what happened that day, what you did, when you saw Beatrice, what you talked about?"

Susan offered Aurora a tissue that she used to wipe her eyes.

"I had pick up some shopping for Mrs Cook and put it in her cupboards. There was some washing up, so I started to do it, Mrs Cook said leave it, but I wanted to help her, she was kind to me, I wanted to help her. A man came into the flat, I did not see him, but I heard her talking to him in the hallway. They were talking about paintings. He did not stay long. Mrs Cook say to me when she come back to the kitchen, 'some people want to make more money, I am happy to gamble it away'. I then cleaned some of her rooms, made her bed for her, tidied up the kitchen. Then about six o'clock, she asked me to leave the flat as she had a man coming to see her. If I was still there, he might ask questions, and I might get reported to the authorities, so I go back to my room."

"Did you see the man?" Martin asked eagerly.

"No, I did not see him, but I heard him saying goodbye to Mrs Cook about nine-thirty."

"Did you see Beatrice again?"

"Yes, the next morning. I go to see if I can help her do anything. I rang the bell but no reply, so I use my key to go in - Beatrice said go in when I want to. But Mrs Cook still asleep in bed, so I go out." Aurora's voice then began to stutter with emotion as she recalled that afternoon. "Later that day there is a police car outside; I think it is for me. I hide, very scared. But they go in Mrs Cook's flat. I hear from neighbour that she is dead. I cried and cried; she was so nice." She began sobbing. Susan hugged her, trying to comfort her.

"I'm sorry to have to keep asking you questions, but when you went in during the morning and Beatrice was asleep, did you notice anything unusual at all?"

Aurora composed herself to speak, her eyes red and wet.

"No, nothing odd. I go to living room; it was untidy as it often is. In the kitchen, the table had been set. It looked as though Mrs Cook had an evening meal with someone and then went to bed without clearing the dishes. There were two plates and two glasses, a lot of empty shells, oysters, I think. People say that she did not feel well. Maybe that is why she left them." Aurora stopped, and both Susan and Martin could see that she was thinking about something. "But," Aurora continued, "the plates she used were not the ones that she used at night. They are the old set that I had never seen Mrs Cook use. The set belonged to her mother. That was unusual. I into the bedroom, but she was asleep. Maybe she was dead at the time, maybe she was alive, and I could have saved her. I see by her bed a lot of tablet boxes; they were kept elsewhere normal. She must have had a bad tummy upset." Again, Aurora seemed to look back into her memory, seeing something that she had not seen before. "I saw the tablets and not her rings; she must have had her rings on her fingers that are not Mrs Cook."

"What do you mean not her rings?" Martin asked.

"I have helped her to bed sometimes when she had too much gin and she always insisted that no matter how drunk she was, she always took her rings off when she slept. She always told me the tale of when she was in India, that a western woman had her fingers cut off so that thieves could get to her rings as she slept. Beatrice said she couldn't care about the rings; she wanted her fingers more. She must have been very ill not to have taken them off. Yes, they were things, no the same."

"So just to be clear, Aurora," Martin said, "the night before Mrs Cook was found dead, she had a meal with someone, used plates that you had never seen her use before, and she must have been wearing her rings while she was asleep, something that she did not normally do."

Aurora nodded in agreement.

"So, what happens to me now? Do I need to leave here?"

"Stay here for now," Martin advised. "I'll try and find out who your landlord is, and then we'll see what we can do."

Martin knew what he was saying, and he saw the look of surprise that Susan was giving him; she had never seen compassion from Martin. She was even more astounded when he withdrew some bank notes from his wallet and handed them to Aurora.

"We'll be back next week to see how things are going. This should keep you going for a while."

* * *

They met just as planned outside Cannon Street tube station amongst the last dregs of the weary rush-hour commuters. Martin was eager and already waiting there when Susan ran up the stairs from the platform. She was late, which Martin was well aware of, but he just brushed aside her apologies. Within his rules of chivalry, it was a woman's prerogative to be late. The renowned Papillon Restaurant was just a short walk from the tube station. If Susan wanted posh, this was going to be it. Two Michelin stars, critically acclaimed food, a relaxing ambience, rave reviews from magazines that mattered. Martin had been there a few times now and had become known well enough for a simple phone call to secure a table even in such a sought after restaurant.

Martin and his female guest were greeted warmly at the entrance and then were calmly ushered towards their crisp white linen-covered table, each place set with sparkling glasses and gleaming cutlery. The Papillon Restaurant resembled a medium-sized church hall with an arched glass roof. It was a false roof that enabled the diners below to wallow in faux midday sunshine whatever the hour or the season; it was one of the quirky features fashionable diners liked to discuss.

Martin was pleased, almost smug, to see Susan looking around like an excited child in such opulent surroundings. She stared at the walls, the glass-domed roof, the large green pot plants that decorated the room, and she looked to be amazed by it all. He had made a good choice.

"Like it?" tentatively he asked.

"I thought there'd be more film stuff about," was all she said, an unexpected answer which threw Martin more than just a little.

"Film stuff?"

"Yeah, I mean if you're 'gonna' name a place after a film, you'd think they'd go to the trouble of putting a few posters up at least. Maybe a photo or two of the stars, I would've done that."

"The film, Papillon?"

"Yeah, you must have heard of it with Dustin Hoffman; too young to see it at the pictures myself, but my dad had it on VHS. Good film."

"This restaurant is named after the French word for butterfly," Martin pointed out.

"Oh, I thought it was strange you wanting to take me to a themed restaurant. The Butterfly, ah, is that why it looks like one big greenhouse in here?"

Martin looked around; he had not seen the likeness before. Now Martin could not help but feel he was eating in an overpriced greenhouse.

They needed a theory. They agreed that the only thing for certain was that Beatrice had died apparently to everyone else peacefully in her sleep. They also agreed that the consumption of oysters, when now added to the fact that Beatrice abnormally used her best china, had two places set, forgot to take her rings off, all indicated that evening was unusual. Susan believed that the old artist in need of some cash went round to see Beatrice and then killed her somehow, intending to sell the painting that he had earlier obtained. Plus, he had been there that very day, maybe he did not leave when Aurora thought he did, or maybe he came back. Martin shook his head, pointing out that the chance to copy more paintings would trump killing the old girl. Susan's next theory was the one she considered to be the most likely. Paige would be the culprit, seeing the money she hoped to get was dwindling away. Martin found that one harder to discount, greed was a strong motive. If Beatrice was entertaining that night, who was her guest? Martin hoped that his next visit to Samuel might offer some answers. Then Martin asked a question that had been on his mind since yesterday.

"I didn't know your mother was dead?"

Susan looked up from her Royal Viceroy, described on the menu as a dessert that mimicked the exotic Viceroy Butterfly of North America. To Susan, it was no more than panna cotta laced with an orange sauce.

"You never asked."

"Well, it's not the sort of thing that one talks about in everyday conversation," Martin sounded a little defensive.

"Well yes, true, you wouldn't ask outright, any dead parents? That would be just weird. But talking to people, taking an interest in their lives, and that sort of thing comes out. You never seem to have much interest in the lives of other people, so snippets of personal information are just left unsaid."

Martin finished his Royal Viceroy, wiped his lips with his napkin, then spoke.

175

"Maybe that is because the lives of other people have little influence on my life."

"That's like saying you live in a bubble."

"The thing is, by not asking, I do not get bombarded by the boring problems of other people."

Susan quipped back, "so why did you give money to Aurora?"

Martin did not want to answer that question. For one, he was not sure of the answer himself; his donation and offer of help had surprised him. Yet the more he thought about it, he thought he might understand.

"Maybe a bit of guilt; maybe seeing first-hand up close and personal the problems someone like Aurora faces every day and her being poorly equipped to deal with them. So, I gave her cash. I would imagine she needs it, and it will help her through what I am sure is going to be a difficult time for her without Beatrice to look after her."

Susan looked at him with a glint of admiration in her eyes.

"I'd come over and give you a big hug and a big kiss, but you have orange sauce on your lips, so I won't."

"Thanks for the offer. So, your mother, how long ago did she die?"

Martin watched as Susan turned her head, looking away from him as if she was watching a void in which, he guessed, she might be visualising her mother.

"Three years," she admitted, her voice showing no emotion.

"How did she die?" Martin continued, convinced that this was demonstrating that he had an interest in Susan beyond work.

This drew her attention, and Susan turned back to look at him. Her eyes still held the hurt after three years.

"My father killed her."

That was not the answer that Martin had expected. Heart attack, cancer, liver disorder, even plain old age, he was imagining one of the more common causes of death, 'my father killed her' was not amongst his list of reasons for someone's mother to die. Unsure of how he should answer, he decided upon, "That must have been terrible for you, losing your mother, and then your father being imprisoned."

As soon as he finished speaking, Martin hoped that her father did not get let off the charge with the help of some tricky lawyer. Martin felt a few beads of sweat on his forehead; he was becoming uncomfortable with the conversation.

"Imprisoned, no, he's free as a bird. Why did you think he was...?" Susan stopped, smiled as if she wanted to reassure a small child, and then continued, "you thought when I said killed, you took that to be he murdered her, I wish others had thought the same as you then he might well be in jail."

"So, he did kill her?" Martin asked tenderly, or at least he tried with such a blunt question.

"Shall I explain? I think you're getting a little confused, most of which is down to me. I'll give you the whole story."

Martin relaxed if for no better reason than he would not need to speak for the next few minutes, just sit and listen very, very carefully.

"My mother was one to stay as fit as she could. At fifty-five years old, she was very active, gym twice a week, cycling ten miles to work every day, nothing like me. She had a figure her daughters envied, a wicked sense of humour, and lived life to the full. On the dance floor, she could ace it, trust me.

"She was cycling home one day from work; it was a dark October evening. The rain had stopped as she approached a set of traffic lights that were at green when a lorry, without any warning, decided to turn left; the driver totally unaware that my mother on her bike was alongside him. There was nothing she could have done; I just can't think of what went through her mind when she realised what was happening. Both her and her now crumpled bike ended up under the wheels of the lorry. Somehow the medics kept her breathing, and the hospital did all they could for her.

"When I arrived at the hospital, she was stabilised, breathing with a ventilator, wires and monitors all over her body, my sisters and father around her, all of us in total disbelief that in the morning she had left the house in high spirits looking forward to pork cutlets in the evening and believing her whole life was ahead of her. Now she lay with one leg broken in three places, broken ribs and a fractured collar bone. Yet, it was the head injury that had left her silent but for the machine breathing on her behalf.

"Over the next few days, the doctors continued to fuss. The family prayed, even me, who is not, as you know, the most religious person. I just wanted things to go back to the way they were. But the doctors soon decided that things would never be the way they were. They concluded Mother appeared to have little brain activity. They made the suggestion that it was maybe a time to consider turning off the machines that appeared to be keeping her alive. Of course, we daughters recoiled from any such thought. She was breathing, warm to the touch. She could not be dead. My father was not so convinced. Even so, we argued with him that Mum could be alive deep in her motionless body, with her sense of humour and love of life still beating within her. The doctors could not deny that they said it was entirely possible, but they just had no way of knowing. They can stick a new heart and lungs into you, but they can't see into your mind. There was some brain activity; what it represented, they could not be sure. We shouted, we argued, we pleaded with our father, who seemed to be set on killing her, or that's how we saw it, killing her not knowing if the future might bring recovery, convalescence, how did we know? We had no idea when we said our goodbyes to her that morning that they would be the last words we would speak to her. He couldn't be swayed and at 10 am on Wednesday, 18th October, the machines were turned off, and my mother died."

Martin was no longer surprised that he could see in her eyes the ingrained grief.

"Your father took a hard decision, I grant you, but saying he killed her is a bit strong."

"Martin, you're a man; you would not understand the bond mothers and daughters have. We knew, we could feel, that deep in her body, our mother, with her sense of humour and zest for life, was still working and scheming to break free of the coma. She just needed time. The time our father took away from her. It was the main reason I left home when I did; I just could not stand to be in the same room as him. It was the same for my sisters; I don't think we have spoken more than half a dozen words with him since."

"And maybe the reason you never fully trust men?"

"You're wrong there, but it is the reason I take life with a pinch of salt and enjoy every minute. The biggest thing my mother's death taught me is when you get up to start the day, there is no guarantee you will be alive to see the night."

* * *

Martin paid for the taxi that dropped them both off beside Susan's block of flats in Tooting, leaving the couple standing facing each other beside the communal door. It was a small block of nine flats spread over three floors, built in the nineteen-sixties, some rented, some owned. Susan's was a one-bedroom flat which now, thanks to her salary at Hayden Investigations, she was keeping for the foreseeable future without the need to sleep with her landlord.

Susan fumbled in her handbag for her key, leaving Martin to break the silence that hung between them.

"Well, as promised, I got you home safe and sound. I hope you enjoyed this evening as tomorrow it is back to work for both of us."

Susan looked up from her handbag, her hand still fumbling around for her key.

"Yes, thanks, Martin; I really enjoyed going to such an exclusive restaurant and being treated like a lady. I hope I didn't let you down or show myself up?"

"No way could you ever let me down. You should have more confidence in yourself when you are at places that are maybe not in your expected comfort zone." He hoped that was taken the way it was meant and not the way it sounded.

Susan wondered if he was saying that she was not of the same class as the others in the restaurant; she hoped not. Even if it was true, your background should not preclude you from eating at a restaurant of your choice, even if the management of the restaurant might 'tut-tut' a few times if she turned up with her pals after a few hours drinking. Maybe there is a time and place for everything. The Papillon was the right place for the first date with Martin. She had not really thought of it that way until the main course arrived, and she felt they were no longer just work colleagues. She had sensed there was something else between them.

Martin took a step closer to her.

"As soon as you have retrieved your key from the dark depths of your handbag, I will let you go and start my way back. We have some real detective work to do in the morning, so a good night's sleep might be called for."

They were now standing very close together. She could feel his warm breath caressing her cheeks; his aftershave filled her head. This was it, that pivotal moment when he was perhaps waiting for an invitation to enter her flat for a night cap and an intimate conversation. She wanted it too; ever since she had heard his voice on the telephone that morning in the café, she had liked him. There was just the one ugly question that hung over her like the sword of Damocles, am I too common? She apparently was not too common to be taken out to a very swish restaurant and be sitting opposite him sharing a meal and relaxed conversation. He had invited her and seemed to be happy to talk to her all evening. Working together had brought her even closer to him. Now was the moment, that time when she might cross the line, ask her boss up to her flat for a coffee along with all the implications that might mean. Sleeping together, she would not object to. Seeing him the next morning back in the office, would that be weird? Would that work? Could they continue? Even though she wanted to sleep with him, she knew deep in her heart that it could go no further than that. He was from a different world, a different background; maybe he even had different morals. For all that he was changing, for whatever reason, he was trying to find justice or at least the truth about Beatrice's death. And then this afternoon, he had handed cash over to someone whom he had only just met. That would not have happened a couple of months ago, of that Susan was sure.

Being a few inches taller than Susan, he looked down into her eyes. From the first time he saw her, it was her eyes that he found so attractive. Not that the rest of her was any less attractive, it was just that he thought he could stare at her eyes for hours on end. They were full of life, innocent expectation and a belief that anything was possible. If only his mother could have seen her tonight not overcome by the glamour and opulence of the restaurant, taking it all in her stride, enjoying every instant. Living as if she was living her last day, the future could always take care of itself. That was one of the things he liked about Susan. It might be regarded as a lack of responsibility, a rashness, but he saw it as an eagerness to live come what may. Would she invite him up, he wondered? He hoped that she would offer an invitation for a late-night coffee; it would make the evening feel complete. Then when the coffee was finished, and the conversation slowed, what then? Of course, he would like to sleep with her. What was there not to like about her, yet should he? If things got that far, could he say no? There are risks at every corner, Martin thought. He edged closer to her.

Ah, sod it, thought Susan, why shouldn't I invite him up, see what happens. If she did not, her friends would listen in disbelief, telling her, 'you didn't invite Martin up to your flat; you're mad!' Yes, they would call her mad, and she would have to agree with them. She took a deep breath.

"Martin, would you....?" Behind her, she heard the door open, then her name spoken.

"Hi Sue, hope you don't mind; I let myself in." Bradley was standing there by the door smiling at her; he leaned forward and kissed her on the lips. "I did call, honest, but your phone went to voice-mail, and it was Man City playing Juventus tonight in the European semi-finals. I thought you wouldn't mind." He then, with a confused look on his face, turned to Martin.

"Who's this?" he asked.

Susan stuttered a little, "Martin, my boss. Martin, this is Bradley, my boyfriend."

The men shook hands in an apprehensive way.

"Pleased to meet you, Bradley. Who won?"

"Juventus, two-nil. Man City just threw the game away in the second half, a bunch of useless, overpaid tossers. You two been out working late?"

"Yes," Susan answered. "Watching someone in a restaurant, it all worked out; well, almost worked out as planned, can't say too much."

"Don't worry, Babe, I understand." He tapped his nose in a knowing sort of way.

"OK, I had best be going now, Susan. See you in the morning." Martin kissed her on both cheeks.

Bradley looked on as Martin walked away from them. "Does your boss always kiss you?"

"He's posh, Bradley; you wouldn't understand how the upper-class act. Come upstairs and make me a cup of tea."

CHAPTER SIX

Watched by Martin, Samuel Parker was utterly immersed in uncovering a file on his cluttered, partly chaotic desk.

"It was here the other day when you last came to see me, so it just has to be here somewhere," Samuel admitted.

Earlier, Samuel had listened closely as Martin explained what Aurora had told him: the use of plates which were not normally used by Beatrice, the fact that she had apparently eaten oysters against her normal practice, the rings left on her fingers while she slept. All small oddities, Martin admitted, that did not conclusively prove anything but seemed to indicate that the night before her death, something odd had happened in that flat. Samuel nodded sympathetically as Martin continued by describing the man who called in to see Beatrice in the afternoon, obviously the painter, who had admitted going to see her that day and who had an arrangement with Beatrice that Samuel had omitted to mention previously. Samuel looked a little sheepish and then became defensive as he told Martin that he had no right to share information within the will. Martin ignored him and continued to tell him about another man who visited in the evening. Who that might have been or the purpose of his visit was open to speculation.

"Maybe that was why she wanted to see me," Samuel interjected. "I called around to see her as planned on that Wednesday afternoon, I rang and rang the bell, but there was no response. Then one of the other tenants came out, and I asked if she had seen Beatrice at all during the day. She said she had not, which was unusual according to her, as she knew Beatrice had been at home the night before and did not often go out. Normally Beatrice would have been sitting having a coffee in the garden on such a bright sunny day, so that's why we were concerned. We tried looking through her windows, but the curtains were tightly closed. That's when we called the police."

"You called the police?" Martin asked, having never really considered the reason why the police had broken into her flat and discovered Beatrice dead.

"Yes, didn't I mention it before? Well, maybe I thought it irrelevant; you seemed to be besotted with who might be in her last will and testament. Yes, I called, and they cracked the lock somehow, and then we all went in. She was in bed still and as peaceful as I had ever seen her. So now I'll never know exactly why she wanted to see me that day."

For some strange reason, the words 'and Chicken Licken never did get to see the King', abstractly echoed in Martin's head.

Knowing that Samuel had not given away much last time, Martin now asked for the full list of people who stood to gain from Beatrice's death. Once again, Samuel resisted, citing that his professional standards did not allow him to. Last time, he said, it had been as a favour for a friend, and he suggested that Martin should take his suspicions to the police to see what they might make of them.

Part of Martin thought that would be the sensible thing to do, pass it on, let someone else deal with it; it was no concern of his. Yet he knew that if he did and they decided to take up the case, then Aurora would need to be interviewed, spoken to, and her lack of paperwork, her status in the UK would be uncovered and no doubt acted upon. She would find herself detained and then deported back to her native Philippines, back to the poverty she was trying to escape from in order to help her family. Susan had seen his unexpected concern, too; that was why she had asked him last night just why he wanted to help Aurora. If he was going to be honest with himself, he was not fully convinced of his own motives. The fact that a family could have live-in maids and manservants working for them, he had always known about, it was just part of his social class. Although never openly spoken about, people knew that the man with olive skin serving your dinner, clearing away the china plates, carefully washing them, and shopping for the mistress of the house, cleaning the silver, vacuuming the stairs, everyone knew they were not really paid anything much, just given bed and board in exchange for their labour. A labour that they could not escape from as they had been brought into the so-called golden land of England under the premise of being a visitor, but who then had disappeared from official records and lived without any status, trapping them in a life of service. Yes, Martin had known about this shadowy labour market for many years. He considered that it was of no concern of his, so why should he question it? Maybe it was the fear he had seen in Aurora's tear-stained eyes that made him see the person, the human being behind those live-in maids. Human beings that just wanted a better life, a chance to support their family and make all their lives better by coming to the UK with dreams and hopes for the future. Slavery had been banned years ago, yet it still existed in the dark corners of London. He could not go and bang on doors, shout and protest as Susan had done, giving the slave-master a piece of her mind. But he could, just as Beatrice did, support and care for a human being. Money meant little to him, so what was wrong with giving her a few pounds to ensure that she would not, like Tala, have to rely on the generosity and charity of a cafe owner.

"Here it is," Samuel proclaimed as he drew a thick buff folder from the bottom of a drawer. He opened it and drew out some papers.

"I am still not comfortable doing this. If you would just wait until after the funeral as was her wish, then all of this will be public knowledge. I'm telling you now I am breaking a lot of

Law Society rules which could see me struck off. All for just a few suspicions that you have based on what some sort of maid has told you, if that's what she really is, as you only have the word of another maid for that and neither of them, I am sure, is going to tell you the whole truth. They just want what's best for themselves, living off the generosity of people with good breeding."

It was either Samuel's reluctance to disclose the contents of the will or the way he dismissed Aurora and her fellow maids as practically sub-human that tempted Martin to punch some sense into Samuel, even though, of course, Martin knew he would not hit out, physical violence was not something that he liked to partake in even with an older man, who clearly would not be much of a competitor.

"Put it this way, Samuel, you've already divulged part of Beatrice's last will and testament, so if you don't give me the rest, I'll call the Law Society myself and tell them what you have already done."

Samuel pushed his glasses back against the bridge of his nose and began to paraphrase what had been Beatrice's last wishes. He talked at length using a number of complex legal terms, some of which he then slowly explained in simple terms to Martin even if Martin already knew what they meant. It was Samuel's way of gaining the high ground and appearing to be the dominant person in the room.

First of all, Samuel repeated the details of the estate agent that he had already shared with Martin for no better reason than he liked to do things correctly as far as it suited himself. Then he touched briefly on the artist, Hugh Alexander, whom Martin had already stumbled across.

The first new name given to Martin was that of the Peterborough Cat Protection Home. A charity which Samuel said, does exactly what it says on the box, protect cats. He said this with a half-smile at his own joke. Ten per cent of any residue of the estate would go to the charity. He explained that this would be a useful way of reducing any tax liability as well as being a good thing to do. Many of his clients liked to leave money to a charity of their choosing, sometimes asking for their name to be remembered somewhere. This was not the case with Beatrice; she had just been happy to give some money to the charity. So, unless the cats had ganged up, jumped on a train and murdered Beatrice, they were not much of a suspect. Martin detected a clearly barbed tone in the voice, which he continued to ignore.

"This one might interest you," Samuel titillated. "Yet another estate agent, James Chapman, of the little-known estate agents: Chapman and Collins. He, too, had taken a stake in Beatrice's property, twenty-five per cent just like the first estate agent when Beatrice needed some extra cash. His share was valued at the time at about a quarter of a million pounds which he happily paid over to Beatrice, rubbing his hands with glee no doubt at the prospect of a fat profit when Beatrice passed away. The thing is, he did come back to me about a month or so ago and asked if there was any way that he could get his investment back. He told me that his company was struggling with cash flow, so it needed a bit of a cash injection. Sadly, the only easy way I could see of him getting back his investment would be if Beatrice handed back his cash and the agreement was torn up, and I, for one, could not see that happening, as I would imagine she would have already passed most of it onto some casino or other. He was extremely disappointed; I can assure you. I can give you his address on the strict understanding that you do not mention me in any conversation or that I have given you his details; that's all I ask."

"And there are no other names mentioned in the will."

"Only Paige, her daughter, or stepdaughter to be precise, she has any residue that is left over once all the other conditions of the will have been met."

Martin took a small scrap of paper from the desk and a pencil that was discarded next to it and then readied himself to write a list.

"The first estate agent, Melinda, she took a ten per cent share in the property, one hundred thousand pounds, the second estate agent, James, took a twenty-five per cent share, about a quarter of a million pounds. The artist's agreement was linked to the painting, so nothing to do with the flat. The charity gets ten per cent, one hundred thousand, and the remainder, which by my calculations is about fifty-five per cent or about five hundred and fifty thousand pounds, goes to Paige. Am I right?"

"Put it this way, your public school education was not a total waste of money."

* * *

On the face of it, Martin thought James Chapman had a reason to speed up the death of Beatrice; it was going to be an interesting conversation with him. Without thinking about it, Martin knew he wanted Susan beside him for no better reason than he liked her company, so he braved the underground and its hot blasts of air to arrive back at the office just before lunchtime.

He walked in through the door and spoke at once, distracting Susan from her computer screen.

"I think we may have found a real suspect with a real motive, someone who needed money." Martin tried not to sound too triumphant. "I'll tell you about it over a coffee. Do you want one?"

Susan stood up and walked towards Martin, gesturing with her hands for him to calm down.

"I think my news might trump yours."

"Nonsense, a man who is in need of money is capable of anything."

"Trust me, Martin, I need to speak first."

Martin saw anxiety in her eyes, intoxicating grey-green eyes that last night he had watched sparkle and shine as together they had stood outside her flat. It was a strange, confusing moment for Martin; his heart was in total conflict with his head. Last night he had put his hands on her upper arms, felt the softness of her skin below the satin fabric of her blouse and then pulled her closer to him. She moved forward without resistance, looking up into his eyes, a look of anticipation across her face. Martin's heart wanted to, and his natural instinct was to pull her even closer to his body, compress and tighten their embrace. Maybe it was for the best that Bradley had chosen that exact moment to walk out and interrupt them; the decision had been taken for Martin.

"Go on then, speak first," Martin offered.

"You have a visitor. He has just popped upstairs, but he will be back in a few moments. I have told him that you were out, and I wasn't sure when you would be back, so if I was you, I'd leave now."

Martin was becoming confused as what Susan was saying made no sense at all.

"So, who is this person that I do not want to meet?"

"Mr Shillingford, I do believe not only the owner of this grand building but also the husband of a certain Jenny Shillingford who you know very, very well indeed."

"Shit! What on Earth is he doing here?"

Before Susan could answer, there was a firm knock, and the door was opened without delay to reveal two men, both of whom confidently walked into the office. They were nearly dressed as twins; brown brogue shoes, slim blue jeans that were fashionably faded, and brilliant white shirts with double cuffs that would do any soap commercial proud. It was only the shade of blue of their linen jackets that marked any clothing difference between the two men. The even more obvious difference was that one of the men was very tall and the other very short.

"Hi, I must be speaking to Martin Hayden." The taller of the two men offered his hand. "Ian Shillingford, and this is Max, my assistant."

Max looked coy as well as a little nervous, no doubt Susan thought, he was used to trailing in the turbulent wake of Mr Shillingford.

"Good to meet you at last, Martin. I have already spoken to your very attractive secretary. I just hope I am not interrupting your day too much; I promise I will not take up much of your time. First, I'm not sure if you know who I am?"

This should be good, thought Susan, and waited to see what Martin would say.

"Not too sure; the name is familiar."

"Well, to be blunt, I am your landlord. Not in the evil Racman sense, I'm not here to get every penny out of you, just a few." The joke was lost on everyone but Max, who dutifully smiled even though he had heard the phrase many times before. "I own this wonderful building located so perfectly in London, enabling businesses to grow and prosper, so I look upon myself as more of a business partner. After all, your success is my success."

Without waiting for an invitation, Ian sat down, at what was, in fact, Susan's desk, as if he owned the place, which he indeed did. Ian held a hand out, and without any form of prompt, Max placed a thin buff folder into the waiting hand of his boss. Then Susan, Martin and Max waited patiently while Ian read through some notes. After a few brief moments, without looking up, Ian stated, "I see that you know my wife." Fortunately, he did not look up or else he would have seen the colour drain from Martin's cheeks.

Susan did see it so rapidly spoke up to admit, "I'm the one who knows your wife, Jenny."

"I also see that you are a charity. Hayden Investigations does not sound much like a charity to me." It was not exactly a question, more of a statement, but even so, Ian was hoping to get an answer. Once again, it was Susan who moved towards Ian, sat on her desk, allowing one leg to casually brush his arm.

"Yes, your wife has kindly allowed us the free use of this office space, and yes, we are a charity, although we need to be very discreet as to how we go about our business, which is that of helping migrant workers who have been drawn into modern-day slavery. I can see by the look in your deep brown eyes that you are sceptical if modern-day slavery even exists; let me assure you it does. Workers arrive from the Asian continent with high hopes and dreams of providing a better life for their families, only to find themselves trapped in households that do not pay them even a small wage but just provide bed and board for a working week that can be in excess of one hundred hours long. That is what modern slavery is all about. We track down these workers, offer them an escape, and seek proper papers for them, as well as protect them from their slave-driving masters and mistresses. Just as a sanctuary for women of domestic violence is hidden away from the public eye, we carry out our charitable work behind the facade of a private detective agency. So far, it has worked well, and we hope that we can count on your discretion in the same way that Jenny has been very discreet about our true purpose."

"Sounds very laudable, Susan, clearly both you and Martin are doing a great job. So how do you finance your charity, given that you need to keep a low profile?"

That question sounded to Martin as if it was leading up a road he did not want to go down, given that Susan had already, as was often the case with her, told a few lies to cover up and found herself in a place that she would have trouble navigating away from.

"Friends and family, very close acquaintances. As you say, we are not the sort of charity that can go around Bond Street shaking a collection tin," Martin answered, not sure why he mentioned Bond Street; it was just an abstract statement.

The response he got from Ian was a broad smile.

"I guess some of those well-heeled types who enjoy giving to charity might not be too keen to give you money only to end up with you taking away their hired help. Good on you, guys, that's what I say, and I am happy that my company can support you."

Ian closed the buff file and held it out, waiting for Max to retrieve it, which he did as if he was an obedient poodle, which to a point would be how he would have described himself. He did not object to being treated like a menial worker; he was well-paid, and Ian trusted him completely; plus, he had total control over the office where he worked and was able to manage it how he wished. Often those in Max's position could see the whole picture; he knew for a fact that Susan was lying through her teeth. If Hayden Investigations was a registered charity, he would be able to claim the loss of rent against the company's tax bill; Max knew he could not.

Max recalled the day that the attractive Jenny Shillingford first mentioned that she wanted to offer a friend of hers an office with a very low rent and would prefer the whole arrangement be kept between just Max and herself. He suspected then that the friend was more than just a friend. There were many rumours about Jenny and her dancing partners, so Max knew that discretion was paramount, which of course, he was happy to provide in the knowledge that Jenny, as a co-signatory on company cheques, would be happy to sign cheques without asking too many questions. That's why he suggested that the rent for Hayden Investigations be nil and logged as a charity which had made Jenny even happier, something he was always pleased to achieve. Max might not be screwing the boss's wife, but he was certainly screwing his business.

Ian and his poodle, Max, left with the same sense of urgency that they had arrived with, leaving both Susan and Martin very relieved to see the door close behind the two men.

"Well, I think we both deserve a cup of coffee," Susan suggested.

"No, a little more than that, I think," Martin added, putting his arm around Susan. "I think we both deserve a good lunch to celebrate our charity! Your choice, my treat; get your coat and let's enjoy ourselves."

Two dates within twenty-four hours, Susan thought, things are looking up.

The Pizza Express in Regent Street was busy; it always was. Any time of day, office workers and tourists provided a constant flow of diners rotating through the doors. Susan and Martin sat at a window table and ordered pizza and wine. To Martin, it felt a little like a celebration lunch. He had just come face-to-face with his lover's husband and survived to tell the tale. He was just sorry that Susan had only chosen the local Pizza Express for their lunch; it was not the sort of place he would have selected. What was it with women, he thought; don't any of them have class and taste? His woman, Jenny, had picked a self-service, allegedly fashionable restaurant over one with waiters and table cloths, and now Susan was waltzing into a pizza joint. It's not that Martin was a snob, well maybe a little, he would reluctantly admit, but a pizza was maybe the worst food to eat. It arrives the size of the plate it is on, too big in his estimation, and you needed a roller blade to cut through it, having to be really careful not to let the slice fly off the plate and across the table. Then eating it in the wedge shape meant that you had to eat the tip of the triangle first and only then work your way around the edge, that is, if you plan to eat it holding it in your hands. Fortunately, Martin was traditional and instead used a knife and fork, cutting the whole thing into squares. That should have made things easier, but for the compulsory cheese that is layered on a pizza, designed by some mad Italian to resemble a sticky web that links the slices together whether you take a bite at it or cut it up into sweet little squares. Nothing about eating pizza excited Martin.

Susan, on the other hand, although she had saved the day with her charitable purpose, wondered about last night outside her flat as Martin began to embrace her. It was no surprise that he would not have been the first man to take her out for a meal, walk her home, embrace her on the doorstep and, depending on the man, she might or might not invite him in. Martin, she would have in the end, after much internal debate, invited in. The meal at the Papillon was totally awesome. Susan had never been to such a posh restaurant, where you get a waiter, a wine waiter and a dessert waiter, that alone had impressed her. Not forgetting the fact that everyone seemed to know Martin, Mr Hayden this, Mr Hayden that; she felt a little like royalty. Plus, the food was pretty good, although she always preferred a pizza with a side salad. Martin and Susan had chatted as they always did, casually and easily, like old friends. Then the taxi ride home to her flat, Martin had insisted that he was not going to let any woman go home on the tube alone. The cab left them standing outside her flat; then things became a little awkward, Susan sensed. She was going to ask him up for a coffee, see where things went, she had just decided, and then bloody Bradley, what is it with that man and poor timing? But then she had thought that maybe it was for the best. If she had spoken out loud the invitation that she wanted to offer to Martin, he had accepted it, and they had tumbled through the door in a passionate embrace, the moment might have become a tad complex with Bradley watching TV. Maybe it had worked out for the best after all.

So here now, the next day, she was watching Martin wrestle a pizza with a knife and fork, which she did not really understand; why didn't he cut it into slices and pick it up? Yes, the cheese would string out across your face, but that was part of the fun of eating pizza. Susan had to ask him, it was going to be a risk, but she was never averse to asking a question that others might consider embarrassing or foolish.

"So why is Jenny Shillingford your only girlfriend when she isn't going to leave her old man?"

Martin looked up from his American Pizza.

"What is it to you who I go out with?"

"I'm just saying, you're free and single, not bad looking, loaded with money, so I guess there would be no shortage of young debutantes who would be happy to go out with you. So why date only a married woman?"

"I like married women, good sex without any long-term commitment. Happy now?"

Susan filled up his glass with red wine and topped her own glass up without speaking. She then sipped her wine as Martin took another mouthful of pizza. Finally, she asked, "Who is Paula?"

They sat silently as Martin finished his mouthful of pizza, drank some wine to clear his palate, and then leaned forward onto the table, his face serious, clearly not amused at hearing Susan mention that name.

"Who told you about Paula?"

"Does it matter?"

"Yes, because depending on whom you have heard about Paula from, the story you will have heard will be vastly different."

"So that's why I'm asking you; who's Paula?"

"Tell me first who told you, and then I might tell you about Paula."

"Jenny."

"The bitch, she is so untrustworthy."

"Martin, she's having an affair as you are more than aware, she lies to her husband, I guess others as well, there is a clue in that that she might not be as pure as the driven snow."

"That maybe so, but why do women have to talk so much to each other and share so many supposed secrets?"

"That's why we go to the toilet in pairs, so we can chat and hear secrets. So now tell me about Paula."

Martin leaned back on his chair, ignoring the last few squares of pizza that remained on his plate. Did he really want to tell Susan about Paula? No, not really. How much had Jenny told her? No more than what he had told Jenny, which was not everything; even he knew not to share everything with a woman, far too dangerous, as he had learnt from bitter experience. Yet he was going to have to feed Susan something to keep her curiosity satisfied, just a titbit so that she would not persist and try and wheedle everything out of him. Slowly he began to tell her about Paula, a story which left them both subdued and quiet sitting on the Jubilee line tube train on their way to see the estate agent, James Chapman.

* * *

Chapman & Collins Estate Agents could be found sandwiched between a dismal chicken and chip takeaway with a cracked window, covered in garish posters on one side, and a very small run-down twenty-four-hour grocery store on the other side that sold everything you might need, both legal and illegal. This explained the continuous flow of down-at-heel, scruffy people who passed through the doors of the establishment, who after a short while exited with their purchases secreted inside their pockets.

It had not always been like this here on Southwark Park Road. A few years back, after the docks had upped cranes and moved downriver to Tilbury, the redevelopment had taken place. Chapman & Collins set themselves up as a bespoke estate agent, happy to serve the young rich bankers who would travel in from the City of London. Surrey Docks and the surrounding areas were up and coming, with prices to match and commission rates that saw Chapman & Collins profits rise and rise. Back in those days, its neighbours were a very high-class fashion shop and a jewellers shop. You could buy your flat, your Christian Dior suit and your Gucci watch within the space of a few yards. Then over the years, things gradually began to change; the novelty of Surrey Docks wore off, and the bankers found other places along the Docklands Light Railway to live away from the tall shadows of the very buildings that they worked in. The fashion shop closed down; the jewellers shut up shop after three armed raids, which just left Chapman & Collins struggling to sell ex-council houses and look after rental properties. Peter Collins decided to give it all up, leaving James Chapman to continue arguing with dissatisfied tenants and show prospective buyers around tower block flats that he would not dream of living in. The golden days of fat profits had long gone.

So, when Martin and Susan walked into the shabby office, James looked up, sensing the couple might be there to find a flat to rent. His heart sank a little remembering the days gone by, but still, he put on a false smile of welcome.

Politely he sat them down in front of his untidy desk, listened to their story and why they were in his office. The reason both surprised and alarmed James; surprised that anyone knew of his arrangement with Beatrice Cook and alarmed that they both seemed to be asking questions that inferred they suspected him of something. He rolled his Biro between his thin bony fingers.

"How is business?" Martin asked, having seen the peeling paint on the shop front, the tired-looking desks and chairs and the outdated IT equipment; on the face of it, business appeared to be very poor.

"We do a good solid trade here. Rentals are on the increase, and more and more people are now buying to let, which works well for me. Add that to some of the larger council properties around here that are now being sold off by the tenants, who are making a tidy sum after the discounts the council has given them, this all means that an estate agent in Bermondsey is still a very profitable business to be in," James replied. He tried to sound convincing even though he was not convinced himself. His accounts and sales figures were delivering just a scant profit.

"So, how did you and Beatrice come to the arrangement of buying part of her property?" Martin asked, deliberately avoiding any mention that Beatrice had died.

The question was not one that James wanted to answer. He pulled his thin-rimmed glasses from his head, placing them on the desk and ran his fingers through his thick hair, a lot greyer than it should be for a man in his early fifties. He wondered just how much these two investigators knew of his meeting with Beatrice. If they knew the truth, he might have to confess, but if he lied, it would place him in a difficult corner from which to escape. The other thing that troubled James was who exactly had employed two private investigators to talk to him about his arrangement with Beatrice. Her family, from what he understood, did not have that much interest in what Beatrice did with her money. Maybe it was the bank preparing to pull the rug from under his livelihood; that would make more sense. They could be collecting evidence from which they could justify closing his account. He would have to lie. If they were from the bank and he told the whole truth, then they would foreclose without a moment's hesitation.

* * *

James's meeting with Beatrice had been fortuitous for them both. She was moaning to everyone around her that her 'bloody daughter' was trying to limit her gambling. So, as he stood beside her in the Sporting Casino in Knightsbridge, he smiled sympathetically at her, then joked: 'slip me a few pounds, and I'll get you some chips to place on the roulette table, a bit like the older boys buying 'ciggies' for the younger boys'. That had started a deep conversation between them. She had seen James at the table on a number of occasions. They shared their highs and lows at the table, talked about their preferred gambling games, the money they won (exaggerated a little), and the money they lost (played down a little).

A client of James had invited him to a small casino, and that had been the first time that James had visited such a place. Lady Luck smiled on him that night, and he left with more than he started with. He then went back alone to increase his winnings which he did, making him feel invincible, and that Lady Luck favoured him, and so he returned again and again, in the belief that making money at the card tables would help his business through the difficult time it was facing. Maybe it was not Lady Luck who shaped his good fortune. Maybe it was Satan himself that had arranged James to win, drawing James into a vortex that he was finding hard to escape from. However much he lost, he returned in the deformed belief that tonight would be his winning night. James could no longer be sure who was on his side. Yet now, this old lady in front of him seemed to have taken a greater interest in him after he had told her he was an estate agent.

They sat at a small table away from the gambling tables, Beatrice with her gin and tonic, James with a scotch on ice.

"So, you estate agents must know lots and lots about property and property investments, so I wonder if you might be interested in an investment opportunity that I can offer you," Beatrice spoke, watching his eyes light up with interest. She continued, "I own a property in Hereford Square very close to Gloucester Road tube station. When I die, which might be sooner rather than later, at my age, there are no guarantees, other people will benefit from the wealth that's locked in my home. I don't know how you would view such a thing; I find it very disappointing that I have all that money tied up and cannot make use of it. I could, of course, down-size, move to the outskirts of London, but to be frank, I would not relish the thought of living in semi-detached land with all those awful people who have very poor standards. So here is what I am thinking, if I could find someone who might be interested in purchasing a part of my property for cash now, then when I do finally stand beside the great roulette table in the sky, that person would not only get their money back, but they would also profit from the rising house prices that seem to be never-ending. Would you know anyone who might be interested?" She, of course, knew exactly who would be interested; estate agents were well-known for their love of easy money.

James could not resist. He at once suggested that he would personally be interested. He knew all too well that at the time, London properties, such as those in Hereford Square, were rising in price all the time, at a rate that showed no sign of slowing. It was just a question of working out how big a percentage he would buy and at what price, and how the legal contract might be written.

James left the club convinced it was Lady Luck shining her light down on him. However, Satan also must have been smiling, knowing James would need to take out a large loan from his bank to purchase part of Beatrice's property.

* * *

"I met Beatrice a while back at a property showing I attended uptown; she was asking about releasing some equity in her house. There were, of course, companies that specialise in such things, but she seemed to want to have more of a one-to-one relationship. The reason, I think, could be the way she was going to use the money, which was not to do an extension or go on a world cruise; hence I agreed to take up her offer. Her solicitor arranged all the documents, and I sent her a cheque, all legal and above board," James stopped and waited for a reaction.

"So, you took a twenty-five per cent stake in her property and recently you wanted out, not enough profit in it for you?" Martin asked, looking directly at James, so he missed the fact that Susan looked towards her boss, who was beginning to sound like Jim Rockford.

James felt himself move back a little towards a corner.

"Yes, I did ask the solicitor if there was any way she might like to cancel the deal, but he suspected that she would have gambled most of it away, so I left it there." That was just a little lie. What he needed to find was a solution to the bank pressing for the loans to be repaid as his profits shrank.

"Why did you want the money back?" Martin continued to ask, his face without any emotion.

James nervously tidied some papers on his desk. If they were from the bank, they would have known exactly why he needed the money, so who were they? It was time to ask.

"To coin a phrase, the answer is commercially sensitive. Who exactly are you working for, one of my competitors?"

This time Susan stepped in to answer. "We are working in the best interests of Beatrice Cook, looking after her affairs. We're concerned that you were trying to cancel the agreement, which as it is a quarter of her house, then she does have an interest. So why did you need to have the money back?"

Martin liked that answer, not so James.

202

"I only have your word that you are working for her. As I said, I need some extra cash to expand my business, so I am not going to go into detail with you as it is not your concern. As far as Beatrice is concerned, a quarter of her house is still mortgaged, she has the money, everyone is happy. So, unless you have any more questions that are relevant, I would like to get on with my day."

Both Martin and Susan were happy to leave; both were convinced that James Chapman was not telling them the whole truth. Although Martin thought, Susan was blissfully unaware that he had not told her the whole truth about Paula, as he knew that if he told her the full story, it would hurt her feelings, and that was the last thing he wanted to do.

* * *

Earlier, Martin had finished his pizza and then, with a wine glass in his hand, began the saga of his relationship with Paula. Just a year older than Martin, she was one of three secretaries that supported the finance director at his father's company. At the time, Martin was working there learning the trade and becoming ever-increasingly mystified about the importance of the helix on a simple screw. Paula was petite, round-faced with short mousy hair and a smile that could light up a room, or at least that was how Martin saw it. At first, he just timed his breaks so that he could sit with her in the staff canteen, talking about the other staff, holidays, and her interests. Slowly they progressed to planned lunches together. More and more people were seeing them as an 'item'. This fact got back to Martin's father, who immediately called his son into his office and told him that it was not the sort of relationship that the son of the owner should embark upon. Feeling like a schoolchild brought before the headmaster, Martin saw his father's point, that is until he once again saw Paula and her smile and decided that how you feel about someone could not be planned, and so they continued to lunch together and started dating outside working hours too.

Paula and Martin had become a serious topic of discussion within the British Screw Company. Some saw the relationship as romantic and sweet; others suggested that Martin was taking advantage because he was the son of the owner and using it to get his 'wicked way' with Paula. While others suspected Paula of sleeping her way to promotion and pay rises. Once again, his father, and now his mother, joined in the chorus that the relationship was not appropriate. Martin hardened his stance and told them both that it was none of their business who he fell in love with. All the while, Paula and Martin's relationship blossomed into weekends away, gourmet dinners and visits to the theatre until Martin suggested that they should get married. To drive home his suggestion, he held in front of her a small box with a large diamond and ruby ring inside. She accepted without hesitation. The engagement only further infuriated his parents; they could not accept that their son was going to marry a secretary. If she had been a company secretary, a solicitor, a director of some sort, even a banker, that would have been fine, but Paula, the secretary, they just could not accept. Even without his parent's blessing, Martin continued with his fiancée to make plans for their wedding and their life together.

It was one cold, wet winter's Wednesday evening as they sat in a Chinese restaurant that Paula asked, in a very timid voice, if she could ask a favour of him. 'Ask away,' he replied, 'we are soon to be husband and wife. You can ask me anything'.

So, she explained that her older brother had got into a little trouble gambling more than he could afford, and now the people to whom he owed money were pushing for payment, which if it was not forthcoming would result in an injury to him down some dark alley. She was at her wit's end and really wanted to help her brother but could not see how unless Martin could help in some way. Any money would be repaid over the next couple of months as her brother planned to do a lot of overtime.

Martin did not hesitate to agree to help. He already had Paula's bank details, having paid for some clothes and shoes for her in the past and promised to transfer five thousand pounds to her to help her brother out of his sticky situation. With a smile, they both continued their meal and made plans for their honeymoon; Seychelles or Caribbean, they were both torn.

So, their romance continued under the scornful eyes of Martin's parents, who had yet to meet Paula's parents as she shared a flat with a friend in London while her parents lived in Bristol.

Three weeks after transferring the money, the first daffodils of spring were bursting into life when Martin saw tears in Paula's eyes.

'It's nothing,' she said.

But Martin could see that something was troubling her. In the end, she confessed that her stupid brother had paid the money back that he owed, and then soon afterwards had got into an argument with one of the moneylenders, which ended up in a fight and her brother being charged with assault. He could lose his job, his flat, everything he had worked for, so her family were trying to afford a good lawyer to represent him in court. Martin asked if he could help, but Paula said that he had helped enough. 'Nonsense,' Martin argued, 'I am sure I can get the very best lawyer for your brother'.

Paula countered that they did not want some high-flying lawyer from London; that they were hoping to get a more local man with a Welsh accent which might help convince the jury that her brother was innocent. So, in the end, Martin agreed to pay for one of the best lawyers in Bristol who had a strong Welsh accent. He could no more refuse to help the woman he loved than fly to the moon.

Court hearings came and went; the case was going to be moved to a crown court. The lawyers and solicitors were working to build the strongest possible defence, as well as submitting their weekly accounts for Martin to settle.

It was when his mother found out he was underwriting the legal costs that the arguments really started. Father, Son, Mother, all at loggerheads, and their loud voices might well have broken up the Hayden family had it not been that Paula did not turn up for work one cold, wet Thursday morning. No phone call and no message to Martin, and her phone was not being answered either. Martin, concerned for her well-being, left work mid-morning and went to her flat.

Susan leaned across the table, listening with an intensity she had not felt before, sprinkled with what felt to her like a little jealousy, an emotion she was not surprised had come to the surface. As Martin had related the story, in her mind, Susan had taken the place of Paula, romantic meals, evenings out, weekends away and then plans for a honeymoon. Susan was not enamoured by either of the two destinations that Martin mentioned; she would like to spend her honeymoon in Rome before travelling down towards Sorrento and Pompeii. Take in all those historical sites that she had learnt about as a child, the Roman soldiers, Emperors, Centurions and a whole city engulfed by volcanic ash. Maybe some people would think it a strange way to spend a honeymoon, but Susan would argue that it would be so much more interesting and memorable than just lying on a sandy beach.

Martin arrived at Paula's flat, frantic. Was she just ill with a simple cold or upset stomach, or had her brother got himself into more trouble, and she had returned to Bristol in a panic? Maybe the rogue moneylenders had taken Paula as retribution for the court case. Martin pressed the bell hard, his finger turning white.

"You must be Martin?" A young woman answered the door in her dressing-gown; she had not been up long. Her face was pale without a trace of make-up. Her wiry hair, in need of a good brushing, was standing up at impossible angles.

Martin asked after Paula and was immediately invited into the flat. He had never actually been introduced to Paula's flatmate; she had always been out when he visited the flat. Martin knew her name was Brenda, and Susan had told him of her Yorkshire bluntness and love of walking around the streets of London photographing old buildings, which was part of the architect's degree that she was about to complete. Today was the first time that he had met her in person. Together boyfriend and flatmate sat down on a well-worn sofa.

"If you haven't guessed already, we've both been screwed over by a bitch called Paula."

Brenda's renowned bluntness was not fiction. The words surprised Martin, who held back for the moment from remonstrating her for calling his fiancée a bitch.

"Paula's gone off to Birmingham. Why in 'heavens name' she would even think of going to such an ugly city, I have no idea? But she has gone off to Birmingham with your money, owing me three months' rent and electric, with her boyfriend, Gary, who I thought she had dumped, or at least that was her story to me when she told me about you. Round-eyed little Paula, in whose mouth butter wouldn't melt, told me she had left Gary, whom she has known since college because she is in love with you. And then she told me about all the help you gave her. I guess now I know she was not exactly telling me about it but just boasting, or at least making excuses for not paying her part of the rent. I saw her doing her online banking on her posh red laptop. 'You've got loads of money, I told her, pay me some bloody rent.' 'Oh no,' she said, 'my poor brother needs the money, and Martin has given me this to help him.' The bitch does not even have a brother. I found out this morning when I phoned her long-suffering parents. Yes, Martin, you and I have been well and truly screwed."

Susan reached out and grabbed hold of Martin's hand.

"Oh, that's so cruel."

Martin agreed with her. He had lost the best part of twenty-five thousand pounds, but that was not his main concern; it was having to stand in front of his parents, who no doubt would be gloating, to tell them, that was going to be the difficult bit. There was another repercussion he had not fully realised at that time; he no longer trusted women.

"But you still go out with women, married maybe, but nevertheless, they are still women."

"Going out with married women or, to be more accurate, having affairs with married women, there is a kind of honesty about the relationship. Both participants know that the relationship is going nowhere, but the bedroom, simple lust, and love does not need to come into the equation at all."

Martin looked at the concerned eyes of Susan. He could see she really felt sorry for him. She was not judging him, just offering her sympathy. So, he felt bad that he had left out a few key parts of the story that he knew, without doubt, would hurt her. Why he did not want to hurt her, he was not totally sure, or maybe he was but did not want to admit it to himself.

* * *

"I know I work for a detective agency as well as you do," Susan pleaded into her phone. "Even so, Becky, we are still good friends, and I am not asking a lot, just a teeny-weeny bit of information about one of your customers."

Susan had been, in her opinion, very observant when she was sitting opposite James Chapman. She mentioned to Martin that she had seen the top of a bank statement and knew where

James banked. Then Susan added that, which she now regretted, she had a friend who worked at that bank, a friend called Becky, so maybe she could find out a little more about James and his financial affairs. Martin thought it a brilliant piece of detective work and watched as Susan called her friend, but even he could see that things were not going as well as planned.

"I'm only asking you to look at a screen and remember some of the figures, that's all." Although Susan guessed even remembering a few figures might be a struggle for Becky, renowned for her short skirts and short memory.

Martin listened with amusement to hear Susan impatiently reason with her friend.

"No, don't email; they can be traced, just bring up the account record or whatever you call it and make a few notes on a piece of paper, the old-fashioned way. The balance, any big transactions over the last year or so, any loans that he might have, a bit like a credit check, that's all."

There was a long silence from Susan as she listened to her friend before she once again spoke in what Martin described as a very cautious tone.

"Well, if you have to, you have to. But I can meet you around the corner from your branch. I'm sure that is easier." Again there was a short period of silence followed by, "well, if no one is here, just leave it in an envelope with the guy on the front desk, as long as it's in a sealed envelope."

Susan now sounded spiteful, which did not surprise Martin, as she had been upset that they had spent most of the morning arguing about who should take the train ride to Peterborough to talk to the Cat Protection Home. Susan stated that she did not want to go and spend the day around a lot of smelly cats and well-meaning spinsters, who regarded the cats as human beings, collecting them from who knows where. Ironically, they were exactly the same reasons that Martin did not want to make the journey to Peterborough either. Of course, he was never going to admit that, as it would only weaken his argument that a feminine touch would be just what was needed.

Susan put down the phone sharply, as much for effect as anything, then turned to Martin, who was lazily drinking his coffee.

"I still think that you should go to Peterborough. You're a man, you'll hold more sway with the people there, plus I'm seeing my boyfriend later."

Martin smiled; he knew full well that she was not seeing her boyfriend later. Thanks to Susan's status on Facebook, Martin knew that the 'miserable little jerk can piss off if he thinks he's watching my TV ever again'. Obviously, he will need to see his next Manchester City match with another girlfriend. The comment, liked with an assortment of emojis by over twenty female friends, was clearly a popular sentiment. Weirdly, the only male to 'like' the comment was one Bradley Wise, who Martin knew was the boyfriend in question who clearly did not live up to his name.

"They are bound to be ladies at the charity, feminine, feline lovers, who no doubt think every one of their cats is a real person. Plus, although I have always wanted a cat, more than one in one house is just not normal. Also, I'm the boss," he added smugly with a wry smile, which only served to annoy Susan even more.

Historically, Susan tended to accept what any man told her. She had never really bothered to try and break down the reasons why; she just went along with what was being suggested. Generally, that would lead to a relationship with a man that her friends would describe as a cul-de-sac relationship. Susan had always been like that, yet something inside her argued that the Martin Hayden in front of her, although her boss, did seem to have his own form in being manipulated by women; something even he would grudgingly admit to, so she gave it a go.

"You might be the boss, but I think we are more equals. It's not as though you are running some high-powered business here; you're just skiving, really. You could say we are partners in crime. So please, I hate cats and trains, please, please let me stay, and you go to see the charity." It was a half-hearted attempt even given Martin's history with women; Susan just did not believe in herself enough to make her reasoning sound stronger.

"I promised you travel in the job advert which you seemed keen to do, and now's your chance."

"European travel, Martin, that's what the advert said. Peterborough is not fucking Europe!"

"Technically, it is," Martin laughed, "and before you start on about adverts being a bunch of lies, your CV was more fiction than fact."

"And the only reason," Susan countered, her voice increasing by a full octave as her anger began to overtake the rationality that she occasionally showed, "you now know it was not totally factual because I have told you it wasn't, that's being honest which is more than can be said for you."

"What's that supposed to mean exactly?"

"Paula, you didn't tell me the whole truth, did you? Jenny had already told me about her, but so has your mother, who did not leave out any of the sordid details at all."

It had happened all so long ago, or so it seemed, Susan had just started her new job, and the regular calls from Martin's mother made her feel at home, almost welcome. Susan was happy to tell Mrs Hayden about Tooting home life, where she was brought up in the Midlands, the schools she went to and her jobs (the last part being a concise reprise of her CV, not a factual account). Mrs Hayden seemed so interested; in turn, she gifted Susan snippets of Martin's early life, not too much, just enough. Enough, Mrs Hayden hoped to make it clear, to show that her son came from a wholly different background to Susan, and without saying it directly, she hinted that Susan was never going to be suitable for her son. It was a subtle hint that Susan did not pick up on at all, which did not surprise Mrs Hayden. She guessed without meeting the young girl that she was both common and stupid, two traits in her own mind she knew go hand in hand. So, the more her son talked to her about Susan this, Susan that, Susan makes the best coffee ever, really good at her job, a real find; she could see that her son was becoming attracted to Susan and memories of Paula came into her mind. There was no way that her son was going to go out with a cheating common girl again. So, she took decisive action as she always did, not always for the best reasons or the best outcome, but for Mrs Hayden the only correct view was her view.

Mrs Hayden planned things carefully for maximum impact. She knew her son would be out all morning for his regular weekly trip to the barber before then going to lunch with one of his useless friends, so Susan would be all alone at the office and happy for a chat. The office clearly was never very busy.

They first spoke of trivial niceties before Mrs Hayden brought into the conversation how much she hoped that Martin would find a nice girl. She worried about him being left alone when she passed away. She could almost hear the excitement in Susan's voice, thinking that she could be that girl. Mrs Hayden liked to tempt her victims with a glimmer of hope before snatching it away, which she did as she started to tell Susan about Paula and what the wicked girl had done to her poor son.

She left nothing out; Susan's feelings were of no concern to her. Mrs Hayden highlighted that Paula was from a very common background, only went to grammar school, and was not a suitable type for her son and hoped that he had learnt his lesson. There was a reason that the upper class were the ruling class; it was because 'we protect our own and stay with our own'. Mrs Hayden heard Susan's voice deflate, not daring to argue with the lady with the posh voice. In Mrs Hayden's experience, common people always capitulated to a well-spoken person.

"My mother told you about Paula?" Martin himself now sounded deflated. He looked across at Susan, someone he never wanted to hurt as she had already suffered too many hurts for a woman of her age.

"Everything, no holds barred, no cloaked inferences, she told it how it was."

"Paula's background was no excuse for what she did; there was no need to mention it to you."

Susan snatched her handbag from beside her desk, pulled her jacket from her chair and made her way to the door.

"I'll go to Peterborough as instructed, not because I want to but because I have been told to by my boss, so I have no choice. We common people need jobs provided by posh people to live."

Without waiting for an answer, she walked out the door, slamming it behind her, leaving Martin alone in the silent office. He was reminded of the times he had spent in the office before Susan arrived. Then the days were simple and straightforward: lunch with his pals, dates with Jenny, the occasional dinner date with other women, nothing too serious. Evening concerts, weekend sports events, once in a while, a few hours in the gym, Martin's life was lived for Martin. Now he was chasing the facts behind Beatrice's death. Telling his single member of staff what to do, having to cajole her into going to Peterborough. Life was becoming too much like real work; was that what he really wanted?

It was Samuel who had sowed the seeds of doubt in Martin's mind.

'Why are you following this up, Martin? I am convinced that you are really wasting your time. Think about it for a moment; there is no hard evidence whatsoever that there has been any sort of foul play. The old lady was found dead in her bed, just as thousands of other older people are each year. The doctor who knows she has a heart problem puts it down to old age. She simply expired as we all do in the end. Don't forget it was the police who broke into her house and found her. They evidently did not have any suspicions, or they would have started an investigation. So, the way I see it, you are chasing a fantasy; all your so-called evidence is based on the word of a maid, who could only have been with Beatrice a few months, if that, no one really knows.

"Then just because the maid tells you the plates were the best plates and that Beatrice had slept with her rings on, and where did this all start? Because you thought that the old lady never eats shellfish. All your evidence is just hearsay. She was an old lady in her nineties, who is to say that she didn't decide to try oysters. That is not unusual. Take me, for example, there was this one weekend when the wife and myself popped into Marks and Spencer and bought a lobster for us. Never had it before ever, so we thought, let's buy one and try it out in the privacy of our own home, plus it was a lot cheaper than going to a fancy seafood restaurant. We hated it, never bought lobster again. People do things like that. You have nothing that suggests to me she was murdered."

If Samuel could see that what Martin was chasing was futile, why did Martin have doubts? He would have preferred not to have doubts. There was something nagging at the back of his mind; he was concerned for others and their plight. He had given money to an almost complete stranger. It was Susan who was teaching him that sometimes you just have to help the person in front of you; you cannot always cross the street and ignore them.

There was a timid knock at the door, and then it opened, followed by the head of the front desk security guy who peered around the edge of the door.

"Sorry to trouble you, Mr Hayden. There's a young lady here with an envelope for you, says she didn't want to disturb you, but I thought you wouldn't mind."

Martin looked at the man, well into middle age, dressed smartly, who always said good morning when Martin entered the building and always said goodnight when he left. He was there every day, rain or shine, at his desk in the hallway fussing around, doing odd jobs around the building and just getting on with his work. Martin didn't even know his name, he had never bothered to ask, but today change was called for.

"Thank you, sorry, but I don't know your name."

"That's alright, sir; I wouldn't expect you to know my name; I'm only a glorified caretaker. But just for the record, I'm Ernest, although everyone calls me Ernie, which I think my father hoped for when he chose Ernest. Shall I send her in, sir?"

"Yes, please do, Ernie, thank you."

CHAPTER SEVEN

She was tall, in fact very tall and willowy. Everything about her was slender, her legs, her waist, her arms, her hands, her fingers. Martin examined every element of her frame, which he guessed to be about six feet two inches, a good four inches taller than himself. Her hair was blonde and draped over her shoulders, a small button nose at the centre of her face, lips which had a little too much lipstick on, her two blue eyes staring out resembled those of an innocent child.

"Mr Hayden?" her voice was timid.

"Yes, please sit down." Martin gestured towards a chair and watched as her short skirt rode even higher up her long legs. Even though he was considering giving up detective work once and for all, if this was a new client, he would be continuing for a while longer.

"What can I do for you?"

"I'm Becky. Susan asked me about one of the bank's customers. She wanted some information on him, a James Chapman." She produced a large envelope and held it towards Martin.

He took it, saying, "I'm sorry you missed Susan; she has just left for an assignment."

"Yes, I know, she updated her Facebook page saying the train has been delayed on her way to Peterborough, wherever that is. It sounded urgent, what she wanted like, so I thought it best if I pop round to see you, I mean drop off the info." She shuffled in her chair and combed her hair with her slender fingers; her nails painted bright red.

Martin waved the envelope in front of him. "Thanks for this, Becky; it is going to be very helpful to our investigation, and please be reassured we will never divulge where the information came from. Is there any way I can thank you?"

Without hesitation, Becky replied, "Well, I've finished for the day, and I could do with an alcoholic drink."

"Ok." Martin was surprised that for someone who seemed timid, she should be so upfront. "There's a bar around the corner; let's go."

* * *

Nothing could have prepared Susan for the stench that flooded over her when Harriet opened the door of her semi-detached house. In addition to the disgusting odours, two cats took the opportunity to dash out into the front garden.

So far, everything she had dreaded about this day trip to Peterborough had come to fruition apart from the free energy drinks that they were giving away at Kings Cross Station, of which Susan managed to grab a handful, saving her having to buy any drinks on the journey. Although the train did leave on time, it was soon stuck behind a local stopping train. Then once that had left the route, signal problems contributed to the thirty-minute delay. The only positive side of the train journey happened to be the woman who sat next to Susan, who spent the whole journey talking to a friend on her mobile telephone. Susan learnt that the woman's husband was not being totally honest when he said he was working late. From the one-sided conversation that Susan listened to, she gathered the husband worked late twice a week, on a Wednesday and a Thursday, and did not get home until after midnight, by which time his wife was in bed, not asleep, but listening so that she would hear when he came in. She pretended to be asleep when he snuck into bed, having first taken a shower, which raised her suspicions still more. Susan wanted to contribute that he was clearly having an affair but thought it best for the moment to just continue listening. The woman had evidently taken the advice of the friend on the phone and gone through his bank statement and credit card transactions, noting that every Wednesday and Thursday, there were charges from the same pub.

The plot deepened. Unfortunately for Susan, neither party mentioned the name of the pub. Apparently, they mutually knew of it, only referring to it as the one with the blacked-out windows, which intrigued Susan even more. The conversation dampened down a bit before the lady corrected her friend, 'No, the swingers pub on the corner, you know', that statement distracted Susan from the signalling problems. 'Yes, twice a week he goes there,' the woman continued, 'when I asked around, he was well known, the bastard, the secrets that he keeps. So, I confronted him....' Here we go, thought Susan, maybe she killed him and was escaping the city, although the Peterborough train did not seem to be much of an escape route for a fugitive from justice. 'Of course, he denied it. You know what he is like. Oh, I'm sorry, my battery is about to die on me, and the signal is breaking up. Tell you what, I'll give you a call later and tell you the rest. Speak soon, Richard, love you.' Now Susan did have a number of questions that she was intent on asking the woman and was hoping to start a conversation on the basis that she had been betrayed by her boyfriend. She really wanted to know, not only just who her husband was swinging with but Richard, who was he? The train chose that moment to pull into platform two of Peterborough station; right then, Susan would not have minded another half-hour delay.

* * *

"Hello, I'm here to talk to you about your charity," Susan said to the dishevelled woman standing in front of her. A rotund woman, maybe in her sixties, with a dirty looking apron covering her equally stained and worn dress.

"You from the council?"

"No, I'm here to talk to you about any donations or legacies that you have had recently. I'd like to find out a little more about how you manage to run your charity."

"If you're one of those office types from the Charity Commission with your papers and forms, you know I don't do that sort of thing. I leave it all to the man at the bank to help me."

"No, nothing like that. It's just that one of my clients wants to leave some money to a cat charity and yours was mentioned. I just want to talk to you first, see how you look after these delightful creatures of yours."

Susan tried her best to limit her breathing and therefore lessen the amount of smell she had to endure, but unfortunately, she did have to breathe as unless she did, she would have passed out and maybe been taken inside, which would not have been her first choice. To her dismay, she was given no choice when the small woman said, "Well, you'd better come in then."

Susan cautiously stepped in, following the little old lady, trying to ignore the fact that there were actual furry cat faeces along with the skirting board.

Harriet Saddlesworth had run the Peterborough Cat Protection Home for twenty-seven years, mostly on her own. She looked a lot older than her sixty-eight years, not through the constant toil that she subjected herself to; it was from the disappointments she had endured in her life. They had weighed her down and aged her beyond her years. Harriet was an eight-pound three-ounce screaming ginger-haired baby in the same living room where she now stood with Susan. All her life, Harriet had lived at 45 Ravenswood Crescent, the only child to have been born alive to her mother and father; two others had been stillborn. Those others could have been her younger brother and sister, but that was not to be. Instead, they were a disappointment for her and devastation for her parents. In her youth, she had had a special female friend who lived a few doors down from her. Harriet had soon realised she liked girls much more than boys, and soon the two teenage girls were discreet lovers. However, her happiness was short-lived as, for her friend, it was just a phase, an experimental time that she was going through. Once the phase was finished, they remained just good friends, leaving Harriet with a love that was not to be, another bitter pill to swallow.

At twenty-four, Harriet was working at a local estate agent. In preparation to leave her parents, she bought a small flat in the centre of Peterborough nearer to her work and closer to the growing gay community that she felt drawn to. It was in her twenty-fourth year, two weeks before she planned to fly the nest, that without warning, her father died from a massive heart attack. Her mother could not cope with a loss that brought back all those memories of her stillborn children. That was a blow to Harriet's plans of flight and left her trying her best to balance looking after a mother whose life was becoming more and more chaotic with her work which now had become an escape for her. Her only two confidants were Thingy and Bob, her tortoiseshell cats with whom she would snuggle up with each lonely night. She did manage to continue working beyond everyone's expectations for two tough years until her mother had a serious stroke leaving her with the use of just one feeble arm and meaning her mother needed feeding and constant care. With little choice, Harriet gave up her job, gave up her life, and accepted defeat. She looked after her mother for fifteen long, tiring years, during which time she buried both Thingy and Bob, who were replaced with Punch and Judy. Harriet was just forty-one when she watched her mother's coffin disappear behind a mauve curtain whilst Chopin's Scherzo no.2 played. Harriet hated the music, but it was her mother's favourite piece. Now alone in 45 Ravenswood Crescent with a few dwindling friends, no life, and no idea what any future might hold for her, Harriet took refuge with her cats.

Susan looked around the cluttered front room with its yellowed bold-patterned wallpaper that she suspected had been put up decades ago. In front of the dusty bay window with net curtains that had greyed with age and showed the scars of cats clawing the filigree pattern, there was a small, similarly scarred sideboard. Susan looked closely at the candlesticks, photographs, and two small porcelain vases with plastic flowers, all of which gave the appearance of a makeshift shrine. A shrine covered in dust and cat hair that had not seen a duster or a can of polish for many years. Susan recalled the words of Quentin Crisp: 'There is no need to do any housework, at all. After the first four years, the dirt doesn't get any worse.' Looking around, she hoped he was right, but maybe he didn't have cats. Apart from the sideboard, the only other items in the room were cat cages, fine-wired cat cages stacked three high. Susan counted fourteen in the room, each one with a cat in it. Some were sleeping, resigned to their confinement, others meowing warmly, calling out to be stroked and cared for; others just howled like tormented banshees.

"You OK?" Harriet inquired, referring to the brilliant white handkerchief that Susan held to her nose.

"Fine thanks, I have a bit of a cold and would hate to pass it onto you," which was a lie. Susan had prepared a perfume-soaked handkerchief, a plan that helped alleviate the odours that filled the house.

"Can I make you a tea, maybe a sandwich?"

Harriet played the part of being a good host as she had learnt as a young woman. Susan pictured in her mind what the kitchen might look like based on the evidence of the front room and decided that taking any form of refreshment here might result in instant food poisoning or worse.

"Thanks, I'm fine. I don't want to take too much of your time, so to business. Do you know a Beatrice Cook?"

Harriet racked her failing memory and answered, "No."

"So, how many cats do you have here?"

"Look, what was your name?"

"Susan."

"Well, Susan, if you are going to ask me a lot of questions, I cannot stand around here. I have so much to do. You had best ask me what you want to ask as I go about my chores."

Without waiting for any form of response from Susan, the little grey-haired lady turned and left the room as she answered the question. Susan could see she was going to have little choice but to follow her.

"No idea how many cats I have, never could see the point of counting them. You can if you want to."

Back into the hallway, past four smaller cages which looked more like hutches and appeared to have either large rabbits in or some sort of furry non-feline creature. Susan was not interested in seeing exactly what she was passing, just getting some answers quickly and getting out.

"Samuel Parker?" Susan asked as she caught up with Harriet, who was now in the room that overlooked the back garden. Again, the room was filled with cages, some containing two cats who were sharing cramped conditions, and hanging in the corner of the rotted French doors was a large birdcage.

"I had a tabby cat called Samuel once, but I am bad with names. Are you or are you not from the council?"

"Not at all; as I said, one of our clients wants to leave you some money in her will, so we are just making sure your charity is doing a good job. Do you do everything around here?"

Harriet pulled three large tins from a pile of cat food tins stacked in front of the French doors; some appeared to be rusty as a result of rain creeping through rotten frames.

"Just me, I do get a little help from a nice woman who normally works for hearing dogs. She pops in once in a while, and then there's young Maggie, a student who comes in on Saturdays and takes any of my little cherubs to the vet if they are under the weather. She has a car, so much easier than the bus, you see."

As Harriet spoke, she walked through an open doorway to the left of the windows which led into the kitchen. Susan looked into the room and then knew she had made a wise choice in refusing anything to eat or drink. If Quentin Crisp did no housework, Susan was sure he would have at least cleaned down the worktops in his kitchen, something that was not part of Harriet's routine. She pushed some ingrained cat dishes to one side and started to open the tins with an old-fashioned tin opener.

"Do you get many donations to help you?"

"Floatations?" Harriet queried.

Susan moved the handkerchief away from her mouth for just a moment.

"Donations." The sweet-smelling cloth was quickly replaced across Susan's mouth and nose.

"Ah, that makes more sense. Some donations, not many, the man at the bank helps me with that side of things. All those daunting forms from the Charity Commission confuse me so much. I own a flat in Peterborough City Centre which I rent out, and that helps a great deal. It's the vet bills that take all the money."

Harriet pulled a spoon from the sink that was overloaded with dirty dishes and cups. Susan wondered just how this stout old lady managed to survive in such a dirt-infested house. With

223

the spoon, Harriet started to empty the contents of the tins onto a selection of dissimilar saucers which she had lined up.

A voice screeched from behind Susan, "Dinner time, slime."

Unaware that cats could speak, she turned, startled, fully expecting to see a talking cat behind her. All she saw were the green feathers of some sort of parrot in the birdcage, which she had thought was empty when she had looked.

"Ignore Halifax; he just likes the attention." Harriet looked up from the mushy wet cat food to reprimand the parrot. "Quiet Halifax; we're talking."

"Navy, gravy," was his only reply.

"Is he talking in rhyme?" Susan asked. Halifax answered first as if to confirm.

"Blue, zoo."

"Be silent, Halifax, or else I'll cover you up. Yes, he does a limited vocabulary, just two words at a time which rhyme."

"Did you teach him?"

"Heaven forbid, why teach a bird to speak? Total waste of time as they only copy what you say, they don't think. He had already been programmed when I got him. And before you ask, he came from a family in Halifax, so that's why I call him Halifax."

"Rich, bitch."

"That's it, Halifax, now you are being an embarrassment."

Harriet cleaned her hands of cat food on her already much-stained apron and walked with a sharp menace in her eye towards the cage. She bent down beside the door, dragged a discoloured and frayed tablecloth from the floor and launched it over the cage, sending poor Halifax into darkness and silence, but not before he managed a quick: "Joker, smoker."

"That's it, you little rascal. Halifax is such a bad boy at times. I often wonder why I ever even consider any other creatures besides sweet cats; it's just that I have such a soft spot for any animal in distress or in danger of being put down."

Harriet leaned in close to Susan, who backed a little away from the old lady with unsurprising dubious personal hygiene. Harriet whispered to ensure that Halifax would not hear, "His owner was leaving the country and planned to just set the poor bird free on the Fens. Having never set foot out of his cage, he would not have lasted the night."

Alongside the now covered and silent cage, hanging from a picture rail (something that Susan had not seen since visiting her grandmother when she was alive), was a framed colour photograph that had lost most of its colour through time. The photograph was of a car, an old-fashioned car that Susan did not recognise; two young women were standing and smiling beside it.

"Is that you standing beside the car?" Susan asked, pointing to the photograph.

"Many years ago, it was Patsy's car; I could never have afforded such a swish car. It was taken a long time ago, a lifetime, one might say. I no longer drive or even go much beyond the end of the road nowadays, there is just too much traffic on the road, and everyone drives so fast."

Now that the perfume was starting to fade from her handkerchief, Susan decided it was time to say goodbye. Standing beside the road, her first few inhalations of the traffic fumes had never smelt so sweet.

Once Susan arrived at the station, she was pleased to see that her train was on time, well so far as that is what the electronic display board was indicating, so a ten-minute wait was nothing too onerous. She pulled her phone from her bag, time to check Facebook and her messages, see what had been happening in the real world as she described the many posts, shares and adverts that popped up on her newsfeed. Michelle had shared a cute picture of a cat diving in and out of a box.

Carol had posted a photograph of her latest yummy cupcakes. Becky had checked into some cool bar off Oxford Street drinking with ...., Susan's heart started racing. She read Becky's check-in once more just to be sure: 'Becky Hunter checked into Gracie's Wine Bar, drinking with cool Martin, lucky me!!!'

Instinctively Susan started typing out a message, well, not so much a message, more of a threatening rant. She was about to post it onto Facebook when her train arrived. By the time she was sitting in her seat, the rational side of her mind had suggested that maybe the tone of the message was not right; in fact, her rational side hinted that it might result in charges of threatening behaviour. Maybe she was over-reacting; after all, Martin was only her boss; it was not like they were a couple. Martin was attractive, the right sort of age for her, had a sense of humour most of the time, clearly had no financial worries, plus she enjoyed being around him. Working together was a pleasure. Even taking into account his strange habit of collecting business cards from everywhere he went and then just leaving them in his top desk drawer. But that balanced out with the fact that he always bought a copy of the homeless paper every time he passed a seller, once she knew he had bought the same edition from the same seller five times in one day. It was those quirky habits, including rubbing his ear-lobe, that endeared him to her. His sceptical approach to horoscopes was something she was sure she could in time erode away, convincing him that star signs do have meaning and should be taken into account. However often she played it out in her mind, his mother's words always echoed around her infatuated head: 'She (Paula that was), was from a grammar school, so my expectations were never going to be that high'. At least Paula made it to Grammar school. Susan was pleased to get out of her comprehensive school as soon as she could. Martin's mum would be even more disappointed if she arrived there one evening with an engagement ring on her finger.

So, if Martin and Susan were never going to happen, then she surmised that Martin and Becky were even less likely to happen. Although Becky was a lot more attractive than her, with longer, better-shaped legs and had always been able to afford clothes that made her look great, well, she had the figure to start with. Stop thinking like that, she told herself, he's your boss, you see him each day. If there was the slightest chance of a one-night stand, would she take it? Yes, without a second thought. Would Becky beat her to it? God help her if she did!

* * *

As he placed the chilled glass of white wine in front of Becky and then carefully placed his own glass of red wine opposite, Martin looked down at Susan's friend who looked up at him, replaced her mobile phone into her bag with a guilty look and then smiled nervously.

"Well, Martin, Sue said you were cute; she didn't mention that you were drop-dead gorgeous."

"That's very kind of you, Becky, but I'm happy to buy you a drink with or without the compliment, however flattering it is. So Becky, thank you for delving into our estate agent's bank account." Martin waved the envelope in front of him. "Before I open it, tell me what he's been up to?"

Becky looked a little puzzled at the question. "Sorry, I don't know."

"Ah, I thought you had some information about his bank account?"

"Oh, his bank account, yes, got it all here," she said, tapping the side of her head. So far, Martin had doubts about just how much there was in there. "I'm better with numbers and accounts than being social, always seem to be putting my foot in it one way or another. For example, are you going out with Susan?"

"Was that an example of a bad question to ask or a genuine 'I want to know' question?"

"A real question. She's keeping very quiet about you and her, so I wanted your take on it."

"Yes, you are extremely good at being blunt as well," Martin commented, which Becky seemed to push to one side while she waited for the answer to her question. "Well, Susan and I have been out but not in the way I think you may be inferring, purely business, a bit like the drink we are having here. Why, what has she told you?"

"She said nothing. We are all promised to keep it secret."

Martin smiled. "All of you promised to keep her 'saying nothing' a secret?"

"Absolutely, not a word. I'm not allergic," she stated as she scooped up a handful of salted peanuts from a white dish that sat on the table. "If I was allergic, I wouldn't eat peanuts, would I? That would be plain stupid."

Martin was trying to decide if she really was stupid, nervous, or already drunk. He guessed it might be nerves as he hoped that a bank would not employ a simple drunk, although, having thought about it, some of his friends who worked in the city banks could be described as simple and drunk most of the time.

"James, our estate agent, what did his bank account reveal?" Martin asked, trying to refocus her away from the peanuts and back onto the only reason he was buying her a drink in the first place.

Becky licked her fingers slowly, which Martin found to be mildly erotic. She then delved into her handbag and took out a folded sheet of paper which she unfolded carefully until it was clearly an A4 sheet of paper with numerous handwritten numbers and words on it. As she used her hands to spread out the folds, in turn, the paper managed to absorb some moisture from the condensation that rolled off her wine glass and onto the table. Martin noticed that as Becky regarded the paper, her eyes seemed to change; her concentration seemed to focus as if she had found her true vocation.

"I guess all those boring regular transactions will not interest you in the least, Martin, just the ones that reveal his lifestyle. There are a number of payments to Mentral (Isle of Man) Ltd, the holding company for an online gambling site where he does spend more than just a few pounds a week, so he is clearly a regular gambler. He drives a Volkswagen, maybe a middle of the range model given his monthly payments to VW Finance. It is, no doubt, a contract hire agreement, very popular nowadays. I have no idea why contract hire is so popular; the car is never yours unless you pay a fat wad of cash at the end of the agreement, which you most likely can't afford anyway, as that was the reason you entered into a contract hire agreement in the first place. Looking at his address and the size of his mortgage, he lives in a very swish house; well, from Google Earth, it looks good. As I mentioned, the size of his mortgage tells me he really can't afford to live there, just needs to keep up with his friends at the golf club. Once again, an upmarket golf club, the Oakwood, which he pays for monthly, so he really can't afford the large annual subscription in one go, not with a mortgage like his. He has a passion for French cuisine, I would say, he dines at least three times a month at La Rustique, a nice little French restaurant, highly-rated, a short drive from his house, although he gets a taxi there and back as against each La Rustique transaction there is a taxi company charge."

"Hold on a moment, Becky; you can tell all this from his bank statement?"

"When was the last time you used cash for anything even mildly significant?"

"Point taken."

"Might I add that he pays several hundred pounds off his credit cards each month, the same amount, so I guess he is trying to get them down, probably maxed out. Although I cannot be sure unless I do some other checks which might flag up to someone in the system and shine a spotlight on me, which I would rather avoid as I am acting as an agent for a private investigator."

"I'm impressed, Becky."

"I am pretty stupid in many ways, but give me money, bank accounts, credit checks, that's where I excel. Sorry about the pun," she giggled.

Martin would not fully understand the geeky pun until he was on his way home.

"As interesting as his life might be, I am more interested in any very large transactions."

"Yes, that's just what Susan said, although I sometimes just can't help showing off and impressing good-looking men." She smiled, took a swig from her glass, almost emptying it in one go. "James, I call him James as I feel I know him so well, which I do in a way. James took out a business loan with our bank. He said it was for expanding the business, explaining that he planned to open another branch along the Dockland Railway Route; the loan was for two hundred and fifty thousand pounds. Yet now I have spoken to Sue, I guess he was pulling the wool over our eyes and was, in fact, buying a share in some old lady's property." Martin nodded in agreement, and Becky continued, "Estate agents are just so crooked, but nevertheless, as an established customer and with a bank manager that he plays golf with, he gets the money without too many questions. Just as I would expect, he has trouble with the repayments, so now it gets passed onto regional staff, not his local friendly, golf playing bank manager. We start putting pressure on him to pay, and then about two months ago, he pays the whole loan off; well, to be perfectly factual, he has a cash injection into his account, two hundred and sixty thousand pounds, so he pays off the loan and outstanding interest in one go. That would have pleased regional staff, big tick in their box."

"So...," Martin tried to speak when Becky raised her hand to silence him.

"So, where did the money come from is your question?"

"You are good at this."

"I have always fancied being an investigator, well not murder or anything violent, but chasing down fraudsters and money launderers would be fun. So, I am kind of living the dream here with you." She smiled. "Back to James, I guessed that you might well ask me where the money came from. Such a large payment is not hard to trace back to an account. It came from the account of...," Becky looked down at her notes, only to see that the vital part of who paid the money into James's account was smeared with condensation from her drink, wiping it with her hand only made it worse. "I'm good at numbers but rubbish at names." She peered at the sodden paper. "A double-barrelled name, I'm sure, Gibbons, I just can't make out the rest. I can check again tomorrow and call you, maybe go for lunch someplace?"

"Florence Gibbons Howard?"

"That's the one. Do you know her?"

Martin nodded, "Yes, I do indeed know her."

Becky emptied her glass and held it up in front of her. "Was that information worth more than just one glass of wine?"

Martin smiled and, without saying a word, took her empty glass and walked towards the bar, wondering if he would be able to shake Becky off before closing time.

* * *

Today it was Martin who was driving towards South Norwood and the cosy flat of Florence Gibbons Howard, with Susan secured safely in the passenger seat. Martin weaved his metallic-blue Honda Civic through the light midday traffic, feeling a lot easier and safer with his own driving than what he had experienced with Susan driving a few days ago. What he did find strange was her quietness; she had hardly spoken a word all morning. She had not even offered to inform him of his 'stars' for that day; he hoped that did not indicate that his death was looming. Their journey began and ended in silence. He knew that she could be moody at times, maybe she was having money worries, or maybe her on-off boyfriend was causing her problems. As they walked up the stairs to the flat, Martin tried to put out of his mind the way that Susan was acting. So she had to take a trip to Peterborough, big deal, and then spend some time in a smelly old house. Some people, he was sure, had a lot worse jobs that they had to do day in and day out.

"This is a pleasant surprise." Florence beamed as she opened her door and, without hesitation, invited them both in, sitting them down in her best comfy chairs before stepping into the kitchen to make tea and serve up a plate of Country Slices.

"Your favourites, I think," she suggested to Martin as she placed them next to him. Once she had ensured her guests had a warm drink, some refreshments and were both 'comfy', only then did she ask the purpose of the surprise visit to her modest little flat.

Martin began, "We are still trying to understand just what happened to your mother and the circumstances surrounding her death, so we have spent the last few days asking questions, trying to make sense of her financial affairs. One of the people who had taken a share in her flat was James Chapman. He paid a quarter of a million pounds for it to your mother. Then it would seem that you paid a very similar amount into his bank account.

I wondered if there was a connection. Did you buy out his share?"

Florence smiled first at Martin and then at Susan before turning her beam back to Martin.

"You are both very good at your job, I must say. I did expect you to mention the payment the last time you were here, so your question is of no surprise to me, and I have no shame in telling you all about it. I guess that Mr Chapman has told you all, estate agents are so untrustworthy. So, what do you want to know?"

"Well, why did you pay James Chapman a little over a quarter of a million pounds?"

"Clearly, he has told you something, just not everything, so here is my side of the story, which I should point out, I have no reason to bend the truth about, and you are getting the facts nothing less. Do help yourself to a cake, Martin." Florence leaned back in her chair and began to speak.

"He called me out of the blue. I thought it was one of those pushy sales calls; he had that sort of voice, you know. He knew me by name and said that he was tracing relatives of Beatrice Cook, saying he understood that I was her daughter by her first marriage. Obviously, he had researched my mother and her background very well indeed. Fortunately for him, he spoke to me first. If he had told Paige that Mother was selling off her flat a bit at a time, Paige would have hit the roof; she is very protective of her inheritance, as you know. Well, he asks if he can visit and talk to me about an arrangement he was in with my mother. Well, even at my age, I know not to invite strange men into my flat, so I arranged to meet him across the road in the little café. I do like a full English breakfast once in a while. My doctor says that it does my cholesterol no good at all. I say, treating myself once in a while improves my outlook on life no end. Anyway, I am sure you don't want to hear about my health. Back to James, who seemed to be very uncomfortable in a greasy spoon café, I would say he is clearly a snob. He tells me that he has purchased a part of my mother's flat, all above board and legally agreed. It was the first I had heard about her selling off the family silver, so to speak, although knowing her, it did not surprise me one iota. He wanted to cash in his investment; it was no good asking Beatrice. She, no doubt, had already frittered the money away at some Casino or other. So, he hoped to be able to offer the share to a family member; he thought that was the right thing to do. I ask you, an estate agent doing the right thing; still, I thought it was sweet of him to think of the family first. The idea of me owning a chunk of my mother's house was ironic, seeing as she had been the root cause of my having to move out of my wonderful childhood home. Plus, there would be a bonus to such an arrangement, it might mean I could force Paige to sell the property or just annoy her that I owned part of it, and she would have had no idea. With all that and the value going up year on year, how could I refuse? Do you want some more tea?"

"No, thank you, Florence. Please continue; it is fascinating."

"Oh, it gets better," she teased. "Of course, no way was I going to give over such a huge sum of money to a stranger, so I spoke to my lawyer, and he drew up an agreement, much like a mortgage, or selling on an endowment policy, just to make sure that he was not going to run off with the money and leave me with just a worthless piece of paper. So I am now a part-owner of a very fashionable property in London."

"Where did you find a quarter of a million pounds?" Susan bluntly asked.

"I married into old money. My first and only husband owned a large estate in Northumberland, forestry and leisure activities which, when he died, left me with a sizable nest egg, which before you ask why I am being very frugal, is because I plan to leave as much as possible to my children. What do I want with a big house and garden at my age?"

Florence poured herself another cup of tea, draining the last of the brew from the rose-patterned, porcelain teapot.

"It was quite by chance that I was on the same coach trip as my mother. As you know, Martin, we had a few strong words. I never actually told her that I owned part of her house; I did not want to let her know in case she took some sort of action to buy out James, with whom she still had an agreement. I did tell her, in no uncertain terms, what she had done to our family. As I recall, the words: 'selfish bitch' came into the conversation. I digress as I have already told you about the heart to heart we had. What I did not tell you was that the next day Mother came to my room looking timid and for some reason full of regret for what she had done to Father and myself. She poured out her heart. I had heard this all before, but this time she did seem to be more sincere. She told me, sitting on that hotel bed with real tears welling up in her eyes, that she had no idea what she might have left by the time they laid her out in her coffin, yet whatever she had, she told me, I would have half, an equal share with Paige. I wanted to laugh, not at the offer you understand, but at the fact that I would get half of what Paige was going to get, depending on how long Mother lived, that might end up being just a few pounds. Still, the gesture was there, we hugged, and she promised when she got back to England, she would amend her will. The money was not important to me; it was the fact that she had said sorry to my face, an apology that had taken decades to be spoken out loud. So now you know as much as I do. I will be attending her funeral, as I should, and I look forward to seeing Paige's face when they read the list of beneficiaries of my mother's estate."

"So, what will you do, sell your share, force Paige to sell the house?" Martin asked before finishing the last Country Slice, carefully holding a plate under his chin to catch the crumbs.

"I don't honestly know; I'll see how Paige reacts to my investment before I decide."

Susan looked around the flat as she listened to Florence tell her story. She looked at the fine net curtains, the deep-pile carpet, the different watercolours around the walls and the sideboard full of family photographs. One photograph caught her attention; she stood and walked across to the dark-wood sideboard, almost seeing her reflection in the highly polished wood. Susan picked up the photograph that had caught her attention and examined it closely.

"Whose car is this?" she asked.

"Mine," Florence told her proudly. "A Triumph Dolomite Sprint, 1900cc, alloy overhead cam producing ninety-one brake horsepower, nought-to-sixty in eleven seconds, which was fast back in those days, the very first car that I bought, and I loved every minute of driving it. I told you I always loved cars; I think I got that particular gene from my father."

Susan handed the photograph to Martin, who looked puzzled, wondering what Susan was getting at.

"So, who is Patsy?"

Florence did not reply at first; her thoughts for the moment floated away from the room before returning. "That is a name I have not heard spoken in many years. Where did you hear it?"

"I spoke to Harriet, she had this exact photograph on her wall, and she told me it was Patsy's car."

"Well, she is right; she called me Patsy. I think it was one of the names her mother was going to give to what would have been Harriet's younger sister, who was sadly stillborn. She treated me like a sister, a younger sister. I, in turn, was happy to treat her like an older sister, someone I could turn to. It was a very difficult time for me; we had just moved from the large manor house into a small, or at least to me, it seemed small, semi-detached house in Peterborough. Luckily for me, just a few doors down lived Harriet, kind, sweet Harriet, who took my hand and guided me through a very turbulent time in my life. She would have told you we became lovers. She seems either just proud, or maybe she did really love me and has never really gotten over it. I suppose it was going to be inevitable; both of us had suffered disappointments in our lives, we became an island for each other on which we could escape. Our affair only lasted a few years; I became a lot more interested in boys, so I let Harriet down as gently as I could; the last thing she wanted was another disappointment. We continued to be friends. We both shared a love of driving cars fast along the country lanes of the fens. As often happens as you grow older, the world that you live in changes, and we gradually saw less and less of each other. Now we only exchange Christmas cards. I do not relish visiting her with all her cats, and she cannot spare the time away from them. So, there you have it, the 'Harriet and I' story. So why were you speaking to Harriet?"

Susan put the frame back from where she had taken it and sat down again. She looked at Martin first and then turned back to Florence, who looked at the young lady in anticipation; well, Susan hoped it was that and not lust. Susan tried to picture a young Harriet with a young Florence together making love. At first, the thought astonished her, but then she began to see and understand two teenage girls looking for stability and comfort in a world that had dealt them a bad hand for two so young.

"Your mother is leaving part of her estate to Harriet's charity."

Florence laughed, loudly falling back into her chair.

"My dear, whoever gave you that snippet of gossip is wildly misleading you. Or was that Harriet recalling one of her dreams, a large legacy for her cats? I do not believe Mother would give any money to any charity; she would rather place it all on a rank outsider at Epsom than give any to a charity. She hated them, thought they were just ways of clearing the consciences of all those rich people who avoid paying tax, helping those poor things who suffer from the resulting cuts. She had strong words for ladies who run charities, trust me, she would not be making any donation to any cause. Plus, I doubt if she even knows of Harriet and her cats, as she never came to our house in Peterborough; Father would not let her."

"That might be so," Martin countered, "but she is leaving money to the Peterborough Cat Protection Home."

"Such a stupid name sounds like a bunch of cats running a protection racket in the neighbourhood; still, Harriet liked it. If the will has not been revealed yet, how can you be so confident that my mother is leaving any gambled money to Harriet and her cats?"

"Her solicitor is a close friend, and when we explained the situation, he thought it wise to share some of the information with us, to help us get to the bottom of your mother's death."

"Well, I am still very sceptical about any sum of my mother's money going to charity, so if you know about the last will and testament of Mother's, is my name not mentioned?"

"Samuel did not mention you, and I am sure he has revealed the complete list of beneficiaries to me."

"Well, maybe I should not be surprised; they say leopards don't change their spots."

They left Florence with, they hoped, not too much disappointment after learning that, in the end, her mother had either not changed her will or had never had the opportunity to amend it. During the slow drive back to Tooting and Susan's flat, they talked about the next move they should make in light of what Florence had said. If Beatrice was planning to change her will, leave more money to her daughter Florence, then Paige would be losing out. Could Paige have found out before Beatrice had a chance to change it? Maybe, Susan suggested, that was why Samuel was visiting Beatrice on the Wednesday he had found her dead because she had asked him to call around to her flat with the intention of changing her will. Would Beatrice have told her stepdaughter? Martin thought it unlikely, as there was no love lost between them. But, Martin added, as he slipped through a traffic light as it changed to red, it was a man we are told who visited her on Tuesday night after the artist had. Paige had all the reasons, they both agreed, to not want her stepmother to alter her will, plus Paige was keen that Beatrice did not fritter all the money away at the roulette table.

"Let's both meet up with my old school friend Freddie. You'll like him, a real character, enjoys a good drink and knows almost everything about everyone. If there's any dirt on Paige, I am sure that Freddie will know and tell us."

"Martin," Susan commented, "you are in a bus lane when you should not be in a bus lane."

"Oops!" Martin turned out of the bus lane into the path of a blue British Gas van. The bearded driver did not appreciate Martin's bad driving and showed it by flashing headlights, sounding a loud horn, and using a hand signal which cannot be found in the Highway Code.

"Martin, I presume you have passed your test?" Susan repeated exactly the same question Martin had asked her a couple of days ago, just to make the point that passing your test does not automatically make you a good driver.

"What driving test, no."

Susan felt herself tense up at his answer.

"You haven't passed your driving test; why not?"

"Because I have never taken one, so technically, I never failed my test either, so it's not all bad news."

"You are meant to pass your test before driving on the road."

Martin braked hard to avoid a cyclist, who was, in turn, avoiding a jaywalking pedestrian, which did nothing to endear Martin to the British Gas driver behind him.

"I know you are meant to; everyone knows that. It was just I never seemed to get around to taking the test; things kept cropping up. In the end, I thought, why worry; I can drive as well as the next person, and to be honest, how likely am I to get stopped by the police at my age? They are more interested in young drivers than us more mature ones. Plus, if I do get caught, what can they do, take my licence away? I don't have one for them to take."

"In that case, I can claim, rightly, that I am a better driver than you," Susan said with a superior air.

By the time they reached Streatham Common, the traffic had ground to a halt around a set of roadworks constricting the flow of traffic.

"Thanks for giving me a lift. Sorry about the traffic."

"No worries, Susan, it's not far and a lot easier than the train."

"Did you enjoy your drink last night with Becky?"

After a slight pause, Martin answered. "Did she tell you?"

"She checked in on Facebook, 'Gracie's Wine Bar with cool Martin', so she said."

Martin edged the car forward; they were making progress, just very slow progress.

"So the whole world now knows that I was having a drink with Becky, whatever happened to the old days of a quiet drink? She is quite a quirky girl, your Becky."

Susan turned away from Martin, speaking to him whilst looking out at the road, the people crowding the pavements and the shops. "She's not my Becky, just a girlie friend. Would you go out with her?"

"I did." Martin teased. If Susan had been looking at him, then she would have seen the small smile breaking across his face.

"I mean on a date. Would you date her?"

"Is that a rhetorical question?"

"Maybe, I'm not sure what that sort of question is. I just ask plain questions."

"No, I would not date her. She's not my type."

"Too common for you?"

"She's just not my type. She's attractive, I'll admit, but going out with her, I cannot really see me forming a meaningful relationship with her, if that is what you are driving at, and if that is what you are driving at, then how come you are suddenly so concerned?"

"I just thought we got on well when you took me out to that posh restaurant. It was almost a date, and wondered if...."

"Susan, we spend a lot of time together, which I enjoy, so I enjoy your company that goes without saying. Dating and all the rest could cause complications, and they might spoil what we have."

Susan did not answer; it was an effective no in her mind. She was fun but not dating material for a posh boy like Martin; no doubt he still worried about what his mother might think.

"Don't forget we're seeing Freddie later; I'll pick you up at about eight."

She stood on the pavement watching him drive off, wondering how best to get him up to her flat, just to prove she could.

* * *

"This is becoming quite a habit, Martin, all these buckshee meals from you. I never really thought you would be so interested in other people's lives unless, of course, they are as attractive as Susan here; no wonder you have kept her close to your chest." Freddie turned to his right where Susan was sitting, trying to eat a simple grapefruit starter. "That is just an everyday saying, a little bit like keeping your cards close to your chest. I would not want to imply that he is keeping you close to his chest in a physical way, although I would not blame him one little bit. You have the most enthralling eyes, Susan."

Susan, embarrassed, blushed, not so much from the flirtatious comments that Freddie was directing her way but from the squirt of grapefruit juice that she had managed to send in Martin's direction as she pushed her spoon into her starter. The only reason that she had chosen the grapefruit was that she thought it would be easy to eat; it was proving anything but.

The three of them were just off the Kings Road in the aptly named Retro Restaurant serving, so the menu explained, 'delights and tastes from the nineteen-seventies', way before Susan had been born, so for her, it was a totally new experience. She had an appetiser of Babycham and salted peanuts as they all consulted the menu, a sparse menu when compared to that of the Papillon or any other modern restaurant for that matter. Freddie assured her that Babycham was a great drink, champagne perry, which to her tasted just the same as Prosecco. But there again, Freddie was consuming pineapple squares that were pinned to squares of cheese by wooden cocktail sticks, so what did he know. Susan thought it must have been all those seventies hallucinatory drugs that created such strange recipes. So then to have half a grapefruit in a bowl with sweet sherry poured over it, topped off with a glace cherry in the middle, did nothing to help her taste buds. Both Martin and Freddie had chosen the prawn cocktail, which she, of course, had heard of and seen in modern restaurants, but which looked nothing like these prawn cocktails. Firstly, she wondered if there were any prawns under the heavy dose of Thousand Island dressing that seemed to fill the ornate glass-stemmed dish, alongside two leaves of lettuce and a quarter slice of brown bread sticking out of it.

"You are such an old flirt at times," Martin commented.

"Less of the old, please." Once more, Freddie turned his attention to Susan. "I am only two years older than your boss."

Susan smiled and, distracted, pushed her spoon carefully into the grapefruit and still managed to squirt Martin with even more grapefruit juice which thankfully he ignored.

Once the waiter had cleared the dishes, Freddie began with a question.

"So Martin, why are you so interested in Paige McLaughlin? Fancy your chances?"

"Now you are being vacuous. I would not even consider a well-attended dinner party with Paige in the room. She reminds me of those scary aunts that used to visit, and you felt duty-bound to kiss, and when you did, they appeared to hug you far longer than necessary."

"Well, I am sure she would welcome the chance of a candle-lit dinner with you, Martin." Freddie turned to Susan and squeezed her hand. "He likes the older, more mature woman."

"Freddie, let's not get into my likes and dislikes. We are here to talk about Paige and what her involvement is in her mother's ...."

"Stepmother," Freddie corrected.

"Stepmother's death. How far would Paige go to protect her inheritance?"

Freddie picked up his glass of wine, a deep red oak-aged Bordeaux, inhaled the aroma and drank. The wine list had recommended a classic seventies wine, a German Liebfraumilch called Blue Nun, which possibly at the time for some households was the pinnacle of wine drinking. Freddie had always despised any wine that did not originate in France, and even today, with the new world wines becoming popular, Freddie was a traditionalist and still would remain loyal to French wine producers. Susan was not so fussy, so when the attractive waiter suggested that she should experience the German white wine, she was happy to oblige; new alcohol always had a place in her life.

Freddie watched Susan out of the corner of his eye as she tried her glass of wine.

"I think Paige would go a long way to protect her inheritance. She has always had a passion for money; she treats it like her...."

"Ugh, that is crap; who drinks this stuff?" Susan interrupted.

Martin smiled at her. "And I believed that you could drink anything which contained alcohol."

"Normally. What is this shit? It's sweet, leaves a rubbish taste in your mouth, plus it seems to burn as it goes down."

"Spoken like a true wine connoisseur, don't you think, Freddie?"

Freddie nodded in delight. "Why do you think I stick to French wine?"

"If this was really popular years ago, then I can understand why so many people took up drugs."

"It was indeed," Freddie explained. "Blue Nun was the de facto wine for the middle class. They served it along with instant mash potato and tinned carrots at dinner parties, all on a hostess trolley to keep it warm, before sitting down to eat around their 'G plan' table. It was the same across all Suburbia. Liebfraumilch, which translates to 'beloved lady's milk', is actually made mostly for export and is known to be a low-quality wine. I think the Germans were just getting their own back after being beaten in the '66 World Cup. Welcome to the seventies, Susan."

"So how come you know so much about it all? If you're just a couple of years older than Martin, then that puts you being born around 1980."

"Well picked up, Susan. Never mess with a private detective; that will teach me. Ok, I admit I was not a total child of the 1970s, but I learnt a lot from my older brothers and sisters, plus you must have seen on YouTube those adorable aliens advertising Cadbury's instant potatoes, 'For mash, get Smash'."

"'Course I have," Susan stated as she pointed to her glass, "but this, ugh!"

Martin tried to bring the conversation back to Paige. "So, enough of the history lesson, let's get back to today and Paige."

"Sorry, Martin, distracted by your PA. Back to Paige, yes, I am sure she would do just about anything to hang on to her inheritance from her stepmother, that is, assuming she has not gambled it all away. Paige, from when she was younger, loved money, getting it, spending it, praising it, boasting about it. The stories are that she spent many years waiting for the right man to come along to marry. The truth, I suspect, was that it took a lot of credit-score checking before she found one with enough money in the bank. Mind you, I do believe that her quest for money and status has made her a little eccentric, possibly bordering on madness. You will have seen the dog walking gym, so that is a little clue."

"OK," Martin asked, "if she learnt that she was going to have to share her inheritance with Beatrice's actual daughter, then she might decide to fight her corner, take steps to secure the money?"

"I guess so; anything Paige does, however outlandish, she justifies as being perfectly correct. Take the way she curtailed Beatrice's gambling in London. Paige was just annoyed that Beatrice would fritter away all her money, leaving her with nothing to inherit, which is daft as she and her husband have more than enough cash and capital to sustain them for the rest of their lives even if they lived for the next hundred years. I think it was just she felt that Beatrice was laying her inheritance money on the roulette table. I guess she would, in the first place, have asked Beatrice to stop, fat chance of that. So, she went straight to the source, the casinos and told them, 'block my mother's gambling habit or else I will go to the papers and the gaming board to tell them how you are fleecing old vulnerable ladies'. She said to her friends that she did it for the good of her stepmother; in truth, her stepmother enjoyed gambling, it was her money, but in Paige's warped reality, she was doing her a favour."

At that point, their main course was served. The two men had rump steak, 'cooked in real animal fat' with deep-fried chips (they passed on the chance to have the instant mash) and garden peas to finish, which were clearly out of a tin. Susan, after seeing the weird appetisers plus the limited menu, was glad that she had stuck with something she knew and trusted: Scampi with chips.

For a moment, Paige was side-lined while Martin and Freddie recalled television programmes from their younger days and the toys they had played with before they tried to recall the characters from the Thundercats cartoon series.

"I think we all liked Cheetara, as pubescent boys, any female was going to be better than any of the other Thundercats," Martin recalled. "I think I must have been about six years old or maybe seven when I had posters of the Thundercats plastered across my bedroom walls."

"And Playboy under your bed!" Freddie teased.

Susan, a little bored by the conversation, looked around the restaurant at the other diners. Old couples who were maybe reliving their youth, younger groups trying out the food from the past, and then the two sitting in the corner; two men who were being discreet and not drinking Liebfraumilch, so Susan thought they must have good taste. They were both laughing and plainly enjoying themselves. She was sure that she recognised one of them, the slightly older one, with a very square jaw, clear skin and short, shaved hair.

"I think it was 'Wacaday' that really formed my character," Freddie admitted. "I always fancied myself as being like Timmy Mallet with his flamboyant clothes and slightly mad offbeat humour. I look upon myself as being a lifelong fan of Timmy Mallet and continue to dress like him where appropriate if that makes any sense."

"Don't tell me you had a pet called Roland Rat?"

"Well Martin, funny you should say that, I did have a dog, a cavalier, who I called Roland Rat, although all my family insisted on calling him just Roland. Plus, there was Michaela Strachan for us older boys," Freddie added as Martin noticed that Susan was both quiet and distracted by two other diners.

"Are we boring you?" he asked.

"The guy over there in the corner with the short hair, isn't that Gary Wallace?"

Both Martin and Freddie looked across to see who she was talking about.

"Who?" Martin asked.

Freddie smiled, "Come on, Martin, do you never watch TV? Gary Wallace from 'Teenage House', don't tell me you have never seen the programme?"

"Never even heard of it. What is it, a documentary?"

Susan looked back at Martin with an exasperated expression.

"You are so not with it, Martin. 'Teenage House', they put six celebrities into a house and treat them like teenagers: it's a reality TV show. They get manky food they have to eat, go to bed at a sensible time, the fun bit is the games they have to play, like charades, truth or dare, spinning the bottle, kiss chase, you know the mad stuff that teenagers get up to, it's fun."

"Sounds it," Martin replied, although he was far from being convinced.

"Martin, you cannot begin to imagine how excruciatingly bad the programme is, yet for all that, it is totally unmissable," said Freddie.

"I just drool," Susan admitted, "when I see Gary Wallace, I get shivers up and down my spine. He is the only reason I watch the show. Do you think I could go over and ask for his autograph, or is that not the 'done thing' in these posh restaurants?"

Freddie put his glass down and stood up.

"My dear, firstly, this is nowhere near being a posh restaurant. Secondly, if you never ask, you will never get it. Thirdly, I know him well, so I will happily introduce you to him personally. Come, let's go and have a chat."

Freddie offered her his arm, and together they walked over, looking like a couple, towards an unsuspecting Gary Wallace.

Martin watched from the table as Freddie, Susan, the man they called Gary and the other fellow, all four of them talking, laughing; enjoying the relaxed chatter no doubt, he thought. Martin felt something; he was not sure exactly what it was while looking at Freddie beside Susan. He had felt this feeling a couple of times before; he would have said it was a hint of jealousy. Yet, that could not be the reason. It was Susan, the girl he worked with. Pleasant as she was, why was he feeling jealous of Freddie as they chatted? She had boyfriends, nothing regular, but she had a life, and Martin was not sure that he could be part of that life. She was sociable, fun-loving and outward in her approach to life. Martin preferred a quieter, more laid-back life. Quiet dinners with a few friends always would be his first choice over a group prowling the bars and pubs all night, laughing, drinking and being loud. Yes, that was the difference between Martin and Susan; she was loud where he was quiet. Even so, he still felt a pang of jealously.

"Freddie has gone outside for a smoke," Susan said as she sat down at the same time as the waiter laid three plates of Black

Forest Gateau onto the table. Martin saw a crumpled piece of paper in her hand.

"Did you get your autograph?"

"Yes," Susan admitted, wincing as she finished the last of her Liebfraumilch. "Get me a large gin and tonic please," she asked the waiter before he left.

"You no longer sound so excited; who was he?"

"It's strange, but for years I have seen him on TV, looked at pictures of his rippling bare torso in gossip magazines and newspapers, I even went as far as cutting out a page feature from the Daily Mirror and stuck it in my drawer. So, you could say I am a bit of a fan of Gary Wallace, and I reckon that if he had contacted me on Facebook and asked me to marry him, I would have said yes without any thought."

"I sense the word 'but', is about to tumble from your lips."

"But planning to marry Gary without seeing him would have been a bad plan."

"Generally, the wise advice is to meet up with the person you marry before you actually tie the knot."

"Yeah, well, I know that now. He stank, not of body odour or sweat, or even a dubious aftershave. He stank of mothballs, would you believe, his clothes reeked of the damn things. What sort of person walks out of their house smelling of mothballs, or more to the point who uses mothballs nowadays, aren't they a Victorian thing?"

"I have no idea Susan, mothballs are not my strong point. Still, I'm sure when you two marry, you'll drive all the moths out of his wardrobe."

Susan sank her gin and tonic in one as soon as it arrived.

"Marriage, I don't think is on the cards either. That was his boyfriend next to him. I need to find a new idol."

After the Black Forest Gateaux had been consumed, they all passed on the offer of instant coffee and instead ordered three large brandies.

"Martin, I didn't pick up on it earlier, but you mentioned Beatrice's real daughter. Have you met her? Gibbons family, I think she married into."

"Yes, Gibbons Howard."

"That's the one, lots of old money, farming money as I recall. So you met her, and she told you her mother was changing her will?"

"Well, she said she was planning to change it. In the end, she never got around to it as far as we can see, so after a few debts, Paige gets the rest."

"Apart from the chunk going to charity," Susan interrupted.

"Yes, but even so, Paige will get several thousand pounds which I am sure will please her."

Freddie rubbed his finger around the rim of the brandy glass, a thoughtful look on his face, and then it broke into a broad smile. "I never thought of Beatrice as the charitable type. What did the old girl leave it to, casino workers benevolent fund!"

They all saw the humorous side of that comment.

"No, some cat charity in Peterborough," Susan informed him.

"Really, what's it called?"

"Peterborough Cat Protection Home." Susan finished her brandy and called for another one.

"Small world, my Aunt Monica, she left a chunk to that very charity last year. Not a great surprise she was a total eccentric, although she never had any pets; we just put it down to one of the mad moments that she had."

Martin and Susan looked at each other. It was Martin who spoke first, "Are you sure it was the one in Peterborough?"

"Of that, I'm certain. We all thought it weird that she had left money to a charity in Peterborough. None of us was even sure if she had ever been to Peterborough. Why would you go?"

"How much did you say she left to the cats?"

"Not sure exactly. By the time the various expenses are taken out of your estate, unless you are in there with the paperwork, you just cannot be one hundred per cent sure, though I'd guess around fifty thousand pounds. Why all the questions?"

"Maybe if we knew a little more about your aunt's will, it might help us with Beatrice's. Who was the solicitor who drew up the will for her?" Martin asked before Susan could; the third brandy was now starting to take effect and slow her down.

"I haven't the foggiest, but I am sure I can find out for you."

"Now?"

"Now, if it is that important to you?"

Freddie, being the good friend that he was, slipped outside to make the call and took the opportunity to have another cigarette as he stood talking to his mother. Inside, Susan noticed she had now drunk a little too much too quickly.

"Twenty quid says the solicitor is Samuel," Martin offered.

"Harriet could still be stashing it away for herself and starving her pussy cats," Susan's voice was now obviously slurred.

"I think I had better take you home soon, young lady, before I have to carry you home."

CHAPTER EIGHT

"I still think you owe me twenty pounds, Susan. As I expected, or should I say correctly predicted without any need to consult my horoscope, Samuel was the solicitor for Freddie's auntie."

Even though Susan had arrived or rather staggered into the office well after Martin, the first thing she did was lie down on the sofa and ask Martin to make her a strong coffee; the hangover was real and vicious.

"Your twenty pounds can wait," Susan told Martin, her voice muffled by the coat she had laid over her head, keeping the light of day well away from her eyes. "What I want to know is how I got home last night?"

"Ah..." Martin sat on the arm of the sofa beside Susan's feet and took her shoes off. Hung-over or not, you don't lie down on a leather sofa with your outdoor shoes on. Martin wanted to tell her, but in the end, he didn't. Instead, he answered her question. "Well, I promise you, you did not drive home, although maybe the vast amount of alcohol you had consumed might have helped your driving ability."

"Very funny, haha! How did I get home, Martin?"

"Another option is your boyfriend Bradley coming rushing to your side, whisking you up in his powerful arms and taking you home."

"I don't do multiple-choice questions with a hangover Martin. Bradley, I discount totally as he is now hopefully out of my life, and there were no football matches on TV last night."

"I took you home, and we spent the night making love."

Susan sat up, the coat falling from her face as she looked at Martin with a frown.

"Just my luck, one time I take home a decent guy, and I can't remember a sodding thing." Then she flopped back on the sofa and recovered her face. "Still don't believe you. Why do I have such a hangover? I don't do hangovers, and I do drink a lot more than the recommended intake for us girls."

"First time drinking German wine?" was the simple question Martin asked.

"Never again," Susan conceded.

In fact, Martin had taken her home; they had taken a black cab to her flat. The cabbie, spending almost the entire journey, threatening that 'if the drunk bint starts to throw up, I want her out of the cab moving or not'. Although Susan was awake, she was totally compliant and did just as she was told, even if she was all for throwing one of her shoes at the driver, an action which Martin was able to convince her would be useless as there happened to be a clear screen between her and her moaning chauffeur.

Why she had decided to overdo the gin, brandy, plus drink a full bottle of German white wine, Martin could not be sure, although he did suspect it was connected to the discovery that her one true male idol was gay. She never had any luck with men, or so it would seem. Martin wondered just why that was; she was attractive, fun to be with, not forgetting a loyal side that would see her fight hard for what she believed in.

Martin had helped her up the stairs, laid her down on the bed in her clothes, where she fell asleep almost at once. The last thing she asked Martin before she slipped into her drunken slumber was, 'How do you vacuum a vacuum?' Why that particular question Martin struggled to understand.

He was going to leave, slip quietly out of the door and make his way home, but then he recalled hearing tales of drunks falling asleep and then during the night suffocating on their own

253

vomit. He placed her on her side, hoping that would help. He considered leaving but was worried that he had not placed her correctly. In the end, he waited just in case, sitting on the side of her bed watching her sleep peacefully.

Martin picked up the well-worn book with the eerie looking cover that was under her bedside lamp: 'Number Seven, Queer Street' by Margery Lawrence. He recalled that Susan had mentioned it in one of their earlier conversations; he opened the cover and started reading.

He read and waited until seven, five hours later. He guessed if she was going to throw up, she would have done it by now, plus he wanted to get home, shower and be back at the office. Freddie had helped them last night, and he wanted to get cracking. The funeral was now only the day after tomorrow.

"I read some of the Margery Lawrence book you have by your bed."

"Ok, maybe I now believe that you at least took me home; thank you for that. Making love to me all night? I hope you wanted to, but I don't think you are the type of man who would take advantage of a drunken woman," Susan sat up again, "however stunning and attractive she might be!"

"Maybe you'll do the same for me one day. I find the best cure for a hangover is work, so let's get on; time is running out."

Last night Freddie had confirmed that Samuel was indeed his auntie's solicitor. He was not sure, but he could see Martin's viewpoint that Samuel might have influenced his auntie as he suggested. She had never shown any interest in cats before. This connection for Susan was conclusive proof that Samuel was guilty of something, what, she was not sure, but she always thought he had shifty eyes and had never liked him from the first time she met him. Martin was not so sure; solicitors often have their own favourite charities, maybe as he was involved in the start of this one, he had it down as one of his favourites, so

if an old lady asked him to suggest a charity to leave their
money to, well the Cat Protection Home would no doubt be
mentioned and encouraged by Samuel. Susan, now sitting at her
desk, was still not convinced; his shifty eyes were all she needed
to see. Martin, on the other hand, from what he had heard from
Susan and Florence, doubted that Harriet would have the
inclination to defraud money out of the charity; she just did not
seem to be that kind. This view was reinforced by Susan, having
already ascertained Harriet's star sign indicating that she was a
kind, homely woman. So, for Martin, Paige seemed to have the
biggest reason to murder her stepmother. She must have found
out that Beatrice was planning to change her will, leaving half to
her real daughter, which when added to Freddie's thoughts and
Martin's knowledge of Paige, he put her down as the chief
suspect.

Susan admitted, which did not come easy for her, that
Paige was a bit strange. When she had first gone around to the
house, she had not been treated well. It did seem that she
became very defensive as when Susan mentioned the fact that
Beatrice did not like oysters, her mood had changed as if she had
something to hide. On the other hand, she argued, Samuel is a
Taurean, born twenty-third of April 1967, his negative traits
being greed and self-indulgence, clear proof in Susan's
bloodshot eyes.

All the while Susan was running down the solicitor, Martin
was searching the internet and had now tracked down, through
the Charity Commission website, the accounts for the
Peterborough Cat Protection Home. The latest, almost two years
out of date, showed very little income, and he wondered how
poor Harriet managed to survive feeding her cats, let alone
herself.

Susan, on the other hand, decided that she would take a
leaf out of the Jim Rockford handbook of private investigation
and dialled Samuel Parker's Office.

"Good morning, I wonder if you can help me, please," Susan had added a tone of authority to her voice which caused Martin to look up and listen closely. "My name is Jane Richards from the Charity Commission; we are carrying out an audit, just like a spot check, on a charity that you have sent a cheque to in the past. Nothing is wrong; it is just that we are testing some of their systems, so we are mapping out some of their transactions to ensure their methods are robust. According to our records, your office sent a cheque to the Peterborough Cat Protection Home in June last year at the request of a...," she hesitated, acting as if she was referring to her notes, which she was in a way as she was recalling how Freddie had described his Auntie Maxine, surname Goldberg, "Mrs Goldberg, a client of yours, who sadly passed away and bequeathed monies to the aforementioned charity. I just need to confirm the date you posted the cheque so that I can see how efficient they are at processing and banking the cheques that they receive. I only need the date it was mailed out."

The office fell into silence as the woman in Samuel's office left the phone and busied herself, pulling out the buff folder from the dusty filing cabinets that Susan had seen when she was last there. Both Susan and Martin waited in silence.

"Yes, I'm still here," Susan answered, at the same time indicating by miming with her hand that she wanted something to write with. Martin grabbed a pen and paper then laid it beside her. "June 21st, wonderful, that helps." There then was a pause while Susan listened and then continued, "Ah, so it was not mailed, it was delivered by hand, so much safer and at least you can be sure that it arrives without having to spend an absolute fortune on postage." Susan listened, this time smiling at Martin. "Well, I think that is most kind, so kind of him. I just wish everyone was like him. Thank you for your time, and I hope you have a very pleasant day."

Susan put the phone down with a triumphant look on her face. Martin spoke first, impressed with her impersonation of an official from the Charity Commission, "What was all that about, plus where did the posh voice come from?"

"A trick I learned in one of the Rockford File episodes. Jim rang up an office to see if they had sent something out. In the episode, it hadn't gone out, so Jim Rockford knew that it had been stolen before everyone thought it had. That was industrial espionage. In our case, the Auntie Maxine's money was sent out from the office of Samuel Parker. I did learn that it was hand-delivered by Mr Parker, who took the trouble to get a train to Peterborough going all the way up there to hand it over personally."

"Well, that does kind of shine the light of suspicion back on Samuel, or maybe Harriet, unless the money has been banked and would not have shown up in the annual accounts yet. Maybe she is saving it up to buy a bigger house?"

"Well, if that is the case, I am not sure how big a house she is saving up for. The lady added a little extra piece of information like ladies do. Mr Parker must like cats, according to the dear lady in the office; it was his fourth trip up to Peterborough with a cheque."

"Fourth cheque?" Martin repeated. "So, I guess he will make that same trip once Beatrice's affairs have been settled."

"That's what she said. It would seem he is a regular little visitor up to the charity. Do you think he is having an affair with Harriet? Oh no," Susan corrected herself, "Harriet is gay."

"We need to delve into the bank account of the charity to see what has happened to those cheques. If Auntie Maxine gave fifty thousand, Beatrice is going to donate one hundred thousand pounds, plus the other donations we don't know about. I would imagine we are talking a lot of money, but I still cannot see how all this fits into Beatrice being murdered. I'll give Becky a call; she did such a good job last time. I hope she is happy to help us again."

"You have her number?"

"Yes, she gave it to me when we went for a drink the other night, in case I needed to speak to her."

"Just make sure she comes to the office this time when I am around."

For a moment, Martin thought that it was his mother talking to him but ignored the thought and called Becky.

* * *

It was just after five in the evening when Becky arrived, having pushed her way through the tourists and hordes of homeward-bound commuters. Dressed as though she was ready for a long evening on the town, not a short visit to an office, nothing was going to stop her from getting to see Martin on time. In the morning, she was dressed a little drab - for Becky, that is - she was still able to outshine her fellow female colleagues, which was one of the reasons no one really liked her that much. So, when she dashed out during lunch and came back with three large shopping bags of clothes from River Island, everyone assumed that she had a surprise hot date that night. This was confirmed to all those around her when she disappeared into the ladies at three o'clock and was not seen again until after four, obviously dressed to impress some man.

She first hugged and kissed Susan then went on to hug and kiss Martin, who felt as though Susan might have been timing the hug, given the look she was sending his way. Once he managed to lever himself free from Becky, he tried to ignore the gentle caress from her hand on his bottom.

Becky had been like an excited teenager when Martin had called her once again asking for her help in investigating people's accounts; she felt just like a real fraud investigator. She had applied on many occasions to secure a job within the bank doing just that. Most times, she only received a polite yet standard rejection letter. On one occasion, she did get to the interview stage of the recruitment process, only to be greeted with three austere looking women who took one look at the attractive young Becky before making a number of secret signals between themselves, all agreeing that Becky was far too attractive to have in the department, too much of a distraction for the young men there. Again, the letter was a polite rejection with the added phrase of 'following your recent interview.' The turn down did surprise Becky as her friend, Susan, had assured her that the star signs were positive and that Becky would get what she wanted. Susan had a knack for knowing what the stars had in store for you, which Becky liked. She often read her stars in magazines yet never really understood what they meant. To her, it was a lot of mixed-up words, so it was Susan who was able to put it all into context for her. So, the turndown was an even bigger disappointment until now, that is; maybe Susan was just seeing the wrong interview, or the timing was different because, as promised in the stars, she was now an actual fraud investigator. Of course, the bank did not know what she was doing while using their time, plus she was bending the rules somewhat; in fact, if she was caught, she most certainly would lose her job. Not just her either, as Nathan would also lose his job for providing her with some data that she could not access. So, if they were caught, they would be both going down, which Becky thought ironic as that was how she had convinced him to help her in the first place.

She thought it a bit much that Martin insisted that he meet her at the office and not the wine bar they had frequented before; that would have been so much easier for her and better to talk than in a boring office. She guessed correctly in the end that Susan would be there watching every move that she might –

no correct that thought – she was going to make on Martin. Everyone had been telling Susan to make a play for Martin, so what was there to lose? Susan was hesitating; 'those who hesitate, lose,' Becky had said, which she thought was some sort of ancient quote. So, if Susan was not going to make a play for Martin, then she would, maybe even get a job with him and then she could leave the bank once and for all. Martin was a lot better proposition than Nathan.

"Grab a seat Becky and show us what you have." Martin ushered her towards the sofa, which she flopped down on, ensuring her skirt rose a little higher than it should.

"Only if you show me what you have," she responded with a broad grin on her face.

"Becky!" Susan stepped into the conversation, at the same time sitting next to her, ensuring there was no space for Martin to join them, so he moved back and sat on his desk looking at the two young ladies now sitting on his sofa. "Can we save the flirting until later? We are looking for any reason that someone might want to kill Beatrice, so what can you tell us about this Cat Protection Home?"

Becky pulled some papers from her bag. "Alright, hold your hair on; I'm just being friendly. We're all single adults here, and we can all have a bit of fun; no point being moody all the time."

"I'll buy you a drink afterwards as a thank you," Martin smiled.

That invitation did not go down well with Susan, who at once responded, "We are investigating a murder here so we don't have time for social drinks. Becky, what do you have for us?"

"Your hangover still hurting?" Martin asked.

"No," was the curt remark Susan gave. "Becky?"

It was a summons to start talking that Becky accepted, closing down any escalation of harsh words that Susan was thinking about saying.

"First, I want to point out to you both that I have had to do some things which I should not be doing to get this information."

"What like Nathan?" Susan smirked.

"No, breaking the rules of the bank, that is what I mean. These accounts are from other banks, so it has been a little harder to get the information."

"That's what I said, Nathan." This time Susan laughed.

"Shut up," Becky told her with a clear threatening tone.

"Who is this Nathan?" Martin asked, feeling that he was being left out of the conversation.

"No one," Becky answered before Susan had a chance. "I found out that when the cheque that represented the money from Mrs Goldberg's will was cashed, it was drawn on Samuel Parker's client account but made out to PCPH, not the full title of Peterborough Cat Protection Home, which I was expecting. Lucky for me, the amount of £51,267 stood out in his client account. The thing is, the cheque was paid into the account of PCPH and not the actual charity account. By that, I mean the account Harriet pays her cat food bills and her vet bills from, her daily current account type, which is not unusual; we all have savings accounts. The odd thing about the PCPH account is that four days later, once the funds were cleared, there was a withdrawal of £51,267 from the account. The current balance is just five hundred pounds. I then looked at other transactions on the account, there were only a few, and if you include the ones I have just mentioned, there are just four deposits made into the account over the last three years since the account was opened. Each time a cheque was paid in from the Samuel Parker client account, and each time, once the funds had cleared, almost the same amount was withdrawn, just leaving the five hundred pounds in the account, which was the amount used to open it. So, if you include all withdrawals, the total amount is £187,376. I am sure the next question you are going to ask me is who signs the cheques to withdraw the money, simple, the only account holder, Harriet."

There was a silence in the office when Becky finished her report. It was Martin who broke it.

"Harriet stealing from her cats, well; I guess it takes all types. It just complicates things; why did she kill Beatrice?"

"Come on, Martin, I spoke to her. I saw the way she lived. Why would she pull out that much cash and live in squalor with a bunch of smelly cats? I don't suppose she is saving it for her old age as she is already old. There must be another answer to this."

"What do you think, Becky?" Martin asked.

"What's it got to do with her? We're doing the investigating," Susan retorted.

"You're such a jealous bitch at times." There was clearly venom rising in Becky's voice.

"Who're you calling jealous?"

"Girls, Girls, let's just calm down and get to the bottom of what is happening at the cat charity. Becky, I know that you have a knack for looking at people's bank accounts and working out their lives, so I was wondering if you had done the same for Harriet."

A fragile calmness worked its way between Susan and Becky.

"As it happens, Martin, yes, I did look into the financial affairs of Harriet. I try and do my work carefully, and that is one of my best qualities," Becky turned to Susan, "not my breasts," she commented, referring to when Susan had carried out her telephone interview with Martin, which she had then told all her friends about.

Martin looked at them, Becky's breasts, that is, and judged that they were not that bad. However, he decided not to make any smart comment for fear of enraging tempers between the two women.

"Harriet pays her bills and not much else. Rates, electric, gas, water, lots of vets, even more to Pets Are Us, I guess for food and supplies for her cats. There are odd other payments, Sainsbury's, Asda, a Robert Dyas, but not much else. When I tried looking for other accounts, I found nothing in her name. So, unless she has other bank accounts under a different name, if she has taken all this cash out, then she must have a lot of banknotes stashed under her mattress."

Martin slumped back into his chair, causing it to turn. He now faced the window, a good place to seek divine intervention or at least some sort of guidance. He was confused. He was trying to think creatively, something his father had always tried to get him to do, 'think differently and do not accept the obvious, look elsewhere'. He once told his son, who appeared to be showing little interest in anything: 'if you have a question, the answer is there, it has to be, like good and bad, light and dark, yin and yang, the answer will be out there, if not the universe is out of balance, and we are all doomed'. Martin thought his father was a little mad at the time, maybe bordering on the edge of being eccentric, but for all that he had loved his father, it was just that he could never admit it, not even to himself. When his father died, Martin had shed a few tears in private, tears he had regretted, but now all these years later, he wished he had cried more tears. His father was worth more than just those few.

"Maybe it's not her; anyone can open a bank account," Susan argued. She was certain that Harriet would do nothing wrong. She had seen her and the way her cats were her only focus.

"That's not exactly correct, Susan. You have to have proof of who you are, utility bills, passport, proper address. Long gone are the days of just walking into a bank and opening an account; you have to prove who you are. Here, I brought a copy of a specimen signature so you can compare it to the signatures on the cheque. I thought you wouldn't believe me." Becky pushed the papers into Susan's hands.

"Aren't you the little Agatha Christie? You weren't so clever when you got caught shoplifting in Harrods."

"I wasn't shoplifting. I just forgot I was wearing it. Don't listen to her, Martin; she is fast becoming an ex-friend."

Somehow Martin could imagine Becky walking out of a shop, forgetting that she had something she had not paid for, although he did not put her down as a thief, more like plain stupid.

"In my defence Martin," Becky began to explain, "I was trying on these chiffon scarves. I needed a dramatic colour to go with an outfit I was planning to wear for a wedding, my sister-in-law's wedding, she came with me to help choose - well, she wasn't my sister-in-law at the time, she wasn't going to be that until after the marriage obviously - it had to be a strong yet not powerful purple. I was trying lots of them on, throwing them around my neck and looking at myself in the mirror, nothing suited. We searched through loads of them before we walked out, chatting away, wondering if we should go somewhere else - the Brompton Road is full of shops - forgetting that I was still wearing one of them. It was totally the wrong shade, so why would I even consider stealing it?"

"They still stopped you both, a shop-lifting gang!" Susan pointed out.

"They never charged me or Heather." Becky began to raise her voice, moving her face closer to Susan. "They just took my name and address, and I gave it back, so it doesn't fucking count as a crime!"

The door to the office opened. Jenny waltzed in, clutching a brace of shopping bags from her expedition along Oxford Street.

"Thank God you're here Martin, some twat has jumped under the tube, and they have closed the frigging tube station. There are no taxis to be had for love or money, so I thought I would seek refuge in here until the world regains its sanity. Who's the new girl?" Jenny dropped the bags beside Martin's desk, hugged him, sat down in Susan's chair and kicked off her shoes. "Don't stop arguing on my account. I love a good bitching session. Who are we running down?"

"The new girl is Becky," Martin offered. "She's not a new girl, just helping us out with a few things. We were just discussing her criminal activities among the chiffon scarves when you walked in."

"I did not I keep telling both of you, mean to steal anything from Harrods," Becky shouted back, regretting it at once as she was very hopeful that she might end the evening with Martin after everyone else had toddled off home, raising her voice was not going to aid that plan.

"Darling," Jenny spoke to console and quieten Becky, "no one in their right mind would ever dream of stealing from Harrods or shop there for that matter. It's like a friggin tourist trap with prices to match. If you need a decent chiffon scarf, I recommend Peter Jones in Sloane Square, lots of choices there. So Martin, caught the villain yet?"

Martin admitted that they had not as yet. The more they delved into Beatrice's life, the more they uncovered, finding themselves with more questions that seemed to have no clear answers, all the time struggling to understand what they learnt and what it all might mean.

Martin looked at Jenny, the body, the person; he recalled the good times that they had together, times when all she had to do was call, and he would be there by her side like an obedient poodle eager to please his mistress. Little chance of that with private detecting now starting to take up time, a lot more time than he had ever planned when he first started his investigation agency. She had called him yesterday afternoon, pleading with him that they go out for a meal and sneak back to a hotel to spend the night together. Martin had never said no to her before.

That word was not in his vocabulary when talking to Jenny; what she wanted, she got. Last night that all changed; he had to see Freddie, have a meal with him, find out more about Paige. For Martin, time was running out with Beatrice's funeral almost upon him. Yesterday afternoon Martin had a choice, pleasure or work; to Martin's surprise, he chose work. Jenny had not been happy to see Martin being so resolute in sticking to his plan and saying, 'no, not tonight, Jenny'.

He continued to look at Jenny, recalling the triangular-shaped mole that she had at the very base of her spine, a spot which he had kissed on many occasions. Now she sat surrounded by shopping bags containing her latest selection of designer clothes that she might wear over the coming months, or which might just be consigned to the back of her cavernous wardrobe and never see the light of day or ever touch her soft skin. Born into money, married into money, she obtained what she wanted when she wanted, and her husband was too busy making money to worry about what or who she was doing. If Martin ever got married, that would not be the situation he would want to find himself in.

Jenny Shillingford, he wondered what was real in her life, what thoughts and worries might make her lie awake at night; he doubted there would be many, if any at all. Then his thoughts turned to Aurora sitting in her rented bedsit, scared, wondering what might happen to her now; she had not been showered with money or privilege. Of course, Aurora wanted those things; that was natural; we all have dreams. That was the reason she had left her family behind and travelled halfway around the world to make her family's life better. She wanted to earn a few pounds so that she could see her own family back in the Philippines prosper, help build a better life for them. She saved what would have been a large sum of money to pay for her airfare across the world, to enter a new world with so many different values and pressures. She had arrived full of hope and full of trust but ended up in a household that did not understand or want to understand why she had arrived at their door. For them, she was cheap labour, an innocent person, a person they ensured was hidden from employment laws and dignity. All the Master and Mistress of the household wanted from her was her toiling day in and day out for no more than a small bed and a few scraps. A maid who did everything without question, even when the man of the house decided to take her for his own pleasure, she, in her vulnerable position, had no option but to say yes. She found herself caught up in the domestic arguments of the household before being thrown out into the streets without any concern about what might happen to her. They might have social status, a tall house in Chelsea, a small country cottage and be invited to Hurlingham Polo or Henley Regatta, but for all that, they had no humanity. Aurora and all those like her were testimony to that.

Had it not been for Beatrice, he did not want to think about where Aurora would have been now. Dirty and abandoned on the streets of London moving from shop doorway to shop doorway, clutching a plastic bag of treasured possessions and a folded cardboard box that she would sleep on. Beatrice the gambler, the mad old lady, despised by her family for what she had done, who did not take well to the social niceties of her class, took Aurora in without question, gave her money and paid her rent, gave her hope and humanity, a chance to get back to her family, escape those cruel households that have for centuries traded in people.

He recalled when he was just thirteen his father at the breakfast table ready for work in his crisp white shirt and a fine striped tie, the pink broadsheet pages of the Financial Times spread across the breakfast table as always, much to the annoyance of Mother. The headlines were of the collapse of Barings Bank, one of the oldest banks in the world. Martin, the ever romantic, commented in his innocence that it was a shame that such a long history was flushed down the pan by one greedy person. His father looked up from his paper, finished his toast and told Martin it was simple justice, payback time and not a moment overdue. He told Martin how the wealth of Barings had been built up in the 1800s with its vast land deals to ensure the slave trade did not go away and that Napoleon had money to fight his war against the English. Banks profit from the misery of people, as do most of the upper classes.

"Times have changed, Dad; the slave trade was ended years ago."

"Has it? Look at me," he said, now folding up his paper, "I have a big house all paid for with a nice car on the drive, well respected in the community, my son attending boarding school, twice a year we go to Italy for a holiday. How did I get all that? Through the labour of those who work for me, those workers who live in small rented accommodation, I pay them as well as I can, I have to make a profit, yet they still have to think before they go out and buy a Sunday roast, whether they should have sliced ham instead that week so they can buy new clothes for their children. Maybe you could describe me as a slave trader."

Martin thought his father was just being dramatic in painting a picture a young teenage Martin did not care for that much. He was going back to boarding school in three days, and all he wanted to do was see if he could meet up with some girls before his return.

Now, all these years later, Martin could see what his late father was saying. Whatever employment laws arrive, however much we think we live in modern liberated times; people still profit from others less fortunate than themselves; maybe that is just the way of the capitalist world. There will always be those who ignore laws and regard people as mere slaves, slaves to help them build fortunes on the backs of those less fortunate. Modern-day slaves who need someone to take up their cause, someone like Beatrice being charitable, or Susan showing her anger, both caring people, both prepared to take action to protect what they believed in. So, Martin thought, in life, you have to do what's right, just like Aurora, who travelled across the globe for her family whatever the consequences.

"Well, from what Becky is telling us, I think that there is certainly something fishy going on with the solicitor," Susan concluded.

"Yet looking at the signatures, I would say it is Harriet taking the cash out; she's signed for it after all," Becky countered.

"If you'd met her, you'd think differently. You know nothing about this case but for a few bank account statements."

"I know lots; Martin told me about stuff, and accounts don't lie. He told me I had a gift, didn't you, Martin?"

Before Martin could answer, Susan slipped in a barbed comment, "a gift for getting laid then forgetting who laid you."

"What sort of stupid bitchy remark is that coming from someone who pays for a boyfriend's van whilst he is screwing someone else in the back of it?"

They now started to trade insults and accusations like seasoned professionals. All of it appeared to have no real purpose or even malicious intent; they both seemed to enjoy raising their voices at each other, waving their arms around, pointing, yet not quite poking each other, verbal descriptions which were either intellectual or just plain crass. However, both Martin and Jenny were finding it amusing, but Martin knew there was work to be done.

"Girls!" He shouted above their ruckus, silencing them in a moment, which surprised everyone, including Martin, "I have no interest in learning about Becky's habit of losing her top when she has had too many cocktails, and as for you Susan, knowing that you once wet yourself on a flight to Ibiza does little to endear me to you. So, let's get back to a dead little old lady."

"If I could add a little to the debate," Jenny started as she began to stand up. "I suggest that Hayden Investigations apply company policy to this investigation, that policy being we do nothing that remotely resembles work. Hand everything you have to the police, who I might point out have a lot more experience in these matters, let them decide what to do and how to do it. Hayden Investigations can then get back to doing what it does best." She threw her arms around Martin and gave him a long lingering deep-throat kiss, holding nothing back, pushing him back against his desk.

"Oh, don't you so want to be her?" Becky whispered; her lips appeared to be drooling a little.

"Well, if I know Martin, that's the end of the dead old lady case." Susan sounded resigned and stood up, walked over to the kitchen, filled the kettle and plugged it in. "Tea, Becky?" she called out.

Martin managed to break away from the surprise embrace, moved from Jenny and looked across at Susan, who was leaning on the kitchen door frame, smiling smugly.

"Beatrice, despite her bad habits, was a very kind person at heart, of that I'm confident. So, until I am certain there was nothing untoward about her death, I am not going to sit quietly. I'm going to knock on doors and ask questions. Once I'm happy with the answers, then Jenny, I'll be a lot more my old sociable self, but for now, Beatrice is the woman in my life. Susan, you can lock up as I'm off to ask a few more questions. I'll meet you tomorrow morning outside Samuel's office at 10 o'clock sharp. Once we have cleared up our worries, we'll go after the truth. It's time to get the hand in the candle. Good night all."

Without another word, he walked out, leaving three women speechless, which is no mean accomplishment for any man.

* * *

"Playing the role of a detective is likely to suit you: not only can you work out a motive, but you might also find something you weren't supposed to spot. Your financial acumen's likely to be working well too. You might also be ready for a detox health programme and/or to tease little grey cells that haven't worked for some time: which might mean reading a book that's complicated or studying to master a technical language."

Susan stopped reading and looked up with an almost triumphant look in her eyes, as if she had just worked out why the apple fell from the tree and that she was now ready to share her discovery with the world.

"The only downside to your horoscope today is that you might have to dump 'Chicken Licken' from your bedside table and replace it with a more grown-up book."

Martin did not look impressed with his horoscope.

"That sounds a lot like you have made it up on the way here to cover up the fact that you are seven minutes late."

"Honest, look." She offered him the screen of her phone: "daily horoscopes, dot co dot UK, you just sign up, and they send you your horoscope, which appears to be accurate in this case. It is yours, not mine, but as I have said before, I'm doing you a favour preparing you for the day ahead and today looks to be a good one. It even mentions that you are a detective: that must help convince you that there is something in these messages from the stars. So, shall we go in and do some detecting work and find out the motive? It's in the stars, you know. Isn't that a song?"

"It's in the stars, next July we collide with Mars', are the lyrics you are thinking of, and Frank Sinatra and company are still waiting for it to happen. Their stars did not work out for them."

Martin held his arm out, blocking Susan's steps towards the office block door just as if he was a bouncer keeping her out of a seedy nightclub, which is something she had experienced on

271

a number of occasions, normally the excuse was that she was simply too drunk to go in.

Today, however, was different. Martin said he had a plan. He was going to see Samuel alone; there was no need for Susan to be there. Martin was going to ask a number of questions that would help to clarify just who might be responsible for Beatrice's death and also throw some light on the proposed donation to the cat charity. Either way, he did not want Susan next to him, potentially shouting abuse or accusations at Samuel, which would only antagonise him and possibly cause him to say nothing. Susan would arrive later at the office, explain to the receptionist that she was due to see Martin after his meeting but that she was early, so could she wait in the office? They would be too polite to refuse, so she would be able to sit and wait for Martin to finish his meeting with Samuel. Whilst she was waiting, she should try and strike up a conversation with the lady in the office and see what gossip and facts might come up.

Susan was not certain of what she was trying to find out. Did Martin want more information about the charity or about Beatrice? How direct should she be? What if the lady gets suspicious or just pulls the confidentiality card? Susan had a lot of questions, but the only advice Martin gave her was: 'you'll think of something'. With that, he disappeared into the office block, leaving Susan to be engulfed by a group of Japanese tourists.

Samuel Parker was blowing his coffee in an attempt to cool it down. Mrs Faversham always made it with boiling water, totally forgetting that Samuel liked his morning coffee luke-warm so that he could gulp it down quickly while he started his day by reading the contents of his inbox or, to be more accurate, pressing delete for the most part as most messages were either spam or requests for his bank details to be sent to so-called solicitors who reportedly had dubious amounts of money for him to claim from non-existent people and companies in faraway countries. Not many of his elderly clients bothered or even understood emails; they relied on the more traditional methods of writing letters or using the telephone.

Still, that was the way Samuel liked to run his business, slowly, methodically with low overheads to make a sensible profit. His elderly clients conducted their business at a similar pace, so everyone was happy. It was just that Mrs Faversham was not that happy this morning. She knocked on his door and meekly opened it just enough for her to poke her head around it. She knew he did not like his first coffee being interrupted.

"I am terribly sorry to have to disturb you, Mr Parker," even after twenty years of working in the same office, she always referred to him as Mr Parker, "I have a gentleman to see you. He is rather insistent. I have told him that you are busy this morning, yet he still insists on seeing you."

Samuel frowned; that did not sound like any of his ageing clients; most would not venture out of the house until after lunch.

"What's he selling?"

"Nothing, or so he says, Mr Parker. It is the gentlemen who visited you previously with that common young lady with the entirely inappropriate attire." She frowned at the memory.

"Is she with him?"

"No, thankfully."

"Good." Samuel tried to hide the look of disappointment he felt might show on his face. He thought she had been dressed entirely appropriately on the last occasion. He also now knew it was Martin Hayden outside, no doubt wanting more information about Beatrice.

"So, to what do I owe another unexpected visit?" Samuel sarcastically asked as Martin sat down.

"I have a few more questions for you about Beatrice and her affairs."

Samuel sighed, placed his fountain pen carefully on his writing pad and leaned back into his chair, the ageing leather squeaking as he pushed his back into the padding.

"Whatever happened to the carefree Martin avoiding any sort of effort that did not involve women or wine? Have you really grown up over the last few weeks and now think yourself a real detective?"

"I have surprised myself in that I actually like working out problems, not like those crappy word search games or Sudoku. I really have taken to problem-solving, lining up a number of facts to see if they stack up, or at least match, in order to give me a true timeline. It's surprising how often things do not sit easily in lines. For example, the cheques that you hand deliver to the Peterborough Cat Protection Home. When you hand over the cheques to Harriet, does she give you a receipt of some sort?"

"What does that have to do with Beatrice?"

"That was not an answer to my question. Does she give you a receipt?"

Samuel sat forward, resting his elbows on the desk. Martin had a serious tone to his normally casual voice. The solicitor intertwined and arched his bony fingers together, resting his chin on them; he was thinking about the question Martin had put to him. Unexpected questions were something he did not relish hearing, especially from someone to whom you had given a favour by sharing confidential information with him simply because Samuel had always been friends with the Haydens. So, this sounded a little like an interrogation from Martin, not the young boy Martin who naively asked where he could find out who would benefit financially when Beatrice died. Like a generous uncle, he had shared some information. Now he was getting quizzed for his trouble. Samuel did not like that one little bit.

"I am a fastidious, some would say cantankerous, old solicitor. I like everything to be carried out correctly and legally.

Yes, she signs a letter for me, a letter that I have provided to ensure that the audit trail from the client to the charity is consistent and correct; that is my job. I can show you if you like?"

"Money is going missing from the charity. None of the cheques you have given her have ended up in the charity account." Martin hoped he sounded dramatic. He had been practising all night, trying to get the phraseology and the manner just right. His mother thought he had a person in his room, although she had thought it strange that the conversation was so one-sided. Still, she never felt sure of the type of person her son might invite home.

"Harriet would not steal a penny; I'd swear on oath, I have known her for years. What makes you think the money is missing?"

"Well, she certainly does not spend it on keeping the house clean. It must be going somewhere; I know it is not in her bank account. I do know that the cheques go into a bank account and are withdrawn in cash as soon as the cheque clears."

Samuel unlocked his fingers and ran them through his thinning hair.

"Don't tell me that you have been poking around in people's bank accounts. You do know you have, without a doubt, broken more than a few laws that could see you get into a lot of trouble. I think I should remind you, Martin, that your investigation company was set up so that you could avoid any real work and still get your monthly stipend from your father's estate. Doing real detective work, apart from being dangerous, has to be done within the law. I would suggest you step away from this. I'll have a word with some friends and see what I can find out about the money. These are very serious allegations you are making which, if proven, will end up in the hands of the police or at the very least the charity commission."

"You'd help out, dig a little deeper to see where the money has gone?"

"I think, as a legal adviser for your family, it is my duty to help you. The last thing I want to see is you being sent to prison for some foolish error of judgement. If you leave it with me, I have some useful contacts, and I will be able to uncover what is going on and then I can, if it is necessary, go to the police if something has been done illegally. To be honest, Martin, I have known Harriet for many years; she is a batty old lady who sees nothing beyond her cats. It would not surprise me in the least that she has a vast stash of money, good old-fashioned ten-pound notes in her untidy house. Harriet is the sort of person not to trust banks."

"Thanks, Samuel, that is a great relief to me. I was sensing that I was getting in over my head."

Samuel stood up, offered his hand to Martin. "My pleasure; I'll speak to you as soon as I find anything out."

Martin did not take the hint to leave but remained firmly seated, looking up at Samuel's extended arm waiting to be shaken.

"So why do your old ladies always give money to the Peterborough Cat Protection Home?"

Samuel dropped his arm back to his side but remained standing; he looked down at his cluttered desk.

"What do you think? You must know I have known Harriet ever since I dealt with her parent's estate. When they died, I thought she was brave to stay and run a charity all by herself, so when one of my clients comes to me wanting to give money to a charity when they die, why wouldn't I suggest Harriet's charity? I look upon it as helping an old friend. It is common practice for solicitors. Legacies are big business for charities. We are always being encouraged to promote this charity or that charity; I prefer the one I know of and trust."

Martin pulled a folded sheet of paper from his pocket, unfolded it back to its original A4 size and looked at it; his face appeared studious and serious. In fact, it was a list of dates: birthdays of his friends that he picked up as he left home in the morning, a prop for this meeting, but he sure as damn was not going to let Samuel close enough to see what it really was, as he appeared to read from the sheet of paper using the style he had rehearsed last night.

"I see my mother is giving money to the same charity when she dies."

"Don't worry, Martin, there is still plenty left for you to enjoy your life."

"I didn't doubt I would be well provided for when Mother finally crosses over to the other side. In fact, I know because I asked her if I could see her last will and testament, the one you helped her draft and notarise. It took her ages to find it - I have always thought her so well-organised - well, she did find it, and she showed it to me. So, I asked her why she was giving ten per cent of her estate to the Peterborough Cat Protection Home. Do you know what she said, Samuel? She had no idea that she was donating any money to any charity, let alone a charity feeding starving cats; it was a total surprise to her. So how do you explain that, Samuel?"

* * *

During their first meeting, Mrs Faversham had taken an instant dislike to Susan. In Mrs Faversham's slightly conservative and very opinionated estimation, Susan had dressed in such a way that Samuel would not be able to keep his eyes off the young torso that was clearly on display to distract him. So, Mrs Faversham was convinced that Mr Parker would make an error of judgement while his thoughts were firmly lodged in the cleavage of this young hussy. The second visit she made was no less distasteful. She might not have been showing as much flesh, but her youth and reasonably slender figure were not what was needed around Mr Parker. Mrs Faversham liked to think that she was protecting Mr Parker from the temptation that young flesh could offer.

So when Mr Hayden had shown up without his young assistant in tow, Mrs Faversham was quietly pleased and offered the young, attractive Mr Hayden one of her warm she hoped alluring smiles. That smile was wiped off her face very quickly when ten minutes later the hussy arrived, all smiles and apologies. Susan told a very dour looking Mrs Faversham that she was early to meet Mr Hayden and asked if she could wait until he had finished with Mr Parker. Mrs Faversham wanted to say: 'no, go and sit out on the street where you belong'. However, she also knew her duty and, with a begrudging smile, offered Susan a chair alongside the photocopier. Coffee and conversation, she had no intention of offering.

If nothing else, Susan picked up on the frosty reception she had from the old lady, who in Susan's opinion should have retired years ago. While appearing to peruse the Metro, Susan looked out of the corner of her eye, observing Mrs Faversham bang away at her keyboard with amazing speed, her eyes affixed to the computer screen. Clearly, Mrs Faversham was not going to be happy or eager to talk. Susan thought back to the three episodes of the Rockford files on DVD that she had watched last night, hoping to get some sort of inspiration. Not one episode involved a grumpy old secretary, although she had fallen asleep soon after the third episode started, the bottle of chardonnay she had drunk taking effect. So, she fell back on what she hoped would be her failsafe conversation starter. "So, what star sign are you?"

The typing stopped; Mrs Faversham looked across at Susan with an expression very much like a schoolteacher that Susan had once got on the wrong side of. That had ended with two nights of detention for her. She hoped Mrs Faversham was not authorised to issue detention notes. "I don't go a lot on those things." She turned back to her computer screen.

"Come on, they are a little bit of fun and help us ladies get through the day. So, what's your star sign, and I'll read your stars for today? These ones in the London Metro aren't that bad."

"Libra," Mrs Faversham offered reluctantly, without removing her eyes from her typing.

"That makes you an air sign. I like air signs; they are peaceful and loving. Your stars for the day are:

'It is time to make a break for it; with the Moon now in your sign of Libra, there is no better moment to start planning your holiday and search for romance.'

"Well, there you go, best get onto your travel agent and get out onto a sunny beach. Is there a Mr Faversham to take for this romantic break?" Susan asked, recalling something that she had been taught during her many retail assistant jobs that she had passed through, always end with a question to keep the sales patter going. Well, she might not be selling anything to Mrs Faversham; but she did need to keep the conversation going if she was ever going to find out anything that might be of use to Martin

"There is a Mr Faversham; it's just that he does not do foreign holidays."

"Why ever not?"

"He has a fear of flying."

"Well, England is not a bad place to go, lots of nice beaches around. Where do you go, south coast or Norfolk coast?"

Mrs Faversham stopped her typing and once again looked over at Susan. "Our holiday is just two weeks in Yorkshire with his brother. We all go in search of the lost railways of Yorkshire."

"Well, that sounds fun," Susan lied. "Do you like trains?"

"I like walking in the countryside." Mrs Faversham now half-heartedly turned away from her keyboard and faced Susan. "It is more the fact that Mr Faversham runs off ahead with his brother taking pictures of disused railway lines and little bridges under which steam trains once ran, leaving me with my sister-in-law who, before you ask, is not that nice a person at all. She always wears dungarees for some obscure reason. I have never liked her."

"I'm sure someone as strong as you can put up with that for a couple of weeks."

"You don't know Mr Faversham. Apart from two weeks in Yorkshire, there are the weekend trips to boring steam railways across the region, which I try and avoid. If you have seen one, you have seen them all. Then every night, he leaves me to load the dishwasher while he goes off to play with his train set."

Susan detected a hint of frustrated sadness in her voice, a resignation to a tedious life.

"And you with Venus as your ruling planet. I bet Mr Faversham still whisks you away for romantic weekends more often than not. Or maybe you whisk him away?"

"Unless he could stoke me full of coal to build up a full head of steam, he is not interested."

Susan tried to ignore what could have been a wonderful innuendo which she guessed was lost on Mrs Faversham.

"So, what does an attractive woman like you do to fill her time?" Susan was not sure how weird that sounded. If someone had asked that question of her, she would have been a little worried about where the conversation might be going. She hoped that Mrs Faversham did not pick up on the creepiness.

In fact, she took it to be a genuine concern for a fellow woman in a loveless marriage, thirty years of boredom and dreary evenings, a loneliness that she never imagined she would have to endure yet endure she did. For reasons she could not recall, she married Mr Faversham, and she took her marriage vows seriously, well, some of them at least.

"We women have to do what we have to do to make the best of a bad marriage."

"Well," Susan commented, "I could never see you as being in a bad marriage, yet if that's what you're stuck with, I bet you cast a cheeky eye around, to see what else might be on offer, a little romance on the side?" Susan gave one of her cheeky, gossipy smiles. She doubted that Mrs Faversham would do anything more than reading a romantic book with her night-time hot chocolate.

"I might have looked once, but when the man you find, who you think will sweep you off your feet, is as disappointing as the one at home, you kind of give up completely on men."

Now Susan thought that sounded just as weird as her line. So when Mrs Faversham stood up and walked towards her and sat beside her, Susan planned that if this old lady started anything funny, she'd be out of the door in a flash. Even so, she held her nerve and continued with the questions.

"So, you found another man, cheeky old you. Who was he?"

Mrs Faversham looked around the office, maybe checking for hidden microphones, which, if there had been any, she should have been already more than aware of.

"Mr Parker and I had a bit of a thing."

"A thing, you and him?" Susan nodded at Samuel's closed office door, "You are the dark horse."

"Well, we were a little younger then; I had, shall we say, needs. I'm sure you understand."

Susan nodded a little too eagerly and was looking forward to this juicy sounding confession.

"Are you two still, you know, at it?"

"Heavens no. As I said, he was a total disappointment, as I am sure most men are in the end."

"I would have thought he would have been ideal material for a bit on the side. Clearly too old for me, I wouldn't dream, but well, you're both a similar age, so what happened?"

Mrs Faversham, for some reason, wanted to tell this young hussy everything about her affair with Mr Parker. She had never told anyone, not her sister or any of her friends. She knew that if she did, they would have judged her, and there would have been the ever-present danger that they would spill the beans when it suited them. Now, here talking to this young hussy, Mrs Faversham thought she could tell all. This little young girl, who looked as if she had been around the block a few times with men, would not think badly of anyone who might go astray, even her, for having taken just the one lover. This could be her only opportunity to get rid of some of the guilt she often felt and share what had happened with another human being. She had confessed to her cat on several occasions, but he seemed to have little interest.

"I know from other people that office romances never work out. Even so, Mr Parker was a smart, attractive man in his younger days. One thing led to another, and I found myself in his arms. I was pretty excited to find someone who actually looked at me with a look of desire in their eyes. So, he took me out a few times."

"Nice," Susan commented then added, "posh restaurants, nights at the theatre, five-star hotel rooms and a night or two of passion?"

"Mr Parker is not like that." Mrs Faversham tried not to make that sound like a reprimand. "I should have known; well, I did know that he was careful with the business accounts. It turned out he was just as careful with his own money, to the point of being bloody tight. Please excuse my French."

Susan never recalled learning the word 'bloody' in her French class at school, although to be fair to her long-suffering

French teacher, Susan was not always there and dropped the language as soon as she could.

Once Susan had nodded to indicate that the use of such foul language did not bother her, Mrs Faversham continued. "Our romantic evenings, if you could even consider them as romantic, were spent at his Oakwood Golf Club in the bar having drinks listening to his conversation with his golfing partners. It might be considered swish by some; I just thought they were a bunch of rich, old, grumpy men. Then at the end of the evening, into his car for a quick fumble, nothing more I should add, just a lot of groping and ruffling of clothes before he dropped me off close to my home. Each time I thought he would move forward, do a little more, maybe actually take me for a candlelit dinner. That did not happen, although to be fair to him, we did one night have chicken in a basket at the bar, and that was the extent of the romance. It became clear to me I was little more than a trophy to sit beside that he could show off to his friends. He was not interested in being with me, so I ended it. As I said, men to me are a total disappointment."

However Susan tried, the thought of Mrs Faversham, even a younger Mrs Faversham, being a piece of eye candy on anyone's arm was very hard to picture.

"Yet you still work together. I would have thought that would be difficult."

"We never speak of those times; mutually forgotten, you might say. Although I guess he is still out there cheating on his wife."

Susan sat up; this sounded interesting, "What makes you say that?"

"Well, it's only a suspicion; I have no proof. He does always do certain things himself. He is often in Peterborough delivering documents to some charity, not that he needs to, Royal Mail does a very good, tracked service, but he always insists on jumping on the train to Peterborough. I think he has a fancy lady up there."

Susan was having trouble imagining Harriet as anyone's fancy lady,

"That's the cat charity?"

"Yes indeed."

They were interrupted as the door to Samuel's office flew open, and Martin stormed towards them.

* * *

Samuel Parker sat back in his chair. The mature Martin that now sat in front of him clearly had a lot of questions that he wanted to be answered, or the way Samuel was considering it, a number of misunderstandings that needed to be cleared up. Martin was being a little too enthusiastic with his detecting.

"I presume that she just forgot, as you will have seen, the document that lays out her bestowals upon her death is about twenty pages long, as I recall. Your father left a very complex legacy which I have tried to unpick and lay out so that in time it becomes easier. The charity was one of a number of tax breaks that we were trying to put in place. Your mother is getting old; it must have slipped her mind."

"Ten per cent of the residue is still a sizable sum of money; it will work out to several thousand pounds, that's a lot to forget."

"I need to place the charitable gift in a certain band to gain the maximum tax benefit; it is all very legal and normal; hence the figures for all the donations will be around the same. If she is unhappy with the donation, we can change the charity or remove the donation in its entirety; it's her money and her choice, I simply advise."

"Beatrice hated charities, and yet she was convinced by you to leave money to one. How long was her last will and testament?"

Samuel did not answer at once. He looked deep into Martin's eyes and then turned his own to his desk, moved some files as if he was looking for something, or maybe playing for time to think; that was Martin's viewpoint. He found it under a pile of neatly folded Daily Telegraphs dating back over the last month. It was a buff file which he threw onto the front of his desk towards Martin.

"Read it," his voice had a threatening tone, "the whole thing, twenty-five pages or so. Beatrice Cook was married twice; hence it is a little longer than your mother's. It is still a very complex document that is designed to keep as much of the family fortune as possible; well, what she had not gambled away. You'll see the entry in there awarding a chunk of money to the charity. You'll also see Beatrice has signed it and that it has been witnessed just as it should. If you are implying that I misled any of my clients as to the donations that they made to charities, then I suggest you get out of my office at once and find yourself another solicitor because if you continue acting out like some TV detective, I will see you in a courtroom, suing you for making such allegations against my professional reputation."

Martin stayed calm as he listened to Samuel's ever-increasing pitch and watched his face become flushed.

"I'm looking for answers, that is all, simple explanations. It's you that seems to be making things complicated."

"That is exactly why rich people like your mother come to professionals like me, to make sure they tread the correct and very fine line between tax evasion and tax avoidance. In the end, all they are doing is trying to preserve their hard-earned money. The Inland Revenue make the rules deliberately very complex, which results in large wordy documents that generally elderly people do not fully understand or even read, for that matter. The jargon is long, monotonous, yet fully legal. All they are interested in is the bottom line: 'when I die, how much money will the taxman cream off?' The smaller that final figure is, the happier they are when they meet their maker. That is exactly why you should let me see where the money is going. I guess there will be a complex trail to follow to find the money."

Samuel paused, then continued, "A minute ago, it was under Harriet's bed, but now you think it could be some sort of fraud. Where is it now? In a Swiss banking account? And you want to investigate it, but you're no financial expert. Unless you already know where the money is ending up, I doubt much will change.

"If you're accusing me of defrauding my clients, I think you had better consider just what you are saying and the consequences of what you're saying. I have done nothing wrong, I assure you. Our conversation ends here, Martin. Get out now and forget coming back to ask me anything else about Beatrice. I trusted you with confidential information; I can now see that was a serious mistake. If you think I am some sort of master criminal, then you had better find yourself a good defence lawyer because I will see you in court."

This time Martin did stand up, folded his birthday list and replaced it in his pocket.

"Just one more question: why did Beatrice want to change her will?"

"Get out now, Martin, before I call the police and tell them you have been dipping your nose into people's bank accounts. I'm sure they would be very interested to hear about your illegal activities."

Martin walked out firmly, closing the door behind him, knowing that he had clearly touched a nerve. Susan was right; everything seemed to lead back to Samuel, Beatrice, the missing cash, the deals with estate agents and artists, even Martin's mother. Everything they had come into contact with had a connection back to Samuel as if he was sitting at the centre of a complex spider's web. Was he the spider waiting there, waiting to trap an unsuspecting victim or was he a victim trapped at the centre waiting to be devoured? Martin hoped that Susan had found out something of value because, as of this moment, all they had were still odd scraps of information. Nothing shone a spotlight on who else the spider at the centre of the web might be.

CHAPTER NINE

"You've got to be kidding me, Martin; it's only just before eleven."

"I thought you could drink alcohol at any time of the day or night?" Martin stated what he knew to be a known fact as he handed Susan a large glass of chilled white wine.

Susan could have rightly argued with Martin that the only time she considered each of the twenty-four hours of the day to be a happy hour was if she was abroad on holiday in her bikini. However, even she knew that there had been exceptions to that rule. Notably when as an impressionable teenager, she had arrived at her place of work with her auntie one very cold and damp November morning, only to discover a padlocked door with an official-looking notice that explained in words of more than four syllables that Zinger Stationery had gone bust. They both sat dejected on the cold concrete steps that led up to the double-glazed locked doors of their now ex workplace wondering what to do next. Susan's auntie, who Susan always thought was both prim and proper, took out a hip flask from her handbag, opened it and took a swig of the liquid that was in it before offering the silver hip flask to Susan, who without hesitation took a large gulp expecting coffee. Just why she was expecting coffee, she had never fully worked out. The malt whiskey, apart from burning her throat, warmed her insides and made her cough loudly. So, sitting here with Martin in a five-star hotel just off Trafalgar Square, sipping chilled white wine from a glass Susan thought was far better than street drinking from a hip flask at eight-thirty in the morning.

As Martin sat beside her, explaining his surprise that even within his own mother's bequests, there was a clause giving money to the Peterborough cats, a clause that his mother did not appear to know anything about. As for Samuel's explanation, Martin did not think that his mother was the sort of person, whatever her age, that would forget handing over a substantial amount of money to cats which were not her favourite pet by a long way. The more Martin thought about it, the more he considered Samuel's reaction of a sudden offer of looking into it himself as odd. Martin was beginning to see with a lot more clarity, and now he was sure of one thing: Samuel was playing a long confidence trick, slipping an innocuous clause into the final request of those elderly women. He liked to boast about being there for them, helping them through the complex legalities of holding onto their fortune. But Samuel also knew that few of his elderly clients would bother to spend the time reading a document full of legal jargon, which to most people was a totally different language spoken by just a few. Samuel would also know his customers well enough that should any potential victim have a legal background or be married to someone in the legal profession, the Cat Protection clause would not be applied to their will. In the worst-case scenario, he could always blame it on a simple clerical error by Mrs Faversham, and she would take the blame. All Samuel needed to do was sit back and wait for his clients to die, and the clause would be accepted by the grieving relatives as a request held close to the heart of their dear departed.

"I always thought he had shifty eyes," Susan concluded as she listened to Martin explaining his theory. "Plus, Mrs Faversham told me he was a skinflint."

Martin continued explaining his ideas to Susan. They both knew that Beatrice was planning to change her will to include her real daughter, Florence. After the French trip, Beatrice might have shuffled through her papers and even read through her own last will and testament, maybe to remind herself who was getting what in order to treat her daughter and stepdaughter fairly. It was then that she might have noticed that when she died, a chunk of her money would be going to the Peterborough Cat Protection Home, which, no doubt, would have been a complete surprise to her. Martin then thought that she would have phoned Samuel to arrange a meeting in order to change her will, arranging it to be at her house on that fateful Wednesday. Beatrice, not being the one to hold back, could well have told him then that she wanted the clause taken out of her will, having never asked for it in the first place.

"And he'd kill her and not blame it on a typing error or Mrs Faversham getting confused with her copy and paste?" Susan questioned. "Think about it, Martin; he'd no reason to kill the old girl."

"People do strange things where money is concerned."

"Like not work!" Susan answered sarcastically before moving on to her own theory. "I still think Paige is the killer. If she heard that her stepmother was going to change her will, reduce it even further, then as your friend Freddie told us, Paige is more than capable of doing strange and terrible things. She has a much clearer motive."

"Maybe it is now the right time to speak to the police, the professionals, let them deal with it. They can dig a lot deeper than we ever can, plus they know what they are doing."

Martin was not admitting defeat; he was just being a realist. More importantly, he wanted to do his best for Beatrice, and if that meant handing everything over to the police, then that was going to be his plan of action.

Susan turned to him, putting her empty glass down. "I know a copper who works out of the Elephant and Castle station. We could pop along there on the tube; ask him for his help. I'm sure he would be happy to. Come on, Martin, let's get cracking."

Martin followed Susan out and onto the tube; he had heard of the Elephant and Castle, he just was not sure that he had ever been there.

* * *

Abigail Eastwood had always wanted to be a police officer. As a young teenager, she continuously prepared to become an upholder of the law, carry the Queen's Warrant. She read crime books, rooted her way through law books and kept up to date with policing trends, right up until the very day when she was old enough to collect the application forms from her local police station. Diligently she filled them out. That was back in the days when she would have been called a Woman Police Officer. She would have worn a skirt and a flat hat and would have had men drooling at her feet. Not that that was the sole purpose of joining the force, although she did privately admit it was a useful side benefit.

Now in her sixties, Abigail was working in a police station at the front desk. She had never worn the uniform she had craved. When she had been an aspiring WPC, her knees were judged to be too close together. She was knock-kneed, a consequence of the rickets she had suffered as a young girl. Back then, the standards the police required for their recruits was high, very high, not like today, Abigail thought when they took just about anyone they could get. The knock-kneed wannabe Woman Police Officer Abigail in the end, spent the whole of her working life as a local government officer, looking after streetlights and street signs, with the occasional foray into drain covers. It was a boring thirty-five years until she was made redundant. On a whim, she then applied to be a civilian receptionist at a police station. Now, at last, she stood proudly behind the front counter of the Elephant and Castle Police Station, where her knock-knees could not be seen.

She looked up and saw Martin and Susan approaching the front desk; it was going to be trouble. Abigail knew that everyone who came through the door and stood in front of her well-polished front desk was trouble. They would be griping about some noisy neighbour, reporting a burglary or theft from their car, a stolen bike – that was pretty common –, a lost purse, even two teenage boys looking shifty in the shopping centre. At least when she was a street furniture supervisor with the local council, no members of the public had approached her.

Susan spoke politely with a smile, "Good afternoon."

"Yes," was the curt remark. Thirty years of working alongside keep left signs had done nothing to improve her public relations skills.

"Is P.C. Tom Ellis available? I'm a friend of his," Susan continued.

Abigail looked up, studied Susan and dismissed her, and then examined Martin, and he too was dismissed; clearly, both were trouble, Abigail thought.

"We don't give out information about officers here; if he is really a friend, then you'll have a number for him. I suggest you contact him that way."

"Well, I knew him a while back," Susan confessed, "so I don't have a number. I just hoped he'd be around; I have a problem that he might be able to help me with."

Abigail nodded in a knowing sort of way, as ever they have a problem just as she had guessed. One day someone might actually come in and tell her what a great job the police are doing in the area.

"As I said, we do not give out details of our officers. If you want to report a crime, then you have to speak to me in the first instance. I will then pass your report on to a Police Officer who will consider what action will be taken."

"We want to report a suspected murder." This time Martin took up the explanation.

Abigail pulled a large form from beside her and began to write, "Name?"

"Beatrice Cook," Martin offered.

Abigail looked up. "Not your friend's name, your name."

"My name?" Martin confirmed.

"Yes, yours."

"Martin Hayden."

Abigail looked up at Susan. "So, you must be Beatrice Cook?"

"No, Beatrice is dead. She's the one we think has been murdered."

"Well, I suppose if she is dead, murder is a possibility. Even so, first, I need your name, young lady."

Together Susan and Martin confirmed their names, their addresses and their dates of birth. Their occupation raised an eyebrow from Abigail as they both stated Private Investigator, but she did not comment. There appeared to be the same lack of interest as they explained their suspicions which might have led to the murder of Beatrice. They also included the money which appeared to be going missing from the charity and how everything always came back to Samuel Parker. None of this appeared to impress Abigail. When you have done more than thirty years in a Street Furniture department, nothing shocks you, or perhaps it was just that Abigail was a hard person to impress.

"I'll pass it on to our sergeant, who will decide what action needs to be taken."

"Shall we wait?" Susan innocently asked, recalling the way things worked with Jim Rockford.

"That's up to you, but I doubt if anyone will want to speak to you until tomorrow at the earliest. We have your mobile number."

"But the funeral's tomorrow," Martin added a bit too aggressively to enamour himself to Abigail. Although, to be fair, even Mr Eastwood, Abigail's long-suffering husband, could not endear himself to her.

"As I said, the sergeant will call you. I have all I need from you," which was a polite way of Abigail saying you are both dismissed.

"If she was poisoned, the evidence will be destroyed when she is cremated. They need to stop or delay the funeral."

"I am sure our real detectives will be aware of such a fact. You have carried out your duty. Leave the rest to us. Now it is time for you both to go so I can get on with moving your report through the system."

This was a less polite way of telling Susan and Martin that Abigail no longer wanted to see them beside her shiny front desk. This time they took the hint and left.

"What a miserable old cow she was. Maybe we should just call 999 and be done with it," Martin said, his head hanging down, his hands buried in his pockets.

"Let's go and get something to eat and think about what we can do. They might well call us later. I'm sure the words 'possible murder' should gee someone up, if not 'Mrs Jobsworthy' on the desk, then one of the coppers who see the report. Have you ever had Pie n' Mash? What am I saying; of course you haven't. Follow me, Martin; I'm going to treat you to the gastronomic delight that is Pie and Mash."

They walked into Goddard's Pie and Mash shop. Martin thought that the tiled walls, floors, and marble tables gave the impression that he had walked into a very large shower room that served food. Everything was simple and plain, even the black and white menu painted on the wall: One Pie, One mash with Liquor or One Pie, Two Mash with Liquor. Martin continued to read the menu, which was any combination of pie, mash and liquor that took your fancy. The only other option was jellied eels which Martin was sure no one had actually eaten since Queen Victoria was on the throne unless they were in the cast of Oliver.

Leaving Susan to do the ordering – she insisted it was her treat – he sat disappointed on the hard, wooden bench, pondering where all the good restaurants had gone. When Susan finally placed his plate in front of him, his disappointment grew. Martin looked down at the well-used cracked plate and the so-called food that was on it. The pie was pie-like, just hardly cooked, or so it appeared, just a light browning around the edges and the centre still pale. Then there was the mash; yes, it was certainly some form of mashed potato. He had seen that before and had eaten it; he just was not sure about the green liquid that the two mashed potato scoops appeared to be floating in. Susan informed him it was called liquor. Now for Martin, the term liquor referred to such things as whisky, gin, vodka, indeed any sort of alcoholic spirit; it did not, anywhere in his book, include a thick green liquid. Following Susan's native advice, he sprinkled a vast amount of salt over the plate, probably enough to give him instant hypertension, if it was not for the equally liberal amount of vinegar that he was instructed to sprinkle over everything. Neither salt nor vinegar seemed to do anything to change the evil look the green liquor appeared to be giving him, teasing and daring him to scoop up a spoonful and consume.

"Are you sure this stuff is edible?" he finally asked of Susan, who had already started to devour the mash, pie and green stuff with a vigour for eating he had rarely seen before. Maybe there was alcohol in the green stuff; after all, that would explain Susan's enthusiasm.

"Best pie 'n' mash around. You are either a Goddard's person or a Manze's person, me Goddard's every time."

"You're speaking another language to me, Susan. Can I eat this stuff?"

"That is the general idea. Try it; you'll love it."

Martin was not fully convinced; he cut open the pie only to see some sort of pale mince that did nothing to alleviate his fear of what might happen to him if he ate it.

"Just eat it, you wimp," Susan instructed, "you ate Indian food after insulting the waiter, so it is not going to be any worse than that."

With mash, liquor and pie on his fork, he tried it, moved it around his mouth and nodded with a smile. "Well, not as bad as it looks."

He then, to Susan's delight, started to eat with slightly more enthusiasm. In fact, Martin had warmed to this south London dish, pleasant, quick and very cheap. He was thinking it could be just the place to put Jenny on the spot and see how she liked real ethnic food.

"So, are you actually ruled by your mother even though you are thirty-five?"

"Almost thirty-five, and no, I am not ruled by my mother. My problem is that more often than not, Mother is right, which is really annoying and, in time, wears you down. I suppose you are referring to Paula. Yes, I loved her, but somehow Mother knew she was not a good choice, and she was right. The advert for your job, that was on Mother's insistence, and I think that has worked out well, better than me just sitting alone in the office. Advert for clients, Mother again. Frustrating as it is, I am finding going around asking questions fun, even though it is nothing like Jim Rockford."

"How would you know? You've never seen the programme."

"I thought it best to catch a few on 'You Tube' to see what you were talking about."

Susan smiled, "Maybe it's just that the women in your life are always right. You seem to be enjoying the Pie and Mash?"

"More than I expected, but I still think you are totally wrong about Paige."

As they were coming to the end of their meal with Martin carefully scooping up the final dregs of his green liquor with his spoon, now not wanting to waste a drop, a familiar voice echoed around the tiled pie and mash shop.

"Suzie Baby, look at you slumming it with us common people. You'll be hanging around the laundrette next. Can I join you two lovebirds?"

Without waiting for a reply, Colin, with his plate of two pies and three mash all floating on what appeared to be a double helping of liquor, sat down beside Martin.

As ever, the other customers comprising mainly of workmen, as well as three old ladies and just one man smartly dressed in a double-breasted suit, turned to look at Colin as he had walked through the door, and their eyes all discreetly followed him until he sat down. Even though it was not that warm outside today, Colin wore a lightweight, blue military blouse with a patterned skirt that matched his top and ended just below his knees. Plain black court shoes finished off his attire. As ever his face was made-up, the lipstick not as bright as Susan had seen before, yet more than bright enough for eating in a pie and mash shop.

"So, how are the inquiries going, Martin, found the culprit yet?"

Martin wondered if Colin actually recalled the last time they had met face to face and the strong words that they had had between them. At this moment in time, it appeared to Martin that Colin had forgotten all about it.

Colin had not forgotten; it was just that he never liked to hold a grudge; life was just too short to be spent keeping resentments. You could disagree with someone, upset them, or just totally piss them off, but there were very few, if any, occasions that Colin felt he wanted to hold a grudge. Colin liked to think of himself as a forgiving sort of person, which he had to be dressing the way he liked to dress. He could see just why

Martin had lost his rag in the office when he learned that technically they had broken into Beatrice's flat, but from Colin's point of view, breaking in was justified as they suspected that Beatrice had been murdered.

It was Susan who took up the conversation and began to explain what they had found out since Colin was last involved. Susan gave him a resume on how the investigation had become more complex with the discovery of a number of old ladies, all of whom had the same solicitor, giving money to the same charity. Susan also added that she never did like Samuel the solicitor with his lecherous eyes and that his astral stars were not that encouraging either. She concluded with how they were now waiting to hear from the police.

"Well, he might have a motive for killing Beatrice but," Colin determined, his clean plate in front of him, his knife, fork and spoon neatly placed on it, "unless she knew that he was doing it to all the old ladies, slipping in a little clause without them knowing, I can't see why he would want to send her off to her maker. Maybe as you say, the old girl was going to change her will, but then he loses one here and there, plus there are plenty more old ladies around to dupe. The daughter, Paige, now still has good reason, her step mum is about to change her will, and she stands to lose out. Maybe you're looking at two villains, one crime covering another crime."

"Are you Gay?" Martin asked the question that he had wanted to ask for a while now.

"That's a bit off-topic." Colin turned to Martin. "Still a valid question. Here I am, sitting close to you in a pie and mash shop. I bet you feel uncomfortable on a number of levels: common people, common food and a cross-dresser next to you. I can see that Suzie Baby has led you very much astray, still all good experience. And to answer your question, no, I'm not gay. Although you're not the first person to ask, and I doubt you'll be the last."

"I thought you were gay," Susan added. "We met in a gay club."

"Correct, young lady, so are you a Muff Muncher?"

"A what?" Martin asked.

"Christ, Martin, if you're going to hang around the seedy areas of south London, you need to learn the lingo, 'muff', ladies genitals as you might say, 'muncher' as in eating, Muff Muncher, a lesbian OK?" Martin nodded; today, he was learning the lingo of south London. "So, Suzie Baby, I know you're not gay, but you were there in a gay club. So why does my being there make me gay? Do I guess my attire might lead you along that train of thought?"

"To be fair, Colin, yes it does." Susan was happy to admit it.

"Well, I'm not gay, and I have two grown boys. I say boys; one is thirty and the other thirty-three, so maybe young men would be a better description of what were my two little babies. I also had a beautiful wife, although I should say, ex-wife. We did divorce about ten years ago, about the time I started sharing her clothes. I think in the end, she just got jealous that I had a better wardrobe than her, which of course, I did." Colin brushed some pie crust crumbs onto his plate and then leaned into Martin. "I am totally incorrigible, never 'gonna' change, unless of course, the Government decides that cross-dressing is bad for your health, which I imagine they will get around to eventually."

Colin gathered the three empty plates together as if he was about to take them away and do the washing up. Colin liked things to be tidy; if he had had a cloth handy, he would have wiped the marble table, cleaning off the odd drops of liquor and pie crumbs.

"So, Martin, I know you don't like me interfering, so I'll direct my thoughts to Suzie Baby. Tell her that the police will get around to looking at your allegations in the fullness of time, which works against proving who takes the money out of the bank account. I doubt there will be any CCTV at the banking desks older than a couple of weeks; they wipe the damn things all the time. There is not a lot that the two of you can do; you have done as much as you can without breaking the law, which I know Martin hates doing."

"So, you've run out of ideas as well?" Martin asked, still wondering at the back of his mind just why a grown married man would decide that wearing women's clothes is a good idea, but still hesitating to ask that question.

"I don't think there is a lot of hope, what with the funeral being tomorrow and the solicitor clearly covering his tracks well. Face it, sometimes you just have to accept defeat and move on, get on with your life and don't let the past taint your future. Hark at me all philosophical. I do have a friend in the charity sector, dresses in a suit and tie yet is as queer as a nine bob note, which proves you can't judge a man by his clothes. I'll see if he has any ideas. If not, I'll ask around. I'll let you know if I find anything."

CHAPTER TEN

Martin liked funerals even though he knew it was something you should never admit to. He suspected that he was not the only one who secretly enjoyed them, although not much fun for you if it's your funeral, that goes without saying. In the same way, it was obvious that if the person in the box was a close relation, then it would be a very sad day for you. It was when you represented the outer circle of friends and distant acquaintances that you sensed the feeling of suppressed enjoyment was there simmering under the polite surface. The men dressed sombrely in well-designed dark suits and dark ties. Women dressed smartly in jackets and skirts, with some even wearing hats. People enjoyed dressing up.

Then there were the flowers that people bought, small sprays, big wreaths, floral letters that spelt out words, Mum, Nan, Bye. Martin thought that it would have been really ostentatious to have a long word spelt out in flowers.

Kensington Crematorium was a small island of greenery in the hubbub of west London. At the epicentre of this green space was the crematorium, dull, square and very disappointing if you were expecting a grand send-off; maybe that was why the deceased needed to be in a box to avoid any disappointment.

Martin stood alongside Susan in the chilly air that hung around the melancholic building. They had joined a number of mourners awaiting the arrival of Beatrice in her hearse. Some stood in silence; some greeted others smiling politely, not a place for a laugh and joke. Just in front of them, Susan noticed the small frame of Samuel Parker with his back to them.

301

"Do you always come to the funeral of your clients, or are you just making sure they are safely dead and buried?" Susan spoke to the back of Samuel's head as he had leaned forward to read the wording on the list of funerals being held there that day. Her voice made him jump very slightly, Susan could tell, yet as he straightened up to his full height, which was not that tall, he had gained his composure and replied without hesitation.

"The same could be said of you, or are you just looking for business?"

"We are just paying our respects to a lady who died without good reason," Susan responded.

"I told Martin that you should not make accusations unless you have something to back them up; it could get you both into a lot of trouble. The death certificate said natural causes, and it would take a lot to change that now that she is in the process of becoming ashes."

Susan wanted just to hit him, a straightforward punch in the face; simple and effective, but maybe not the best course of action at a funeral.

"Maybe we cannot prove anything, but we do not give up."

"Susan, my dear," Samuel looked into Susan's eyes, ignoring Martin completely. "Can I say how attractive you are when you are angry. Sometimes I wish I was a few years younger, and then I would certainly invite you out for a romantic meal. However, I am a little too old for that sort of thing, and I imagine you would not be inclined to accept such an invitation from me. Oh, and for the record, there is really nothing to prove. You are just misguided young people caught up in the excitement of playing detectives, as that is what Martin does best, play at being an adult. Even with your maturing influence, Martin does not worry too much about other people."

A familiar voice interrupted their conversation.

"Suzie Baby, you look so drop-dead glorious in that black outfit. All I had to wear was this boring grey business suit, although tell me you like the slit on the side of the skirt and please tell me it is not too much for a funeral." Colin arched his leg a little to accentuate the split. He had decided against black tights, thinking it would not go well with the grey of the skirt, so he decided to stick with taupe and just plain black court shoes, always his preferred footwear.

"It looks fine to me," Susan commented with a hint of admiration in her voice.

"I was in two minds to come along, fearing I might upset some of the old dears in there, but I thought, sod it, the old girl sounded a really good laugh, and I bet she'd revel in the fact that an old 'tranny' like myself turned up to see her off. So, who's this chap you are chatting up, Suzie Baby?"

"Not chatting up, just sharing some of my thoughts with him. This is Samuel Parker, the solicitor we have spoken about before."

Colin offered his hand towards a very surprised looking Samuel.

"Pleased to meet you, Mr Parker, or can I call you Sammy. I think Sammy suits you a lot. I'm Colin."

"Is that Colin or Coleen?"

"Sarcastic little solicitor, aren't we? I prefer Colin."

"Then I prefer Mr Parker if you don't mind."

"Suzie Baby was right; you are a bit of an arsehole."

"I think I have had enough of this pathetic conversation." With that, Samuel walked away towards a short old lady in a wide-brimmed hat who was dabbing her eyes with a small tissue.

"He is a bundle of fun."

"So, what are you doing here?" Martin asked.

Colin smiled, "I do love a funeral. I bet they will say a load of crap in there about the one stuck in the coffin who can't stick up for herself. Funerals can be so cruel." He continued with,

"Well, I can't comment on his star sign as I'm no expert, but his eyes are clearly not trustworthy."

"So now you've seen him, shall we just kill him?" Susan whispered, ensuring that Martin could hear her flippant comment.

"Well, I suppose if you are going to kill someone, then here is a good place to do it. Just a short drag of the body to the oven out the back there, neat and tidy," was Colin's contribution to Susan's conspiracy.

"That sounds like a lame reason to attend a funeral for someone you have never met," Martin offered, as he noticed more and more pairs of eyes looking towards the three of them.

"Come on, Martin, loosen up. Susan never met her either, and I feel that I am almost part of your team now that we have shared a meal of Pie and Mash like true brothers and sisters. Plus, I know how disappointed you must feel not having found the culprit. We can't always win these things, so I thought I'd come along and give you some moral support, even give you a hug, but somehow I don't think that would help you much."

Even though Martin could not deny enjoying funerals, Colin was right; he was disappointed. This funeral was different; it represented a failure to help Beatrice, maybe she would not have been disappointed, but he felt disappointed in himself.

Martin had always been a disappointment to others. That was just how his father had described him when it was clear that Martin had no intention of taking over the family business. And that was the reason that Martin never tried anything too hard, or for that matter, involved himself in other people's lives; it always ended in disenchantment.

He never really wanted to embroil himself with Beatrice, her life or her death, somehow Susan had persuaded him, and she had shown faith that he could succeed. He looked at her standing beside him, God she looked sexy, he thought, but then recalled that he should not be having those thoughts in this place. He turned back to his depressed side; maybe she was thinking how much of a failure he was; Colin had already expressed that thought, so he could not blame Susan for thinking the same. Maybe their working life would return to the simple timetable of coffee, chats and lunch; no more investigations, no more working, no more involving himself in the life of anyone else. It was futile; Martin was born for a simple life, nothing complex, no challenges. Maybe that was how things were planned for him, just floating through life, taking him where the tidal currents took him. People like Aurora had a different plan; they fought against the tide, had the strength to oppose the sometimes overwhelming waves that threatened to engulf them. He wanted to try and help Aurora, try to find a home here for her or ensure that she could afford to return to the Philippines. The latter outcome attracted him much more; giving money away was easy, he could do that. Fighting for her to stay in England would, he was sure, end in disappointment.

"Martin, it's my job to look morose, not yours, lighten up a bit." Florence stroked his arm the way that a mother would reassure her child. She looked at Colin, who was the primary reason that she had approached the trio in the first place, wanting to know how the man dressed as a woman was related to Beatrice. "I'm afraid I don't know you." She let go of Martin and offered her hand to Colin. "I'm Florence, Beatrice's daughter."

Colin shook her hand softly; it had taken him a number of years to refrain from his normal vice-like handshake.

"I'm Colin, a friend of Susan's. I'm here to support my grieving friend. But if you're the daughter, then how come you're not riding in the big black 'limo' that should be here soon?"

"Long story but abbreviates down to a family rift."

"Well, it's good that you have come anyway; there should be no hard feelings in death."

Florence smiled at him. "Oh, I still dislike my mother. Dead or alive, she never seemed to keep a promise and only seemed to think of herself. I had very little contact with her, which suited me, and I think, suited her. Did Martin tell you the last time I saw her, we kind of made-up, or at least papered over our differences? She even promised that she would change her will to include me, which never happened, so in the end, she did not change much."

Florence turned again to Martin. "I know I sound bitchy and unforgiving, but then parents do not always include you in the full truth. As you know, my father left my mother once her gambling became a problem, he never spoke well of her after that, and I had to listen day in and day out to him, putting my mother down. What I never learnt until many years after he died was that Beatrice only started gambling when my father had an affair with a woman at his company. It devastated her, something I never knew, and she never told me. I couldn't bring myself to mention it when we last spoke as the hate over all those years would not go away; plus, I think maybe she did not need reminding of it. Yet all this has spurred me into going up to Peterborough next week and seeing Harriet. The differences in our lives should not keep us apart."

* * *

Martin and Susan took their places towards the back of the high-ceilinged faux church.

"I know this is a funeral," Susan whispered, "but you look really miserable. I do hope you're not going to start bawling your eyes out."

"If I do, just hand me a wad of tissues before you deny knowing me."

"Oh, I will; there's nothing worse than seeing a man act like a little girl. I see that he has a front-row seat," Susan nodded towards the front pew. Alongside Paige and her husband, there Samuel Parker sat, examining the order of service they had all been given when they walked in.

"I guess he wants to ensure everything goes according to plan, and he gets his next cash injection. Look at him sitting there as if he was one of the family." Martin's voice had a tone of defeat in it that stirred Susan. She had seen the days before when Martin seemed to just want to give up, and she did not like seeing him like that.

"We must have missed something along the way, a misjudgement or something that we overlooked."

"This is real life, not a TV detective series," Martin added, opening his own order of service while some insipid music played and the last of the mourners settled down. Then there was a moment of silence as the canned music stopped, and next, the organ started playing some hymn that Martin did not recognise. The music heralded the entrance of Beatrice's coffin, being carried down the aisle towards the altar.

"Even so," Susan continued, her eyes burning towards Samuel as if she was trying to bore into his mind, "he is ripping off old ladies, creaming off part of their wealth, on the face of it to give money to a charity which he somehow transfers into one of his deep and rich pockets. What I don't understand is that he does not show any outward signs of being rich or flashing any cash around. Mrs Faversham said he was mean, just like Scrooge, so why defraud old ladies? Then why decide that Beatrice had to die? Did he think she was going to expose him, ruin his reputation? If that had happened, he would never be able to practice again."

"All I know is that once Beatrice's coffin slips behind that purple curtain and is committed to the oven, any hope of proving he killed her will have gone up in smoke. We will have let her down; she will remain just another old lady who died of heart failure."

"Maybe Colin is right; maybe we are looking at this the wrong way around."

"How do you mean?"

"Beatrice would have needed to prove that he was ending up with the cash from the charity. The fact that he slipped the charity clause into her will was not going to harm him too much; after all, as he said to you, the old lady got confused and forgot about the donation to the rich cats of Peterborough. And we know how hard it is to untangle the bank accounts of anyone, so why would Beatrice even consider it? But if Beatrice was going to change her will, Paige would lose out a lot; she would have the motive to make sure that her stepmother died before she changed her will. So, what if Paige, who likes to be attractive to men, was having an affair with Samuel? Once he heard that Beatrice was changing her will, he would have told her and together, not separately, they decided that Beatrice had to die."

"Now that does sound like a TV story. Paige likes young men."

"From what I've heard, rich old men trump young, poor men."

The hymn music stopped, and from the front, a deep voice began to speak. "We are gathered here today to celebrate the life of Beatrice Cook."

"Think about it, Martin," Susan whispered, "with Samuel defrauding the money, we both agree that if any of his victims found out about it, he could easily put it down to a clerical error. Why take the risk of killing someone when there is no need to? But if she had told him that she wanted to see him about changing her will, then maybe she had also told him that she was going to split Paige's share between the two daughters so that he would have the papers ready for her to sign on Wednesday. If Paige was, say, very friendly with Samuel – after all, since when does the family solicitor get to sit at the front – he would have told her that she was about to lose maybe a hundred thousand or so, more than enough motive to kill for."

"That still does not sound sufficient of a motive. A hundred thousand pounds to Paige, okay, she would not be happy, but I can't see her killing for what, to her, is not a lot of money."

Colin had been listening attentively to their conversation; sitting next to Martin, he had little choice but to hear it and now wanted to join in. Speaking in a hushed tone, he leaned in towards Martin, pleased that they were towards the back and that their conversation was not disturbing the other mourners.

"I do agree with Martin on this one, but which will are we talking about?"

"Beatrice's," Martin snapped back at him.

"I know that just which one of her last will and testaments are we talking about?"

"She only has one," Susan replied. She had leaned in closer to Martin, who now had two heads almost in his lap.

"No, dear, she had two. The one that sorts out her liquid assets and other odds and ends, the one where she pays back the estate agents and anyone else she owes money to. Maybe there would be a few thousand or so leftover for Paige, but I'm talking about her property will, the bricks and mortar of where she lived."

"What are you talking about?" Martin asked this time, in an attempt to get both Susan and Colin out of his personal space, but not succeeding.

"It's complex and very legal, and I'd rather not discuss it facing Martin's crotch. It can wait till afterwards."

"Colin, tell us more," Susan pleaded.

"Patience, Suzie Baby, after the service."

Colin and Susan resumed their correct sitting positions, much to the relief of Martin, who wondered what exactly Colin had been talking about: two wills?

Martin listened to the words being spoken about Beatrice by the Reverent Williams, whose eyes looked uninterested in what he was saying – it was his third service of the morning. Then Paige stood and spoke of the love she had for her stepmother. She talked about the life that Beatrice had led, making no mention of gambling or losing family fortunes to the roulette table. The praise continued with Florence, who avoided any mention of the way her mother had forced her to live in Peterborough, a nightmare for their social class. The songs and words, religious and of no relevance or reflection to the life that Beatrice had lived, were just what was expected, kind words and sympathy. Martin wondered what Beatrice would have thought of the whole affair.

The words, the music, the false adoration and the kind memories all led to the conclusion when the notes of J. S. Bach's 'Sheep may safely graze' echoed around the room, and the coffin began its slow, dignified journey behind the purple curtain. At that moment, all Martin could think of was the one fact he had learnt at school about J. S. Bach, which was that the composer had twenty children. The fact had stayed with Martin since his schooldays with the wonderment as to just when J. S. Bach had the time to compose anything at all.

Family, friends and other bystanders were ushered towards the flowers that the undertakers had arranged for mourners to gather around. Reverend Williams dutifully thanked people on their way out of the exit door, secretly hoping to get at least a minute or two before the next body was carried in on the shoulders of strangers dressed in black suits.

* * *

The moment the three of them were outside, Susan pulled Colin to one side.

"Well, what's this about two wills?"

Martin joined in the demands. "A property and an odds and ends will; what are you going on about?"

"Please, Dearies, calm down. I'll explain."

Colin took them to one side away from the main throng of guests and began. "Beatrice had two wills that she was involved with. The first is the one you seem to know a lot about; that's the one that contains the agreements with estate agents, artists, cat charities and an odd selection of others. It also gives the breakdown of who gets what of her personal possessions. The estimates of the residue of that one work out to about twenty thousand pounds plus a load of old furniture, 'tutt' and nice paintings which all go to Paige. So as Martin said, even if she changed that will to include Florence, her real daughter, then Paige would only be missing out about ten thousand pounds. Not a vast sum nowadays by any stretch of the imagination. I know some people who spend that on getting married. I digress."

"That can't be right," Martin argued. "I have seen most of the will, and her property alone is worth about a million, so the residue after all her debts will be more than a mere twenty thousand."

"What is wrong with you people?" Susan interrupted. "Ten thousand, twenty thousand pounds, we are talking about money here, real money, lots of it in my poor eyes."

They both ignored Susan. Colin continued answering Martin's question. "That's where the property will comes in. You say a million; I guess you are thinking about her flat on the ground floor?"

Martin nodded; that was where she lived, after all.

"You'd be wrong; it is the bloody whole building, four floors and a basement of valuable real estate, worth about eight million pounds. Now that is a lot of money, Suzie Baby."

Colin went on to explain to the dismayed couple that the building in Hereford Square was solely owned by Beatrice's second husband. When she had married him, he knew full well what she was like; her penchant for gambling was well-documented in their high social circle. So, he had a rather complex will drawn up around the house that he owned, meaning she had never actually owned it at all. In the eyes of the legal profession, she was no more than a tenant in the building with no legal rights over the property, so that in her second husband's lifetime, if she was made bankrupt through her gambling, then the house could not be considered as part of her assets and therefore claimed by her creditors. Once her husband died, Paige's father's instructions meant that Beatrice would be allowed to continue to live in the house and that her income would be the rents from the other flats in the building, and that income she could do with as she wished, including spending it at the roulette tables. The house was now legally held in a trust and not owned by her at all. There was, Colin had found out, a small clause in the will that had been written by Samuel's father many years ago that allowed Beatrice to borrow up to ten per cent of the value against the property, but any creditor could not consider selling until she died, and then only with the consent of the majority owner, which was always planned to be Paige. There was also some very ambiguous wording, as there always is in legal documents, which allowed Beatrice to add blood relatives to be beneficiaries of the will. Colin had understood that the clause was included by Beatrice's second husband in order to allow Paige to alter things for her children so as to avoid inheritance tax. That one clearly backfired on him, as legally Beatrice could add Florence, her blood relative, as a beneficiary of the will; thus the eight-million-pound house would be split two ways, and Paige would be losing out on four million pounds, more than enough, they all agreed, to be a motive for murder.

"So, I was right; Paige found out that Beatrice was going to change her will and would be losing out on four million pounds, so she killed her stepmother before she had a chance to change it. I am so good at this."

"Well, I would not go as far as that Suzie Baby, regarde et apprends, look and learn."

Colin gestured with his hand towards Paige and Samuel, who were talking beside some elegantly displayed wreaths and flowers. Samuel had a reassuring arm around Paige as she wept gently into an embroidered hankie. They were joined by Florence, who embraced Paige briefly in a friendly manner before stepping back a little and talking to her. She said just a few words and then smiled and walked away. Samuel moved closer to Paige. They chatted softly as other mourners milled and moved around them, looking at the flowers or reading the small cards of condolence. Paige smiled at Samuel and held his hand.

Two men dressed smartly in black suits joined them and offered sympathy to Paige. Everyone seemed to be sharing the grief that hangs over a funeral. Then the three men, including Samuel, stepped to one side, allowing Paige to engage with some other mourners while they continued talking.

Martin, Susan and Colin watched the conversation that Samuel was having; it did not appear to be sympathetic or friendly. There appeared to be conflict as Samuel raised his shoulders, opening out his arms and shaking his head. Then the slightly broader man firmly gripped Samuel by his left arm, discreetly guiding him away from the flowers, the chatting mourners and the cold crematorium, to lead him towards the busy car park. The three men left together, quietly, without fuss, no goodbyes, just three mourners leaving a little too early.

"Who are those men?" Martin asked as he watched the three disappear amongst the cars.

"Christ Martin, you can be totally naïve at times," Colin told him. "The one with the thinning grey hair is Dave

Thompson; the broader one doing the leading away is Paddy Wood, both of them are police detectives. Sammy boy has just been nicked." Colin smiled broadly, satisfied with the entertainment that he had seen. "Well, I enjoyed that," he admitted before he continued. "Now even if Paige had been so kind as to have invited us back to the wake with, I guess, tea and curly white bread sandwiches, can I suggest we return to your humble office with a couple of bottles of champagne and some smoky bacon crisps, as I think we should all celebrate."

* * *

"I need to ask you," Martin spoke as he cautiously poured from the champagne bottle into three white plastic beakers, which were all they could find in the office to drink the 'champers' from. They did consider using their normal tea and coffee mugs, but for some reason, they all agreed that using those would seem to be irreverent to the champagne producers. The plastic beakers, although not perfect, were a necessary compromise. "Why the smoky bacon crisps?"

Colin replied without any form of hesitation. "Some people dip strawberries into their champagne, which I am sure is alright for some people, but as you might have noticed over the last couple of weeks, I am not 'some people'. Now the bacon crisps, once dunked into the bubbles, not only make the crisps softer and more alcoholic but conversely leave a hint of smoky bacon flavour in the champagne. And before you judge me, people stick all sorts of fruits and stuff into their alcohol, so why not have flavoured champagne?"

All three had slipped away from the funeral, grabbed a taxi back to the office of Hayden Investigations with just a brief stop at a corner convenience store to collect a supply of champagne and smoky bacon crisps. Throughout the whole journey, Colin refused to say any more about the apparent arrest of Samuel Parker until he had a glass of champagne in his hand.

Finally, Colin, after first speaking for a short while on his mobile phone, was holding a plastic beaker when he jumped onto a desk to sit beside Susan. He kicked off his court shoes and raised his beaker high above his head, the full beaker splashing a little of the champagne down his arm.

"A toast to Hayden Investigations and their first successful case. Cheers, all!"

Beside him, Susan smiled and joined in quaffing down a large mouthful of champagne. Martin, who was leaning back on the soft leather sofa, was a little more subdued. He sipped his champagne politely and was about to ask a question when Colin cleared his mouth of champagne and spoke first.

"Well, I have just got off the phone with Detective Inspector Wood, that was the one with thinning grey hair, and he told me that Samuel Parker has just been charged with four counts of fraud by abuse of position, plus a selection of other charges regarding the bank accounts that he opened and laundered money from, a good day's work, I think."

"How come you and this D.I. are such good friends that he shares all this information with you? And just why did they turn up at the funeral and arrest Samuel?" Martin asked.

"And what about the murder charges?" Susan added.

"Ok, hold on, my dears, just one question at a time, please." Colin slipped off the desk, grabbed a large bag of smoky bacon crisps, pulled it open and dipped a large crisp into his champagne, then proceeded to eat the soggy crisp. "Mmmm, nice," he concluded, licking his fingers.

"So, explanation time," Colin declared as he walked over to the sofa and sat beside Martin, patting him on his knee. "First, I shall tell you both a short yet heart-warming story. A good few years ago, in the days of Thatcher and the miners' strikes, a young man joined the police force full of ambition and drive, which saw him rise to the heady heights of Detective Sergeant. A career crushing problem arose when he decided he preferred to wear women's clothes and not the usual suit and tie of a detective. Given that the number of investigations where male detectives had to dress up as women were few and far between, there was a conflict. They could not get rid of the cross-dresser easily as there are many employment laws that protect such people. So, a compromise was reached, the cross-dresser took early retirement and left his appropriately dressed colleagues to fight crime."

"You're a copper?" Susan asked in disbelief.

"A policeman?" Martin added, just in case there was any confusion about the question being asked.

"Was a detective to be correct. For your information, policemen and 'coppers' wear funny-shaped hats. Might I add that I was a bloody good detective too but for my fashion preferences."

"And there I was thinking you were a villain. I thought you knew too much about breaking into homes and about the law," Martin offered.

"It's amazing what tricks you pick up when chasing villains. They have no qualms about breaking the law, so at times I had to tread a fine line between what was and was not legal."

Susan dipped her hand into the crisp bag, pulled out a handful of crisps and dunked them in her drink, managing to drop half of them into the champagne, the other half she just about managed to squeeze into her mouth. Speaking as she finished the champagne-tainted crisps, ignoring the mess she had made of her drink. "What about the murder? Are they going to charge him?"

"Before I tell you about that, let's recharge our plastic cups, although I would suggest Susan that you wash yours out first, and next time, darling, just dip in one crisp at a time, please."

With his plastic cup refilled, Colin continued. "I often pop in and see my old colleagues at the Elephant and Castle 'nick', you know the one next to the pie and mash shop, with that dopey cow Abigail on the front desk. I have a chat – not with her – and a cup of tea with my old mates and learn all the gossip. I think they were a little sorry to see me leave when I did, so my occasional visits are treated as a break from the normality of the day. Plus, they use me to wind up some of the newbies, telling them that they will have to spend time undercover dressed like me. It always shocks me that some seem a little too happy to volunteer to don ladies' clothes, although not as shocked as I was to see Martin dining with the common people of south London in Goddard's Pie and Mash shop. I was interested to learn what you both had found out, which, from what I heard, made it obvious there were some illegal activities going on. Once I left you, I popped back to the 'nick' and had a word with some of my friends. It is truly amazing what you can find out nowadays: the internet, mobile phones, online tickets, computers, social history sites, we all leave an easily traceable trail across the web, however much we think we don't." Colin lubricated his voice with a large swallow of champagne before he continued. "We did pretty much the same as you, checked his bank accounts, spoke to the Charity Commission, made a few phone calls to the bank security department, sadly all the CCTV of the days that the cheques were deposited and then later withdrawn were no longer available. What we were able to find out was that Samuel's mobile phone had been located in the bank, or at least very, very close to it on the days the cheques were paid in. So, he did not give them to the cat lady at her home. In fact, his phone was nowhere near her house, although, from what Suzie Baby said about the state of the house, no one in their right mind would go anywhere near it. His phone also turned up in the bank or, as I said, nearby on the same days the money was withdrawn, so there was a good chance he was there on those days too. The strange thing is that when the cash was both paid in and paid out, the name was Harriet Saddlesworth, the lady from the cat charity, who had signed the cheque for cash. Even odder was when we looked at her passport record, which ran out seven years ago, the signature was completely different. Harriet, to our minds, was not taking the money out. Therefore, Samuel looked the most likely culprit."

"But how could he be Harriet? The bank would see that he was not a 'her' if you see what I mean." Susan tried to explain as the bubbles, and the alcohol began to take effect.

"Our thoughts exactly, although in the real world, I am occasionally mistaken for the opposite sex, can't think why? The other thing that should have been flagged up is paying in large sums and taking them out. These transactions are brought to the attention of the bank's LRO, and before you ask, that stands for Laundering Reporting Officer, a legal requirement. In this case, the LRO was also the bank manager. So, we looked into his background, turns out that he at one time worked in Rotherhithe, south London, before being transferred up to Peterborough after screwing up a loan with an estate agent."

"And that estate agent was James Chapman?" This time it was Martin's turn to ask the question.

"Yes, the very same. So, we now have the solicitor, the estate agent and the bank manager, all of whom happen to frequent the same golf club. It was not rocket science to deduce that Samuel was on very friendly terms with the bank manager in Peterborough, making it easy for him to cash a large cheque, a percentage of which, I guess, will have found its way into the pockets of the bank manager. I'm not sure which is worse: Masonic Clubs or Golf Clubs. Anyway, as you both correctly worked out, Samuel does indeed appear to be slipping a clause into old ladies' last wills and testaments, giving a chunk of their cash to the Peterborough Cats' charity, and then ensuring the money does not reach the charity. Instead, he ferrets it into a bank account; no doubt he will be describing it as his retirement fund. I am guessing that now he'll be inside for the best part of seven years, which will do his business no good whatsoever."

Martin stood up and went to his desk to top up on champagne. He had another question of Colin. "What I do not understand is that Samuel told me the flat was worth about a million pounds. He even gave me a breakdown of the figures, including the one hundred thousand pounds for the charity. Yet ten per cent of the whole property, eight million pounds, is a lot more."

Colin patted the sofa once more. "Come and sit down, and I'll explain a little more. Don't forget, Samuel is a crooked solicitor."

Once Martin had settled back on the leather sofa, Colin started to enlighten him.

"First of all, look at things from Samuels's viewpoint. Of course, he knew about the two wills. He knew that the property was held in trust. He knew Beatrice did not have many assets but for some valuable artwork. He also knew she had died. What he did not know the first time you visited was what you might know.

"The easy and most sensible option would have been to tell you nothing as he had no obligation to tell you anything. But, with an attractive young lady sitting opposite him, he liked to show off. So, to impress Suzie Baby, he acted out the part of helping a friend, taking a risk. So, he told you about an arrangement that Beatrice had entered into. His legal mind was not telling you anything about her will as the arrangement with the estate agent was connected to the property in the trust. He had known you for years, so guessed that you would do nothing with the information he was passing on to you. Martin Hayden

319

do something, never in a million years, he thought. Well, he thought wrong."

Colin paused, drank some more champagne, then continued, "So when you returned asking more questions, he was a little concerned, but he could not backtrack. He still had no idea of what you might know about all the arrangements, so he gave you some more information, including the charity bequest. Letting you do all the figures and make all the assumptions, and not correcting you when you thought one hundred thousand pounds was going to the charity. To do so would only raise more questions from you. He hoped the extra information would become a burden to the socialite he thought Martin was. The old Martin might well have put it all to one side, but the new Martin returned a third time to tell him you had uncovered a fraud. With your finger pointing his way, he knew that he had underestimated you, and now he was in deep shit.

"When the police arrived at his offices, they found Mrs Faversham had been given the task of removing thirty bequests for the cat charity that had been surreptitiously inserted into the wills of a range of his elderly clients. That added to his guilt."

Susan stood, holding her champagne in one hand and a handful of crisps in the other, speaking before she filled her mouth. "But he can't just change people's wills without them knowing, can he?"

"Of course not, but he would just call them up with that smarmy voice and say there had been a typing error. Could the client come in and re-sign. They all trusted him; they had no reason not to."

Susan asked, "So what about him murdering Beatrice? Or was it Paige, like I said, and you being very polite and not nicking her until after the funeral?" She was being a lot more careful with her crisps, as yet not totally convinced that smoky bacon flavour champagne would catch on.

"There was no murder. Beatrice simply died of natural causes in her sleep."

"That's utterly impossible," Martin argued, "she never ate oysters, used her best china, did not take her rings off, and she was visited by a man that evening. Nothing was right about that evening; she did not die naturally."

"I love it when you get angry. Everyone says about you that you are so laid back, not bothered about anyone else but yourself. They are wrong, Martin; you do care about people, those less fortunate. It's just that you've never believed that that is what other people wanted you to be. I spent years thinking about dressing up, repressing something that was in me just because I thought people wanted me dressed as a man because I was a man. I was wrong. Once I stepped over that line and wore dresses and tights and spent the best part of an hour doing my make-up, most people were not that bothered, and if they were, they were not the sort of people I wanted around me. My ex-wife didn't want me like I am, so she left. Now my tough macho mates in the force, they couldn't care less; they could still tell it was me under the clothes. So Martin, you should simply be yourself, not what you think other people want you to be."

"Whatever you say," Martin shrugged off the comment. "But it was murder of that, I'm positive."

"I have to agree with him," said Susan joining forces with Martin.

"Beatrice might have been stenophagous, yet she was also adventurous and would happily fight for the underdog," Colin said, waiting for the question that he was sure Susan would ask, and she did.

"Steno what?"

"Stenophagous," Martin answered, "eating a limited variety of food."

"Very good Martin, maybe public school does have its benefits after all. We are normally happy sticking to the food we know unless the occasion merits otherwise. When was the last time you had smoky bacon crisps and champagne Martin?"

"Never."

"There you go, but you still tried this concoction. Now thinking about Beatrice and her oysters, I'm afraid Hayden Investigations failed in a basic investigation technique; you didn't go door-to-door, did you?"

Martin just shook his head in answer. Making door-to-door enquires was something he was not comfortable with. He admitted, "Well, we started, but once we had spoken to the maid, we left it at that."

"Thought so, if you had asked around the building, you would have met a sweet, retired old Judge who was shocked and horrified to hear that Beatrice had been found dead. Even more so as he had been having a meal with her the very night she died, making him the last person to see her alive."

"He killed her!" Susan almost shouted out. "Why?"

"Suzie Baby, this is not a Jim Rockford episode."

Martin opened his mouth to speak, but Colin raised his hand to silence the question. "It would seem that Beatrice was, how shall I say, 'befriending' the Judge, 'flirting with him', 'getting to know him better'; I think you get my gist. Well, it would seem that she did not actually want to get her leg over him but was after a big favour from the Judge, and that was why he was round her place that night. At his insistence, they were sharing a plate of oysters that he bought for the occasion. She dragged out her best china for the old man. Maybe he thought the oysters and the champagne would get her in the mood if it's ever possible to get in the mood when you're ninety. They spent the evening together, chatting and eating oysters. Even though it has been shown previously that Beatrice did not relish eating oysters, she was sacrificing her instinct in order to get the Judge on her side in a matter that was concerning her.

"I'll break there to take questions while I refill my cup. Shall we pop another bottle? Well done, Susan, buying three of them. On the company credit card, I hope?"

Martin pulled the cork from the second bottle and asked his question, first pointing out, "If Susan had a company credit card, Oxford Street would not know what hit it. So, what did Beatrice want from the Judge?"

"She wanted him to pull a few strings in order to get her maid, Aurora, leave to stay in the UK indefinitely. Sweet, I think, fighting for the underdog by eating oysters, although I guess if you didn't like them, it would be more of a sacrifice. I, for one, love the way they slip down, so decadent. The sad thing is the oysters she ate did not agree with her at all. They must have given her a real tummy ache, stomach cramps, very uncomfortable. No wonder she couldn't be bothered to take her rings off. As both doctors agreed, that triggered the heart failure during the night. The stomach upset, that is, not the rings, obviously."

Susan stood beside Martin, holding her cup out for a refill, convinced now that the champagne and crisps were best kept separate.

"That is so sweet, don't you think, Martin? Trying to help Aurora, eating something you totally hate to eat, plus, I guess preparing to defend yourself against a randy old Judge. She was quite a character, was our Beatrice, not just the habitual gambler everyone tarnished her with. So, what's happened to Aurora now?"

"Well, I have only heard this second-hand, but they plan to deport her. She has overstayed and has no connections to the UK. So, it's onto a plane back to the Philippines for her."

Martin sat back on the settee next to Colin.

"So that was why she lived upstairs to Beatrice, the flat was in effect managed by Beatrice, she gave her the flat, and I

323

guess never charged her any rent. Is there nothing I can do for her, assuming Aurora wants to stay?"

Both Susan and Colin looked mildly surprised at Martin, hearing his genuine offer of help. Colin answered him, avoiding any comments about him caring for other people, turning over a new leaf; although the temptation was strong, he managed to resist it.

"Well, as I understand it, she is keen to go back to her homeland, the problem is that she has no money to pay for her flight, so the Government will pay for it, but that will mean she'll probably never be allowed back into the UK ever again, assuming she ever wanted to come back that is. Now, if someone was prepared to pay for that flight, I'm sure she'd feel better and if she ever did want to come back...."

Martin interrupted, "I'll pay for her ticket; just tell me who I should speak to in order to arrange it. Plus, we need to look to see how best we can help Tala."

He looked across the office towards Susan, standing still enjoying the champagne without the crisps. She smiled. "For a 'poshie', you're so sweet at times."

"Social class has nothing to do with how nice a person you might be. It's more about your life experiences and how people react towards you."

There was a timid knock at the door. All three turned around to see it open wide.

"Ernie," Martin called out. "Come in and join us in our little celebration; have some champagne."

"Well, thank you, Mr Hayden, I shouldn't really as I am on duty."

"Come in, close the door, and we'll all keep it between ourselves. Susan, grab a cup for Ernie, who does a fine job here keeping the place spotless."

"Well, just a small one, please, Miss, I can't be away from my desk too long. Someone's birthday, is it?"

"Nothing of the sort." Colin ushered Ernie into the room, closing the door. "Martin and Susan here have just cracked a case that spanned the whole of the UK, well Peterborough at least, and have brought justice where there was none. That's all we can say, confidentiality and all that." Colin put a reassuring arm around Ernie. "What I can say to you, Ernie, is that young lady over there still owes me tea at the Ritz. However, being the generous person I am, this scrumptious feast of champagne and crisps is all the repayment I need."

"Congratulations then, sir. I bet that female disguise of yours helped a lot with the case. Bottoms up as they say." Ernie then emptied his plastic mug in one long draft.

"So, what can we do for you?" Martin asked.

"I'm sorry, sir?"

"You knocked and came in; I thought you had a question or needed to tell us something."

"Of course, sorry the champagne and your celebrations distracted me. I just popped in to tell you that your mother and a friend called in earlier. I said you were out, to which she only said, 'it was a little early for lunch', not too sure what she meant by that. Anyway, she said she would call back later today."

"Who was her friend?" Martin asked cautiously.

"Not too sure, she only spoke to your mother, saying: 'are you sure he can help me out?' All your mother said was, 'My son's a detective, of course, he can."

Author notes.

I do hope that you have enjoyed reading about Martin and Susan as much as I have enjoyed writing about the first of the many exploits and mysteries I have planned for them. If you did enjoy it, I would really appreciate it if you could do one or more of the following:

- Tell a friend, even strangers on a train.
- Post a review on Amazon and/or Goodreads.

This helps me and aids other readers when thinking about their next read.

You can find more about me, the books I write, and what I am up to on my website www.adrianspalding.co.uk or find me on my Facebook page Adrian Spalding Books.

The Reluctant Detective is a humorous jaunt. However, the aspect of modern slavery I have highlighted is sadly not total fiction. People like Aurora and Tala do exist within the highest levels of society. Working for little or no pay, they are trapped in a world they have little control over and little hope of leaving. The reason is their masters are people that are often held in high esteem. Maybe that is why reports of this type of slavery are almost non-existent. I hope this book will help raise awareness of this issue.

Bye for now,
Adrian.

Sleeping Malice

by Adrian Spalding

Your past never forgets.

When journalist Helen Taylor landed her dream job on a newspaper, she could never have imagined that her first assignment would become her worst nightmare.

Travelling to France for a simple story, Helen encounters Phillip, a puzzling Englishman who avoids contact with anyone. When she meets him, she feels there is something dark about him, which may provide her with a major scoop.

Greg, an out-of-work journalist, also arrives in the village asking questions about a missing man. With the appearance of two journalists, one English family fears they are being hunted for the secret they hold.

So when Her Majesty's Government stretches its merciless talons across the English Channel, Helen and Greg have to work together to discover just what has been hidden in the village.

As they begin to uncover the facts, their own suppressed secrets start to emerge. They learn that when your past comes back to haunt you, no one around you is safe.

Available now from Amazon

The Night You Murder

By Adrian Spalding

When you know the truth, can you see the lies?

The day Thomas de la Mer saw an old flame walk through the door of his antiques shop, he had no idea that his life was going to change forever.

Laura offered him the opportunity to make a large profit on a rare figurine. Hoping to impress her, he agreed to help finance the deal, even though he was going to have to borrow a large sum of money to do so.

As events unfold, Thomas begins to learn that her reappearance in his life was not just by chance, and he starts to worry that she has too much knowledge of what lies behind the innocent façade of his shop.

His concerns grow when she disappears with the figurine and the money, money he borrowed from a criminal who will stop at nothing to get it back.

Will Thomas find her before the loan deadline expires? Why did she seek him in the first place? Will saving his own life mean sacrificing hers? In the end, can he avoid revealing his true identity?

Available now from Amazon

Printed in Great Britain
by Amazon